# FLIGHT FOR SANITY

KATHRYN JACOBS IS a top-ranking FAA official in charge of drone regulation. But her proposed research has exposed a nerve deep within the walls of the FAA. At the same time, her best friend, airline pilot Darby Bradshaw, is fighting to promote a safety culture at Global Air Lines. Darby was warned by many not to report, but her determination to do the right thing has manifested into a nightmare she may never escape.

Aviation safety is at stake—especially if the pilot job is eliminated.

*Flight For Sanity* is a thriller that reads like a mystery. But there is no mystery about the corruption behind the scenes of the world's largest airline and within the walls of the FAA. The lengths to which powerful people within the industry will go to destroy these women will shock the nation.

It's time the world learns the truth, before it's too late, and automation replaces pilots.

Truth is scarier than fiction.

# FLIGHT FOR SANITY

# Inspiration. Motivation. Plane Stuff.

*"Sometimes truth is scarier than fiction"*

By Karlene K. Petitt

at

## Flight To Success

www.KarlenePetitt.com

# FLIGHT FOR SANITY

Karlene Petitt

JET STAR PUBLISHING INC.
SEATAC WA

"THE WORLD IS A DANGEROUS PLACE,

NOT BECAUSE OF THOSE WHO DO EVIL,

BUT BECAUSE OF THOSE WHO LOOK ON AND DO NOTHING."

*Albert Einstein*

# DEDICATION

*Flight For Sanity* is dedicated to all the people who demonstrate courage to speak out against injustice, expose corruption, and possess inner strength to do the right thing, despite personal ramifications. Your love of humanity and effort to improve the lives of others will never be forgotten. I am proud to stand beside you.

***Change does not take time...***
***Change takes people with integrity, courage, and fortitude.***

# FLIGHT FOR SANITY

# PROLOGUE

JOHN MCALLISTER SHIFTED in his first class seat as he stared out the window, Puget Sound coming into view in the distance. The Cascades were barely visible above the low-level drizzle that blanketed the city and surrounding area. The city was encased in a gray haze, and visibility was low. The Pacific Northwest convergence zone played havoc at times, but when the sun shone bright there was no city more beautiful than Seattle.

He pressed the flight tracker button on the screen in front of him and then glanced at his watch. They would be landing ten minutes early, and he couldn't get home soon enough. The meetings had been long and tedious. If any of this were real, it would be a hell of a lot easier to swallow. As of now, it was a means to an end. He glanced across the aisle.

The secretary of the Department of Transportation had been buried in paperwork the entire flight. *What was so consuming?* He wondered. Whatever it was, it had government written all over it. Unfortunately, John was unable to secure the seat next to him. Yet, 2B remained empty. Interesting for an oversold flight.

"Would you like another coffee, sir?" the flight attendant asked and John jumped, startled by her presence.

"That'd be nice." His night would continue well into the darkest hours after the rest of the house was asleep. Within minutes he had a fresh cup of coffee in his hands.

Global Air Lines had started a Seattle to DC non-stop flight about three months earlier. He would have preferred a larger plane, as a six-hour flight was a bit much for a Boeing 737. Yet sitting in first class, he supposed it didn't matter the size of the aircraft.

Global was pushing their presence into the Seattle market with force. Interestingly enough, the FAA was creating a larger presence there, too. Nothing was ever a coincidence.

Just as he finished the last sip of his coffee, a pilot announced they would be beginning the descent soon. The flight attendants began their duties cleaning up the cabin. He handed his cup and napkin to the young lady who had taken excellent care of the front cabin, and she smiled warmly.

That was one thing Global did well—they had one hell of a service. Their flight attendants were top notch. But, he could not help to wonder if this could be construed as deceptive marketing. Hell, he didn't have to wonder, he knew. Beautiful marketing package with great service, but a tumor grew within the inner workings. He was getting close, and at least one finger pointed in Global's direction.

John glanced across the aisle again, and this time the secretary's gaze drew a slow smile when their eyes caught. John nodded to him—perhaps the only obstacle to everything they needed to accomplish. He looked away first.

He held no judgment on the secretary's ethics, per se. But, he wasn't as effective as he needed to be. Yet again, none of them were.

John returned his attention out the window, wondering why the secretary of the Department of Transportation was visiting Seattle.

They had chatted in the business class lounge prior to boarding. Despite what he'd told John, top industry officials did not go to meetings across the country, meetings came to them. He should know, as he had taken the trek back to DC far too many times to count. Someone powerful sent him this direction. The question was who, and why.

Clearing his ears, John scanned the horizon. They were landing to the south, and buildings protruding the cloud base below caught his attention. His eyes narrowed. They were flying high, too high for their location. He would have thought they were being vectored for the downwind to land north, but instead they were descending for a southern landing, and far too fast.

DON WAS SITTING in the right seat of his Boeing 737 inbound to Seattle, playing the part of a good Global first officer. He had finally reached the epitome of his career—employed at the most elite airline in the industry. He glanced left, and rolled his eyes. He wasn't sure that the performance level of some of the guys he flew with matched that rating. With the image of Global pilots, he'd thought that there would be more substance and professionalism. Yet some were incompetent assholes. Those with the biggest attitudes were also some of the worst pilots he'd ever flown with. Unfortunately, big egos in airplanes opposed safety.

Don made the cut for Global, yet was surprised due to the career path he'd chosen. Never having touched the military, he went the general aviation route. He had attended an ab initio college, where students earned their flight ratings and a college degree at the same time. He got good grades, graduated, instructed until he had enough hours to fly with a commuter. He chose a commuter with the quickest captain upgrade time, money be dammed. He had planned well, taking out as much money as possible for college loans. Then he saved as much of that money as he could to survive his first airline job. He upgraded quickly, got his hours, and within no time he had a Global interview.

Global hired very few commuter pilots; they hired military. He was one of the lucky ones. Then he glanced left again, and wondered how lucky he actually was. This guy was not only an asshole, but a crappy pilot as well. Any pilot who thought he was hot shit because he hosted four stripes on his shoulders had an idiot for a captain. Four stripes did not make the captain—*it's what's inside the uniform that counts*. In this case, there wasn't much there.

There was also nothing Don could say or do about his captain's performance or behavior. Not only was Global Air Lines a *captain's airline,* Don was still on probation.

Probation was serious airline business, where a first officer had to keep his mouth shut or he would be fired. For one year he could not stand up to a screwed-up captain, call in fatigued, or complain about shitty training. Far too many times Don had found himself rolling his eyes at his elite airline. Hell, his commuter airline's training program had put Global's to shame. But what could he do? Nothing.

He sighed, shifting his attention to the instruments. Once again, his captain was behind the airplane. *Did he even have a clue that he couldn't fly?* Don wondered. That old joke about being the only survivor in the crash finally made sense. This guy was so far behind his airplane, if they crashed in Seattle, Sky God would still be over Yakima, 100 miles away from impact.

They were on the Ephrata Seven arrival and had just passed over the HETHR intersection, and turned to a heading of 250 degrees. They were high. He was always high or fast, or a combination of both. Except when he was attempting a visual, then he would get too low.

"Global 42, turn left to a heading of 180, cleared for the ILS 16 right approach," ATC said.

Don replied to the clearance. The captain spun the heading bug. The localizer was coming in, yet they were still well above the glideslope.

"We're high," Don said, attempting to hold the contempt from his voice, as they intercepted the localizer heading inbound. "You're cleared for the approach."

The captain reached over and selected approach, but they were still above the glideslope. They were inside of CELAK, a point on the arrival ten miles from the runway, and could descend to 3200 feet—they were at 6000 feet.

"You're above the glideslope."

Modern day Boeing 737 aircraft had software available that, if activated, enabled the aircraft to capture the glideslope from above— Global's was deactivated. They would have to fly the plane down to the glideslope to capture it, and he was doing no such thing.

"Oh fuck!" the captain said, and selected vertical speed, and began diving for the glideslope. He started at 1000 feet per minute and then increased it to 1500 feet per minute. "Gear down, flaps 15, landing check!"

"Speed," Don said, as he dumped the gear. He waited for the captain to dial the speed back, and then pulled the flap handle aft. He began to read the landing checklist to final flaps and then said, "Flaps."

The captain responded, "What? Huh?"

"Do you want final flaps?"

"Shit. I said flaps. Flaps 25. Ummm. Flaps 30. Dammit!"

Don glanced at the speed. "We're too fast for final flaps." Then he glanced at the vertical speed, and said, "Sink 2000", which was not followed by a response. They were diving toward the glideslope, then diving through the glideslope, and screaming in, too fast for the flaps. *Fuck. No job was worth death.*

"Go around!" Don shouted.

The captain repeated, "Go around," in a conversational volume, but nothing happened. They were still diving toward the ground.

"Go around!" Don shouted again, this time louder, scanning the instruments. The captain had disengaged the autopilot. He had not selected the go around button.

"It's broken," the captain said. "It's not working!"

"Then fly the fucking airplane," Don yelled, while attempting to pull back on the controls. But the captain held tight, his arms were locked holding the controls forward. *Was he trying to kill them?*

JOHN NEVER FELT more helpless. He glanced to the guy next to him, who was still sleeping. Nobody else appeared to be paying attention. His eyes darted back to the window. They were flying toward the ground. Uncontrolled. *God, I cannot die. Not like this. Not today.* He wanted to close his eyes, but he couldn't. He would watch until impact. Trees, buildings, and cars, and they were heading toward them, and fast.

DON PULLED BACK on the controls to no avail. The captain's face was frozen, his eyes unblinking. But moments after the trees came into view, impact imminent, the captain pulled back and the aircraft began to climb.

"Go around thrust, flaps 15," Don said, as he pushed the thrust levers forward, and raised the flaps. Those procedures should have been the captain's. Don stepped over the lines of a first officer, but he would be damned if he would allow the captain to stall the aircraft.

"Global 42 is on the missed," Don spoke over the radio. The captain reached up and engaged the autopilot.

"Global 42, climb to 2000 feet and turn right to a heading of 340. We'll vector you for a close in right base to 16 right." There was a pause, and then the radio came alive. "Global, do you need assistance?"

Don was dialing in 2000 feet on the mode control panel as he said, "Global 42, climbing to 2000, then right turn to heading of 340. I'll let you know. Thanks."

He watched the instruments as the aircraft leveled at 2000 feet, and then he turned the heading bug to 340, despite the fact that the captain was supposed to be the pilot flying. Instead, the captain stared out the window at nothing.

Don's heart sped wildly. *What the hell had just happened?* Whatever it was, he would not allow it to happen again. He sucked a deep breath and then said. "I've got the airplane."

"The hell you do!" the captain snapped, his attention snapping back into the aircraft. "I've got this. I'll do it."

"Do what? Fucking kill us!" Don's heart raced, pounding behind the wall of his chest to where he could feel it within his throat. He had tolerance for anything, but not death by airplane. "I'll fly this aircraft with you alive or dead. I don't fucking care." Don pulled the gun out from his holster and pointed it at the captain.

"You've just kissed your career good-bye."

"At least I'll be alive to see the event." Don sucked a deep breath, and pressed the microphone, "Tower, Global 42 requests runway 16 left. We'll need the area cleared for an autoland."

Don held the gun with his right hand resting on his lap, pointed toward the captain. His left hand programmed the new approach. "I'm flying, you're sitting on your hands."

"Fuck you."

"Global turn right heading to 070."

With his left hand Don pressed the interphone/mic select switch to mic and said, "Right 070 for Global 42."

It would be easier if he killed him now. He had the voice recorder of what was said, and they would have the FOQA data showing the performance of what the aircraft had done. That would be proof on his side. For all intents and purposes, this asshole was trying to kill them all, and chickened out on the first go. There was no way in hell he would give him a second chance.

"You're going to jail for this."

"Sit on your hands," Don said again. "Now!" He was half expecting a fight as the captain stared his way. Then the captain slid his hands under his ass.

JOHN'S HEART RATE had yet to slow. The aircraft had pulled up at what appeared to be less than a couple hundred feet, and gone around. But the missed approach was anything but normal. The momentum of the aircraft began upward prior to the application of power. The next arrival and approach were perfect. Neither pilot gave a PA telling the passengers what had happened and not to worry, or explained why they missed the approach, which was unusual. Especially for Global.

He sat in his seat, and waited for all the passengers to disembark. Some appeared frightened and others were oblivious. The cockpit door remained closed. Once everyone had left, the first class flight attendant said to him, "Sir, we're here. It's time we *all* get off this plane." She smiled. Exhaustion and fear emitted from her eyes.

John stepped into the aisle, and pulled down his bag. He then retrieved his briefcase. "I would like to talk to the flight crew."

The flight attendant hesitated a moment, and then smiled and said, "Of course." She lifted the handset, pressed a couple of buttons, and spoke. Her expression changed, as she gazed out the door. John looked left. Suits were coming down the jetway.

"Sir, we're going to have to ask you to deplane," the leader of the suit pack said.

John pulled out his credentials and displayed them to the man who requested that he leave. The man's composure changed slightly, a bit of red working at his neck. He clearly searched for the words to tell the head of the Seattle National Transportation Safety Board he had to deplane an aircraft that *should have* been an accident.

Within seconds the man's composure shifted again, this time from aggressor to friendly—the power of credentials. Yet, a normal reaction should have been one of tension. Instead, this man reversed his demeanor to jovial. The other suits stood silently behind him, obviously knowing their places.

The flight attendants from the back of the aircraft excused themselves as they passed by, and left the aircraft with bags in tow. Silent, and faces ashen—they knew how close to death they had come. The first class attendant was off the handset, and standing with her bag beside the closed flight deck door. There was no indication she was going anywhere soon.

"Mary, you can go now," the man said to the lead flight attendant. "We've got this."

The flight attendant and John exchanged a glance, and he gave her a slight nod. "Thank you for the great service," he said. She blushed and their eyes caught a second time before she left. Hers spoke of gratitude, yet she was clearly shaking.

John returned his attention to the man in charge. "Now gentlemen," he said, intentionally disregarding the man in power. "It looks like we have an interesting situation here."

The man in charge, who had released Mary, stood taller than the others, and if John didn't know better he expanded his chest. "This is company business, and nothing that necessitates the NTSB."

John was far too tired for this shit, and there was something about almost dying that destroyed his patience.

"Who are you?" he asked.

With a broad smile, the man extended his hand, "I'm the manager of flight operations."

"I didn't ask what you did, I asked who the hell you were," John said, taking his hand and shaking firmly.

John knew exactly who he was. He'd been watching him for months.

The look in his eyes shifted ever so slightly, but the smile stayed plastered in place. "Captain Rich Clark."

Once John forced his name, he released the hand. "I want to speak to the pilots now, followed by a full report on my desk Monday morning."

"Report?" Clark said. "About what?"

"This plane damn well nearly hit the ground," John said, his voice low and firm. "I want to speak to the pilots. Can you get them?"

Clark shifted his weight, and placed his hands on his hips. He glanced at one of the men at his side, as if giving him permission to speak.

"I'm the Seattle union rep, Captain Phil Jackson." He extended his hand and John took it. He also knew exactly what was coming next. "I've got to talk to the pilots before…"

John raised a hand. He knew how this worked, and didn't have the patience to listen to why he couldn't talk to the pilots. This could turn into a battle, and nothing would be accomplished here. He assessed the group, and then handed Clark his card. Excusing himself, he worked his way up the jetway.

He moved toward the window outside the jetway that provided clear visual of the flight deck. He pulled out his phone, and snapped a couple photos. He then walked across from the gate and sat at the bar. He ordered a double scotch and removed his jacket. He pulled his tie free, stuck it in his briefcase, and rolled up his sleeves. With his seat angled toward the gate, he waited.

The warmth of the scotch worked, soothing his nerves. Finally, the suits with crewmembers in tow walked out of the jetway. John's camera was in motion. The captain's face was expressionless. Then Clark said something, and everyone laughed. Everyone except the first officer. John clicked a few more pictures.

As the group walked into the tangle of bodies in the terminal, John brought his scotch to his lips. He replayed what had happened to keep it fresh. He rewound the events and jotted a few notes onto the cocktail napkin. He then thought of the secretary of the Department of Transportation, and wondered if this event had been in the secretary's honor, or his.

# CHAPTER 1

S PLASHES OF YELLOW, red, and brown darted from branch to feeder, ignoring her presence on the other side of the glass. Theirs was a world where flight was a necessity, and death would come to those who couldn't spread their wings and soar. There were times that she thought she, too, would perish if she couldn't touch the sky. Darby Bradshaw shifted her attention from the window to her cell phone.

She'd give him five more minutes, before getting back to the business of enjoying her day. Somehow he'd heard about her attempt to gain a meeting with Sinclair, and wanted to talk to her first. He had *grave concerns*. Hell, Darby had grave concerns about her union rep.

It had been four months since Global nearly buried an airplane at the north end of the Seattle airport, but they were doing nothing about it. She could not get the event out of her mind, and she knew that incident was a sign of things to come. The fact that John was on the flight had made the event all the more real.

John had been instrumental in saving her life on more than one occasion. More than that, he and Jackie had just announced their engagement, with their wedding planned for September, and a baby on the way. Jackie's first husband had died in an airplane crash, and if John were lost that way too, she wasn't sure Jackie would survive. Jackie was one of her best friends.

Ray walked into the room with a steaming cup of coffee. "What are you doing?" he asked, sitting on the couch beside her. He handed her his cup.

Darby was a first officer on the Airbus A330 and Ray a mechanic for Global Air Lines. They had merged into the essence of an old married couple, which was inevitable since they had been dating for about a year and a half. They spent many days and nights together, yet they still weren't officially living under one roof and each had a place of their own. They were both nervous about giving up their identity, so nothing was ever mentioned about that next step.

"I'm waiting for Phil to call," she said, taking his cup, and then sipped his coffee. *Yummy.* "Not too bad for a guy."

He held out a hand for the return of his beverage. "I share. I don't give it away."

Darby grinned, "And you're really good at sharing, too." She handed Ray his coffee, and said, "Phil heard about my plan to get a meeting. I suspect a little pillow talk has been occurring in the Seattle office."

"Joel?" Ray said.

"No less."

Joel Iverson was the Seattle chief pilot and good friends with Phil. Unfortunately, Phil lost sight of the boundaries of what he should and shouldn't talk about with management, despite a friendship from the past. Joel and Phil had both been Coastal pilots. Today, Joel was bought and paid for, and the company owned him as a chief pilot. She sighed, wondering how many people had a price tag on their ethics.

To the pilots, Joel complained about being a glorified secretary, and would roll his eyes at upper management. Yet, Darby wasn't so sure where he stood, and if that was an act or not. Either way, Phil should not be discussing anything with him.

"You guys have the most fucked up union," Ray said. "Sounds like they're on the corporate payroll."

"They are, literally," Darby said, reaching for Ray's coffee when her phone rang.

"Saved by Phil," Ray said, pulling his cup back. "Tell him I owe him one."

Darby leaned over him to pick up her phone off the end table, and as she did, she kissed Ray on the cheek. Then she answered. "Hey Phil, what's up?"

"I heard you're trying to get a meeting with Sinclair."

"Yep. Who told you?"

"That's not the issue. The concern is this meeting screwing up your career."

"Reporting safety issues is going to screw my career?" Darby grinned at Ray, and pretended to hang herself with an invisible noose. "How so?"

Ray laughed and took her phone. He pressed speaker, and then set it on the coffee table.

"Let's just say, you've been… an irritant and you've pissed off a few of the wrong people. They're not happy."

"Who's not happy?" Darby asked, leaning against Ray. He slid a hand inside her shirt, and she pulled it out, and slapped it. "Besides, since when is our goal to make management pilots happy? I thought safety was the vision."

"You've already talked to them."

"I talked to Clark and his boys about SMS."

"The social media policy?"

Darby closed her eyes and shook her head. "SMS is safety management systems, not social media," she said. "Unfortunately current operating practices indicate that we don't have a positive safety culture to support it. These guys violate FARs as well as company policy. They work around rules, and don't get me started on the training department."

She leaned forward, arms on her knees, and added, "Our recency process is nothing more than a pencil-whipped legality dance." Ray placed a hand on her back and rubbed.

A 'recency' was the currency requirement for a pilot to obtain three takeoffs and landings in ninety days. Many international pilots went months without flying, and one guy she knew had gone a year. Yet, when they visited the simulator, they did nothing but rush the pilots through the process, in the shortest amount of time, to check the currency box.

"You should let the union take care of this."

"Ya think?" she said sarcastically. "Our union should have addressed these issues years ago."

"You don't know what these guys are capable of."

"Then enlighten me."

"I'm afraid this will turn into a section eight action," Phil said. "Odell, Clark, Wyatt, and that damned director of training should all be fired." His voice had escalated to the point of yelling. "I hate them all."

Darby whispered to Ray, "Where the hell did that come from?" She then said to Phil, "Uh… those guys were let go a month ago. All but the director of training, that is."

"Oh… of course," he said. "But Sinclair is no better."

What the hell was Phil so mad about? And why did he really care if they were going to nail her or not? *Guilty conscience,* she thought. Maybe he'd shared a bit too much information, and learned what they were going to do. Besides, she didn't hate any of them. She didn't care enough about them to feel hate. She wanted a safer system.

"If I give him a written report, he can't ignore the issues."

"Don't do this. I'm telling you, you've got a target on your back."

Ray cocked his hand like a gun and then pressed it against her back, and she raised her arms. "Don't worry. I walk to the gym with a thick book hidden under my coat for protection, in case someone takes a shot."

"I don't trust any of them," Phil said. "Clark is the worst kind of evil!"

"Evil or not, we have to do something at our company," Darby said and rolled her eyes. "Besides, Clark is doing his evil elsewhere these days. He's gone."

"What if we give them the report a piece at a time, but in a way that they think it's their idea?" Phil suggested. "Let them take the credit. It will take time… years… but it's the best way to make this happen the right way."

"The right way?" Darby jumped to her feet. She placed her hands on her hips, and with her voice loud enough for him to hear her with the phone lying on the coffee table, she said, "We don't have time. We're going to have a crash. That 737 in Seattle was a friggin' wake-up call that something needs to be done. That plane should have been buried thirty feet deep. We had 20,000 safety reports last year alone. We're flying on borrowed time."

Ray patted the couch beside him, and she sat. He wrapped his arms around her, and pulled her close and whispered, "Don't let him get to you."

"Will you at least talk to the union attorneys first?" Phil asked.

"Of course." Darby leaned forward again. "If you could tell me one thing. Why do you have your panties in a bunch over my giving a safety report to management?"

# Chapter 2

SEATTLE'S WEATHER GREW crisp overnight, and Darby could smell snow in the air. They were due for one hell of a winter. She pulled her coat tight, and then ran up the path and jumped onto the porch. Knocking on Kathryn's backdoor with a couple loud taps announced that she was there, but opening the door and stepping inside gave credence that she was family.

"I finally did it!" Darby said bounding into her kitchen.

"What? Recover from your hangover?" Kathryn asked with a laugh.

"I wish," Darby said, and headed straight for the fridge. She opened it looking for something to drink. "I've been way too boring for far too many weeks."

"I made a fresh pot of coffee."

"Do you mind if I just grab a Diet Pepsi instead?"

"Of course not." Kathryn pulled down a large glass from the cupboard and filled it with ice, and then set it on the counter. Darby opened the bottle of soda and filled her glass, then returned the bottle to the fridge.

She had just finished a good workout and needed something cold. Water should have been the beverage of choice, but her low caffeine light was flashing bright.

"So what'd you do?" Kathryn asked, filling a plate with homemade chocolate chip cookies. One could always count on comfort food and chocolate at Kat's house.

"I finished my report," Darby said, sliding into a chair at the kitchen table. "I want you to read it. But first you have to make me a promise."

Kathryn sighed. "Depends on what that promise is." She set the plate on the table in front of Darby.

"Thanks," Darby said, taking a cookie. "There will be no depends. I need your thoughts, and you have to take off your FAA hat for this one."

Kathryn Jacobs was her best friend and a kick ass FAA inspector. She was more than an FAA inspector; she was a top administrator that had power to do something of importance. She was also the one who would use her powers wisely. She had perseverance, dedication and brains—a powerful combination. The FAA was fortunate to have her, and Darby was lucky to have her as a friend. But there were times like this that the line between friendship and work blurred.

Kathryn sat across the table and reached for Darby's report. Darby pulled it back, out of Kathryn's reach.

"No. No. No. Not until you promise that your FAA hat is off." Darby sipped her Diet Pepsi and added, "You may only read this report as my friend and confidant, one who supports and encourages me to uphold the highest standards of..."

"Cut the crap," Kathryn said with a laugh, folding her arms. "Seriously, what is that?" She nodded toward the papers clutched in Darby's death grip.

"A safety culture report. Well, actually a report of how Global violates a safety culture as well as FARs and policy, etc. I requested a meeting with Sinclair, three months ago. He's the new director of flight ops. Anyway, at the time, he said he wouldn't talk to me unless I talked to EO first, but…"

"Why would he want you to talk to equal opportunity?"

"One can only guess," Darby said, taking a bite of her cookie.

"Are you going to talk to them?"

"Hell no," she said with a mouth full of chocolate. "I told them that this was not a girl issue, this was a safety issue."

The FAA was mandating SMS, and in order to comply, it required a positive safety culture. Safety culture included a reporting culture, just culture, learning culture, and an informed and flexible culture. Thus, Darby had written a book—*Inside the Iron Bubble*. Yet, in hindsight, she realized that Global's flight operations management had no clue what a safety culture was, thus, how would they ever manage safety management systems? They wouldn't.

A key feature of a safety culture was not only to have processes in place that supported people to report safety issues by encouraging them to report, but to make it easy.

"Sinclair finally agreed to see me."

"Playing devil's advocate," Kathryn said, leaning back and folding her arms. "You already had an SMS meeting months ago. What more could you tell them?"

"That's the point. I had an *SMS* meeting," Darby said, emphasizing SMS. "But, you can't have a safety management system without a safety culture. I think it's time to give them an official copy of their screwed up processes, and explain why their behavior doesn't meet a safety culture, and how that will impact the SMS."

Kathryn sighed. She lifted a spoon and tapped it on the table. "While that appears logical, I'm worried about you kicking that hornet's nest. Have you talked to your union rep about this?"

"Yep. Three months ago," she said. "Phil doesn't want me to do this. Said I should give it to the union to handle, or slip it to management in bite size pieces so they could take credit over the next few years."

Kathryn laughed. "Now that's a strategy I hadn't thought of."

"Yep. But the problem with feeding babies a bite at a time is they spit half of it out in the process." Darby sipped her drink and then said, "Anyway, he warned me they were going to give me a section eight."

"What's that?" Kathryn asked, reaching for a cookie.

"Remember that show MASH, where Klinger was trying to get discharged?"

"He's afraid you're a cross-dresser?"

"Funny," Darby said choking on her bite of cookie. "But he did go on a tirade how much he hated all the managers."

"He hates the *new* guys too?"

"Appears so," Darby said. "Nothing's changed."

A couple months after Darby's book had been released and hit the best seller's list, she had been invited to a meeting with the head of corporate safety and the director of training, as well as Wyatt, Clark and Odell—pilot managers at the director level. She had discussed SMS. Wyatt, Clark and Odell were subsequently removed from their management positions. The replacements had no leadership skills either. They replaced the old crew with the same type of people.

"Why didn't you tell me nothing had changed?" Kathryn said, clearly pissed. The exact reaction Darby had hoped for.

"We were all busy with Jackie's wedding," Darby said, placing her report on the table. "I didn't want to take anything away from her."

"I get that." Kathryn's eyes glanced to the report. "How many pages is that beast?"

"Fifty-four. Single spaced, with twenty pages of supporting documentation."

"How many FAA violations are in there?"

"Let's just say… if violations were murders, we'd be looking for a serial killer."

"Dammit Darby!" Kathryn said, and closed her eyes. "If anyone knows that I read this, and did nothing about it, my career is toast." She opened her eyes, and sighed. Staring at Darby, she shook her head, but Kathryn's wheels were in motion.

Darby hated putting her friend in this position, but she wanted Kat to read it so she would understand how bad things were, and why the FAA-mandated safety management system would fail if something weren't done about the lack of a safety culture. It would be nothing but lip service if they were allowed to continue as is. She also knew Kathryn would edit it in the process.

"First, who does anything proactive within the FAA?" Darby took a sip of her drink, eyeing Kathryn over the brim of the glass. "Besides, you have to admit that nothing happens quickly at the FAA. So your reading and not saying anything wouldn't be noticed."

"Maybe not, but the notification should be done." Kathryn's foot began to tap under the table—a Kat trademark. "You did the best you could, what if—"

"But I didn't do the best I could, because I was stupid," Darby said. "Unless the system is changed, nothing will change. You put the same people into a broken *system* and they will do the same thing. I thought getting rid of managers would solve the problem, but I was wrong."

"You weren't wrong. Getting rid of egotistical snakes was *exactly* what was necessary. Changing the system will not necessarily fix the problem either. The problem now is the *new* team. Had they put servant leaders into those positions then things would have changed. You were right the first time; people change the system."

Darby picked at the chocolate chip on a cookie, and thought about that. It made sense.

"They made the entire pilot management team take leadership courses. But I suspect they either skipped their classes or they're just slow learners." Darby sighed. "Either way, all that effort was for nothing. It was just for show."

"I'm afraid to look at this," Kathryn said, nodding to the report.

"No you're not. You're not afraid of anything," Darby said. "And despite my union rep's warnings, the company can't retaliate against me for reporting safety issues. I'll be fine."

"Why not give this to me officially, and we'll let the FAA fix whatever is in here?"

"First, rumor has it that the regional FAA office is filled with retired Global captains, and they are part of the club. It's also been said that Global is the tail that wags the dog. Playing devil's advocate, if they did anything at all, it would be to fine them for what's in this report, but that wouldn't do anything." Darby spoke rapidly, with many concerns.

"Global made 1.7 billion dollars last quarter. A fine for Global would be like fly shit in pepper. They wouldn't even notice it. It would mean nothing and they'd press on as always. We have to fix this, not fine them."

Darby was afraid if she didn't do something, Global would have an accident. She had to say something to the management team. John's near crash should have been a wake-up call, yet nothing short of changing innocuous procedures came of it.

Numerous incidents occurred daily, and one of the Global management pilots declared an emergency because his autopilot and autothrust failed, and he was flying in visual conditions. Manual flight should be a pilot's minimum performance level, not an emergency—definitely another wake-up call.

Kathryn sighed, and said, "Okay. FAA hat is off for the day."

"Thank you!" Darby said, sliding the report across the table. "You won't be sorry."

"I'm not so sure about that."

"I have one more thing to tell you. It's kind of big."

Kathryn leaned back in her chair and folded her arms. She raised an eyebrow, and then said, "Can it wait? I'm thinking I might have my hands full here."

Darby laughed. "Yep. It's not going away."

# CHAPTER 3

THE DICHOTOMY OF good versus evil lurked within the cracks of his life. A life defined by moments—a statistic, a vow, a birth. John McAllister embraced the tranquility of his current moment with his bride. Warmth enveloped them in the whirlpool in the Presidential Suite on the 35th floor of the Embassy Suites Hotel in Niagara Falls. He and Jackie were at opposite ends of the tub facing each other.

John massaged a foot of the woman he loved. Surrounded by bubbles, Jackie's head rested on the edge of the tub, her eyes closed and face serene with a peaceful smile spread across it. Moaning emitted occasionally. John could not believe how lucky he was.

Yet, luck had nothing to do with his success, and everything to do with a life filled with sacrifice. He had given up the opportunity to have a family, and committed everything to the National Transportation Safety Board.

Dedicating thirty years of his life to the NTSB, his old boss had promised to recommend him for the presidential nomination to the board. Despite John's active involvement in solving Bill Jacob's attempt to control the industry by crashing planes, Walker ended up dead and John was promoted. But not to where he deserved to be.

"Mmmm, that feels so good," Jackie said, opening her eyes, "but I think the left foot is getting jealous."

"We don't want that to happen," John said, and he placed her big toe into his mouth and sucked.

"Oh, God," Jackie said, squirming, as she giggled. "Stop. Don't stop!"

John gently placed that foot into the water and lifted her other foot. His fingers kneaded her right foot. "I'm sorry to take you on a working honeymoon sweetheart."

"Are you kidding?" Jackie said, her eyes glistening. "Besides, this is our *second* honeymoon. Who gets two honeymoons in the first two months of marriage?"

"I don't think three days in Hawaii would be considered a honeymoon."

Due to his schedule, the best he could do was a long weekend. This time he had to work it around a DC trip. After the baby, it could be a long time before they had time alone again.

"You made me an honest woman. And besides, I loved house hunting. But, I'm not sure if Sandy appreciated me christening the bathrooms at each house we visited."

"Oh, I'm sure the commission she gets will make up for you puking in all the houses."

"Toilets. I made every one," Jackie said, reaching for her glass of champagne. "If I ask for more than one glass, you have to be the responsible one and stop me"

"I'm on it," John said. "And I've got powers of distraction that you've never seen."

Jackie laughed, and placed her glass on the edge of the tub. "Well, you've got a lifetime to show me all of them."

"I'm counting on it." John set her foot in his lap. He reached for her hand, and then pulled her to him. Turning her around she nestled in between his legs and he wrapped his arms around her, and nibbled her ear. She made the most delightful noise. It was part purr and part moan, and it drove him crazy.

"So which area did you like best?" Jackie asked.

"Sweetheart, I am good with anything you want. If I get the appointment, where we live will be your choice." He hated lying to her.

"Seattle?" she said jokingly. "Seriously, as long as I'm with you, I don't care where that is. All the neighborhoods were beautiful."

He kissed the top of her head. "As long as I get to come home every night to you and the kids, I'll be in heaven," he said, his hand sliding over her abdomen, and then back up to her other breast.

Jackie was five months along, and the baby was sucking its thumb. He had read every baby book he could find, and the baby-making process amazed him. It also scared the hell out of him. He could not imagine being a father in his mid-fifties, but he was more worried about Jackie. A woman in her forties had more complications than those who were younger. However, he could also afford the best care money could buy, and he would be with her every step of the way to assure nothing happened to the love of his life.

"Well, I kind of liked the Kensington area," Jackie said. "Sandy said it was the safest in the DC area, and I really loved all those little shops and antique stores." She covered John's hand with hers as he massaged her breast. "But what I really liked best is that Chris could walk to school while I'm taking care of the baby."

"That's definitely a benefit."

John was destined to spend many long days, and even longer nights whether he had the job or not. Moving her away from her home and life in Seattle would be problematic. He wasn't sure how long she would put up with being isolated with a baby while he was out at business dinners. He hoped forever.

More importantly, he hoped to hell he could balance the insanity of what he was doing and a new family, all at the same time.

"I don't want to break the bank," Jackie said. "You're going to have three mouths to feed."

"Not a worry," John said. The added money was just around the corner, and cash always gave the best buying power. He lifted her hand and kissed her palm. "You know I would turn it down if you wanted me to."

Jackie broke into a hearty laugh. "Like hell you would. Besides, I'd never let you."

"But you'd be giving up so much moving to the other side of the country."

"I'm not giving up anything. I have you," she said moving his hand to her abdomen. "I have the baby. I have Chris. And I have Kathryn and Darby who will come and visit as often as they can. And Linda promised to Skype."

"Then we'd need a really big house," John said, theatrically. "With WiFi."

He loved Chris, and had enjoyed watching him grow into a nice young man. But now he was fifteen, and John could see him pulling away. He knew a move would add to that behavior. His mother was going to need him. Kathryn and Darby were definitely part of the big package he had married into, and he couldn't ask for a better support system than Linda and Niman.

John had wanted Kathryn to come back to the NTSB, but she was in position to do something big at the FAA. There was more going on behind the scenes than anyone suspected. He felt guilty lying to her, but he had more worries with the overall operations of the Federal Aviation Administration than he did losing a friendship.

There had been continual consternation between the NTSB and the FAA. He also had a great deal of concern about what had happened on that Global flight, yet progress was moving slowly. Too slowly, as far as he was concerned. He'd also been ordered to remove himself from that investigation—a complication that could be worked around.

John had to remind himself daily that all his actions were for the greater good. Sometimes sacrifice was what it took, and if that meant sacrificing your ethics in the process, well then, that would be the price he would pay.

"Five bedrooms, at least."

"Huh?" John said, shifting his attention back to their conversation.

"We'll need a five-bedroom house," Jackie said. "Maybe six."

John grinned. "Why don't we get four, and if they come to town all at once, we'll put them in a hotel. The twins would love that."

"No, they'll want to play with the baby."

"Good point," he said, his hand massaging the area that got them into trouble in the first place. Her fingers lightly stroked his hand, as he found pleasure touching her.

"Are you sure you'll get that position?" Jackie asked. "I mean the current guy has only been there for three years."

"The new president will appoint a new candidate."

"What happens if you don't get it?" She asked. "I mean, what if they decide to give it to Diane Nobles because she's a woman."

"I don't think that would happen," John said. "Besides, there have already been two female department secretaries, so that's not a new thing. I don't think anyone would stick someone in just because of gender." He thought for a moment and added, "Actually, I think if anyone would give it to a woman for the sake of being a woman, it would be Drake."

"Well, maybe Darby's book helped to show them who Nobles really is."

"The best sellers list didn't hurt," John said.

Diane Nobles was the head of human factors in the FAA and she had skeletons in her closet. One of them Darby had brought forward in her book. She had found an FAA human factors report dating back twenty years that identified problems with training, pilots lack of understanding due to aircraft complexity and automation, shitty training programs, and that pilots were losing their flight skills. Nobles had been the committee chair, and she buried the report.

Yet, she continued to move up in the FAA. Now, twenty years later those exact problems were more pronounced than ever. That report had been spot on and she could have done something back then. She should have done something. He was now beginning to understand why she hadn't, but there were too many pieces to the puzzle laid out before him.

He could only hope Darby's book would be enough to take her down, but so far she held strong. While John had never planned on becoming the Department of Transportation secretary, he was the best applicant. Unfortunately, he was in a precarious spot with his current assignment.

"Promise me one thing," Jackie said rolling over and wrapping her arms around his neck. He moved forward so her legs had room to wrap around behind him.

"Anything, my love," he said, his lips gently touching hers.

"That whatever happens, you keep focused on what's important in life."

His hands slid down to her lower back and he rubbed. "I do know what's important," he said. Trickling kisses around her neck.

She giggled. "Don't ever forget that."

John and Jackie climbed out of the tub and into the king sized bed and made love with the roar of Niagara Falls outside. She had fallen asleep in his arms and snored gently, yet he could not find sleep.

Everyone got someplace through buying someone off, manipulation, or climbing into bed with another—literally or figuratively. It was damn time he toughened up and played hardball with the real world. The benefit would far outweigh the cost. However, what he'd learned over the previous four months was painting an ugly picture, and he didn't know quite how to deal with it or which direction to turn.

John knew what was important. He pulled Jackie closer and felt her heart beating against his. She and his baby deserved to be protected every time they stepped onto an airplane, but at what cost? Everyone deserved to be safe.

Every airline ticket came with an implied contract—that passengers would receive safe passage to their destination. Many airlines were not honoring their side of that contract. The FAA was not doing due diligence. And everyone appeared to be in bed with someone—Diane Nobles was no exception.

Global Air Line's Boeing 737 that nearly impacted the ground, hit a chord like none other. That situation may have been nothing short of the endemic problem of inadequate training that left pilots less than proficient, the hell with competency. *Or was it?* He still wasn't sure, but he waited for the process. Answers were always there if one looked, listened, and had patience.

There *would* be a new secretary of DOT for 2017, and why couldn't it be John McAllister?

"I swear to you my love, I will not let you down," he whispered. "I will not fail this time." He kissed her forehead and placed a hand over his baby. He *had* to become the United States Secretary of Transportation—lives depended upon it. He would do whatever it took to make that happen. He would no longer care about violating principles. The new generation of business and government was nothing more than strategic manipulation. A game he would learn to play.

# CHAPTER 4

WITH HER HEART soaring, Darby pulled off Rainier Avenue and turned onto Airport Way. She headed south toward Rainier Flight, a fixed based operator located at Renton Airport. She could not believe how perfect life was. Kathryn was willing to read her report. Jackie and John were married. A baby was coming. All the kids were doing great. She glanced up to the Cessna 172 that was on downwind, and she thought about the man she loved. She wanted to tell him their great news, but she was nervous as hell.

She pulled into the parking lot, found a spot and then put her car in park. She tossed her purse on the floor and covered it with her coat, and locked the door. Placing her sunglasses in position, she stuck her hands in her jeans pockets as Ray's aircraft turned final for landing.

Ray had been a little off lately—off being grumpy. He was a mechanic at Global and loved his job. *So he said.* She suspected his getting kicked out of management hit him harder than he thought it would. Granted it gave them more time together, and he also liked working on the planes better than management duties. But something was amiss. Whatever it was, her news would either snap him out of it or make it worse. Life was a gamble when playing with emotions. But a risk everyone should be willing to take.

His plane touched down on the numbers. Shortly thereafter, he pulled off the runway and taxied toward the ramp. Darby waved and did a little happy dance, then walked toward the plane. She waited until he shut down the engine and then ran to the left door. He smiled without much joy behind it.

When he opened the door she said, "Good morning. I missed you last night."

They had been spending most nights together, except when he worked late or she had an early flight. Yet, there was a time early in their relationship their schedules didn't matter. Last night he'd said he needed some time. Which was good for Darby so she could finish her report.

Ray climbed out of the plane and gave her a quick kiss. Then he walked to the aft door and pulled out the tow bar. "Here, put yourself to work," he said handing her the contraption.

"With pleasure," she said taking the bar. She walked around by the propeller, knelt and connected it to the nose gear. "Ready?"

He grabbed a wing and she angled the nose to align the plane with its parking spot and they pushed the plane backwards.

"Hey Ray boy!" Someone shouted from across the ramp. "Now I get it!"

Ray flipped him off, as they pushed the plane into its final position.

Darby unlatched the bar and returned it to the baggage compartment. She grabbed a rope that was tethered to the ground and looped it to through a ring on the left wing and tied a knot. Ray did the same on the right wing.

When done, he grabbed his iPad and headset from the front seat of his plane, then closed and locked the door.

"What was that about?" Darby finally asked.

"Nothing," he said, with a slight shake of his head as they headed toward the office.

"I finally got a response from Sinclair. I get my meeting."

Ray stopped walking and turned. "Are you sure you want to mess with these guys?"

"I'm not messing with anyone. I'm just identifying areas we need to fix, to Sinclair. Granted, it's every department in flight ops, but they're really screwed up down there."

"Screwed up or not, you're going to ruin your career."

"So I've been told."

"Maybe you should listen."

"Excuse me?"

"Sweetheart," Ray said, relaxing a bit and shifting the load in his arms, clearly searching for better words to get his ass out of the doghouse.

"Maybe I should listen? *Seriously?*" Darby folded her arms. Thank God she was wearing glasses and he couldn't see the f-you look she was giving him. Yet she suspected her body language spoke volumes.

"That's not what I meant. They're going to screw with your career if you make life too uncomfortable for them."

"I'm a seniority list pilot. What the hell could they do to me?" Darby said unfolding her arms and splaying her palms. Frustration took hold. Ray had initially supported her, but over the previous month he had been slowly shifting his support to the dark side, attempting to convince her to not report. He also parroted much of her union rep's warnings. Thus, she stopped talking about it, but her mission never wavered.

"You'd make an excellent chief pilot. Play the game, and get that position."

"Like you did?" The minute that came out of her mouth she regretted it. "I'm sorry."

"No. I deserve that."

Darby sighed and removed her sunglasses. "I have no intention of playing games with people's lives by pulling the shit these guys do, to make a buck or climb the management ladder." She placed a hand on her hip and extended the other. "What they are doing is wrong. If I don't tell the director what I know, I'm just as bad as they are."

"He already knows what's going on."

"We don't know that for sure," Darby said. "Okay... Let's play devil's advocate that you're right. If I give him a report, in writing, a message of—you have just been served—then he won't be able to play dumb. He'll have to start fixing things."

"Why the hell do *you* have to be Joan of Arc?"

Darby grinned. "I'm not. I'm just a girl. Standing here, telling a guy that enough is enough."

Ray laughed. "You are going to be the death of me." He pulled her into his arms. "I just worry about you, sweetheart."

"I'm golden," she said, melting into him. "But, I haven't told you the best news."

"We definitely need some good news," Ray said, holding her tight. Then his phone rang, and he released her. "Just a sec." He walked a foot away, and spoke in low voice shaking his head. As hard as she tried, she couldn't hear him. He turned and then said, "Can I meet you at your house in twenty minutes?"

# CHAPTER 5

"YOU TRYING TO kill me or are you training for the Olympics?" Darby said, bent over with hands on knees while attempting to catch her breath. She normally could outrun him, but whatever happened during his twenty-minute phone call put him in a definite mood to kill and conquer. Either she or the pavement was his victim, she wasn't sure.

Hopefully this was not a sign of things to come.

Ray was breathing equally as hard, pacing along her porch trying to catch his breath, too. "Ah, finally something I can do better than you."

"I know a lot of things you can do better than me."

"You make *that* hard," he said under his breath.

Darby stood upright, and walked toward him and placed a hand on the front if his shorts and said, "Not yet, but there's potential."

"You watch *way* too many movies."

"Are you kidding?" Darby said, placing her hands on her hips. "Some of my best lines come from great movies."

"*Pretty Woman* is great?" Ray said, raising an eyebrow.

"What is wrong with you?" Darby said, turning from him and unlocking the door. She stepped inside, and he followed her into the kitchen.

When she and Ray met, he had been the director of maintenance at Global Air Lines. However, due to his knowledge of a maintenance issue that he'd ignored, more like a Ponzi scheme, he was demoted back to mechanic. One could hardly blame him for his silence back then, as Global had anything but a reporting culture. They all knew what would have happened to him if he'd come forward.

When it was all said and done, he was actually lucky to not have been fired. She often wondered why he hadn't been. But, he loved working on planes and had appeared happy with the shift in position and change in responsibility—until recently.

"Sorry," he said. "It's just... I've got a lot on my mind."

"Yep. That mind's been filled for a while now," Darby said, opening the fridge. "So, who was on the phone back at the hangar?"

"Nobody important."

She sighed. At first she thought his attitude was due to all the attention to Jackie and the wedding, and Ray getting nervous that Darby would catch the bouquet. Then she thought it was the time spent working on her report. Perhaps she had become a broken record, as it seemed like all she talked about was fixing Global problems. But he should care as much about safety for the airline as she did.

When the girls were whining, Kathryn always said to just ignore the behavior, it would go away. She'd tried that strategy out of convenience with Ray. But now he was trying to kill her by running her to death, and it was time to end the problem, one way or another. With what she was about to face, she needed everyone on her team—especially Ray.

"You're eventually going to have to tell me," Darby said, handing him a bottle of Coors Light. She had grabbed a bottle of water for herself, and then headed into the laundry room and picked up a couple of towels, and yelled, "Hot tub?"

Within minutes they were lifting the lid off the tub. Proper protocol after a run would include a shower first and tub second. But they would never make it to the tub if the shower happened first, and they needed to talk. They stripped out of their jogging clothes, and climbed in.

"I'm sorry for all my attention on that damn report," Darby said, sitting across from him. She sipped her water and stared at him. "So what's been up with you anyway?"

"Nothing." He took a long drink of his beer, and then said, "Everything. I don't know."

"Male menopause?" She grinned.

"More like a mid-life crisis."

"Don't let me hold you back," Darby said, and took a long drink of water, eyeing him. Her heart sank ever so slightly at the thought.

"That's not what I meant." He raised his beer to his lips and took a long swig and then said, "Work has been a bitch lately, and…"

"You should become a pilot. You've got the hours."

His eyes held hers for a moment, and then he said, "I'm concerned about you meeting with Sinclair."

"What's he going to do? I'll be fine," Darby said with a wave of her hand. "Besides, Kat's got the report and—"

"Kat has it?" Ray asked. "Were you going to let me read it?"

"Of course. I want to know what you think, but you were flying this morning."

"I *think* you should let it go, your career—"

"Broken record." She grinned. "I'm a seniority list pilot, and I'll move up when my seniority can hold it."

"What's the point?" Ray took a sip of his beer, and then set the bottle on the edge of the tub. "They're never going to change. They'll screw with you."

"Okay Mr. optimistic, the point is… I want to leave the airline better than I found it."

"You'd have more success sticking your head into a moving propeller."

"But it's my head," Darby said with a grin. "But thank you for that visual."

"Babe, you're going to get hurt."

"Then you can protect me," she said, in the best lady in distress voice she could muster.

Ray laughed. "I'm not sure if there is *anyone* who could take on that job."

"Seriously, is this what's been bothering you?" she asked assessing his tells

"The guys down South aren't playing on a normal field."

"So I've heard," Darby said, just as her phone rang. "I'll be right back."

"Seriously?" Ray said. "Can't it wait?"

"It might be Kat."

"Of course it is," he said, and reached for his beer.

"Don't roll your eyes at me," Darby said, climbing out of the tub. "Give me a minute," she said grabbing a towel, and then ran toward the kitchen. Shivering, she wrapped the towel around herself, picked up her phone, and pressed callback.

"So, what'd you think?" Darby asked.

"I should never have agreed to reading this."

"Pretty incriminating, huh?"

"Incriminating? This airline should be shut down."

Darby climbed into a chair and pulled her legs close to her chest, and hugged them to stave off the chill. "Lawrence Patrick couldn't possibly know what's going on."

"But he should be held accountable," Kathryn said.

Lawrence Patrick, Global's CEO, had taken two bankrupt airlines and turned them into one mega beast. The airline had created an image of the most elite airline in the world. If you flew on Global, you were flying the best. However, she agreed with John—the inner workings were nothing short of a tumor that could suck the life out of the organization.

"This is nothing to play with," Kathryn said. "I'm not sure you talking to them is the solution. How could anyone possibly know what's happening and allow this to occur?"

"That's why I think they don't," Darby said, adjusting the towel.

"This goes far beyond safety culture. You have an entire flight operations team that's flat out violating regulations."

"That's what I've been saying," Darby said, climbing off the chair. She opened the refrigerator and grabbed a Diet Pepsi. "So, what do you think? Besides wanting to shut them down."

"It was well written. Shocked the hell out of me. But, I'm not sure if you should give it to them."

"Why not?" Darby opened the lid on her soda and took a drink.

"When you put something in writing, you can't take it back."

"Well, it's all true. And I want to make sure they don't take anything I say out of context." Darby sighed. "But I am nervous."

"You should be effing scared," Kathryn said.

"I just want them to do the right thing." Darby knew that passengers' lives were at stake.

"Can we talk about this tonight?" Kathryn asked. "You still want us all for dinner?"

"Of course, to both questions," Darby said, glancing at the time on her oven—the only thing her oven seemed to be good for. "See you in two hours."

With a chill crawling deep within her skin, Darby headed toward the back patio with Kathryn's words sinking deep—*You can't take it back.* Maybe that was exactly why she was doing this. Pull the pin and throw the grenade, you couldn't take it back. She'd had that exact thought when she wrote her book, and nothing came of that.

Besides, this was an internal report, so why would any one of them care? She would just give it to them. Her reporting duty would be complete, and they could do with it what they wanted. But, she couldn't live with herself if they had an accident, and she hadn't done everything she could in attempt to prevent it. The thought of losing John made her sick.

Darby stepped on the patio, and said, "Sorry about that." But Ray was gone.

# CHAPTER 6

HOLDING THE GUN to her head, she pulled the trigger. Warmth of the air and vibration in her hand instantly soothed her nerves. Darby wasn't sure if a hairdryer in the shape of a gun was politically correct, but it reminded her how short life was every time she used it. It also got the job done quicker than any other dryer she'd owned—efficiency at its best.

Ray was downstairs watching television in the living room, and if she didn't know better, he was pouting. Well, she did know better and was losing patience with his mood. She had such incredible news, and he was ruining it.

He had slipped out of the hot tub and had walked past her in the kitchen without her seeing him, and went to take a shower alone. *Men.* She swore that if they weren't the center of attention, they had their one little feeling hurt. She wasn't sure how he would take her news. She kind of wanted to cancel dinner.

Darby shut off the hair dryer. She dragged a brush through her hair, and then pulled it into a ponytail. This news was going to impact Ray more than anyone else. Their life together would change. What the hell had she been thinking giving a group announcement about something like this?

Adding a touch of mascara to her lashes, she sighed. *This is as good as we get tonight.* Darby stared for a minute, assessing the woman who returned her gaze. She knew what she had to do—tell Ray her news before everyone got there. But she was such a damn chicken.

The truth was, she wanted Kathryn and the girls there for moral support. They would all be happy for her. God, she wanted Ray to feel the same joy she felt. Darby swallowed her fear, and headed downstairs.

He was sitting in the easy chair with his legs extended. She hesitated at his side a moment, and then climbed into his lap. He wrapped his arms around her and kissed her forehead. Ray loved her, and he would be happy for her.

She laid her head on his chest, and said, "I want to tell you something before everyone gets here."

"Uh, huh?" he said with about as much interest as a limp dick. As if a limp dick had interest in anything other than hanging there. Her stomach grumbled. She glanced at the television to see what was so enthralling—something about the presidential election. The election was beyond heating up; it was so overdone. The truth was, the world may just see the first multi-billionaire businessman as the president of the United States. But at the moment, there were more pressing issues.

Darby reached for the remote and pressed mute. "What I have to say will be quick."

*Just give it fast like medicine and it's over,* she thought. What surprised her most was her fear that Ray would not feel the same excitement she did. God, she hoped her fear was off base.

"So, I have really good news…"

The doorbell rang, and Ray said, "Saved by the bell."

"Ha. Ha. You're always saved by something." She climbed off his lap and went to the front door.

She opened the door and Sam stood in front of her. "Hey Darby, big order tonight."

Darby laughed. Not from the fact that she was on first name basis with the Chinese food delivery guy, but he knew the size of her order. Not that size was an issue. "Dinner party, and I'm cooking," she said, grabbing her purse. She'd paid with a credit card over the phone, but pulled out a $20 bill for his tip. Sam always snuck extra cookies and hot mustard into the bag, and he never forgot her chopsticks.

"Wow! Thanks," he said.

She grinned, as this was the game they played each delivery. She thanked him, and then she set the bag of food on the dining room table. Her stomach grumbled again. God, she was hungry. Opening a small box at the top, she pulled out a slice of barbecued pork and took a bite, and then headed back to the living room.

The volume was back on the television.

This time Darby sat on the couch opposite him. She didn't say anything, but just watched him, and ate her pork. He glanced her way and smiled, and she gave him one of those closed lip smiles. *Damn. Why was this so hard?*

Ray stood, and turned off the television. He tossed the remote onto the chair and moved to the couch and sat beside her. He held her hand. "I'm sorry."

"For what?" One eyebrow rose with a mind of its own, curious as to which part of his behavior he would apologize for first. *This should be good,* she thought.

"I've been an ass," he said, lifting her hand. He turned it over, and placed his lips on her palm. Then he pulled away and added, "Self-absorbed." He kissed her palm again, and said, "I'm totally here for anything you want to say."

Darby pulled her hand back, and stood. She placed her hands on her hips, and sighed. And then she grinned. "Okay, if you really want to know. I…" A pounding at the front door interrupted her sentence, and was followed by Jessica and Jennifer pouring into the house laughing, with Kathryn and Chris in tow.

"We're here!" the twins yelled.

"Chinese?" Kathryn said. "This must be really good news."

Chris went into the kitchen and opened the fridge, and Jessica said, "Can you get me a Diet Pepsi?"

Jessica opened the bag of Chinese food and began removing cartons and setting them on the counter. "Aunt Darby, if you're home next weekend, will you drive with me?"

Darby glanced at Kathryn, who shrugged. "Sure. Mom making you crazy?"

Jennifer laughed. "To say the least. Can you work me into your schedule too?"

"I'll be home on Friday," Darby said.

She loved her open floor plan, with a kitchen as an accessory to the living room hosted by a dining room table between the two rooms—a perfect design. She pulled plates out of the cupboard. Kathryn opened the drawer and began counting forks.

"Stop! What the heck are you doing?" Darby waved a handful of chopsticks.

Kathryn rolled her eyes.

"Don't roll your eyes at me," Darby said. "Girls, now I know where you got *that* maneuver."

Darby was not really the girls' aunt, but she had always been Aunt Darby as long as she could remember. She loved them all. Ray walked into the kitchen and said hello to everyone, then shook Chris's hand.

"How's life with the ladies?" Ray asked Chris, as he grabbed himself another beer from the fridge. Chris shrugged, but the grin told all.

Chris had been staying with Kathryn and the girls while his Mom and John were on their East Coast honeymoon, and Darby knew he was having the time of his life.

"You want driving lessons too?" Darby asked.

"That'd be awesome!" Chris said. Darby laughed. She knew the way to a man's heart, but a teenage boy—offer him a chance to operate a machine and he was all in.

Darby waited until everyone's plates were full and they were seated. "Now that I have you all here. I have some great news."

She felt like a fool putting herself on stage. But the moment she learned of the news, early that morning, she did a happy dance.

"Aunt Darby, spit it out already," Jessica said, stuffing an eggroll into her mouth.

She breathed deep. "I got a captain bid on the Boeing 757 in Seattle." The room silenced, and her guest's mouths hung open. Not the response she'd expected. "What?"

"What the heck?" Jessica said, "I thought you were pregnant!"

"Holy cow. Me too," Jennifer said, toasting her Diet Pepsi to her sister.

Darby's eyes went wide. "What?" She looked at Kathryn in question, and said, "You too?"

Kathryn nodded. "I was beginning to wonder."

"What the hell. Baby? Me?" Darby began laughing. "No way. The only baby I want is one that I can fly."

Darby loved flying more than anything. She lived and breathed the moment she could get into the sky. The opportunity to hold a Seattle captain bid was long overdue, and took her flying to the next level. Not only would she be a captain, but she would also be flying a Boeing again. She loved flying the Airbus, but sitting reserve, on the Airbus A330, she rarely flew.

She would still be on reserve with the 757, yet the reserve system between an international aircraft and a domestic aircraft were two different worlds. As a captain flying a domestic aircraft she would actually get to fly more. More than likely she would fly all the time, and she could hardly wait. Granted, the trips would be red-eyes, as nobody wanted to fly in the middle of the night. But there were always sacrifices. Unfortunately, she and Ray's quality time together would shift, and he knew it.

Darby looked at Ray and said, "Surprise," with hands spread wide.

"I didn't know you bid it," Ray said.

"I never removed the bid off my card. It's been there for years."

"You never give up on your dreams, Ray," Jessica said. She dumped a scoop of Moo Shoo pork onto her plate.

"I always thought you *were* a captain," Chris said, and Darby laughed.

"I am so happy for you," Kathryn said, hugging Darby. When she pulled back, her eyes were moist eyes. "You gave up so much for the girls and me. It's time you got back in the left seat. You deserve that."

After the merger Darby allowed her fourth stripe to be ripped from her shoulders in order to remain in Seattle. She stayed to help Kathryn with the kids after psycho Captain Bill Jacobs, Kathryn's husband, went to jail for killing hundreds of people orchestrating airliner crashes. There was no way Darby could leave them, not even now. Patience was a virtue and she knew if she waited long enough, her time would come. Now was her time.

Sometime during Kathryn's hug, Ray took his plate and walked out of the kitchen.

# CHAPTER 7

AN AWKWARD SILENCE filled the room, as Darby pulled her sports bra over her head. She tossed it into the hamper and stared Ray's direction. He was lying on the bed watching *Real Time with Bill Maher*. He had eaten his dinner in the living room. Alone. She had not looked for him until after everyone had gone. When she took his empty plate back to the kitchen, he didn't follow.

She cleaned up the kitchen, and then found him upstairs. Whatever was eating him, he would have to work it out himself. But one thing she knew, when Ray went silent, it was like an airplane in flight with a double engine failure—it wasn't good.

Darby climbed out of her black lace undies and threw them at him. He caught them in midair and smiled glancing her way, and then pulled his attention back to the television. Her report lay beside him.

"Did you read it?"

"I did," he said.

Darby glanced at the report, and back to him. She felt naked and vulnerable. Probably because she was—the naked part anyway. There had been a time if she were wearing nothing more than her skin that he couldn't keep his hands off her. How time changed everything. With hands on hips, she drummed her red nails. She wanted to cheer him up, but had no idea how. She rolled her eyes, and headed for the bathroom instead.

Darby turned the faucet on her tub to full hot, and then poured a double dose of rose scented bubble bath into the water. As bubbles began to fill the tub, she pressed the power button on her stereo. Jimmy Buffett came alive singing, "Changes in latitudes, changes in attitudes, nothing remains quite the same." *Isn't that the truth?* She pulled her hair high on her head, and then wound it in a scrunchie.

She dumped face cleanser into her hands, added water, and with eyes closed rubbed it onto her skin. She then splashed handfuls of water on her face to rinse the soap away. With eyes closed, she patted the counter, feeling for the face towel. When she couldn't find it, she opened them, and jumped. Ray was leaning against the door jam, holding her towel.

"Looking for this?"

"Thanks," Darby said, taking the towel. She pressed it to her face and blotted. She wasn't sure why blotting was the method of choice for drying ones face, but now that she was getting older, she would do anything to help the age from setting in.

She glanced at the filling tub, and then stepped past Ray as she ducked into the bedroom. Pulling on her bathrobe, fuzzy side in, she asked, "Want a glass of wine?"

"No thanks," he said, moving into the bedroom.

She went downstairs and poured herself a glass of Merlot, taking her time to fill it. Not exactly sure what was up with him. She had her suspicion it had to do with money. She already made more than him, and making a captain salary would further that gap. *Men,* she thought with a sigh.

"Oh shit!" Darby said, remembering her tub. She turned and ran toward the stairs, as quickly as she could without spilling her wine, and yelled, "Ray, check the tub!"

By the time she returned to her bathroom, she froze. Ray had not only saved her bathroom floor, but he had lit candles surrounding the tub.

"What's all this?" she asked, setting her wine on the counter.

He pulled her to him, and gave her a long hug. And then put her at arm's length, and untied her belt. "You're beautiful," he said opening her robe.

His lips found a home on her neck. *Oh God, that feels good,* Darby thought. Ray was back. She could only hope. But then, his bipolar behavior was something she would not accept long term. Sometimes he was such a teenage girl. She giggled. Maybe that's why she loved him.

"Why are you still dressed," she asked tossing her robe to the counter and stepping into the tub. She slid down into water with bubbles up to her chin.

"I'm not going to steal your relaxation, too." He reached for her glass of wine, sipped, and then handed it to her. "I stole your joy. I'm sorry."

"No you didn't," she said eyeing him over the brim of her glass. "The joy will be when I get in that left seat again, and fly."

He sat on the edge of the tub, which was big enough for two. A marble ledge encircled it that was wide enough for glasses, plates, candles, or butts. The twins and their friends had spent many afternoons soaking their feet after a basketball game. But tonight there were bubbles, candles, and Ray.

He was wearing a white t-shirt and a pair of running shorts, and he looked so cute. But he was so much more than his looks. He was such a goodhearted man. She wasn't sure how she got so lucky to have met him, despite his mood swings. She never thought she would fall in love again, and truly thought that love only struck once. The third time was definitely her good fortune.

Ray placed a washrag on her back. He bent down and kissed the top of her head and began washing her back. She set her wine on the ledge, and wrapped her arms around her bent legs. Closing her eyes, she hugged her legs and melted into his touch.

"I'm sorry I've been an ass," he said. "When I heard you got the upgrade, I was pissed you hadn't told me."

"You knew?" Darby said, looking up. "I just found out today."

"I'd heard four weeks ago. I thought you knew too. I had no idea you had bid it." He kissed her shoulder and then slid the rag to her lower back. "More than that, I had no idea what you've been going through with this company."

"What do you mean?" she asked, turning her face toward him, resting a cheek on her knees.

"Your report," he said. "When you talked about some of the issues, I had no idea how much crap had been going on, and for how long." He reached for her wine and sipped, then returned it to the edge of the tub.

"Yeah, it's been a fun time," Darby said closing her eyes. She placed her forehead against her knees again while he massaged her neck.

"What's been going on is pure insanity. I knew these guys were assholes, and violated regulations and shit, but..." He sighed. "I never knew everything they had done to you. Well, I knew, but when it's written in a report in context of the big picture, it kind of puts it into perspective. It's hard to believe how stupid they are."

Darby laughed. That was one way to put it. She sat upright and turned towards Ray, and crossed her legs. She sipped her wine, thinking about his words, and then handed him the glass. "I couldn't agree more. But the thing is, I can take whatever they throw at me. I just couldn't take it if an accident happened and I kept quiet. Much of that report is from other people who are afraid to come forward. Nobody should be afraid. Not in today's world."

"I'm just not sure telling them will matter."

"Maybe not, but once I give the report to Sinclair, he'll put it into context and will get it."

"Sweetheart, he's done nothing yet, and besides—"

"My point. How could he possibly know?"

She had to give Sinclair the benefit of the doubt. The flight operations department was a structured hierarchy with a chain of command, not the open door policy written in the operations manual. There was zero communication between departments. The entire system was a series of silos that went up, not out. The entire structure opposed a safety management system designed with a flat structure and open communication—a system where employees on the ground floor could report safety issues.

"I have to believe he doesn't know because the system is designed to keep everything out of the ivory tower. He inherited a huge problem."

Ray sighed. "In a perfect world. But, they built that structure to keep all the crap out of the top offices so they could plead ignorance if anything happened."

"But Sinclair hasn't been there that long. It was Wyatt and Clark's doing, and they're gone."

"I have to tell you something—"

"What's that smell?" Darby said. "Something's burning."

Ray jumped off the edge of the tub and turned, the back of his shirt was on fire. "Shit!"

"Stop. Drop. Roll," Darby shouted, and then she began to laugh.

Ray stuffed a towel under his shirt and pressed his back against the wall, smothering the flames.

"You are so hot!" Darby said, still laughing. "Come here baby and light my fire."

"Ha. Ha." He pulled off his singed shirt, wadded it up and threw it at her. "Did I burn my back?" he asked turning his back toward her.

"Come closer so I can see." She worked to stifle her laughter. "Sit," she said, patting the edge of the tub.

He sat with his back to her so she could check out his wounds. Darby inspected his back, lightly trickling her fingers over it, and then leaned in and kissed it gently. "Looks really good," she said, sliding her arms around him. She gave him a big hug and then pulled him into the tub, on top of her. He ended up in her lap, bubbles flying everywhere, and legs hanging over the edge. His moment of shock was replaced with joining her in laughter.

"I'm a so glad you're here to save me," Darby said wrapping her arms around him. "My knight in burning armor."

"You think you're so funny," Ray said, working out of his shorts. He tossed them out of the tub, and pulled his legs in. He rolled over and got on all fours straddling her, and then leaned over her he blew out all the candles.

"Taking baths is not for wimps," Darby said. She reached up and put her arms around his neck, and pulled him towards her. She kissed him long and hard, and when she came up for air, she gazed into his eyes and said, "Your love burns my soul."

"You're never going to let this die, are you?"

"Nope. Not for a very long time."

# CHAPTER 8

FOUR WEEKS HAD passed since Kathryn had read Darby's report, and the words still haunted her. She was sure that many of the events were not isolated to Global, but more than likely occurred at multiple airlines. The problem was, how to address this mess. Then she thought of John's flight, and it all made sense as to what happened. It was nothing but poor performance fueled by inadequate training.

Darby had allowed Kathryn to give John the safety report, and when he officially took office as the secretary of the DOT he could do something. He needed to understand the magnitude of the problem with airline operations and training to create effective change.

For now, Kathryn was stuck with overseeing drone regulation, which was a challenge all unto itself. Her mind shifted to Jim Drake, the owner of Drake Industries, and his campaign for president of the United States.

Drake Industries was leading the pack for drone technology. When the world had a grasp on security, Drake would make billions with that technology alone. Hell, if Drake solved the security issue, those billions would double. *What the hell was he running for president for anyway?*

She was beginning to wonder when the public would think that ground control of aircraft would be better than pilot control, based on how bad pilot performance had been. Yet, was poor performance really the pilots' fault? Human error would be at the heart of ground-based drone technology, too. That was something that could not be avoided.

Kathryn pushed back from her desk, and walked across her office. She placed a raspberry chocolate flavored coffee pod into her Keurig machine, and closed the lid. She set her mug in place and pressed start. She performed this coffee ritual far too often in her day, but it gave her a chance to get out of her head for a moment, and think. As the hot black liquid filled the mug, she folded her arms and worked to get rid of her feeling of unease.

When brewing was complete, she added a yellow packet of fake sugar followed by a splash of cream, and then slowly stirred the mixture. There was no reason to be on edge. The kids were doing great in school. Albeit she would have to face them driving soon. Jackie was still having morning sickness, but that happened to many women during the entire pregnancy. John was about to get the job of a lifetime. Darby was home studying for her captain checkout. Everything was great, yet something didn't feel right.

"Kathryn." The voice from the doorway made her jump. "Everything okay?" Jason Bernard asked.

"Couldn't be better." Kathryn smiled. "Sorry about my reaction," she said to her boss. "I was thinking and didn't hear you come in." She raised her mug, "Can I get you a cup?"

"No, thanks. I'm good," he said. "I just wanted to bring you this report." He set it on her desk. "I sent you an electronic copy, but took the liberty to print it as well. I need your help."

Kathryn walked behind her desk, and glanced down. "Global?" Her heart rate increased ever so slightly.

He nodded. "Apparently an isolated incident, but they're taking it seriously. Changed their procedures to ensure this would never happen again. Blah. Blah. Blah."

It had been seven months and they finally completed the report. Kathryn sat heavily behind her desk, and lifted it. Her heart was now running a marathon. This was the report about John's flight, from the NTSB. She wondered why John hadn't sent this to her. He hadn't even told her it was close to completion.

"Is there a reason you're putting this on my desk?" Global Air Lines, as well as incidents that had nothing to do with drones were normally off limits to her.

Her boss glanced over his shoulder, then stepped back and closed the door. "Yes, there is," he said when he turned her way. "I'm not telling Rob I gave you this, but I want your perspective."

Rob's responsibility was to review violations and incident reports submitted by the NTSB, and to write the FAA recommendations for further investigation, or provide recommendations to the airline's principle operating inspectors based upon the NTSB's assessment.

Kathryn was not alone to have noticed that Rob never challenged anything. Any report that came past his desk denied most NTSB recommendations. No reports ever required further investigation as far as he was concerned. She just grew to accept that as part of a system flaw. At one time she had thought he was being paid off to look the other way, but after she got to know him she learned he just didn't want to make waves. Not a good attitude working in a safety environment.

She pushed her opinion on his attitude and complacency as far as she could without getting herself fired. If she didn't have a job, there was nothing she could do to fix the system. She only prayed John got the DOT secretary position. Then things would be different. She could assist him in fixing this mess, and many more.

"Do you think there is more to this than meets the eye?" she asked.

"I'm not sure," Jason said, "But this one was a bit too close to home."

Kathryn knew exactly what he meant. She could never imagine losing John, but the current secretary of the Department of Transportation was on that flight as well. Not that the other lives were not equally as important—every life deserved safe passage.

The thought of losing anyone through a needless accident was something that she fought daily to stop. The loss of another person she loved was unacceptable. Her ex-husband having been involved in so many deaths still haunted her thoughts.

"How close to rumor was this?" she asked.

"Let's just say, I had no idea how close that plane was to impact."

She nodded and her foot took a life of its own, tapping beneath the desk for a moment, and then she said, "How do you want me to deal with the analysis and report?"

"Write it up. Word doc. Then print. Just walk it over to me."

"Can you send me the voice recorder?"

He sighed heavily. "Global said that voice recorder was inoperative. No recording. All they have is the FOQA data."

"What the hell?" Kathryn said. *How utterly convenient for them,* she thought.

"My reaction as well."

"Get me your thoughts, and Rob and I will go over the concerns, that he will more than likely overlook. I want to keep your name off of it. This is only between you and me."

"When do you want it?"

"Yesterday," Jason said, with a chuckle. "But I won't have Rob's report for a month. You have time."

Jason Bernard left the office and Kathryn shook her head with dismay. Darby was right about one thing—nothing at the FAA worked quickly. She began to read.

A LITTLE OVER an hour had passed and Kathryn finished the first read. *Holy shit.* She stood, dumped her cold cup of coffee down the drain and made another cup. Then she returned to the report.

She opened the folder and turned to the page where she highlighted details. She circled the word IMC, meaning they were flying in the clouds. The decision to go around was made at 700 feet. But when one of the pilots decided to go around, he inadvertently hit the autothrottle switch instead of the TOGA switch, meaning he removed automatic thrust. TOGA was the acronym for takeoff and go around power, and would have given them guidance and power to execute a missed approach. However, the flight director stayed in the approach mode and they continued to follow it heading straight for the ground.

A go-around in the Boeing 737 should have given them a pitch of about 12 degrees with power of about 90% N1. N1 was the rotational engine speed, likened somewhat to RPM. Instead they were still flying at a 3-degree pitch with 54% N1 power. Apparently, neither pilot noticed they were still headed toward the ground.

Why the hell they didn't identify the pilot flying was interesting.

These pilots did not have situation awareness beyond the flight director that was providing guidance for the approach. When they conducted the procedure for a missed approach, it was obvious the plane didn't perform with the command they had given it. *Why didn't they notice? How could they not see that the pitch and power didn't change?*

The plane got within 186 feet of impact and was flying toward the ground at 2000 feet per minute. The ground proximity warning system had to have been screaming in the background during the excessive closure toward the terrain with gear that had been raised. Sadly, she couldn't hear it, or any other dialogue in the cockpit because the cockpit voice recorder was inoperative. *Hmmm.*

Kathryn pushed back from her desk, and this time she walked to the window. A Global flight had just rotated. She watched it climb, and folded her arms to stave off the chill. Every day millions of people put their lives in the hands of pilots and flight attendants, expecting to be delivered safely to their destinations. She wondered if the 135 souls on board the flight on her desk ever realized how close to death they were.

Airlines sometimes gave passengers vouchers for delayed and canceled flights, but she wondered what kind of value they gave to those who came within seconds of dying.

Darby had once been in a jumpseat with a blaring ground proximity warning, and autothrust increasing the power to maximum, while the plane sank toward the ground because the pilots had an improper configuration. The captain and a check airman did not react either, and they were in visual conditions. Kathryn sighed. What was preventing these pilots from reacting properly? Darby saved that flight. Who saved this one?

She glanced back at the report. The next step would be to closely read each paragraph to see what they were missing. On the surface it appeared these pilots just messed up the missed approach procedure, making human error by pushing the wrong button and not identifying the error. But the truth was, these pilots were behind the aircraft from the onset of the approach and into the arrival.

Was this near crash a result of an improperly written procedure? Or was re-writing the procedure a Band-Aid of a more endemic problem—poor training.

A ringing phone broke into her thoughts, and she stepped toward her desk and answered. Cell phones were off limits, yet she conveniently forgot to turn hers off because of Jackie's condition.

"Kat, John here. I've got to go back East for a meeting. Can you keep an eye on Jackie for me?"

"You just got back yesterday. Are you sure you're not a pilot?"

John laughed. "I don't know how they do it. Wipes me out crossing the country twice in a week."

"Does Jackie know you're calling me?"

"No. But, I—"

"I'll keep an eye on her. But seriously, pregnancy is a normal body function and she has done this before."

"I know, but I worry."

"You should worry more about what flights you take."

"Did you get the report?"

"I did. It ended up on my desk today." With her arms on her desk and her forehead in hand, she added, "This was ugly. You better damn well get that job."

"Uh... I'm doing my best. That's why I'm heading to DC again."

"When do you leave?"

"I'm at the airport now."

"I'll see if Jackie can join us for dinner tonight."

"That'd be nice. And Kat... is there any way you could send me a copy of that report?"

"I've got an electronic copy in my inbox. Consider it done. But why didn't you get it?" John's access at the NTSB was one of the highest, and this report originated from his office.

"I've been given marching orders to stay away. Some conflict of interest bullshit," John said, and then added, "Make sure you delete the path."

Kathryn chuckled. "When you get to the big office, you'll have to clean up your language."

There was a great deal of talk about deleted emails in the media during this election year. If the public only knew the extent of what people in high power had sent via email that was subsequently deleted... What this election did, however, was to make sure everyone cleaned up their act, and opened their eyes to the possibility of email hacking and recording when they least expected it.

She opened her secure email and found the link, downloaded the report, and then sent it to John's private email, which was safer than his government address. He had all the protections, and nobody from the government could see the activity.

"You've got it. Path is deleted. Now have a good flight and don't worry about your bride. She's in good hands."

# CHAPTER 9

AS MUCH AS Darby loved studying her plane, she was glad to break away for a night and was looking forward to a girls' dinner with Kathryn and Jackie. She had only a couple of days off and would head back to Oklahoma City on Saturday for two additional training sessions before her checkride. But tonight, she ditched the training manuals, brain dumped aircraft limitations and would let her hair down. She turned on her blinker, glanced into her rearview mirror, and switched lanes.

It felt like years since they had a girls' night. Now Jackie was an old married woman with a baby on the way, and she was in the middle of training focused on her plane. At least Kathryn hadn't given up cooking. Her stomach grumbled on cue.

Seattle weather was turning cold and she had missed seeing the change, spending too much time out of state with training. She loved fall in Seattle. The colors were brilliant, and the scent of the damp earth was like no other. Now, most of the trees were bare from early and strong winds. Clicking on her blinker, she pulled into Kathryn's driveway. Jackie had just arrived, and was heading for the front door when she saw Darby's car and waved.

Darby parked her car and jumped out. "Hey momma bear!" she called.

Jackie lit up the moment she saw Darby, and they hugged, long and hard.

"How's training going?"

"It's going," Darby said noticing how much Jackie was showing. "Five months? Really?"

"I might have been wrong on my original date," Jackie said wrapping her arm inside of Darby's. "Let's go find food. I'm starving."

"I like the way you think."

Before they reached the front porch, Kathryn had opened the door. She handed Darby a glass of red wine, and gave Jackie a hug. "Let's get you both inside. It's freezing out here."

The warmth of Kathryn's home embraced Darby like a hug, and something jazzy played from the speakers. The house felt calm, probably because the twins were at basketball practice. After practice they would be going to a team party, and Chris was sleeping over at a friend's house. That manifested into time alone with her friends.

The women moved to the living room and Kathryn handed Jackie a glass of sparkling cider and then lifted her glass of wine. "To friends," she said. "Life would not be the same without you."

"Cheers," Jackie said, her eyes filling with tears.

"How long will your emotions be like this?" Darby asked, raising her glass.

Kathryn said, "For the next thirty some years," doing a double take at Jackie's gut as she settled into the couch, and her eyes widened in surprise.

Darby shrugged. "She goofed up the dates."

"How far along are you exactly?" Kathryn asked.

Jackie laughed. "Are you both calling me fat?" she said, rubbing the tummy that clearly indicated baby on board.

"You look great! And you're not fat," Kathryn said. "You just look a bit further along than five months."

"I was so excited when they told me, I got confused," Jackie said. "Last time I did this baby-thing we talked about it in months. Now they do everything in weeks."

"How many weeks?" Darby asked.

"Twenty-four, I think," Jackie said, and sipped her apple cider. "My doctor said she's due on January twelfth."

"She? You're having a girl!" Kathryn jumped off her chair and hugged Jackie.

"Wait a minute," Darby said. "Twenty-four weeks? You're more like six months along?"

"Give or take a day or two," Jackie said.

"Well here's to hoping with math skills like that, John's the baby daddy," Darby said with a wink, and then ducked the pillow that came flying her way.

"You're horrible!" Jackie said,

"I hope you're both hungry," Kathryn said, before anything else went flying in her living room. "The lasagna is ready."

"I love you." Lasagna was Darby's favorite Kathryn meal, but something she didn't partake in often. Tonight she looked forward to a little indulgence.

They made their way into the kitchen. Kathryn had outdone herself with the dinner. Salads were on the table, candles were glowing, warm French bread was in a basket, and the lasagna bubbled in the center of the table.

"This looks wonderful," Darby said. "But let me tell you about the last time Ray and I played with candles."

By the time she finished with the story, the girls were laughing so hard that Jackie said she was going to pee her pants. Once the bladder crisis was alleviated, Kathryn asked Darby how training had been going.

"It's been okay. But only because I've flown the plane before." She stabbed a bite of lasagna and spun the cheese onto the fork as she continued. "But the train-at-home thing was interesting. Not that I don't love reading at home, but there was nobody available to answer questions."

"You trained at home?" Jackie asked.

"The classroom portion, yeah."

"How the heck can that be effective?" Jackie asked, stuffing a bite of lasagna into her mouth.

"Effective might not be the point," Darby said. She proceeded to tell them about the Airbus A340 instructors and their computer based training program. The instructors had to listen to someone read the systems knowledge portion to them, via the computer. They also had to do it hooked up to the Internet, so they were limited as to where they could study.

Darby sipped her wine, and said, "So when they took the computer test, that replaced the oral, they all failed at least one module, and in some cases more than one."

"Are you kidding?" Kathryn asked, narrowing her eyes.

"No joke. And they were all instructors who had previously flown an Airbus before."

"How did you do on your test?" Jackie asked.

"I did fine, but only because I flew the plane for years. We also did a mini-review before the test." She stuffed the bite of lasagna into her mouth, and held up a finger while she savored the morsel.

After she swallowed she said, "But any of your kids could have memorized the facts and passed our test. It doesn't mean they understand what's happening, or how to use that information on the plane. I really think understanding the inner workings of the new generation, computer operated, aircraft is the key to safety."

"How are your sim sessions going?" Kathryn asked.

"We've had a different instructor every night. Most often these guys argue. And the simulators don't work half the time, and we never have a thorough debrief. Ten minutes at best."

"Doesn't sound like much of a training program," Kathryn said, and sipped her wine.

"Nope. They're not really performing under the AQP guidelines. But it's FAA approved." Darby grinned. "I feel bad for my sim partner."

AQP was the advanced qualification program that most U.S. airlines trained under. Airlines could design their own programs with a reduced, train-to-proficiency footprint and make pilots teach themselves the systems at home. There were a few requirements—crew concept, training devices emulating the aircraft, and operational realism. They also had to gather data to show the effectiveness of training.

"The principle operating inspector approved that?" Jackie asked.

"The Feds overseeing Global are retired Global captains," Darby said. "Which explains so much."

"How can that even be legal?" Jackie asked Kathryn. "I mean it sounds like they're protecting their buddies."

"It's a system that's not monitored," Kathryn said. "We're the kinder, gentler FAA," she said sarcastically.

"But on the flip side," Jackie said, "if the pilot who worked at the airline knew what was going on inside, and went to oversee the operation they might know what to monitor, and then could be a positive force."

"In a perfect world," Darby said with a laugh. "But Global is a good ol' boy system, and I think that club has extended to the FAA."

"How can they be objective?" Jackie asked.

"They can't, and that's the problem." Darby lifted the bottle of wine, and filled her glass.

Kathryn was staring at her plate, and was nothing short of abusing a perfectly good piece of lasagna with her fork. Darby broke off a piece of bread and tossed it onto her plate. Kathryn startled and looked up.

"I'm sorry." She looked directly at Darby. "I was just thinking about a safety report I read today."

"Global?" Darby asked.

Kathryn nodded. "It was the report from…"

"The flight that almost killed John," Jackie said. "What the heck happened?"

"You heard about that?" Darby asked. She and Kathryn had intentionally kept it from Jackie, because sometimes what you didn't know couldn't hurt you. She didn't think John had told her, either.

"Oh, I hear all sorts of things. Apparently with my being pregnant, John thinks I have hearing loss too. Besides, I snoop a little." She grinned. "A lot."

"Are you mad we didn't say anything?" Kathryn looked mortified.

"Oh, no. I totally understand why you both kept that from me. And John… he's so concerned about the baby. For me… all I can do is pray that he comes home safely, and know that he will."

Kathryn emptied her wine glass, and reached for the bottle. "After reading that report, he was in fact saved by the grace of God."

Relying on God was not the answer for safety. Besides, if he had ultimate control, he would not allow any planes to crash and people to die. He would not have allowed Brian to die in the Cali crash, or Keith to be murdered. John was just one of the lucky ones.

Kathryn proceeded to tell them what she learned from the report. After Darby heard the details, she changed her mind, deciding that maybe Kathryn was right. John and all those people had been saved by the grace of God—this time.

They were seconds from death. However, God or luck should never be relied upon for safety. Something needed to be done. Despite Jackie's cavalier attitude, Darby couldn't help but notice her eyes moisten. Greg's death by plane still haunted them all. Love continued, yet it was never replaced, and memories always remained. Darby knew that better than most.

"What's bothering me," Kathryn said, "especially with this damn train-yourself-at-home program, is that the underlying problem for that flight may have been training. Pilots only know what they know."

"Unconsciously incompetent," Darby said.

"What?" Jackie's brow furrowed.

"They call it unconsciously incompetent if pilots make an error because they didn't know what they didn't know."

"How do you know this stuff?" Jackie asked.

Darby shrugged. She also knew that pilot error was blamed for ninety percent of all accidents. However, an accident was never one thing, but many. Multiple factors were always part of the event. Unfortunately, nobody looked at how many times the pilots *saved* the flight.

A critical analysis of the accidents creating those statistics identified pilots as the last line of defense. Thus, they were ultimately blamed, despite multiple contributing factors such as inadequate training, poorly contrived and written procedures, fatigue, systems failures, technology failures, and unexpected weather, to name a few problematic areas.

Yet, thousands of pilots used their experience, knowledge, instinct, and innate skills daily to prevent accidents. Nobody ever heard about the decisions made by the humans in an aircraft who stopped a catastrophic accident. Those pilots were unacknowledged heroes. Until Captain Sully that is, and they still attempted to fault him. Had he died, that event would have been attributed to pilot error.

Her concern was that when those heroes retired, substandard training would not prepare the new generation of pilots to handle the task.

"This 757 training program would have been pretty hard to navigate if I hadn't flown international, or flown the plane before. Boeing is so very different from the Airbus."

"Did you ever get your meeting?" Jackie asked, buttering a large piece of bread.

"Oh, yeah… I did. But, let me just say it wasn't easy. It took me three months. It had to be on my own time, because, as they said, this was *not company business.*"

Kathryn choked on her wine. "You never told me that. Reporting safety is not company business? Since when?"

Darby laughed and spread her arms. "I rest my point on the non-reporting culture."

"What's with our airline?" Jackie said.

Jackie was no longer working for Global, but she'd been a flight attendant, scheduler, and flight attendant training instructor, thus she had her fingerprints all over the company and had a vested interest. This was also the airline that put her first husband into an early grave. Well, actually, Bill had done the dirty work, but he had been a pilot for Global, too.

"It's not really the airline's fault," Darby said. "It's just a few incompetent, sucky, bad managers." She had many more adjectives for them, but she decided to keep it PG rated for the baby. "Anyway, I decided to meet with them after my training's complete."

"That's a good idea," Kathryn said. "Do you have a date?"

"Yep. I confirmed it this morning. Tuesday the fifteenth. I wanted it right after my checkride, which is Monday. But, they gave me ninety minutes the following morning. The good news is that'll give me a chance to talk to the union first."

"That's probably a good idea," Kathryn said, nodding slowly.

"I'm not so sure. My captain rep wants me to, but I seriously feel they are double agents down there." Darby sipped her wine thinking about how little the union had done over the years since the merger. Not to mention not standing up for her when management put that bogus letter in file. *Social media violation, my ass.* "However, if I can get one of the attorneys to read it, they could tell me if there is anything I shouldn't say."

"It's all true, isn't it?" Jackie asked.

"Absolutely," Darby said. Kathryn and Darby exchanged a glance. How true it was made it scarier than hell.

"Then you should give it to them in writing," Jackie said. "But I can't believe it's taken them this long to meet with you."

"You and me both. The good news is, with the delay I have firsthand training issues to add to the report, mirroring everything everyone had told me about it." Everything always worked out for the best, and this was one of those times.

"After reading the Global report," Kathryn said, "I more than ever think you should let me run with this. The connection to the Flight 42 incident can't be overlooked."

"I have to do it. I'm not running to the FAA and ratting out Global." Darby said. "I just really want them to close up their holes, to mitigate risk. I think we will have a better chance for change by letting them do it."

Darby appreciated Kathryn's help, and Kat gave her the courage and strength to press forward with this. Kathryn Jacobs was her safety net if she fell. Between John and her, the aviation world would be a safer place. But she knew, by giving Global the report, this would be the quickest way to make change.

If they were willing to listen and learn, that is.

"By the way, where's is John tonight?" Darby asked scooping another portion of lasagna onto her plate.

"He had to go back to DC for some meeting about the position."

"To John, and his success," Kathryn said, raising her glass.

They all raised their glasses, with the unspoken words hanging over the table. Jackie would have to move across the country, and days like this would be few and far between. The glasses kind of hung there with the cloud, and they all fell silent.

Jackie started crying first. "I'm going to miss you both so much!"

# CHAPTER 10

THE DAY OF meetings had been long after a very short night, and John was not looking forward to the evening ahead. Resting on his bed with legs extended, he read the report Kathryn had given him for the third time. He had stopped at a twenty-four hour Kinkos to have it printed prior to arriving at the Fairmont. Somehow a paper copy brought tangible reality to the event.

Pulling Kathryn into this web without her knowledge was something he wasn't proud of. Time would tell what would come of his deception—if he were lucky, absolutely nothing. Unfortunately, luck was tenuous at best. Yet after reading the report he realized how damned lucky he had been cheating death.

Glad to be back in his room, with pen in hand he jotted a couple of notes in the margin, of the pages. *To hell with the safety of our system.* When incidents like this happened, they were equal to an accident. The only difference was that nobody died and the public was kept in the dark. What happened in this event was greater than a problem of two pilots making a human error.

*Was there a connection? Or was this a coincidence?* He wondered.

John lifted his wrist—8:45 p.m. He was scheduled to meet Diane Nobles downstairs in the Juniper restaurant in fifteen minutes. Diane was the head of the human factors group at the FAA, and she had been working her way up the ladder for thirty some years. She also worked closely with flight operations management at Global Air Lines.

*Dr. Nobles a human factors expert?* Her education, from undergraduate to Masters and then a Ph.D., was in computer science. She graduated from George Washington University, in the heart of DC, and was undoubtedly well connected. But what the hell was she doing in human factors with the FAA?

Granted, aircraft technology overpowered pilot operations, but the human factors position was not about the operation of technology, but the concern for the human and their interaction with that technology. He sat up and pulled one shoe on, and then the other.

Darby learned of Nobles' oversight of that safety report from 1996, and nothing had been done. Twenty years later, when those exact issues were at the heart of aviation concerns, John did a little investigation of his own.

He learned that Ms. Nobles had no right to be in her current position. She was a computer science geek, leaning and vying for automation. This made sense as to why she did nothing when they learned of the human factors problems so many years before. She didn't know what to do because that was not her domain. This shifted the essence of his investigation.

John had no doubt that she was put into place for a reason, and had been groomed and positioned along the way. She sure as hell didn't get there on her own. But by whom, and how far would they move her? Was this position just another step in the ladder for her? Time would tell. It always did. He hoped to hell that he could remain objective.

John walked over to the closet and pulled on his sports coat. He turned, facing the mirror to adjust his tie. He'd contemplated wearing a pullover sweater or sweatshirt to downplay whatever Nobles was up to tonight. But he had to play the part of the Washington club. One never knew who was watching.

He ran a hand through his hair, and then glanced at his watch. He had five minutes to get downstairs. He would be on time, but hell if he would be early and waiting for that woman. There was something buried deep within her psyche that he couldn't quite figure out. Darby clearly exposed her lack of follow through, yet that didn't appear to matter to anyone of importance.

John set the report on his desk, and placed his computer on top, then stuck his room key into his pocket. He put the do not disturb sign on the door and closed it behind him. He walked down the hall toward the elevator.

*What the hell am I doing?* he wondered, pressing the down button. The investigation was proving nothing. But if he actually got the job, then his time was not wasted. The nation's safety depended upon his success one way or another. He reminded himself to stay focused as he stepped off the elevator.

John walked into the restaurant and said to the host, "I'm meeting Diane Nobles."

"Yes sir, right this way." The host walked him to a table in the far corner of the room. She was sitting with her back to the wall, facing the room. The moment she saw him, she lit up with a smile that probably fooled many, but not him.

"John," she said, standing. "Great to see you again." She moved around the table and gave him a hug before he knew what had happened. A flash snapped off to his left. He glanced that way, but could not identify the person behind the camera. He knew that anyone taking photos of this meeting would utilize a high-powered camera with no flash required.

"Nice to see you again Miss Nobles," he said pulling back from her embrace.

She smiled, "John, please. Call me Diane." She said, sitting once again. "It's time we move to a first name basis."

"Diane it is," he said taking his seat, glancing at the drink sitting before him.

"I took the liberty. Twelve-year-old Balvenie. I hope that's okay."

John lifted the glass and tilted it toward her, and then he sipped. It was more than okay. "Thank you, nice choice."

"I'm glad you like it. Now, let's order," she said. Lowering her voice she added, "I'm starving. I could eat anything."

"Maybe we should stick with the cows tonight."

Nobles laughed at his comment, a little too hard, and a bit over zealous. But the warmth of the scotch and the atmosphere relaxed him for the first time of the day. He lifted the menu and surveyed his options, and decided that the evening might not be a total waste.

When the waiter arrived, they ordered Caesar salads and filets. Hers was four ounces and well done, his was ten ounces and rare.

"I understand congratulations are in order," she said sweetly. "Married. Baby on the way. A teenage son. Aren't you just the immediate family man?"

"Thank you." He sipped his scotch, ignoring her sarcasm. "Did you ever marry? Kids?"

"Heavens no. With a career like mine there was no time for a family."

"I suppose not." John had lived a similar life. But when he met Jackie, he realized that love and the opportunity for a family should never be sacrificed because of a job. His love for Jackie, Chris, and their unborn child was the reason he had to see this through.

He'd always had a duty for safety, but not until he had a family of his own did he understand the loss when an aircraft went down. The loss was more than the souls onboard the aircraft, it was those left behind to survive without their loved ones. Those families deserved to know why their life was ripped apart needlessly. His family and close friends gave him a deepened passion he never thought was possible.

The waiter arrived with their salads and a bottle of wine. He poured a healthy glass for John, and gave Nobles less than a couple fingers. She had this meal planned to the last detail, and he was curious to see where it would go.

He sipped his scotch while his wine breathed, and stuck a fork into his salad. He had not realized how hungry he was until he took his first bite. *Delicious.*

"What do you think about the election?" she asked, between bites.

That was a loaded question. The presidential election was days away, and they had two interesting options—a billionaire with no filters who would undoubtedly send an impact through the financial community, or a politician who lied, covered his stories, and buried bodies.

"Well, we don't exactly have exceptional options this year."

There was no doubt that Drake had his share of bodies buried, with equally as many lies told. But this election was nothing but politics. The vote would have to be the lesser of two evils.

"Do you think it will make a difference who they select, for the department position?" she asked.

"Probably not," he said, sipping his scotch. "Whomever is elected, they'll choose the best person for the job. Looks like you almost got it by default."

"What do you mean?" She asked, without blinking.

"Global Flight 42."

"Yes, the report came across my desk." She lifted her wine and said, "Have you read it?"

"I didn't need to, I was on it."

"That's not what I asked," she said.

John smiled, and lifted his glass to his lips.

Diane thought she and John were vying for the same position. Yet he wondered who was moving the pieces on the game board. He knew one thing, however. If Nobles thought she had this locked up, he doubted she would have called this dinner meeting. This was the information he needed.

"What'd you think when you read it?" John asked.

"Pilot performance is a huge issue, and one of the first things I'll address when I'm the secretary," she said, as she stuffed a bite of salad into her mouth.

"Yes, it is," he said, raising his fork. "But one I would have thought you'd already addressed over twenty years ago."

Without blinking she said, "Change takes time."

A young man picked up their salad plates, and John finished off his scotch, and gave him the glass. Within seconds, dinner plates were being set before them. John thanked the waiter, as he stuck his fork into the beef and lifted his knife.

"Why did you call this meeting?" he asked, as he slid the knife through the meat, blood red juice flowing onto the plate.

"I think we both know that answer."

"Enlighten me," he said, stuffing a bite of filet into his mouth.

"We can't both have the position," she said, cutting her meat. "I was thinking… if you stepped back, I could assure you *any* position. I could make the salary and conditions worth your while.

You wouldn't have to move from Seattle. We could both have what we want."

John stuffed a second bite of filet into his mouth to buy time. She was getting nervous. Meaning, she may not have a president in her pocket.

She smiled warmly, and then continued to eat her meal.

"Doubting yourself?" he finally said.

"Negotiations are part of Washington."

"What I can't figure out is your end game."

She smiled. "I don't play games, sweetheart. It's all business."

They ate in silence until John said, "Why the offer? Why now? My guess is that you might only have one presidential candidate in the bag, and you're getting nervous he may lose."

"It won't matter who's elected. It only matters who's on your team."

"Perhaps you should focus on what's good for the safety of the industry." John stabbed the knife through his steak with a little more force.

Nobles smiled and then sobered quickly. She leaned forward and lowered her voice. "You have no idea who you're playing with."

"I think I might." John took a long sip of wine. When he set his glass on the table he said, "But I can't be bought."

This time she chuckled, and then reached forward and touched his hand. "Then you're in the wrong city."

He recoiled from her touch. "Times are about to change. This city will change. The people are sick of corruption, sick of being lied to, and the politics of it all. At the end of the day, safety will prevail."

"You're so goddamned righteous, sitting there with that smug look. You think this industry is based on safety? You're ridiculously naïve. Aviation is about one thing only—making money. When you get that into your brain then maybe, just *maybe*, you'll have a chance."

"Smug or not, I'm willing to wait it out," John said. "We're not as ignorant over at the NTSB as you think."

She raised an eyebrow. "Your point?" she said, with a look that ran his blood cold.

"My point? There's a problem with airline operations—the FAA, and you appear to be at the center of it."

Moments ticked by with neither moving their eyes from the other. John would not play his entire hand, but he had hit a roadblock and needed to throw a stick of dynamite to stir things up and keep moving forward. This woman seemed to be a connection somehow, but he couldn't prove anything.

She lifted her glass of wine and rotated it, staring into the red liquid sloshing in the glass. "You don't want this job. Not with a family." She sipped her wine and then added, "It's dangerous in DC."

Anger rose from the core of John's being. Nobody threatened his family. He calmed his heart. He would not allow her to see she hit his one and only button. He calmly folded his napkin and placed it over his plate. He stood and walked around to her side of the table. Towering over her, he said, "Don't you *ever* fucking threaten my family."

"John, you completely misunderstood," she said, pushing her chair to the side, attempting to move from his space. She moved back just far enough to look up at him. "I'm just saying the west coast is much *more* family friendly."

He placed a hand on her shoulder, and when she tried to move he squeezed, tight. Then he leaned in, with a hand on the table and his lips within inches of her ear, he whispered, "You do not want to see what I'm capable of."

# CHAPTER 11

LIFE WAS TOUGH when you belonged to the cat family. Darby breathed deep, opened the door, and inspected the damage. Thankful her tail was still intact, she pulled it inside the car where it belonged. Sticking her hands inside the top of an overly low cut, perfectly tight-fitted leopard body suit, she adjusted her boobs. She had teased her hair to a wildness that only Halloween could handle. A tiny black nose and whiskers were the final touch. If she could survive the night without snagging the fishnets, life would be perfect.

The good news was she got to be home on Halloween. The bad news—they delayed her two days of training by a week, and then pushed her simulator check back, yet another week. It felt like an act of God to get her meeting moved, to coincide with the day of training, but everything was back in place. Her crazy schedule meant a major training inconsistency that manifested into party time—at least for one night.

"Meow," Darby said backing down her driveway. The party was at Kathryn's house and a small event. Jackie, John, Linda, Niman, Ray, Kathryn's boss was attending, and two couples from Jackie's Lamaze class.

Ray was meeting her there, and she had no idea what he was going to be this year. The year prior he had been the most awesome pirate, but that was because she was a mermaid. She suspected he might show up as a hunter, or something to complement her being a cat. He was creative, and loved Halloween as much as she did, which made the holiday all the more fun. Not to mention chocolate was involved.

Darby was a couple of blocks away from Kathryn's house, keeping a watchful eye out for trick-or-treaters. She clicked her blinker on and turned left, then drove down Kathryn's street. Kathryn had told the twins they could have a get-together at Jackie's house with Chris and some of their friends, but to keep it clean, no drinking, and that they would be checking on them. *God, Kat had her hands full.*

She was less than a block from Kathryn's house, when lights flashed behind her. *What the heck?* That's just what she needed, but, if she were ever going to get out of a ticket, this outfit would do it. She turned on her blinker as if she were pulling over, but with Kathryn's house in sight, she slowed but kept pressing forward. Kat's driveway was full of cars, so she pulled over on the street. The officer's motorcycle pulled in behind, lights still flashing, and siren blaring.

He walked her way, with hat and glasses in place, and thumbs in his belt. Darby rolled her eyes, unbuckled her seat belt, and reached for the glove compartment to get her registration and insurance. Just as she leaned away, the door opened and he grabbed her from behind.

Darby screamed, and fought as she was pulled from the car, but he was stronger. A witch, a devil, a couple of pregnant angels, and a zombie were standing on the lawn watching, but nobody moved.

He pulled her away from the car and kicked the door closed. She yelled, this time because he put a foot on her car.

Then he pushed her forward, facing against the hood of the car, his body pressing a little too close. Either he was happy to see her or that damn tail was in the way again.

"I didn't do anything. You've got the wrong person," Darby stated with a calmness she didn't feel. She did not want to go to jail. Kids were now standing on the sidewalk, watching.

He pulled her right arm behind her back and then the left, and cuffed her hands together. Darby's heart was racing. At least when her ass was hauled off to jail, there would be a bunch of witnesses who would come to bail her out.

With her wrists cuffed, he turned her toward him and then lifted her onto the hood of the car and spread her legs so he could move in closer.

"What the hell?" Darby said, and then she began to laugh. "You bastard."

"My being a bastard has nothing to do with your being arrested for being so damn hot." He reached a hand under her butt and lifted her, then freed her tail. Then he opened a book, and began to read. "You have the right to wear clothes or not. Anything you say can and will be done to you. You have the right to have someone watch, or join… but she better be cute."

Within moments, a witch came flying around the front of the car. "Ray?" Kathryn said, and then she began to laugh. "There will be no judging tonight, you win the prize."

Kathryn always had a great prize for the best costume.

"Damn right." He pointed a finger at Darby and said, "Freeze." Then he went to his motorcycle and shut off the lights and noise. He walked back to the car and opened the door. He grabbed her purse and keys, and then closed the door. He returned to her side and dropped the keys into her purse and handed it to Kathryn.

Ray lifted Darby with one quick swoop, putting her over his shoulder with her scantily clothed butt and protruding tail sticking in the air.

"Put me down," Darby cried, but she was laughing too hard to say more than that.

He slapped her butt, then touched his hat and nodded at Kathryn. "Where shall we deposit the prisoner?" Kathryn extended an arm toward the house, and he headed that way.

Ray put Darby down on the couch and asked, "Does anyone have keys to these things?"

"Paybacks are hell," Darby said, as Ray pulled keys from his pocket and unlocked the cuffs.

Once they were off, she rubbed her wrists. Handing them to her he whispered, "We'll play with these later."

Darby should have noticed that police would not use fur-lined cuffs. But then again, everything happened so quickly she didn't know what to think. Her only problem was she was aroused as hell… unable to do anything about it for hours.

Kathryn had made an incredible buffet of creature-like food. Darby wasn't sure what half of it was, but it looked scarier than hell and tasted incredibly delicious. Stories were told, drinks flowed, and the charades in costume were hilarious. Jason Bernard came dressed up as a zombie, and he turned out to be a really nice guy. He was married, but his wife had been in an accident and needed full-time care. She had been bed-ridden for over ten years, mostly in a vegetative state.

It saddened Darby how she had judged him without really knowing him. People had a horrible habit of doing that. She had thought Jason

Bernard was a pig, and was after Kathryn. The truth was, he was just a nice guy who seriously needed a break from his reality, and he was funnier than hell after you gave him a few drinks. Okay, so he probably was after Kathryn, but Halloween, let the monsters run wild.

They all took turns answering the door for the trick-or-treaters until they had a few too many drinks, then the sober pregnant angels took over. When the clock struck ten, Jackie headed home to check on the kids. It was a school night after all. She had convinced John to stay at the party. Jason Bernard and Jackie's prego friends left at the same time Jackie did.

Kathryn made a pot of decaf coffee, and brought out a bottle of Baileys. "Nightcap anyone?" Then she brought out a tray of pastries in the shape of spiders, and set them on the coffee table.

"I'll have one." Darby raised her hand, knowing that if she didn't get her butt out of the chair, Kathryn would get it for her. Kathryn handed Darby her drink and a spider. "And this is why we need a woman in charge, because they take care of you."

Everyone laughed, and John said, "That may be so, but I'm not sure if you can trust 'em."

"Ouch." Kathryn whacked him on the head with a rolled-up napkin, and handed him a cup of coffee. "You're just saying that because Jackie's not here."

"Of course. I'm not stupid."

Niman laughed, and Linda asked, "So who do you think's going to win the election?"

Linda had come as the Statue of Liberty, and Darby nodded at the appropriateness of her question, as she glanced toward John. This election would determine the course of aviation for years to come, since the president would select the Department of Transportation secretary.

"I'll vote for whoever's going to make John a secretary," Darby said. "Can we rig the election?" She grinned and dipped a spider into her coffee and took a bite.

"I think that would be Drake," Kathryn said, sipping her coffee. "He might be the only chance of not making it a political position."

"Oh man," Darby said. "He kind of scares me."

"Why?" Kathryn asked. "He actually reminds me of you."

"How so?"

"He speaks his mind. He's not afraid of saying what needs to be said. He's got courage."

Darby laughed. "I'm going to take that as a compliment."

"He has business sense," John said, "If he'd put his accountant in charge of the budget, we could change the financial trajectory of the country. Not to mention, it might buy me the position, too."

"We need Kevin Kline and Charles Grodin," Darby said.

"Huh?" Ray said.

"Now that was a great movie," Linda added. "It was about a fake president who had his accountant fix the U.S. budget overnight."

Darby grinned at Ray, who rolled his eyes. He seriously did not appreciate good movies.

"I'm voting for Drake," Kathryn said. "A businessman might move efficiency into the government sector, and change would happen quicker."

"He's a sexist pig," Darby said. "We need someone who's passionate about the country like Linda. My vote is for Baxter."

Linda raised her torch high. "I'm with Darby." Lowering the torch, she said, "I keep running the psychological profiles of these two candidates. We know that Baxter screwed up on his taxes. He made an error, and I don't think he'd do it again. I'm also sure

Drake has made a lot of errors. But that just makes them both human."

"True," Kathryn said. "But Baxter lied."

"Show me a politician who hasn't," John said.

"Good point." Kathryn added a splash of Bailey's to her mug. "So, what's the profile on Drake?"

"That's what I can't figure out," Linda said. "He's a money man and his decisions are based on finance. Yet something is off."

"How so?" John asked, leaning forward, reaching for his coffee.

"It's about character. There are things he did for money while conducting business, because there was a legal loophole and he could get away with it—but not ethical decisions for the good of the people. For the power of a buck, he does the wrong thing and then blames the system for allowing him to do it. Not much accountability."

"It's like the airlines," Darby said. "They *could* train for competency and do what it takes to make sure everyone has the skills to fly. Despite knowing that good training would improve pilot performance to improve safety, airlines do the minimum because the FAA allows it, and it's profitable."

Kathryn sighed. "You know it's wrong. You do it anyway, and then blame the government from not stopping you."

"I'm just saying, it's all about accountability and integrity," Darby said.

"We need a president who has the integrity to do the right thing, for the right reason," Linda added.

Linda was amazing. Her first husband was a pilot, and killed himself and hundreds of others in a plane crash thanks to Bill. Because of that, she went back to school and became a psychiatrist and met a neurosurgeon in the process. Darby liked Niman way better than the murdering pilot, despite never having met Linda's first husband.

"I think they're both crooks," Ray said.

"Harsh," Darby said with a laugh. "My question, of many, is… Why does Drake want to be President of the United States anyway? He won't have control like he did with his company, and it might give him a coronary if he doesn't get his way."

"You're the one that says, don't sit around and bitch about something unless you're willing to change it," Kathryn said to Darby. "The bureaucracy and the BS he's had to put up with for years, running his business, would drive anyone crazy. I wouldn't be surprised if he'd just had enough and decided to change it all."

"He said cutting taxes would create jobs," Ray said.

"Do you think if Global Airlines gets a tax break they would use that to create new jobs or improve training? Not a shot in hell," Darby said. "They'd put it in their pockets."

"That's an interesting point," Niman said, leaning back and folding his arms. "While 'tax cuts create jobs' is a valid business theory, when businesses want to grow they do it with or without a tax cut, and employ people as needed. The growth as an investment provides the tax break."

"Not many people do something without a motive," Linda said. "Once you know what that is, the story unfolds."

"I know what Ray's motive was with his costume," Darby said, dangling the fur-lined handcuffs in the air. Ray grinned, and she added, "Did I ever tell you the story of the night I was taking a bubble bath?"

Ray pulled a pillow over his head and groaned

Darby laughed. "Paybacks are hell."

# Chapter 12

DARBY'S FIRST GRADE teacher had filled a jar with marbles and asked everyone in the class if it was full. They had all said yes, but then he poured a cup of sand into the jar. He asked again if the jar was full. Once again everyone said yes, but then he poured a cup of water into the jar. Kathryn was Darby's water—no matter how full Darby's life was, there was always room for Kat.

Pulling into Kathryn's driveway, she glanced at her watch. Three hours was more than enough time to find out what was bothering Kathryn before Darby jumped on her flight to Oklahoma City. She turned the ignition to off, dropped her keys into her purse, and climbed out of her car. The living room lights glowed from behind the curtains.

She threw her purse over her shoulder, and pushed the car door closed just as rain began to fall. Pulling her bag close to her body, she ran up the path toward the front door. She jumped onto the porch, knocked a couple quick knocks, and then opened the door and stepped inside. The living room was empty and the house was oddly quiet.

"Kat, you alive?" Darby called, and headed toward the kitchen.

"Thanks for coming," Kathryn said, wiping her hands on a towel, and then tossing it on the counter. "Seriously, this could have waited." She walked around the counter and gave Darby a long hug.

"Of course." When she pulled back, Darby looked in the pan. "So, were you mashing these potatoes or just trying to kill them?"

Kathryn laughed and said, "Not sure." She sat at the kitchen table and refilled her wine glass. "Are you ready for your check?"

"As ready as I'll ever be, with my do-yourself training program."

Kathryn closed her eyes, and shook her head. "That's part of what's bothering me."

"My shitty training program?" Darby said, sitting at the table beside Kathryn. She reached for Kat's glass, and took a sip of her wine. Then slid the glass back in front of her.

"I'm not sure," she said, tapping a finger on the table. "I'm worried about John. He's not been the same since he returned from DC, and he was home for a couple of days and left again. Jackie won't talk about it, but something's up. And then, that damn report from the Office of Inspector General keeps haunting me, not to mention the final report from the plane that almost killed John." Kathryn stared her way. "And, yes… your training, program."

"Are you thinking there might be a connection?" Darby asked, in mock surprise, and winked. The Office of Inspector General's report stated that pilots lacked flying skills and the ability to monitor their equipment.

"One could only surmise," Kathryn said.

"So, if you brought me over here for a recap of events, I'm hoping that food's involved."

Kathryn laughed. "Would I ever let you down?"

"Never. That's why I love you." Darby stood and pulled a bowl from the cupboard, and then scooped a large portion of mashed potatoes into her dish. She grabbed a spoon, slid back into her chair and said, "Shoot."

"To begin with, we're going to have serious problems when NextGen goes full speed if pilots aren't getting better training."

NextGen was the next generation of aviation where automation would control most operations, but at the same time, increase pilot demands. Such that, instead of air traffic control providing separation guidance, pilots would be responsible for their own aircraft separation, among additional challenges. Complexity would be added to an already complicated aircraft, leaving more room for human error. Understanding aircraft systems and operations would be essential for a seamless operation. If Global didn't get their shit together soon, they would be involved in the first of many NextGen accidents.

"You're preaching to the choir," Darby said, playing with her potatoes. "But I'm hopeful that after I talk to Sinclair, and show him what's been going on within the company, we can change things at Global, at least."

"Perhaps." Kathryn paused, assessing Darby for a moment and finally said "What I'm concerned with is they're going to mess with your checkride."

Darby waved a hand, "I'll be fine."

"That could be a way to discredit you. Ninety percent of your report focuses on training issues. If they fail you *before* you talk to them, they could just say you're complaining because you failed."

"I thought about that. But the truth is, I've never failed a check or needed additional training. If they fail me, I'll use that to validate their shitty program."

The truth was that anyone could fail someone in a simulator for anything if they wanted to. And she was the employee non-gratis not only for writing her *Inside the Iron Bubble* book, and then giving the flight operations managers a lesson on SMS, but now she was forcing a meeting to point out areas where they lacked a safety culture, too. Sadly, most of it revolved around the training department.

Darby reached for Kat's wine, and took another sip as a trickle of fear ran down her spine.

"I'm glad you had your Coastal experience."

"Me too," Darby said. "But what about the pilots who've never flown a 757 before? We've got new hires coming onto this aircraft. We need to give them a solid foundation. My first officer is struggling something terrible."

Darby had been a Boeing 757 captain at Coastal Airlines before the merger, and she'd had the benefit of a great training program, as well as her experience as a captain. For her, the Global training program was, at best, a review.

"The airline is growing rapidly, and you will be flying with pilots that may be less than, let's say competent, because they haven't been given enough of or the right kind of training,"

"We don't actually have to be competent anymore." Darby grinned. "Rumor has it that the FAA says we only have to be *proficient.*"

"Ha. Ha." Kathryn sipped her wine, but the concern remained in her eyes.

"They might screw with me, but I won't go down without a fight." Darby returned her attention to her potatoes.

"I'm not so sure a pass or failure really matters," Kathryn said, standing to turn the oven buzzer to off.

"Excuse me?" Darby's eye went wide and she placed a hand to her chest. "My heart be still. Failure matters."

"Let me rephrase," Kathryn said with laugh. "Passing doesn't really mean anything if you don't have the knowledge and skills to go along with that success. I think the reason pilots aren't manually flying is because they've lost their flying skills."

"I think they're losing their flying skills *because* they aren't flying," Darby corrected.

"Chicken or the egg. Which came first? Why aren't they manually flying?" Kathryn grabbed two potholder mitts.

"Good point. But the FAA has known this was a problem for a long time. Hell, Nobles knew it twenty years ago, and did nothing. If the FAA does nothing, and they're in bed with the airlines, I'm not sure what we can do. So, what's the point?"

Kathryn placed a hand on her hip. "Touché. Then tell me again why you are risking your career by reporting safety culture issues?"

Darby raised her middle finger and rubbed her nose, and then laughed. "Okay. Okay. But if we don't try, then nothing will be done."

"My point exactly," Kathryn said. "So, here's the deal… nobody is asking *why* pilots aren't hand flying."

"I don't think they have the confidence to kick off the automation."

"Exactly!" Kathryn said opening the oven with mitted hands. She lifted the pan and set the baked chicken on the cutting board. "I also think that they are reading the flight mode annunciator, but they just don't know what the heck it is telling them."

"I couldn't agree more," Darby said. "Man, that smells good."

"Are you sure you don't want to stay for dinner?"

"I wish I could." Darby licked her spoon, while glancing at her watch. "But I have a flight to catch."

"Okay. So, what we need to do is improve training."

"I've been saying that for years," Darby said. "But they won't do it without quantitative data proving the necessity."

"Exactly. So, let's give it to them."

"How? Our POI's a putz and is allowing this shit to go on."

The POI was the principal operating inspector and every airline had one. As far as she could tell, Global's was worthless. Unfortunately, he was one of the good ol' boys, and as best Darby could see, he had no clue about training. Hell, he had even retired before glass cockpits came into reality.

"How do you really feel about him?" Kathryn asked with a grin. "He's not *that* bad. Can you cover that?"

"The hell he's not," Darby said, standing to pull a roll of foil out of the drawer. She ripped a large piece off and covered the chicken. "Some of the training programs coming out of the Global school house are nothing short of embarrassing."

Kathryn removed her potholders and tossed them onto the counter. She grabbed a wooden spoon from the drawer, and began scooping potatoes into a ceramic bowl. "That flight came too damn close to crashing. Nothing has shaken me to the core like this since Bill..." Kathryn dropped that sentence, took a deep breath and continued a different direction. "Jason says I'm too close and making it personal."

"It should be personal," Darby snapped. "It was John! It's our industry. Families, neighbors, and maybe the person who is supposed to find the cure to cancer could be on one of those planes."

Kathryn ripped a sheet of foil off the roll and covered the potatoes, placed the bowl into the oven, and turned the knob to warm. "The pilots didn't know the autopilot was off. But how couldn't they? What the hell were they looking at? What were they thinking?"

"They weren't. Or they were, and they were so overloaded because their heads were up their asses," Darby said.

Too many loved ones were dead because of a needless crash. Darby's 757 training program sucked. The safety culture report, the OIG report, the industry issues, and Nobles ignoring the ramifications of what was in progress were all pieces to a puzzle that, if put together, would create a picture of a horrific crash.

Darby understood Kathryn's concern more than most, because she was living in the same nightmare.

The pilot training system was broken. The more advanced the aircraft, the shorter airlines' training programs became. And the FAA allowed it. They had it backwards. Greater complexity required more training, not less. The thousands of pilots flying on the autopilot, who didn't have the confidence to manually fly because they didn't understand their aircraft, was growing at a rapid pace. When the plane broke, those pilots would be in trouble.

Now that Drake was the President of the United States, Darby only hoped he would give John the DOT position. If so, change would happen.

"How are you going to get the data to prove that airlines worldwide need to improve their training practices?" Darby asked.

"I have an idea," Kathryn said. "But I don't think it's going to be easy."

"Life wasn't meant to be easy. If it were, it wouldn't be as much fun to play," Darby said, setting her bowl in the sink. "What's the plan?"

"I'm still formulating the details." Kathryn leaned against the counter and folded her arms. "Knowing what to do and doing it are not mutually inclusive events."

"Neither is fair and just." Darby rinsed her bowl and put it into the dishwasher. "Where are the girls?"

"Basketball practice."

"Did you let them drive?"

"Hell no!" Kathryn said.

Darby laughed. The girls had turned sixteen the day before, and Darby had taken them to get their licenses, and then out to a birthday lunch. Her diligence in giving them driving lessons had paid off. They were both exceptional drivers, and one day Kathryn was going to have to let them go on their own. "They're good drivers."

"It's not them I'm worried about." Kathryn's tone told her this was the end of discussion.

Darby grabbed another wine glass off the rack and poured an inch of Kat's wine into it. She handed Kathryn's glass back to her. Extending her glass, Darby said, "To courage. It's never the easy path."

Kathryn touched her glass to Darby's, "No, it's not. But it's the right path."

Kathryn's phone buzzed. "Jackie," she said to Darby, and answered. "Hey, sweetie."

Her eyes went wide. "Okay, calm down. You're going to be fine. Uh huh." Kathryn walked to the window and said, "Get in here."

Darby followed Kathryn to the window and peeked out. "How long has she been out there?"

"I'm not sure. But she thinks John is having an affair."

"She thought Greg was too," Darby said. "John wouldn't. Would he?"

Kathryn shook her head and opened the back door before Jackie had time to knock. "Sweetie, come in and sit. Why were you sitting in the driveway?"

"I didn't want to bother you two."

"You could never bother us," Darby said. "What the heck's going on?"

Jackie sat heavily in a chair and set a metal box on the table.

Helping Jackie out of her coat, Kathryn asked, "What's that?"

"I found it in John's office. Bottom of a drawer." Tears began to fall again. "I was going to try to open it, and I couldn't. Then I broke the lock. He's going to be so mad."

"What's in there?" Darby asked.

"Photos."

Darby exchanged a look with Kathryn. *This can't be good.*

"Did you look at them?" Kathryn asked.

Jackie shook her head no. "I chickened out. But I broke his lock, and he's going to know I know."

"What do you know?" Darby asked, grabbing the box, and opening it. Then she pulled out an envelope with a stack of five-by-seven color photos. Patrick Lawrence was in one with some woman. And then Clark... "What the hell?" and then she pulled another, "Oh my God. What's this? I know him." She handed to photo to Kathryn.

"I don't know," Kathryn said, looking at the photo.

"That's Don Erikson. The first officer from John's flight."

"John must have taken these after the flight. But why?" Kathryn looked at the others and scowled. "The CEO of Global, shaking some lady's hand. The crew. Some guys in suits."

"That's my union rep Phil, and our chief pilot Joel," Darby said, pointing. "That one is Rich Clark, the director who was supposed to have been fired."

"The incident occurred in March, when was Clark let go?"

"I don't remember," Darby said with a fear she hadn't felt in a long time. "Did the NTSB ever talk to the crew?"

Kathryn shook her head. "No. The pilot union wouldn't let them. They got the FOQA data, but that was it. Apparently, the voice recorder wasn't working."

"I'm not surprised ALPO wouldn't let them talk, but..." Hairs on the back of Darby's neck stood on end. "I'm going to call Don."

"Do you think he'll talk to you?"

"Hell yeah. He's a super great guy. Great pilot, too." Darby set the photo down. "He's not someone who'd make multiple errors and almost bury a plane."

Jackie reached for the photos and looked at them, and began to cry again.

Darby pulled up a chair in front of her. "This is one time I'm glad you snooped. But the tears and your fear about John, I think it's the hormones." She glanced at Kathryn who nodded. "John is not cheating on you. He's doing his job and he's keeping everything secret for a reason."

"I didn't know anything about this," Kathryn said. "And we're *not* going to tell him."

Darby stood and placed a hand on Jackie's shoulder. "I'm going to head to the airport, and leave you in good hands." She squeezed Jackie's shoulder. "When does John get home?"

"Three days, I think," Jackie said.

"Good, then tomorrow Kathryn will help you find a place to fix this lock, or replace the box."

"But John's key won't work."

"Good, then he can break the lock," Darby said.

"Darby's right," Kathryn said. "Stay for dinner. Tomorrow we'll fix the lock, put this back, and John won't be the wiser. Text Chris and tell him to come home with the girls. They're getting a ride from Mrs. Peterson."

Darby hugged Kathryn and Jackie, and walked out the door. Once in her car she unlocked her phone. Choosing her words carefully, she sent Don Erikson a text.

# CHAPTER 13

SOME SESSIONS WENT well and others just went—this had been one of those other sessions. Darby unbuckled her seatbelt, and stood. She reached over her seat and packed up her belongings. The instructor was already out the door. Her first officer was unusually quiet as he packed up his stuff.

Nathan had a few problems during his approach, but nothing that couldn't be fixed with a little effort. Besides, their checkride would be a team effort and she planned on being the pilot flying. The worst thing about the AQP checking process was a weak pilot could pass without ever flying the simulator.

"Do you think he's going to let me take the checkride?" Nathan asked, still in his seat.

"You're military, of course he will."

He shrugged. "I'm not sure even *that* could help me."

Nathan was a new hire. Thus, on probation and he could be fired for anything. But that rarely happened for performance once the pilot was into the simulator training phase, especially if he had a military background. Not because the training department was filled with compassionate people, but rumor had it, the guy in charge of pilot hiring was a Global God and he would never be made to look bad for hiring the wrong person.

"Military pilots are family," Darby said setting her bag on the floor. She glanced out the door, and the instructor was no longer in sight. "I think they'll take care of you." But there was always a first time for everything.

"Yeah, but I feel like an idiot. I bid this plane because they say the bigger the plane the easier they are to fly, but I had no idea." He sighed, climbing out of his seat. "I didn't know what I was supposed to study, what was important, or even how to prepare for this."

"Why didn't you tell me this earlier?" Hell, she couldn't even get him to have a beer with her after training, or a cup of coffee before their session. She had assumed he was just focusing on his studies and didn't want to be distracted.

He scratched his head and said, "I... well, I... felt like an idiot, and after each session I just wanted to get the hell out of here. I have a forty-minute drive home, and..."

"Okay, sit your butt back down. I'm going to show you how to prepare for this checkride. You've got two days. I've watched what you're doing and it's fixable."

She climbed back into her seat, but they sat facing each other.

"It looks like you are hesitant because you don't know what you are doing. What I think's happening is, you're trying to find what button to push, and are spending too much time thinking about it." She gauged his demeanor as she spoke.

No pilot liked the realization they weren't sky gods. "You're having to think too much, and that's creating a delay. Words go into your head, you think about it for a few seconds, and then act. If an emergency were really to happen on a plane, stress would short circuit your memory even more."

"But I've tried to go faster, and then I mess up."

"You don't need speed. You need to be efficient. You need automaticity."

"Huh?"

"Your knowledge needs to be at a level where you don't have to think about what to do. Your response is automatic. You just do it, kind of like breathing. You need to automatically know where every switch is and its purpose. So, you're not speeding up to go fast, but you actually know what you're supposed to do and where the buttons are, which makes you move with more efficiency."

"I've read every procedure. I know them all. But I get in here and it doesn't come out of my brain like it's supposed to."

"So, let's change that."

"If you can fix me before our checkride I'll give you my first born."

Darby laughed. "Uh, a beer after our ride would be good enough."

"Anything," he said, looking desperate.

She understood what he was going through. If he failed this ride, they'd let him go and it would impact the rest of his life—compliments of Global's less than stellar training program.

"When you get home, I want you to make a note card for each phase of flight, each approach, and each maneuver. On the front of the card write takeoff, or engine failure, ILS approach, TCAS, GPWS, or VOR etcetera. Then, on the back write the exact steps of what you will do, and say."

"I have everything written on a sheet of paper."

"That's good. But it doesn't test your memory. When you write these, you're going to test your memory in the process.

Write the phase of flight or event on the front of each card. Then write the steps on the back from memory. See how well you know them."

He nodded as she spoke.

"Then you're going to sit in a chair, a hot tub, or get your butt to the gym on an exercise bike or treadmill and—"

"You study at the gym?"

"Heck yeah. Do you have your panels on the wall at home?"

"Yes."

"Does your wife have an exercise ball?"

"Yep."

"Okay, phase one—write cards. Phase two—sit on the ball in front of the panel and rehearse, touching the buttons on the panel. Make sure you bounce."

He laughed. "You're nuts."

"Maybe. But it works." She turned forward in her seat. "Studies have proven that motion helps form memories. So, with your butt on the ball and the panels in front of you, you're going to practice by reciting and touching." Darby grinned. "Pick a phase."

"Uh, how about a go around."

She turned into position in her seat and said, "Go around, flaps 20." She touched the thrust levers and then the flap handle as she spoke. "Positive rate, gear up." She touched the gear handle. "400 feet. Heading select." She pointed to the altimeter and then touched the heading bug. "1000 feet, set speed 180." She pointed to the altimeter as she said 1000 feet and then pointed to the speed bug. "Flaps 5. Flight level change." She touched the flap handle again, and then pointed to the FLCH button.

Darby was theatrical, loud, and touched everything with zeal. "This is what you are going to do at home, over and over again.

But you're going to be touching the paper panel. Double check the back of your card to make sure you don't miss anything."

"That's it?"

"Nope. When you got that set, you move to phase three." Darby grinned. "My favorite part—fantasizing. You can do this in the hot tub or at the gym. But if you do it in public you have to risk looking like an idiot talking to yourself."

The truth was most of the world looked like they were talking to themselves with cell phone headsets, thus not an issue and definitely not the point.

"Seriously?"

"I couldn't be more serious. Once upon a time they called this armchair flying. Well, they still might, but I think fantasizing adds a little more flare. The point is, if you can visualize where the buttons are then you really know your stuff. That's why I live by limitations on flash cards. If I'm only reading something, it doesn't mean I could regurgitate it, if needed. Not until I read the question, and have to come up with an answer, do I really know that I know."

"That makes sense."

"If I were you, I'd go to the closest store, get some three-by-five cards and then go to Starbucks. Write them up before your drive home. Then you can study on the way home."

"You read and drive too?"

Darby laughed. Perhaps she should not be telling him to study and drive. Men were not quite the multi-taskers that women were.

"No reading and driving. But after you get your cards written up, you'll have them in your mind. You know the phases of flight. Start with pushback, then taxi, takeoff, and so on. Just talk to yourself the entire drive home. You can think and drive. If you can't remember something, check it out when you get home."

"I'll do that," he said. "Then I'll have more time to study them at home."

Darby assessed him for a moment and then said, "I'm going to tell you something that I don't think I have ever told a man before—the faster the better."

"Excuse me?" he said with a grin.

"You want to do this in your sleep, without thinking. I want you to recite without hesitation and quickly. Really know it. I don't want you going fast in the simulator or airplane, but for reciting, you need to have zero hesitation. Then in the plane you can add a potato between each step; you know, one potato, two potato. Also, when you're driving, I want you to tell yourself *why* you are doing each step."

"What do you mean why?"

"When you go around, why are you adding thrust? Why bring up the gear? Why push heading select instead of VNAV? If you know the *why* to each step, you've moved from rote memorization to adaptive expertise. You'll know what *needs* to be done, not just memorizing a step that'll apply to any situation." She glanced out the door. "We'd better get out of here, in case the boss wants to debrief the session."

"Why would he start now?"

Darby laughed. "You noticed, too?"

They left the simulator and headed for the briefing room. The instructor was sitting in the room, with a Coke and an opened package of potato chips on the table, and he was typing grades into a computer.

"Do you have anything for us?" Darby asked as they entered.

"No. You'll be fine," he said with a wave of his hand. "But Nathan, you need to learn your procedures a little better."

Darby and Nathan exchanged a glance.

"I'll work on that sir."

Darby and Nathan left the room, and headed down the hall. Once they exited the building Nathan set his flight bag on the ground, and stuck his hands into his pockets and said, "I owe you an apology."

One of Darby's eyebrows rose with a mind of its own. She wasn't sure she wanted to hear it, but if a man wanted to apologize, she definitely wouldn't discourage that behavior. "Lay it on me."

# CHAPTER 14

A MEETING WITH Sinclair was going to be a worthless waste of time. What kind of games were they playing? And what gave any of them the right to talk about her to the other pilots! Darby sat on the bed in her hotel room and fell backwards. She kicked off one shoe and then the other, with a phone pressed to her ear waiting for Ray to answer.

Sinclair had the nerve to schedule a meeting with her, while at the same time his boys warn a guy on probation to distance himself from her. Nathan hadn't said it was Sinclair, per se, but who else could it be? He'd just said, "they". She wanted to scream at the absurdity of it all. Sinclair pissed her off something fierce, and she hadn't even met him yet. At least now she had a couple of days to...

"If this is phone sex, I'm in," Ray said. "Unless you're only going to breathe heavy without any action."

Darby startled at Ray's words. "Depends who is this," she said, responding quickly and back in the moment.

"The man of your dreams. What are you doing?"

"Lying on my bed, lost in thought and calling some guy."

"You got the right one," Ray said. "So, how'd your session go?"

"The after session went great. Had a little tutoring session for my first officer, and I learned a few interesting things myself."

Darby told Ray about Nathan's warning, and how nervous and behind the plane he was. Mostly he was afraid to ask for help. Then she said, "But he finally got his balls on, and fessed up."

"Dammit, Darby. If this doesn't flash a neon warning light, I don't know what does. I'm telling you, cancel your meeting with Sinclair."

"Are you kidding me? This makes me want to do it all the more. Who the hell does he think he is, the Grand Poobah?"

"More or less."

Sinclair could think as much of himself as he wanted, but that didn't change his responsibility to the safety of the industry, the crewmembers, and the passengers. Sinclair was playing a dangerous game that he'd inherited, and he had but one option—fix it. Why the hell wouldn't they just do the right thing? It was so damn easy.

"Can you do me a favor?" Darby asked.

"Anything."

"Will you find out what really happened to the flight recorder on Flight 42? Kat told me it was broken."

"It wasn't."

Darby sat upright and said, "You knew?" Her mind spun an entirely new direction.

"Someone erased it."

"Crew?"

"I don't think so. If that were the case, they would have blamed the crew for erasing it, instead of saying it wasn't working."

"How'd you know it was erased?"

"Well…" Ray hesitated a moment. Sucking of breath emitted through the phone, and then he said, "When I heard that it was inop and had been pulled from service, I kind of went back into work that night, found it, and ran a few tests of my own."

"You're the man," Darby said standing. "Why didn't you tell me?"

Ray made some guttural sound and said, "Someone lied to cover up what was on that recording. I didn't want you to stick your nose into this."

"Dammit Ray!" She walked across her room, opened the mini-fridge, and pulled out a Diet Pepsi. "Are you going to report it?"

"Hell no."

"Ray!"

"I need this job."

"You're not going to get fired for telling the truth." God, sometimes he frustrated her so much. Why did everyone at Global think they were going to get fired for telling the truth to solve problems? What was this, the eighteenth century?

"The hell I wouldn't."

"They didn't fire you last time."

"You don't know the half of it."

"Then enlighten me." She sat on the windowsill, and took a long sip of her drink.

"I only kept my job because I kept my mouth shut so long. My hand was forced, and they got that. But to them, I'm an asset. I'm one of them."

"And you're telling me this why?"

"Because I don't want anything to happen to you."

Darby screwed the lid back into place and stuck her drink back into the fridge. She slammed the door.

"Darby?" Ray said, during her moment of angst.

"Yep, I'm here." If this day could give her any more surprises it would be considered the worst surprise party of the year.

"You mad?"

"About what? My boyfriend lying to me?"

"I haven't lied," Ray said. "I just didn't openly provide information."

Darby rolled her eyes. "Did you document what you found?"

"Yep."

"Did you take that voice recorder?"

"I will plead the fifth."

"Will they find it in inventory?"

"Nope."

Darby laughed. "Okay. You're forgiven."

"Insurance policy. But it doesn't really matter anyway," Ray said. "Whether it's broken or not, it was wiped clean. If challenged at the end of the day, they'll say the crew did it."

"Point taken." Darby's brow furrowed thinking about this new bit of information. She glanced to the bedside clock. "Oh shit! I'm meeting Nathan in the lobby in ten minutes."

"Oh yeah?"

"He said he wants to make it up to me. He bought two nights in the hotel to study before our ride on Monday." She grabbed her shoes. "Probably wants to pick my brain."

"Don't stay out too late. It's a school night."

Darby laughed. "No kidding and I have a lunch date with Don tomorrow."

"Don?"

"Don Erikson, the first officer from Flight 42. He lives in Oak City, and—"

"You know him?"

"Oh yeah, he used to fly the kids free flights program with me a few years back."

Ray sighed. "Is there anyone you don't know?"

"I'm sure there is, but that's not important now. This time I got lucky." Darby headed into the bathroom to touch up her mascara. "It's better to be lucky than good."

"So they say," Ray said quietly. "I'm going to go play poker with the guys tonight. Maybe that theory will work for me. Call me after you talk to Don tomorrow."

"Of course."

"And Darby… be careful."

# CHAPTER 15

DARBY STEPPED ONTO the elevator and pressed the down button, with Ray's words of warning, "Be careful," echoing in her mind. When the doors opened, she sucked a deep breath, walked off the elevator and headed toward the bar. Standing at the entrance she glanced around the room. Music was loud and voices were even louder. Nathan sat at a tall table in the corner alone with a bottle of beer in front of him.

Darby headed for the bar and ordered a Jack on the rocks, an order of chicken wings, and then gave the bartender her room number for the bill.

"What are you drinking?" Nathan asked as she approached.

"Whiskey," she said. "On the rocks. Unless it's the good stuff, then I wouldn't be thinking of killing it with ice." Being they were in a crew hotel, the options were limited and usually, included ice. "It's on its way with an order of wings. You hungry?"

"Yeah, kind of," he said. Then added, "I'm sorry I listened to those assholes."

"You're on probation. What were you going to do?"

The waitress dropped off her drink, and when she was gone, Nathan said, "What could I do? Grow a set."

Darby laughed, and raised her glass. "To balls! Better late than never."

He clicked his beer against her glass, and then said, "What'd you do to piss them off anyway?"

Darby unlocked her phone, typed Amazon into her browser, and pulled up a photo of her book—*Inside the Iron Bubble*, and showed him the photo. "Or, it could be they're pissed at me for helping my friend Kat take down their plot to rape the company by cutting training and pocketing the funds, years ago." She sipped her drink.

"How'd that go?" he asked, raising an eyebrow. "I mean… training at this airline seriously sucks. And I'm not just saying that because I'm behind the airplane."

"No shit." When he gave her that wounded puppy look, she clarified, "I wasn't talking about you being behind the airplane, but training. All I'm saying is it was a horrible time, and a few people ended up dead in the process."

Nathan's eyes widened and he theatrically slid his chair back a foot from the table. "Waiter, bill please!" he called, with a wave of a hand.

"Shut up. I didn't kill them," she said. "But most of them deserved it."

"Oh, okay." He pulled his chair back. "As long as they deserved it."

"They killed my boyfriend." Tears sprung to her eyes without warning. She looked down and sipped her drink, working to lose that moment.

"I'm sorry," he said, his humor shifting to compassion. "I'd heard about all that in the news, but didn't realize…"

Darby blotted under her eyes with a napkin. "Allergies" she said. "That was then, and this is now." She lifted her drink and took a long sip and then said, "So who warned you about me besides

Sinclair?" When he gave her a funny look she said, "You said *those* guys. There had to be more than one."

"Oh. Our first instructor said to distance myself from you. That you had a target on your back, and it would be best for me to not get in the crosshairs. Then our second instructor pretty much said the same thing. Then our third instructor—"

"I get the message," Darby said. "Wow, I didn't know I was so famous."

"Infamous, I'm thinking."

"I thought Sinclair had warned you."

"Who?" he said, lifting his beer and taking a long drink.

"The manager of flight ops. He took Clark's place. A few guys sort of went away because of my book. But apparently, Clark might be haunting the jetways."

"Your book was about Global management?"

"Not per se. I wrote about SMS, and may have used some examples of their behaviors."

"Our management's into bondage, and you wrote about it? Holy shit! No wonder they're pissed."

The look on his face was priceless, and Darby began laughing. This time the tears were for another reason. When she could speak again, she said, "Not S & M. This isn't a sex bondage thing. SMS is safety management systems."

He turned a shade of red. "Okay, now we both know I'm an idiot."

"Don't worry. I knew that when you tried to fly an ILS with the VOR tuned." Darby was still laughing, and it felt good.

He flipped her off, and then joined her laughter. The waitress arrived with their wings, and set them on the table.

"I'll have another beer and whatever she's drinking," Nathan said, digging into the wings.

When the waitress looked her way, Darby said, "Jack Daniels on the rocks. And may we get some ranch dip, please?"

"Of course, I'll be right back."

"So, you didn't write a sex book about management, what's their problem?"

"I didn't really say that," Darby said, reaching for a wing. "I have no doubt there's fornication at the management level. But, I'm just not sure if they're tying anyone up these days. Kind of old school." Darby took a bite of her wing and then said, "Actually, I think they're pissed because I had the nerve to schedule a meeting to discuss safety issues."

"You're going to talk to Sinclair about safety?"

"Mostly about all the shit they're doing that doesn't meet a safety culture. I thought they'd connect the dots with my book. They allegedly removed a few people out of position, so I thought they were taking this seriously. I was wrong."

The waitress dropped off the dip and drinks. Darby thanked her and continued. "Look at how we're being trained. We haven't had a debrief this entire program."

"Nathan, you need to learn your procedures better," Nathan said, mockingly. "Does that count?"

"That's about the size of it." Darby dipped a wing into the ranch dressing and said, "I also don't think they have any subject matter experts designing training programs."

"Shouldn't the POI be overseeing all this?"

"Yep. But then again, he doesn't necessarily have any experience either. Most of those guys are retired airline pilots and they're old school. The principal operating inspector is no different. They know nothing about SMS or NextGen, don't understand how people learn, and have never flown a glass cockpit aircraft."

"If our training was like this in the Navy, we'd all be dead," Nathan said, tipping back his first beer and reaching for the second. "It's kind of a screwed-up system."

"That it is. I decided to go to Sinclair and give him a heads-up, in hope we could start creating change." Darby sipped her whiskey, and then poured the remains into the new glass, filling it to the brim. She stuck a baby straw into it, leaned forward and sipped it to a manageable level. "I've been warned by many to watch my back."

"How does someone actually do that?" Nathan asked. "I mean, seriously, your back is behind you, so you can't exactly see it?"

"Makes it quite difficult, for sure." Darby dunked her wing into the dip again, and asked, "Did you get anything done after our session today?"

"Made the cards. Tomorrow I'll study them."

"That was a good idea to get a room. I mean it's your career and all." She sipped her whiskey and observed him over the rim of her glass. "But aren't you worried being seen in public with me? What if someone rats you out?"

"Ahh, fuck 'em," he said with the wave of a hand, tipping back his beer.

Just then a pair of arms wrapped around Darby from behind. "How's it going sweetheart?" Jake gave her a squeeze and then pulled up a stool to their table, and set his beer down. He helped himself to a wing.

"Nathan, this is Jake. Jake, Nathan." Darby sipped her drink. "Jake's a check airman on the A330. Nathan's my sim partner."

"How's training going?" Jake asked Darby. "Ditching us for the Boeing… I'm not sure if I can forgive you for that one." He lifted his beer and took a swig, eyeing Nathan as he did.

"It was a captain calling. Our check is the day after tomorrow," Darby said. "But it feels good to be back in the Boeing." She definitely missed the Boeing. But more than that, she missed flying as captain.

Nathan finished his beer and said, "I'm going to head back. Long day of studying ahead." He waved for the waitress.

"I've got this," Darby said. "Already on my room."

"Are you sure?" he said. "I mean after all…"

"You're paying for your room, and you're on probation. Of course I'm sure. Have a good night and I'll see you Monday morning."

Once Nathan was gone, Jake said, "What's the deal with that one?"

"New hire. Million miles behind the plane, and nobody in training knows how to fix him. I gave him homework." She grinned.

"What'd you do?"

"I gave him beginner's lessons on how to ingrain all procedures into his little brain, so he could pass his check."

"But isn't Monday your LOE?"

Darby grinned. "Yep."

"You're evil," he said, and sipped his beer. "But in a good way."

"He needs to know his stuff. Albeit overkill for the checkride."

The checking event would be a line oriented examination, LOE, where they would have a normal flight, experience an emergency and he would have to read the checklist, per her command. She would fly, and guide him as to which checklist they would need, depending upon the emergency. A solid captain could carry the weakest first officer on a checkride. The problems began when both pilots were weak.

"Does he know what the checkride entails?"

"Nope."

"Like I said, evil." Jake grinned.

Darby laughed. "Well, I am feeling a little guilty now, because he paid for a hotel room for two nights to study. But then again, I'm going to have to fly the line with him, and I need my first officers to know their stuff. At least the basics."

Nathan was based in his hometown, so the company would not pay for a hotel room. Unfortunately, they would not pay for the hotels for instructors either, even if they commuted across the country. Which became problematic because many of the good guys wouldn't take the job because of the added expense, unless they lived locally. Except for Jake. He was pretty darn awesome.

"So, I heard you're giving a safety report to Sinclair on Monday."

"Tuesday." She grinned. "Word travels fast."

"There's not much around here I don't know." Then his face sobered. "You need to be careful. Word is they don't want to hear anything you have to say."

"So I've heard." She looked into her drink, and then up again. "What I don't understand is why?"

"Sweetheart, it's nothing you've done. It's the culture. The good ol' boys don't have a clue how to pull their heads out of each other's asses. Just be careful."

"I will." She lowered her voice and said, "A good friend of mine was on Flight 42, the 737 we almost buried in Seattle."

"Ouch." He sipped his beer and then said, "I worry about you."

Darby stirred her drink slowly with the mini straw. "I'll be fine." She sighed. "But three different instructors warned Nathan to distance himself from me. This was the first time I saw him outside the simulator since we began working together."

"Shit. I know where I know him from." Jake set his bottle on the table. "He was coming out of Sinclair's office yesterday."

"Are you sure? He said he didn't know who Sinclair was."

"Damn right. And, you didn't hear it from me, but there have been Clark, Wyatt and Odell sightings throughout the building."

She wasn't sure what surprised her more—Nathan coming out of Sinclair's office and feigning that he didn't know him, or confirmation that the group of dullards were back.

"Did they think I wouldn't find out?"

"They're just a bunch of little dickheads, not enough room for brains."

"This is all so stupid," Darby said. "All I'm trying to do is improve safety."

"I know. That's why I love you." Jake raised a hand toward a guy who just walked in. "My student. Want to join us?"

"No, thanks. I'm going to go watch Erin Brockovich and get inspired."

Jake laughed. He introduced her to his student, and then she said her goodbyes. She was headed toward the elevator, but turned right instead, and went to the front desk.

"Hey Darby," the front desk clerk said. "How you doing tonight?"

"Great. It won't be long until I'm free to fly around the world."

"We're going to miss you."

"I'll miss you too. But I'll be back for recurrent." Darby stuffed her hands into her jeans pockets, and asked, "Could you do me a favor? My sim partner checked in today for his last two days of training. He's a new hire and I want to make sure the company is paying for his room. Sometimes they like to mess with the new guys because they don't have a voice."

"What's his name?"

"Nathan Marconi."

The clerk's fingers danced upon the computer, and then she said, "Here he is. Not to worry, they've got him on direct bill."

# CHAPTER 16

POKER IS A game of inadequate information where statistics and psychology provide a competitive edge, somewhat similar to the airline business. Captain Rich Clark flipped the first three cards on the center of the table—king of diamonds, nine of spades, and two of hearts. Lifting a corner of his cards he assessed the damage—king of spades and the king of hearts. Damn blind luck didn't hurt either. He laid his cards face down, and stood. He walked to the bar and pulled a bottle of scotch off the shelf. Not his best stuff. That would come later.

"Anyone want to join me?" he asked.

"I'll play," Wyatt said, doubling the big blind. "Hit me on the shot too."

"Yeah, pour me one," Sinclair said, pushing his chips forward. "Calling."

To manage potential liability of Bradshaw's book, Sinclair had taken Clark's place as the manager of flight operations at Global. The move was never intended to be permanent, but he suspected Sinclair had forgotten that fact. Nothing ever came of her book, other than a little noise. Yet he could not allow her behavior to continue. She was nothing short of a liability.

Clark removed the lid and poured gold liquid into one glass, and then the next. He had been the manager of flight operations for years. Nobody, not even some little twit, would take him down. However, he was strongly encouraged to go away—for a while. He stepped back out of the office, fixed a knee that had been giving him a problem, and now he was back, with business as usual.

Wyatt, on the other hand, left town for an extended vacation to some island. He had two years' worth of vacation. Clark was hoping he'd stay out permanently, yet was not surprised at his early return. As far as bosses went, Wyatt was as good as anyone. Clark continued to pour scotch into the other glasses.

"Damn," Odell said under his breath, placing his cards face down. He slid them forward. "I'm out. I'll take a double."

Captain Odell had been a chief pilot at Coastal, and they inherited him. He began his alliance in the pilots' union, and after he proved himself, Patrick moved him over to the management side of the house. Apparently, he was Lawrence Patrick's boy at Coastal. It paid to be in the CEO's pocket. Thus, he had moved up rapidly at Global, and was now the director of flying. They sent him over to Jet Star Air, Global's subsidiary, for a temporary shift. Once a management pilot was demoted, they normally left the airline, but a lateral move to another airline meant nothing except business as usual.

The fact that Odell was still sitting at the table with him was an interesting sight, and surprised the hell out of Clark. He and Wyatt had lulled him into the illusion that he belonged, when he was forced down their throats. Yet his acceptance was the reward for a job well done when he nailed Bradshaw and stuffed that letter into her file years earlier.

They knew Odell openly trashed Clark and Wyatt to the Coastal pilots in the early days. But time, promotion, and power had bought him. Clark was sure Odell was standing by to wipe out either he or Wyatt, but he had done everything they'd asked, and it was difficult to buy loyalty like that in today's world.

"Miner?" Clark asked, raising the bottle.

"Please." Miner matched the bet, stood, and lifted two of the filled glasses. He set one in front of Wyatt and the other in front of Sinclair.

Clark smiled at Miner's behavior. Dick Miner had been acting director of training since Frank Dawson got himself killed. Dawson had been involved in some fiasco with a guy over at the FAA, and they had been careless. He ended up dead for nothing. Greed ruined everything. Greed and stupidity, that is.

One thing a management pilot never did was to threaten the hand that fed him. The damn Coastal pilots were a pain in the ass, especially the women. If they weren't bitching about one thing it was another. Most recently demanding a place to pump their milk. *Seriously?* Clark knew the challenges were just the beginning. There were only two places women belonged—the kitchen and the bedroom. Unfortunately, they were being shoved down his throat where they didn't belong—his airline. To make matters worse, some retired pilot was making his life hell with her insistence that Global needed to improve their female numbers. *To hell with them all.*

Clark handed Miner a glass, and another to Odell. Then he returned to the table. "I'll call," he said matching the bet on the table.

Wyatt lifted his drink and said, "To being back." Everyone extended a glass, as he said to Sinclair, "We'll find you another spot."

Sinclair, for all intents and purposes, covered both Wyatt and Clark's positions. But Clark solved many airline *problems* from the comfort of his home, and he was amply rewarded. It was good to be one of Patrick's protected boys. Odell's position had been filled with a line guy who had already been sent packing. Unfortunately, the new guy was a far better replacement, for many reasons. Time would bring him back.

Clark flipped the next card over on the center of the table—a nine of clubs.

Sinclair tipped back his drink. Eyeing his hand, he said, "What's the deal with Bradshaw?"

"Legal said we've got to make time for her," Wyatt said, mouthing an unlit cigar.

"You in?" Sinclair asked Clark.

"Check." Clark set down his cards. He was in this game for the long haul. He leaned back, folding his arms, and assessed the group. The day Bradshaw requested the meeting he began setting up an insurance policy. That task, however, was more difficult than he'd expected. He raised his glass to his lips, and sipped. *No man has ever reached greatness without difficulty.*

"Check," Wyatt said. "Bradshaw won't be a problem." He glanced Clark's way.

"Planning on messing with her checkride?" Odell asked.

Wyatt harrumphed. "She aced the systems test, and all her instructors said she looks like she's been flying the plane for years."

"She was a captain on the fifty-seven at Coastal," Odell said.

"We've scheduled the new first officer to get his ride first," Miner said. "He's weak, so that'll give her a good workout flying seat support. After he passes his check, then she can take her ride with him. We got Bob, the new instructor, to give her the ride with Fhimi checking Bob."

Clark smiled. "The perfect storm." A four-hour checking event was a lot for any pilot to handle. When a weak pilot was included in the mix, it was a set up for failure… but Fhimi too? "Won't that appear obvious?"

"Hell no," Miner said. "We schedule like this all the time."

Both pilots worked and trained together as a crew. However, since neither pilot was legal until after their checkride, airlines would often have a qualified pilot to fly seat support, for the pilot being checked.

Most airlines utilized an instructor pilot as a qualified individual for the check, ensuring a competent seat support pilot and not to exceed two hours. However, Global decided to check the first officer first, with the captain-in-training in the left seat, then allow the qualified first officer to fly the captain's check for the type rating.

The principal operating inspector approved it, and no probationary first officer would complain. This process saved time and money, and they didn't have to pull an additional instructor into the process. Twenty crews per day—it added up. Having a clueless director of training didn't hurt matters either. Clark glanced at Miner.

"Don't you have to get the first officer in the left seat for a type-rating?" Wyatt asked.

"We got him scheduled two days later," Miner said. "This'll give him a chance to see a type-rating ride."

"Good kid," Sinclair said, glancing Clark's way. Clark nodded.

"I don't think she'll fail," Odell said playing with his chips. "But it will piss her off. When's the meeting?"

"Tuesday," Clark offered.

"You guys going to join us?" Sinclair asked.

Wyatt glanced at Clark, and then checked. "Haven't decided yet."

"Don't let her talk," Clark said, turning the final card over—an ace of spades. He checked. "Run the conversation."

"She scheduled ninety minutes." Sinclair leaned back. "I'm not sure how I can keep her from talking during that length of time."

"Cut the meeting short," Miner said standing. He opened the fridge and helped himself to a beer, and popped the top.

"Turn the conversation against her," Wyatt said. "Put her on the defensive, and she'll kill a few minutes defending herself."

"Be prepared she's got a temper," Odell said.

"A nice ass, too," Clark said, under his breath, with a grin. "You guys in or out?"

"That's one you don't need to knock up," Odell said, and the room silenced.

Clark flipped him off, and everyone laughed.

Clark's assistant ended up pregnant, and then she went away. From the office that is. She eventually went back to the flight line. Money could buy anything and besides, she was in love. That always helped. She had been a probationary pilot for the airline, and did a nice job keeping him warm on the road during base visits. But everything comes to an end.

"All in," Wyatt said, pushing his chips forward.

It would cost Clark another fifty bucks to see what kind of player Wyatt was. Yet he suspected he already knew. A person could tell a lot about another's behavior by how they played cards. Wyatt and Clark had been playing in the airline business for quite a while, but Wyatt had been getting soft.

"I'll call," Clark said, counting out his chips. "Let's see what you've got."

Wyatt flipped his cards over displaying a nine and an ace. "Full house," he said, with a smile.

Just what Clark thought, Wyatt was a fisherman. Not a good strategy with so much on the table, in a game or business. Clark looked at his hand for posterity. A full house, kings high. Wyatt was no competition, and never had been. However, there was a time to play and a time to wait.

Clark turned his cards face down and slid them forward. "Good game."

"Power is in the knowledge," Wyatt said, pulling his chips toward himself.

Clark knew better. Power was the lack of knowledge. Survival was all about plausible deniability.

# CHAPTER 17

THERE WERE MANY ways to kill a perfectly good morning, and Darby knew them all. Her day started early, but between a workout, followed by a study session and a way too long shower, she somehow managed to kill every bit of extra time. She grabbed her purse, threw it over her shoulder and ran out the door and toward the elevator. The doors opened to the lobby with two minutes to spare, and she headed out of the hotel.

Don was standing beside a white Bronco blocking inbound traffic. With a wave, she ran toward him. "How the heck are you?" she said, opening her arms and going in for a hug before he could object. Not that he had ever objected before. "Thank you so much for meeting me."

"My wife gave me a free pass today." Don looked past Darby toward the front door, then back out to the street. "Climb in, I know the perfect place."

"Wife?" Darby asked while climbing in. "When did you get married?"

"Year and a half ago, and we're expecting a son in two months."

"Congratulations," Darby said. "Family, job of a lifetime, looks like everything's going your way."

Don gave her a sideways glance. "How about you?" he asked.

"Same old stuff. But I just got a captain bid in Seattle." She played with the radio and said, "Not married. No kids."

"Never thought otherwise."

"What's that supposed to mean?" Darby said, sounding utterly offended, in the most mocking voice she could muster. Don knew how much she loved flying, and that had always trumped a family. Truth be told, flying and her pilot community was her family. They were the first real family she ever had. That was enough for her, and that made Don her brother.

"Do you like Chinese?"

"A man after my own heart."

Fifteen minutes later they were sitting in a booth, a plate of barbecued pork and two large beers in position. "So, what the hell happened on that flight?" Darby asked dipping a piece of pork into a dish of hot mustard. "Word is that ALPO won't let you say anything, but you guys tanked it pretty bad."

He lifted his beer and took a long drink. Then set it down. "Yep, the union won't let us talk, but my wife told me that I should tell someone." His knuckles turned white gripping the handle on his beer mug. "This is all fucking bullshit."

"I like the way your wife thinks," Darby said. "But what the hell happened? I mean you're one of the best pilots I know."

"I pulled my gun on him. I pulled my fucking gun on the captain and took the plane from him."

"What the hell!" Darby thought nothing surprised her, but she was wrong. "You high-jacked the ship. Like in mutiny?"

"If you want the unabridged version, no interjections."

"I'm just saying, you pulled a gun on the captain, erased the CVR and…" He gave her a look that told her to keep her mouth shut. Darby pulled her fingers across her closed lips to zip them shut, twisted at the end and tossed the key. Then she reached for another piece of barbecue pork, and swirled it in the mustard.

"How'd you know it was erased?"

"I'm sleeping with a Global mechanic." Darby stuck the pork into her mouth, and winked. "We're actually in love, but that's not the point."

"I didn't erase anything. I *wanted* that recording to prove what happened," Don said. "They fucking act like it was a non-event. Don't talk. Don't tell. Nothing happened. Nothing will happen." He tipped back his beer, and the waitress arrived with their food. Darby's moo shoo pork was placed in front of her, and the sweet and sour prawns were placed in front of Don.

Once the waitress was out of earshot, Don said, "I'm going public."

"With what happened during that flight?" Darby's heart was racing hyper speed now, running all the possibilities through her mind. Ray's warning her to be careful moved to another level. "But if you pulled a gun on the captain, are you sure you want to tell the world? Why the hell did you *have* a gun?" The last question was stupid. She knew why he had a gun—the same reason she did.

He stabbed a prawn with his fork. "I'm an FFDO. The captain tried to kill me and everyone else on the fucking airplane. What was I supposed to do?" He stuffed the deep-fried chunk into his mouth.

An FFDO is a federal flight deck officer. They are pilots authorized and trained to carry a gun. The rules are if the gun is pulled, it is to kill. Designed for the bad guys breaking into the cockpit. *But to be used on a fellow pilot?*

"Holy shit." Darby set her chopsticks on the plate. "I'm surprised they didn't throw you in jail."

"You'd think." Don proceeded to tell her the details of their entire trip, and the events of that night. When done, he tipped back his beer and waved to the waitress for another. "They want to pretend nothing ever happened."

"How the hell can they hide this?" Darby said lowering her voice, shocked by what he had said. "You guys were in an effing two-thousand feet per minute rate of descent and pulled out at 186 feet!"

"Exactly. That's why I wasn't going to give him a chance to do it again." Then Don scowled at Darby. "How the hell did you know that?"

"I've got a friend in the FAA. Not important," Darby said with a slight wave of her hand. "Do you think he did this on purpose?"

Don nodded. "I did... I mean I do. I know it. But then they said he got behind the plane." The waitress brought his second beer and once she was gone, he continued. "Now I'm not so sure." He closed his eyes for a moment, and when he opened them there was fear woven within the red lines.

"I know what I know. But then they pulled me into a room for eight hours telling me over and over what they said had happened—the captain was behind the plane. He inadvertently pressed the wrong button for the missed. It was pilot error. Blah. Blah. Blah." He tipped back his beer and emptied half the glass. "It's always pilot error."

Don pushed his prawns around his plate. Darby feigned patience. This was something she hoped she'd never hear again, but now she knew for sure—the captain may have done this on purpose. A chill wormed through her body and she rubbed her arms. It was Bill all over again. She knew that Global's training sucked, and far too many pilots were less than proficient. Yet intentional and error were two entirely different things. For Don to pull a gun on the captain, he had to have had a hell of a reason.

She prayed Bill was not reaching his arms from prison. Everyone had thought he'd acted as a lone ringleader, but she always had her doubts. His friends had taken their lives, and hundreds of lives along with them as they crashed their aircraft, pushed over the edge of mental instability by Captain Bill Jacobs. Never did Darby think Bill had done all that on his own. Nothing was ever that simple.

"I think he was intentionally trying to kills us."

Darby had not realized that she was holding her breath until Don spoke, and then asked, "Why do you think that?"

Don stuffed a prawn into his mouth and stared her way while chewing, his wheels were definitely turning. He swallowed and then said, "He *was* a shitty pilot—always high and fast, or low and slow. Every leg he was behind the airplane. And he was a screamer. Everything he did wrong was someone else's fault."

He lifted his beer and stared into the glass for a moment and then looked up. "It was the look on his face. Like he wasn't there. He was crazed. Not until he saw the ground did he pull back. I think he had a plan and backed out because reality hit."

Darby stared into Don's eyes, each deep in thought with their own fears. This could not be happening again, but it was. The only question was *why?* Why kill everyone on the flight? Then she thought of John, and the battle he would be up against with Diane Nobles.

"I couldn't risk giving him a second chance, so I pulled my gun. Held him at gun point and we did an autoland." He sipped his beer and then added, "Then a bunch of suits showed up at the gate."

Darby had seen the photos. She already knew who was there. But he continued.

"Regional Director. Chief Pilot. And some idiot from Oklahoma City was in town... Ah, fuck, umm, Clark. That's it. He did all the talking. Told us that we would work this out. Nothing would come of it. We just want to be team players."

Don sighed and mixed his rice into his sweet and sour sauce, and scooped a bite into his mouth. "The captain went from yelling at me saying I would be fired, to immediately agreeing with what the management pukes were saying. All I know is something weird is going on."

Darby glanced at her plate. She'd never thought it was possible to have Chinese in front of her without touching it. But there was a first time for everything. Her stomach rolled. "Okay. So, they don't want you to tell the world you pulled a gun on the captain. Why not?"

"Hell if I know. Maybe they would have to admit what he did?"

Darby nodded, "But why would the management pilots at Global give a shit about him?"

"That's what my wife said." Don sighed. "I'm on probation."

"They can fire you for anything."

"Exactly." He nodded. "I need this job. Baby coming. Mortgage. You know the deal. But..." he glanced across the room, and then toward the door.

"But what?"

His attention shifted back to her. "The hell I'll keep quiet about this. Either one of two things happened," he said. "We have a captain who can't fly worth shit and froze. Or we have a captain intentionally trying to take a plane into the ground." His hands balled into a fist. "I'm not sure which is worse."

"The guy who's incompetent," Darby said.

"That's what I said. But my wife says the psycho was worse."

"No way. With a psycho you only have one. With incompetence we could have thousands."

Don lifted his glass toward Darby. "My thoughts exactly."

"So, what are you going to do?"

He lowered his voice and leaned in, and Darby followed his movement.

"I've been telling them what they want to hear. Doing what they request. I've been the best fucking employee they've had. But as soon as I'm off probation, I'm going to the media and telling them exactly what the captain did, and how I pulled a gun on him. One month, and three days to go, give or take a few."

Don was her kind of guy. Go bold, or go home. "Would you be willing talk to my friend at the FAA about this? She won't say anything to anyone. But when you go to the media, you'll have an FAA paper trail."

He thought about it for a moment, and then nodded. "Yeah. I'd be happy to. Only if you're sure she'll keep it under wraps until I'm off probation."

"I can guarantee it. You'd be surprised what I've told her."

"At the end of the day, the union's going to be pissed. Probably won't represent me anyway."

"You won't be missing much."

Darby proceeded to tell Don about Kathryn and all she was attempting to do, and then filled him in about her pending meeting with Sinclair. She even told him about the warnings her first officer had received about keeping his distance.

Imagine what they would do if Don went public. If this were pilot error, Don's detail of the events would be supporting information for Kathryn and her plans to impact change. John would find this fascinating, too. But if this were intentional… that would change the story completely.

"I'm not sure if the FAA can help with this one," Don finally said. "They're half the problem."

"You and I both know it."

The waitress packaged Darby's food into a box, and Darby picked up the bill. It was the least she could do. They drove back to her hotel in silence.

He pulled up front, and put the car in park. Darby opened the door, turned toward him and said, "You're doing the right thing by speaking out. Far too many people won't say anything because of fear. But, I get what you're doing, and I understand why you're doing it."

"We can't live with ourselves if the worst happened," he said, flatly.

"Exactly." She sighed and stepped out of the car, and then turned toward him and said, "Be careful."

# CHAPTER 18

B Y THE TIME Kathryn got halfway to the office, her nerves were far from being back in check. Sitting at the light, fingers drumming on the wheel, she flipped on her turn signal. Turning left, she pulled around the corner and headed toward her new destination—Starbucks. Sometimes she felt like such a Darby. Delay the problems with a coffee detour.

Kathryn wished Darby would listen to her, and step back from trying to educate Global. If Darby would allow the FAA to deal with this, Kathryn could stop worrying about her. She wasn't as trusting of the inner workings of Global as Darby was. There were far too many signs that indicated Global management was not happy with Darby pushing for a meeting.

Granted, Darby officially going to the FAA would cause problems of a different kind. Yet the players at Global were anything but authentic. Putting Global on the side for a moment, if Kathryn's idea worked, they would have data to prove that training needed to be improved, and they could make that happen at all airlines, including Global.

Scanning left and then right, she drove across the parking lot toward her destination. There were only three cars in line and she pulled into position.

When John got his promotion, between the two of them, they could put Darby's focus back into flying, with confidence that change would be underway. God, she hoped he'd get that position. Darby could be their eyes, and they her voice. Together they would make a change for the better.

*But what the hell is John up to?* Kathryn wondered. She and Jackie had the lock fixed, so he would be no wiser that they saw the photos. Those photos were innocuous at best. Why hide them in a box? A bit melodramatic, but then John always had a reason for his actions. She just wasn't sure if she should confront him or not. She wanted to know who the hell that woman was—time would tell.

Pulling forward the voice spoke from the machine, "What can we get you?"

"Grandé pumpkin spice latte, please."

Within minutes she had her drink in hand, and was headed toward the office. Somehow sipping the sweet warmth unraveled the last of her nerves. *Those girls.*

She wasn't being unreasonable about their driving, and she would not bend. They needed six months of experience before they could take the car alone. It had only been three days since they earned their licenses, yet she wasn't sure she could do battle like this for another six months concerning, as they said, "exercising their rights as licensed drivers." That language had to have come from one person only—Darby.

Kathryn pulled into the office parking lot, and then into her spot. She sipped her drink and looked out the window, glancing up the side of her building. So much opportunity was possible within those walls, but so little accomplished. Apathy in the Federal Aviation Administration was equivalent to automation complacency on the flight deck. Placing a hand on her briefcase handle, she squeezed. There was a way.

With her purse over her shoulder, she climbed out of her car and grabbed her briefcase. Kathryn closed her door and locked the doors with the key fob. She headed for the building with coffee in one hand, and the solution to the industry problems in the other.

Jason Bernard was a good guy, and she was glad he could make it to her party. She had refused to use that opportunity to discuss work. He needed a break. He'd also trusted her enough to hand her the review of Global's flight mishap, with careful gloves to not hurt any feelings, and ensured they would take most of the NTSB's recommendations. That would be a first, but there was always a first time for everything.

His only problem was, he wouldn't take no for an answer. She figured if she invited him to the party and he met her friends, he would see that she wanted nothing more than a friendship. There was a time and a place for socializing, and work wasn't it. He was also married.

The elevator took her to the top floor, and she headed straight for her office. She locked her purse in the side drawer and then opened her briefcase. Three copies of the initial proposal were tucked inside. She glanced at her watch—ten minutes until her meeting with Jason.

Kathryn sipped her coffee, as she thought about what was at stake. Safe airline operations demanded that pilots understand their equipment and have the skills to manually fly the aircraft, as well as the confidence to kick off the automation. A great deal of research from their office, as well as the NTSB, had identified the problem, yet nothing had been done. She could see how Darby thought Diane Nobles was behind much of this, and Kathryn wasn't sure Darby was too far off base with that one.

If Nobles became the Department of Transportation secretary, instead of John, nothing would change. Kathryn had never thought Nobles neglect was intentional, but more the bureaucracy they all had to work within. Nobody in their right mind would intentionally keep pilots deficient in skills. The world was full of mysteries, yet there was no mystery that airline safety depended upon pilots being properly trained, and Kathryn knew that they were far from that—at least at Global.

She finished her coffee and then made a fresh cup in her office, and poured it into her Starbucks cup. She added cream, then grabbed her briefcase and headed out of her office, closing the door behind her.

The walk to the boardroom felt longer than usual. She wasn't sure why she was nervous. Jason Bernard was eager to help impact change, and she had an opportunity to know him better on a personal side. Perhaps it was because she invested so much time and energy into the proposal, committing her nights to research. But there was too much at stake to give anything less. If he didn't go for this, she wasn't sure what she would do.

Jason was waiting in the boardroom when she arrived. He had papers stacked high and was deep into reading something, with a scowl on his face, when she walked in. She set her briefcase on the table and he startled slightly.

"Good morning," Kathryn said. "You started early today."

He set the document he was reading down, and looked up with a broad smile. "We could work 24/7 and never catch up."

"Well, thank you for making time for this," Kathryn said opening her briefcase removing two of the folders. The document he'd been reading was placed face down.

"Of course. Thank you for having me over the other night. I had a great time." He poured himself a glass of water. "I'm excited to see what you've come up with."

"I'd like to interview pilots to assess their knowledge and confidence level, in addition to observing if there's any correlation with aircraft understanding, confidence, and their willingness to disengage the automation, to determine if there is any connection to AQP training."

"That's a mouth full," Jason said with a laugh. He folded his arms and leaned back. "English, please."

Kathryn laughed. "Sorry. I had this speech and it kind of rolled out with a mind of its own." She took a deep breath and started over. "We both know there's a preponderance of evidence, much of what has come out of our office, that pilots are deficient in knowledge, procedures, skills, monitoring, and basically situation awareness necessary to make the best decisions."

"You're planning on proving there's a problem?"

"My goal is not in the proof, per se. Proof is in the performance. Basically, I'm going to ascertain the pilots' level of understanding to determine if that's impacting confidence, and if in turn, the lack of confidence is influencing their willingness to disengage automation and reluctance to manually fly." His brows furrowed so she said, "Check out page twenty-two and you'll see more of what I mean."

Jason turned to the page, and he read the questions. His head slowly nodded in the process and his expression remained open. She was over the first hurdle.

"I'm hypothesizing that pilots' lack of understanding, or knowledge of the aircraft they fly, is influencing confidence, and that lack of confidence is influencing performance. Page four has a detailed list of six hypotheses."

Jason turned to page four. "This is interesting."

"We both know that nothing will change without quantitative data." Kathryn sipped her coffee, measuring her speech. "We also know there *is* a problem. That last report from the Office of the Inspector General was frightening, and broadcasted to the world pilots lacked flying skills and the ability to monitor their instruments."

"They lack flying skills because they never do it," Jason said.

"Yes, and I think they can monitor; they just don't understand what in the hell they're looking at. Our 2013 report identified these same issues, but…" Kathryn stopped before she put her foot into her mouth. Much of the problem came from the top where Jason's office existed.

"But what?" Jason said, setting the proposal on the table.

She breathed deep. "Nobody is doing anything. We know there's a problem, and yet there has been no guidance as to how to solve it."

"Not true. The Transportation Infrastructure Committee created the Airline Safety and Pilot Training Act."

"Which never passed the Senate, and that was seven years ago, and what has it accomplished?" Kathryn asked. "Granted it brought the 2010 Extension Act, but I don't think that's enough."

"We've mandated that all airlines conduct upset recovery training, stall training, fly hand flown arrivals." He hesitated and then added, "Oh yes, training how to get out of a bounced landing. Not to mention slow flight."

"Yes, by 2019." A lifetime away, as far as she was concerned. "But modern day automated aircraft are designed with protections to avoid those areas of excessively slow flight. And pilots should possess skills to avoid bounced landings," Kathryn said. "This is absolute insanity." She breathed deep. "Okay, if automation fails and the pilot has no flight skills to fall back on, they could put themselves into those unusual conditions, then it would be useful."

"My point exactly," Jason said.

"But prudence would dictate that we should provide pilots the training to *prevent* stalls, unusual attitudes, or managed flight to avoid bouncing the aircraft on the runway. We need to teach pilots how to fly. All we're mandating would be excellent training as a failsafe, but pilots must have core skills first. Where's that training?"

"We're making progress. Look at the efforts against fatigue since the Regional 39 crash in New York."

Kathryn's blood went cold. That was the first crash of Bill's destruction. Granted that investigation brought to light pilots commuting and fatigue issues. Yet Global had booked Darby on a positive space ticket across the country on her own time, to match her up to an international trip, not more than a year ago. Global scheduling operated under the premise that if they didn't pay their pilots, then it wasn't construed as duty, and they were legal—despite violating every FAR concerning duty time.

"But what are we accomplishing? Look at Global's fatigue program. They add a module explaining circadian rhythm and sleep cycles that has no bearing on the pilot who is in the hands of scheduling." She sighed. Jason returned his attention to the proposal.

"SMS is also mandated to be in effect in a year," he said without looking up. "That should fix things."

"Don't get me started on that." Kathryn finished her cold coffee. "Unless these airlines have a safety culture in place, safety management systems will be nothing but lip service."

Kathryn thought of Darby and how long it took to get a meeting to report safety issues. Three months, and they said it *wasn't* considered company business. Without a solid safety culture, safety management systems and risk mitigation strategies would be as worthless as the paper they were written on.

Global worked around rules and regulations as if they were stones in a path to be stepped over or kicked aside. There was every indication they would work around any policy they could under the construct of safety management systems, as they did for everything else.

"Without a safety culture, safety management systems will be nothing but a shell." Kathryn tapped the end of her pen on the desk, and added, "My concern is that airline resources will be focused on creating an image of a beautiful system that will do nothing for training."

In 2007, the NTSB recommended that all airlines create a safety management system, mandated to be in effect in 2018. They were slowly moving in the direction of safety, but slow was not what they needed—an accident was knocking at the door. Training wasn't improving and that scared the hell out of her.

"It will have been eleven years from the NTSB's SMS recommendation to mandate," Kathryn said. "That's a decade of accidents and incidents, while we attempt to get our shit together."

"Nothing works quickly in a bureaucracy."

"They say that an unprecedented set of accidents will occur between 2020 and 2025. We need to speed up the pace," Kathryn said flatly. "Training is the underlying problem, and while we mandated stall and upset recovery training, no mandates were initiated to teach pilots how to fly, or to help them to understand their systems so they *don't* get into those conditions."

"Remedial training was part of that legislation."

"The best part," Kathryn said. "But if you notice the focus was on flight training. Meaning in the simulator. Yet nothing is being done about learning and understanding the aircraft."

"True. But change takes time."

"As it is now, the airlines are doing nothing to bolster training. Pilots are learning systems at home, and they don't really understand how the current generation aircraft operate. Hell, even a director of engineering at Airbus says pilots use less than 20% of the computer's capability. Airline training programs are leaving pilots short on knowledge, and that's resulting in a lack of confidence."

"Point taken." Jason removed his glasses, and squeezed the bridge of his nose. "So, what's the overall plan?"

"I'm going to see if there is a correlation between training, AQP standards, confidence, knowledge, and pilots' reluctance to hand fly." She reached for the pitcher of water and poured herself a glass. "Nobody has looked at why pilots are not hand flying, just that they've lost their skills because they don't."

He returned his glasses into position and said, "This all sounds good, but I can't see how you plan to get that data?"

"We'll utilize LOSAs to identify when pilots are manually flying their aircraft. Then after each flight, we'll give the pilot who flew the leg a twenty-minute oral to assess his, or her, knowledge on basic operational items, as well as assess the level of confidence."

A LOSA was a line operations safety audit where a trained individual would sit in the jumpseat and observe a flight crew in aircraft operation.

"Demographics?" he asked.

"Time on equipment, type of training, be it traditional ground school, or at home computer based training, how often they flew, etcetera, would all be included. Then I'll construct a structural equation model to demonstrate how the latent variables influence each other."

"Latent variables?"

"Sorry, uh… the unobserved variables. We can't really see confidence so we have to ask. The same with knowledge."

Structural equation modeling was a multivariate technique that combined an aspect of factor analysis and multiple regression that would enable her to simultaneously examine the interrelated relationships between measured variables of hand flying, did they or didn't they, and the latent constructs of what they couldn't readily see.

"Naturally I'd start with existing literature and observed data to test the relationship between the latent and observed variables, to identify if the constructs represent the variables."

Kathryn spoke rapidly, excited about the possibilities to put her research background into motion, but Jason's expression indicated he had no clue what she was talking about.

"Those are just procedural details that can be dealt with later," Kathryn said. "But the point is, if we can show a relationship between training, or lack thereof, with pilots' confidence and their reluctance to disengage the automation, then we'll have the power to mandate improved pilot training."

"This might be exactly what we need," Jason said.

Kathryn's heart beat a little faster. "This will give us the power to create the change we need. Actually, it will give us the strength that would make it hard pressed for any airline CEO to fight it."

Jason pulled his glasses from his face again, and used a corner of his jacket to wipe a lens. "It's going to take a lot of money to fund this."

"Yes, it is. But worth it." Kathryn sipped her water, and watched Jason play with his glasses. "I've also got some interesting news." She hesitated, chewing on how much she should tell him… more to protect him if something were to come of her unorthodox meeting.

"Go on," he said, placing his glasses back into position.

"I've scheduled a meeting with the first officer from Global Flight 42. Apparently, there's more to that story than the FOQA data portrayed."

If Kathryn didn't have his attention before, she captured it with that statement.

"Have you talked to him yet?"

"Minimally. But he's agreed to meet me next Monday at noon. He's got a flight into Seattle with a three-hour layover. I'm going to the airport and meet him for lunch."

"Union coming?"

"Nope. I've also agreed to keep anything I learn quiet for another couple of months until he's off probation."

"Record it. I want a copy."

"I will," Kathryn said. "So, should I press forward with this proposal? I could have it ready to submit for funding within a week."

"Yes. But not at the expense of your current workload."

She nodded. "Then give me three weeks." There would be some long nights ahead.

He glanced at his watch. "I've got a conference call I've got to take. Can we discuss this further at lunch?"

She smiled, a forced smile. "You just don't give up, do you?"

"A trait, I think, we share."

# CHAPTER 19

NOT EVEN THE warmth of the sun could thaw the chill that crept under Darby's skin the day before and gripped tight. It didn't help that the temps were dropping into the low thirties. Sitting outside the training center, she pulled her coat tight and sipped her coffee, thinking about what Don had told her. She glanced at her watch. Thirty minutes before her checkride, and she needed to get her head together. Yet, too many thoughts were bouncing around like a pinball machine, theories whacking the ball from side to side, ending up in one spot—Bill Jacobs.

She had called Kathryn immediately when she returned from lunch with Don the day prior, and told her what he'd said. Unfortunately, she and Jackie were in the middle of Lamaze class, so it was a short, one-sided conversation with a lot of panting on the other side of the phone. John was back east again. She ended up logging onto her computer, wrote it all out in a document and emailed it to her Yahoo account, an account she used to retain private emails and reminder notes, and then forwarded a copy to both John's and Kat's private emails. Then Nathan slithered into her mind.

"Darby," a voice said.

With sunglasses in place, she looked up from her front step perch. "Ah, speak of the devil," she said with a grin.

"May I?" Nathan sat beside her, before she could say no. "Why didn't you return my calls yesterday?"

Darby shrugged. "Got smart." She raised the cup to her lips. He had left four messages throughout the day asking for her to call him. Apparently, it was something really important. But she had more important things to do other than getting played, so she never returned his calls.

"I know who Sinclair is. He paid for my hotel room at company expense."

"I know."

"But how?" His moment of question was replaced with remorse. "I wish I could undo it all. It's just…"

"Just what?" Darby said, going from calm to pissed. "I wasted my time to help you, and you're what, uhh… setting me up? Spying on me? I don't even know what the hell you're doing."

"I'm not sure either. He just said to see if I could get you to change your mind about the meeting. Apparently, he doesn't want to meet with you."

"So I've been told," Darby said, standing. She tossed her empty cup into the garbage can.

"Why doesn't he just cancel?" Nathan asked, as he stood.

"My guess… they ran this by a company attorney who more than likely said they can't avoid a meeting if an employee wants to report safety issues. But they sure as hell can try to get that employee to cancel on her own."

Darby opened the door and held it for him. Then she turned toward him, "Let's go get this check out of the way."

DARBY AND NATHAN walked into the briefing room, but the check airman wasn't there yet. They had five minutes until they started the brief. When Darby had been an instructor, she had always arrived early, was organized and ready to go before the students arrived. A calm relaxed atmosphere put the students at ease for better performance. This was anything but relaxed.

They each pulled out a chair and sat. Silence ticked between them. Nathan looked a horrible shade of gray.

"You okay?" she asked. "More specifically, how's your mood?"

"Remorseful. Worried. Kind of feel like my career is over."

She assessed him for a moment. He was sucked into the club without a choice. Yet he came clean, despite putting his career on the line. Not many people would do that.

"Do you know that if you have a good mood before testing you'll do better than if it sucks?"

"Shit. Then we *are* in trouble," he said theatrically.

"I'm serious. They did tests and showed half the group videos of some criminal getting torched in an electric chair, and then showed the other group a video of a puppy playing. The first test played downer music, the second played upbeat." Darby reached into her purse and pulled out her phone. "The group who was upbeat did way better than the other group."

"And you're telling me this to make me more depressed?"

Darby laughed. "Hell no. We need to liven up this party." They were already into ten minutes of their briefing time, and who the hell knew when Fhimi would arrive. She wouldn't tell Nathan details about the guy. There was no need to depress him even further.

Darby stood, and closed the door. Then she set her iPhone on the table and opened iTunes and found the perfect song—*Because I'm Happy*. "It must be crazy what I'm about to say…" Darby sang out of tune with the song. Her feet and arms were moving, as she got into her groove.

Nathan started with a smile and then began to laugh. "You are crazy."

"So I've been told," she said. "But we're about to pass our checkrides." Darby's arms waved over her head, body bouncing with the beat. "This is a good day."

He was grinning and his leg was bouncing to the beat. She had him, so she reached a hand out and he took it. Then she pulled him to his feet. And he began dancing.

"I can't believe I'm doing this."

"Believe it baby. No better way to get in a good mood but to get your groove on." The song ended and Darby pressed play. "One more time, just for the fun of it."

This time they were seriously attempting to one-up each other on the moves. Nathan's gyrations far outdid hers. He was funnier than hell. They were both laughing so hard that Darby's eyes watered, and then the door open and slammed against the wall. Nathan stopped and stood to attention, but Darby froze with a hip pressed forward, one arm extended with a hand pressed out and the other hand behind the back of her head with hair lifted.

"What the hell is going on in here," Fhimi spat, with a guy following him, eyes wide, music still playing.

"Dance party." Darby came out of her pose, shut off the music, and extended a hand to the guy standing beside Fhimi. "Darby Bradshaw."

He shook her hand. "Jack. I'm getting checked out as a new instructor, I'll be running the ride today. Fhimi will be observing."

"This is hardly professional behavior of a Global pilot," Fhimi said, sitting heavily.

Darby placed her hands on her hips, and then theatrically lifted an arm and looked at her watch. "Hmmm, about as professional as showing up twenty-five minutes late for report time for a qualifying exam." She glanced at Nathan, and back at Captain Fhimi. "We, at Global strive for on-time performance."

Fhimi glared, Nathan's face showed no expression, and Jack fought a grin that his eyes couldn't hide.

"We don't need the full session for the brief," he said with a flick of his hand. "I've got this down to sixty minutes."

"Well then, you just cut *my* brief time for my crew by thirty minutes. Want to play tit for tat? Or do you want to get this checkride started?"

Fhimi ignored her comment and turned his attention toward the computer. Darby glanced at Nathan who gave her an eyes wide, fake scared face with as much teeth showing as possible. She winked at him and Jack began to laugh. Fhimi's head jerked toward them, and then he glared at Jack.

"Sorry boss," Jack said.

"I can fail you, too!" he snapped.

"Perhaps," Jack said. "But then we'd have to do this all over again because, technically I'm supposed to give the entire session. Not one that starts thirty minutes late." He turned toward Darby. "I waited for him in the lobby, per his direction, because he wanted to brief *me* on how this would go tonight."

He and Darby exchanged a glance that told her that brief included something that needed to be said out of student earshot. Normally the brief included the students, as they were part of the process.

"How will this go?" Darby asked. "Would you like to share the brief with the rest of us?"

Fhimi glanced at Nathan and brought his attention back to Darby. "I need your licenses," he said.

"Shouldn't I be doing this?" Jack asked.

Fhimi thought for a second and then pushed back from the computer for Jack to take a seat. Darby fought back a laugh.

There was no doubt that Fhimi was scheduled for one reason only—to play with them. Play all he wanted, but she had a foundation of a real airline, whose training program was solid and, apparently, Jack was not going to play his part. Which didn't hurt their odds. It was hard to believe that this shit really went on in the world's most prestigious airline. *Truth is stranger than fiction.*

Jack conducted the oral and asked the questions they were responsible to know—limitations. Fhimi, on the other hand decided he was going to continue with the process as he attempted to play "stump the dummy." Darby was quite amused, especially when he asked questions that he didn't know the answers to.

Once the debate was complete, he gave them paperwork and told them they could review it for ten minutes. Then he and Jack left them alone.

"How'd you think that went?" Nathan asked.

"Excellent. The music was great, moves were good and..." He gave her a scowl, and she said, "Fine. We did fine. He clearly knows less about this airplane than we do."

"Less than you," he said.

"He doesn't know any difference."

"Half the time you answered for me."

"Yeah, but he doesn't know that you didn't know. He just thinks I interrupt."

Darby knew what was covered during training, and what would have been impossible for a new guy to know without having flown the plane. Whenever one of those questions came out of Fhimi's mouth, even if it was Nathan's turn to answer, Darby would respond and then apologized.

The funny thing was, Darby believed these orals should come back. But they had to make it part of the program, standardized, and ensure the instructor understood what he was asking. More importantly, the students needed to know what to expect.

"Well, thank you," Nathan said.

"You're welcome. Now, we're flight planned from Seattle to Narita, with an APU generator inoperative."

"I'll check the MEL."

The MEL was the minimum equipment list that would direct the pilots on how to configure the plane with the inoperative item, and if they were allowed to fly without the component. An inoperative APU meant that they would not have an auxiliary power unit as a backup generator, but they could dispatch. They did a quick brief, took a restroom break, and then they headed toward the simulator.

# CHAPTER 20

THE SHOW WAS about to begin. Darby sat in the left seat and Nathan in the right. They began their respective preflights, taking their time as they systematically set up the simulator for their checkride. Each of them located numerous switches that were out of place, and the left engine needed oil. After the preflight checklist was complete, Nathan called for a clearance.

"Ground, Global One would like to push, gate Bravo."

"Global One cleared to push," Fhimi said.

Darby smiled. Fhimi just couldn't give up control of the session to Jack. Observing a new instructor meant just that.

"Pushback checklist," Darby said. When it was complete she placed the rotating beacon on, and called to the ramp. "Brakes released, cleared to push."

Simulator motion came alive and the visual, out the window, indicated the plane was pushing away from the gate. The weather was reporting two miles visibility, but clearly that was not the case. They had no more than a quarter-mile based on what they could see out of the window.

"Can you check the weather again?" Darby asked Nathan. "Looks like there's a bit of a discrepancy as to what's being reported."

"Tower, can you give us the current ATIS?"

"Altimeter is 29.92, the wind is 190 at fifteen knots," Fhimi said. "Uh, visibility is, uh… two miles."

Darby looked outside, then back to Fhimi. "No it's not. Look outside."

"Shit. I told you to change it," Fhimi snapped at Jack.

"You told me to not touch anything."

"You're supposed to be running the session."

"Then get out of that seat, and stand back there and watch," Jack spat.

Darby glanced at Nathan and rolled her eyes, and said, "Before start checklist."

Once both engines were started they began taxiing toward runway 16 left. This time the weather dropped to zero visibility. Darby stopped the taxi. "Will you see if low visibility taxi procedures are in place?"

Before Nathan could make the call Fhimi said, "Negative. You've got half a mile."

"No we don't," Darby replied.

"Shit!" Fhimi snapped. "Okay… uh. How's that look?"

"Better," Darby said and continued the taxi. Seconds later the left engine generator tripped off line. Darby stopped the aircraft's movement. "Talk to ground and let them know we have a problem and see if we can remain on the taxiway," Darby said to Nathan. Then she called maintenance.

"Uh, go ahead and reset the generator," Fhimi said. He was now playing maintenance controller. "Looks like this aircraft has had a continual problem with a generator tripping, uh… every couple days."

"We'll come back to the gate," Darby replied. "I'll let the company know."

"Negative! You're good to go."

"No sir. I'm returning to the gate."

"If the generator reset, you're legal to fly," Fhimi snapped.

"I'm not taking an airplane across the ocean with a history of an engine generator tripping, without our backup generator. Check the records, the APU is inoperative."

"Uh… records show it's been, uh… ten months since the engine generator last tripped," Fhimi said.

Darby glanced back, and Jack was standing behind Fhimi with his arms folded shaking his head.

She accepted the new information as their current reality and they continued the taxi. Once at the end of the runway, Fhimi said, "Global you're cleared into position and we want the first officer to fly."

Darby raised a hand to stop Nathan from responding. She set the parking brake and turned in her seat. "You heard us brief that I was flying. I don't think that controllers can state which pilot should take control. Not to mention, last minute."

"But I do," Fhimi said. "Nathan will fly. You're cleared into position."

Darby turned her attention forward and keyed the microphone. "Ground, we'd like to hold in position for a pilot brief."

"You're cleared into position; we need the taxiway."

"We're showing less than a mile visibility, and I will not sit on an active runway while we conduct a pilot brief," Darby said. "Didn't you hear about Tenerife? If you want us to move our aircraft from this location, provide a taxi clearance."

"You're cleared to hold in position," Fhimi said.

*Of course we are.*

Tenerife was one of the worst airline accidents in history, where a Boeing 747 was still on the runway after landing, and another Boeing 747, attempting to takeoff without a clearance, slammed into it. The details of events that led up to that accident were complex, but the results were two planes on the same runway in the fog, and 583 people died. Far too may near misses occur daily, and a simple avoidance strategy could include *not* taxiing into position prior to departure clearance, when there was a perfectly good taxiway to wait it out.

She picked up the PA and said, "Ladies and gentlemen, we're going to hold in position for a few minutes to conduct a last-minute pilot brief, due to an unexpected clearance from air traffic control. We'll be in the air shortly." She set the PA handset back into the cradle and turned toward Nathan. "Whenever you're ready to brief the takeoff and departure, I'm all ears."

Nathan gave the brief, talking through precisely how he would conduct the departure, with speeds, altitudes, and turns, reciting the cards she knew he had made, and included the details of their departure. "Any questions?" he asked.

"Excellent brief. But how about you brief an engine failure at V1, too." Darby would be certain to cover all bases. "With that generator issue, weather fluctuations, the training, and confusion in the control tower, this might *not* be one of our luckiest days. Better to be fully prepared."

Fhimi said something under his breath that almost sounded like a growl, at the same time Nathan began reciting his engine failure actions at V1.

If the plane was flyable, V1 was the speed at which it would be preferable to take the airplane into the sky than attempt to abort. This was the pilots' action speed, as the decision should have already been made prior to this point. These big birds flew quite well on one engine if the pilot knew what they were doing, and speed was on their side.

After Nathan finished his brief, Darby said, "Ready?" He nodded and she keyed the microphone. "Global one is ready for takeoff."

"Global One, you are cleared into position. Cleared to go," Fhimi said.

"I got this," Darby said to Nathan, as she raised the microphone. Normally the first officer would do all the talking if the captain were taxiing. But nothing about this ride was normal. "Ground, please confirm that Global is cleared to depart runway 16 left."

"That's what I said," Fhimi spat.

Darby was pushing his buttons on this point, but he damned well better learn how to conduct a checkride. Besides, she wasn't quite sure if he was just waiting for her to step off the cliff through the gate he was opening, pushing her for a bust.

Darby turned toward Nathan and said, "Don't ever accept a half-ass clearance. You want to know precisely what runway they are clearing you onto. Even if you think you know what they mean, you definitely want it on the CVR," she said pointing to the cockpit voice recorder. "Sometimes you'll hear this crap overseas, but make sure you state the clearance correctly, or don't go onto the runway."

Nathan nodded, and lifted the microphone. "Ground. Confirm that Global One is cleared for takeoff on runway 16 left."

"Confirm," Fhimi said.

"Global One, you're cleared for takeoff runway 16 left," Jack added.

Nathan repeated the clearance, and Darby taxied into position. She gave the thrust levers to Nathan, who then advanced them to takeoff power.

Everything was normal during the takeoff, which was disconcerting. Silence during a checkride in a simulator left the most experienced pilot questioning what they had missed. Passing through 10,000 feet she selected the autopilot to on.

Passing through 12,000 feet the right engine surged, the EGT spiked, and Darby said, "I've got the plane." She pulled back the thrust lever to control the surge, and pressed the microphone switch. "Control, Global One is leveling off, and would like to receive radar vectors to sort out an engine problem." Then she said to Nathan, "Engine limit, surge stall checklist."

Nathan already had the QRM, the quick reference manual, in his lap and had it opened to the page. The EGT, or exhaust gas temperature, measured the temperature of an internal combustion engine, and a spike in temperature identified something was wrong. Together they confirmed which engine it was, determined the EGT was not stable, and then shut down the engine per the checklist. The checklist also directed them to start the auxiliary power unit, but the APU was inoperative—they would have no emergency backup power.

"Control, Global One is declaring an emergency. We lost an engine and would like to return for landing," Darby said.

Fhimi attempted to give them a slam-dunk—a high-altitude, high-speed, rush to the runway maneuver. But Darby would have no part of that. While they had declared an emergency, there was no hurry. The weather had improved to visual conditions, and the flight attendants needed to prepare the cabin. They had more than enough fuel and time to manage a stable and safe arrival to landing.

They had descended and were holding at 4000 feet, when during the second turn in the holding pattern the flight deck lights went dark, simultaneously as the autopilot kicked off, and red lights flashed and warnings screamed of their new condition. They still had lights, but not what they should have had. They were on standby power.

"We just lost all electrical power," Darby said. "I've got the airplane. That left generator tripped again. Will you see if we can get it back on line?"

Nathan did as requested. Power came back up for a moment and then tripped again. "It didn't hold."

"Okay, let's do the loss of all electrical power checklist," Darby said. She got on the radio and contacted the tower. "We would like vectors toward the runway. We lost all electrical power and need to expedite our arrival. Please state current runway conditions."

Fhimi gave them vectors out of the holding pattern, and away from the runway, heading northbound over Boeing field on an extended downwind for SeaTac. She would allow this only because the weather was good, and she had options with Boeing directly underneath her. But twelve miles would be her limit with the direction he had pointed them.

Visibility was clear, and winds were 190 at 15 knots, but they had a maximum of thirty minutes on standby electrical power, and that was no guarantee. She started the timer on her watch, not sure if the aircraft clock worked or not.

Nathan was flipping pages, and then turned to the front again. "I can't find it. There isn't a loss of all generators checklists."

"Okay. Let's think about this. We never saw this in training, but… oh, look under AC power."

Nathan's finger slid down the index. "Nope. Nothing."

"Do they have anything for one bus off?"

"Nope."

"Look under the L section for the left AC bus off," Darby said. "If that's not there, check the right." Then she picked up the PA. "Flight attendants prepare for landing."

"I think I got it." He flipped to the page and said, "We have left bus off. Then right bus off… and here we go. Both AC busses off."

"Control, Global One requests a vector to 16 left." She turned her attention to Nathan and called, "Flaps 1."

Nathan moved the lever, and then said, "The flaps aren't working."

"They are working," she said. "The gauge is not powered." Under the current stress, not many pilots would have noticed the lack of movement on the indicator. He was paying attention to details—that was good. "We've got hydraulics and there's no reason they shouldn't be coming out."

"Global One turn right heading 140 to intercept the ILS 16 left, cleared to descend to 2000 feet."

"Flaps 5," Darby said to Nathan, and then confirmed the clearance and turned the aircraft toward a 140-degree heading. Nathan lowered the flaps. Darby keyed her mic. "Global One. Emergency aircraft will maintain 4000 feet until glideslope intercept. Confirm Global One is cleared to land 16 left."

"Cleared to land," Fhimi said.

Jack immediately clarified. "Global One is cleared to land runway 16 left. Altitude is your discretion. Emergency equipment standing by."

Fhimi said, "The first officer is supposed to be flying."

Darby responded to controller Jack, as she intercepted the localizer. Only her radio and instruments worked on standby power. Fhimi was officially an idiot. They were eleven miles out and just below the glideslope at 4000 feet.

"Here we go. Loss of power on both, start APU… It says what to do if power was restored, but not where to go if it wasn't."

"Continue reading down that checklist and see if you can find where it says if you can't restore power."

"Oh… Got it."

"Okay, tell me what items we don't have available that could impact landing, and any cautions."

"No autopilot, no flight director, no flap indicator. Oh… do not arm the speedbrakes, and make sure you don't raise the speedbrake handle manually until the nose wheel is on the runway. Some anti-skid inop."

The glideslope was coming alive, and just prior to intercepting Darby said, "Gear down, flaps twenty. And we'll do the landing checklist in the QRM."

Nathan lowered the gear, and then the flaps and said, "Oh, and neither of your reversers are going to work."

"Thanks. Let's get that landing check complete."

Nathan's finger slid down the page, and he said, "There's a descent and approach check in this procedure, too."

"Okay, read the change items."

"Uh… Autobrakes off." He moved the selector to the off position, and then they confirmed gear and flaps were out, and the speedbrake handle was not armed.

Darby landed the crippled aircraft without incident and stopped on the runway. Then the motion turned off and lights came on bright.

"We'll leave it here for a quick break, and reposition when we come back for Bradshaw's checkride."

# CHAPTER 21

NAPOLEON HILL ONCE said, "Patience, persistence, and perspiration make an unbeatable combination for success." But Napoleon obviously never met Fhimi. There were a few other realities in life, and one of them was a person's limit with patience for assholes. Darby's limit with Fhimi ended about two hours earlier, but she persevered to landing.

She and Nathan climbed out of their seats, and Darby pulled her flight bag out of the slot. She grabbed her purse and jacket, and looked around the area to see if she had missed anything.

"You're leaving?" Nathan asked.

"Oh, we're definitely done here."

AQP training and checking required operational realism. The system also required a standard checking profile, not to be adjusted per the instructor's whim. There were multiple profiles they could choose from, but they could not make them up along the way.

Not only did the weather not fluctuate in real life in the manner it had during the evaluation, but the inconsistent generator discussion, instructors arguing in the simulator, and multiple failures—inoperative APU, engine failure, and loss of dual AC busses, indicated one of four scenarios. One—whoever wrote this LOE did not understand the FAA requirements of operational realism. Two—the instructor was playing with Darby and Nathan, or both. Three—Fhimi was just an effing idiot. Or four—all of the above. All options were equally unacceptable.

"Join me in the briefing room after you take care of business," Darby said.

Then Darby headed to the bathroom, more to gain her composure as much to ensure she would not pee her pants with what was about to happen next. After business was taken care of she found the break room, purchased a Diet Pepsi for herself and a Pepsi for Nathan.

"Guys, I would like to have a talk with you both in the briefing room at your earliest convenience. I'll be waiting," she said to Jack and Fhimi.

"Will you be dancing?" Fhimi said, snidely.

Darby turned toward him. "If you take a thirty-minute break, you just never know what we'll be doing," she said, and headed out the door.

She walked into the room and Nathan was sitting, and she handed him his drink.

"Thanks." He took the bottle and opened the lid, and then said, "How the hell could you prepare for something like that?"

"You can't," she said. "This was a bullshit ride with a capital B. I'm going to say a few things, and you don't want any part of this. Let me do all the talking. Remember, you were never dancing. You pulled out of that so fast when the door opened, he saw nothing. It was all me."

"I'm going to be fired."

"No, you're not. You just play with Sinclair and tell him you did everything he asked. But when you do, record it with your cell phone."

"But policy says we're not allowed to—"

"Yeah, I know. But it's your career."

He nodded and raised the bottle to his lips, just as the door opened.

After the instructors walked into the room, Darby stood, and walked over to the door and pushed it closed, firmly. She extended her hand to the chairs and said, "Sit, please."

Fhimi glanced at his watch and said, "We only have forty-five minutes for your checkride. If you want to waste time in here, it's all yours. Or we can call you an incomplete."

"Incomplete my ass!" Darby snapped. Fhimi's eyes widened, and Jack folded his arms and gave her a subtle wink. "I've never had a more unprofessional checkride since a dipshit sat in the back and texted during my recurrent years ago. But in this case, you're dealing with initial students!"

Darby placed her hands on her hips and drummed her fingers, silently counting. Hoping to make it to ten but she only got to three. "To start with, do you have a clue what constitutes AQP qualifications? Do you know how many violations of our *approved* program you made today?"

"You don't—"

"Don't interrupt," Darby snapped. "I'm not done. Not only did you screw with the program, but your lack of professionalism showing up late, your lack of understanding of the systems in that bogus oral you gave, and then your deviation from an approved script with those multiple emergencies was bullshit. But to top it off, at the very minimum you should understand proper ATC phraseology and procedures before ever being allowed to step foot in that simulator as an instructor."

Darby walked toward the desk and lifted her drink and unscrewed the top, not removing her eyes from Fhimi, and she took a long drink. He folded his arms and glared at her, their eyes locked. The silence in the room was thick. She replaced her lid without looking away from him.

Then she sighed. This was a friggen waste of time. "Do you have any debriefing items for us?" she asked, setting the bottle back on the table.

"Only that you're combative with ATC, and you have a problem with the word no, and—"

"I wouldn't allow *anyone* to put my passengers in danger."

"It's a fucking simulator!" he snapped.

"No sir, it's not. It's a high-fidelity training device that replicates the aircraft, and the machine that the FAA has anointed, in lieu of the aircraft, for checking events. And you, sir, are to follow the approved program, obeying all standard protocols and procedures."

She turned to Jack and said, "Was what we did here today part of the approved program?"

"No. It wasn't," Jack said.

"Did we handle these non-standard events with professionalism, following standard operating procedures, complying with all FAA regulations, with understanding of our aircraft systems while maintaining situational awareness, and utilizing the highest level of crew coordination?"

He grinned broadly. "Actually, I could not have said that better. Yes, you did."

Darby turned toward Fhimi and said, "I think we're done here."

"If you don't get back in that simulator, I'm not giving you a type-rating."

"I already have a fucking 757 type rating, you idiot. Uhh… I mean, sir."

# CHAPTER 22

THE SLAMMING OF a door in the hallway jolted her awake. She rolled over, opening one eye to check the time. Memories of why her t-shirt was on the nightstand came flooding back—sometime around midnight she had pulled it off, and had thrown it over the clock to block the light. She lifted her shirt and glanced at the time, then dropped her feet to the floor. The day she'd fought for was finally here. Darby pulled the shirt over her head and stuffed her arms into the sleeves.

Closing her eyes, she sighed, and fell back on the bed, her legs still hanging off the edge. The thought of a five-minute nap sounded really good. Five minutes was all she needed. *Five minutes… maybe ten.* Pulling her legs up she snuggled under the covers just as the alarm clock came alive with a screaming buzz, and then her phone began chiming across the room. She rolled over and smashed a hand onto the clock to stop the noise, and jumped out of bed rushing to kill the noise on her phone. That's when she saw a text message from Ray.

*Remember… you are smarter than Sinclair… you fly a better airplane… you have integrity. Don't let that asshole rattle you. But then again… you are really cute when you're mad, so that might be a good tactic to distract and conquer. Go get 'em girl!*

Darby grinned and pressed reply. *I will dazzle and defeat. Thanks for the pep talk!*

With the thought of napping a distant memory, she pressed start on her coffee pot. Pulling off her t-shirt, she wondered why she had put it on in the first place. In no time, she was attired in her sports bra, shorts, and tennis shoes. While the coffee brewed, she dumped some fake creamer and yellow junk into her travel mug. *Where was Starbucks when you needed it?*

After filling her travel mug with the best coffee a hotel room could produce, she grabbed her room key and her cell phone, and headed to the gym. Her meeting was at 0900 and she was prepared. Now all she needed was a motivational workout to pump confidence into her brain and strength into her heart.

Darby sat on the floor and stretched while she drank her coffee.

Once the caffeine kicked in, she set the half-full mug in the treadmill drink holder. She grabbed a couple five-pound weights and climbed onto the treadmill. She pressed start and began walking, upping the speed until she got to three miles per hour. Headphones in place, she played Josh Groban—*You Raise Me Up*, while she lifted the weights over her head. She told herself to be strong. But despite her overt courage, in truth, she was nervous. Yet she would never speak those words aloud.

Taking this report to Sinclair, despite her union's warnings, was nothing short of sailing on stormy seas. Groban's words gave her faith that she was not alone in this battle. She had Kat, Ray, John, Jackie, and Linda.

Clearing her mind, she told herself over and over she would be strong, confident, and concise. She would hold her temper, despite that fact she looked cute when she was mad. *Yeah right.* A smile spread across her face. The next time she was pissed at Ray, she would certainly ask him how cute she was. Then her mind drifted to her union attorney. She pressed the speed up to four miles per hour.

She had met with him after the checkride. Not only did she share her report, she also expressed concern over the way they conducted the checking event. ALPO legal had no comment on the shitty training event other than they would look into it. The attorney didn't want Darby to give Sinclair the report because he didn't like putting things in writing. He also said, "Sinclair makes me nervous because he's so… corporate."

Darby smiled now, as she did then. Giving him a copy of the report was essential. She did not want to be taken out of context or forget anything she had planned on saying. She also wanted to make sure that if they ran out of time he would still hear everything. Besides, he could reference back to the report when she was gone. There was no downside to giving it to him.

There was a bag full of doubt about her union representation. ALPO, the Airline Pilot Organization appeared to be working on behalf of the company, not the pilots. The only reason she went to see them was because her captain representative recommended it. Which turned out to be a waste of three hours. Well, not a total waste. She learned, without a doubt that the current contract administration guy was nothing short of a double agent. Tapping the speed button, she worked the number up to five miles per hour. Lowering the weights, she pumped them at her side.

When Darby asked the contract administration guy if his kids were going to be pilots, he had vehemently said the job sucked and he would never allow that to happen. Meaning, he did not like flying. He parked his ass in a union job that enabled him to be home every night and was paid more than he could get flying. If he gave the company what they wanted, then he would do what many of the ALPO representatives did—move from a union job into a management job, making a shitload more than they could on the flight line. Darby was breathing hard now.

There was something inherently wrong with any union rep being allowed to move into a management position. She dropped the weights on the floor, kicked her speed up to six miles per hour and began to run.

The conflict of interest was like a raspberry jelly stain on a pair of white pants—noticeable. Darby glanced at the time, forty-five minutes had passed, and she slowed the machine to a walking pace to finish her cold coffee. Once done, she stepped off the machine, and pressed stop. She returned the weights to the rack and grabbed a towel. Wiping the back of her neck, she noticed a familiar face across the room.

"Hey Brent," Darby said. "What are you doing here?"

"Captain upgrade on the 737."

Brent had been a first officer at Coastal, and she had flown with him often. He was a good guy. Smart, hard-working, and a great first officer. Darby was glad he had seniority to hold a captain position.

"How's training going?" she asked, filling her mug with cold water.

Brent shook his head. "Pure insanity. The manuals aren't in color, so I've got to use two computers to study. I had to Google to see what colors the speed tape indications were."

Darby rolled her eyes. "Only at Global."

Modern day aircraft were dependent upon color as many of the symbols were the same, with the only distinguishing feature the color. If they could get someone in training management who understood there were some areas they should not cut corners, learning would improve overnight.

The truth was that the only reason the colors were stripped from the manuals in the first place was to reduce printing costs. Now, everything was on line so what was the point? *Oversight.*

"What are you doing here?" he asked Darby, lifting weights over his head. "Recurrent?"

"Nah. I just finished my check yesterday. Captain upgrade on the 757."

"Congrats. I hadn't heard."

"Well, you had enough on your plate navigating a Global training program." She glanced at her watch. "I've got a meeting with Sinclair today. Presenting a safety report."

Brent lowered his weights and said, "Be careful. These guys don't play right."

"So, I've been told, many times." They said their goodbyes, and Darby rushed back to her room to get ready for her meeting.

AN HOUR LATER Darby was walking off the crew bus, and heading into the training center. The corporate offices were in the same building as training, but on the third floor. Darby found her way to Sinclair's office, but his door was closed.

"It should only be a few minutes," Jane, his secretary, said.

Darby sat on the couch and lifted a magazine, but her mind wandered. Despite all the warnings from everyone, this was the right thing to do. She knew that with all her heart. Maybe, just maybe, if Sinclair didn't know what was going on, she would give him the information to begin change.

Five minutes later Sinclair's door opened and out walked a tall slender man, gray at the temples, with glasses perched on his nose. He glanced over his shoulder toward the office, and then strode across the room toward Darby.

"You must be Darby," he said extending a hand. "Captain Sinclair. Heard you had quite the checkride."

"Yes, one might say that," Darby said with a smile.

"Why don't you go make yourself comfortable in my office," Sinclair said extending a hand toward the open door. "I'll be right with you."

"Okay…" Darby said, with an involuntary eyebrow lifting. She watched Sinclair make a hasty exit.

"Can I get you a cup of coffee?" The secretary asked breaking into her moment of *what the hell was that?*

"What?" Darby said, "Oh. No thank you. I'm good."

She headed toward Sinclair's office and entered the room. Not more than a foot inside she froze. If this were a cartoon, the bubble coming out of her head would be a bold, capital WTF!

"Please, have a seat," Wyatt said, extending a hand. "Nice to see you again," Clark added, neither of them rising from their chairs.

These assholes were supposed to be gone, off property, and replaced. Granted, her sources told her they were back. Yet, she never expected to meet them here today. Maybe she had an inkling they could be there, but that thought never manifested into reality. The truth was—reality sucked.

"Will we wait for Captain Sinclair?" she asked.

"That won't be necessary," Clark said.

Buying time to regain her composure, or bite her tongue… she wasn't sure which, Darby walked behind Sinclair's desk, her eyes scanning until she saw what she needed. Pressing the button, she said into the speaker, "Jane, I think I will take that coffee after all. Double cream and some stevia." She released the button and said, "Gentleman, can I get you anything?" Clark's glare was answer enough. Another press of the button, "That'll be all. Thank you."

She moved around from behind the desk and sat in the chair that had been saved for her. In no time, Jane tapped on the door, opened it, and handed Darby her coffee. Jane exited the room as quickly as she had entered, and closed the door.

Wyatt began talking first. He told her about Global's expansion, and then began quoting the same presentation that she'd heard at her last base meeting the previous month. Darby sipped her coffee, listening respectfully.

"We work closely with Diane Nobles," Clark said, his eyes boring into Darby's.

"Diane Nobles knew of these problems for over twenty years and did nothing," Darby said setting her empty cup on the table.

She removed two copies of her report from her computer bag, as Wyatt continued talking. Thankfully, she had the printed copies, as she would not get through half of what she needed to. One copy was supposed to have been for her and the other for Sinclair, who was obviously not returning. *Coward.* When she finally glanced at her watch, forty minutes had passed.

"Guys, we have multiple problems with safety culture," Darby said, interrupting Wyatt talking about the Airbus A340 program. She began with the lack of a flexible culture, and merged to a just culture.

"If you had a problem," Clark said, "You should have gone to your chief pilot."

"He *was* the problem."

"You need to take responsibility," Clark snapped. "If you had a problem, you should have called your chief pilot. That's what he's there for."

If this conversation had been a sitcom she would be laughing. But as it was, if Ray were correct, she was getting cuter by the minute. How the hell did they derail this to a singular point from eight years earlier, when they had a book of important issues to discuss?

"Just to get this straight, and not have any confusion," she said. "You're telling me that I should have said, 'Excuse me chief pilot, but I have a problem with you. So, I'm going to hang up now, and I will call you back and report you to yourself?'"

Clark opened his mouth, but then closed it.

Wyatt, however, jumped to Clark's rescue and said, "There are a lot of people who like to sit in the back of the room and throw spit wads."

Before Darby could respond, a rapid knock came at the door and Jane poked her head into the room. "Gentlemen, your noon meeting is about to begin. The boardroom is filling."

The door closed and Darby glanced at her watch. "I thought we had ninety minutes."

"We didn't think that was necessary," Clark said, with a wave of his hand.

"Not necessary?" Darby snapped. "You have instructors falsifying records. It's a common practice to violate the federal aviation regulation concerning duty time limitations. The head of human factors declares an emergency because he didn't have an autopilot. I think necessity speaks for itself."

She stood, thinking that the energy it took to stand would diffuse what was coming out of her mouth. She was wrong.

"You do know that the FAA is recommending we fly *without* our automation. Worse yet, your head of human factors wrote to me and said that Global pilots as a group can't hand fly, nor can we manage the automation in the current environment. He also said you have the data to prove that. What are you doing about it?" She waved the reports. "You're cutting training. You put your buddies in charge who are anything but subject matter experts. And you change procedures like you change your underwear, thinking that a new procedure will help save the day. Not to mention, you have idiots conducting checkrides."

Darby silently counted to five and placed her free hand on her hip. The other hand grasped the reports. "You have performance problems, and instead of addressing them you create a video telling our pilots to declare an emergency if they lose their automation." She was mad, but not mad enough to see that she had their attention.

Jane poked her head in again, and Clark's glance sent her closing the door without question.

Once she was gone, Darby said, "There are so many problems with what's happening in this airline, it's hard to know where to begin. We need to fix them before something happens."

Clark stood, and Wyatt followed.

"We should get you into training," Wyatt said with sincerity.

Clark added, "Maybe we could make you part of the ambassador program."

*What the hell?*

"Gentlemen, the overall culture at this airline defies a safety culture. There's no way we'll meet our SMS requirements." Darby handed them each a copy of the report. "It's all in here, and then some. Every day something new comes up that flags a problem."

"I'll read this tonight," Clark said, having switched from attack mode to charming.

She turned to Wyatt and said, "You know, sir. Not even in third grade did I sit in the back of the room and throw spit wads. I sat in the front and paid attention."

Thank God she had pressed record on her phone before she entered the room, or no one would ever believe this.

# CHAPTER 23

SEATTLE'S REPUTATION HELD strong, as large, cold, drops fell from the sky. Instead of complaining about rusting, Seattleites should learn to dance in it. Besides, without rain there wouldn't be rainbows. Darby pulled her hood over her head, and ran toward the building. Once inside, she removed her jacket and shook it. Dripping on a basketball court was never a good idea. She headed straight for the popcorn stand and purchased four cartons, three bottles of water, and a Coke.

She could not believe what had happened, and couldn't wait to tell Kathryn and Jackie. More than that, she wanted to do a happy dance. But then again, she had promised the twins to stop embarrassing them when they had turned fifteen, and a promise was a promise. It was hard to believe a year had already passed.

Darby donated her change, gathered her goodies, and stuffed bottles into her purse. Juggling the popcorn and coke, she headed for the gym. The game was about to start and she didn't want to miss a moment of the action. In no time, she spotted Kathryn and Jackie waving her way.

She climbed the bleachers squeezing between people and gave the ladies their treats.

"Where's Chris?" Darby asked.

"Behind us, left, top row," Jackie said. "But don't look. I'm not supposed to know him."

"Teenage boys," Darby said, with a smile.

"Boys? Are you kidding? They're a piece of cake compared to girls." Kathryn took a bite of her popcorn. "Thank you."

"Of course," Darby said. "I'll be right back." She climbed the bleachers with the Coke and a carton of popcorn. When she and Chris' eyes connected, he grinned and shook his head. "Hey sweetheart," she said, leaning in and giving him a kiss on the cheek. "Can't let my favorite guy go hungry."

"Thanks," Chris said, turning a shade of red, taking his Coke and popcorn, but loving every moment.

Darby headed back down the bleachers and then squeezed in between Kathryn and Jackie. She took the carton of popcorn from Kathryn and retrieved the water from her purse.

"Why can *you* do that?" Jackie asked. "He doesn't want to have anything to do with me."

"Because I'm not his mother," Darby said, waving to Jennifer. "So… I got a call from Clark today. Now he wants me to come to Oklahoma and give a safety culture presentation to his divisional leaders."

"Oh, my God," Jackie said. "That's incredible."

"Yep. Everyone was wrong. I didn't get fired, and they're taking this serious."

"That would've never have happened if you hadn't left a copy of the report," Kathryn said. "You had a good hunch on that."

"Go Jess!" Darby screamed, when Jess went in for a layup. The ball went in, two points scored, and the teams were running down the court in the other direction. Everyone screamed.

"I'm so proud of you," Kathryn said, squeezing Darby's hand. "You've gone through so much with this company, and they're finally taking this seriously."

"This is turning into the best day ever," Jackie said. Then she leaned forward and tossed a kernel of popcorn at Kathryn. "Tell her your news."

"What happened?" Darby asked. "You got laid?"

"Darby!" Jackie said. "That was so inappropriate."

"What's more inappropriate is that Kat's... go Jen!" Jennifer stole the ball, ran the court, passed it to her sister, and Jess scored. They all stood and yelled, and the ball headed the other direction.

Kathryn laughed. "This time I'm saved by the ball." She sipped her water, and then grinned. "Jason's agreed to allow me to run the research."

"You don't have to date him in exchange?"

"Of course not," she said, with a wave of her hand. "He just wanted to have lunch and talk about the logistics."

"Yeah. He wanted to seriously discuss it in your bed. With you on top."

"Darby!" Kathryn said.

Jackie began laughing. "I think she's right. Poor guy is probably lonely."

"Oh hell. You're both right, but we're good." Kathryn sighed. "He asks. I say no."

Jennifer got fouled and went to the line. "Way to go!" Darby stood and yelled when Jen sunk the ball.

"I hope you're good," Jackie said.

"If I were a guy and we met for dinner, there wouldn't be an issue," Kathryn said. "Our society sucks."

"Let me ask you one thing." Before Kathryn could say no, Darby said, "When you worked for John, did you ever feel uncomfortable meeting him anywhere at any time?"

"Never."

"So you met him, whenever, wherever."

Kathryn nodded. "Your point?"

"My point is, you have excellent intuition, and I'd follow your gut. There's nobody who wants you to get laid more than I... but if you feel uncomfortable going out with him, go with that." Darby sighed, "But I really like him a lot. He's super funny, and despite his being married... he seems like a good guy."

Kathryn sighed. "It's just that..." she lowered her voice, and added, "I don't know what to do with his continual advances."

"You're hot and he is acting like the typical pervert at work who won't take no for an answer."

"Hey you two," Jackie said. "Stop with the pervert talk. Darby, you weren't fired for your report. Instead, you were asked to give a presentation to the bigwigs at the airline. Kat, you were approved to do you research." She placed a hand on her abdomen, and smiled. "John's going to be home for Thanksgiving. We fixed the lock, so he'll never know I broke it. Things are good. We need to celebrate."

Darby and Kathryn exchanged a glance, raising their bottles of water. Jackie lifted hers.

"To good days ahead," Kathryn said.

"And to making the skies safer," Darby added. "Holy cow! Did you see that shot?" Kathryn and Darby jumped to their feet and cheered, while Jackie yelled from her seat.

# Chapter 24

H E LAY STILL, breath measured, eyes closed. Footsteps walked past his head, and stopped. Something was lifted by the nightstand. *A key? His phone?* The footsteps moved away and he glanced left, his phone was still there. He closed his eyes and held still, but continued with an audible breath. Rustling in the bathroom was followed by footsteps back into the room. They stopped at the end of the bed. Silence. Then the closet opened. *What the hell?*

Lying there, feigning he was asleep was the coward's way to behave. But sometimes that was the best of all options. Ignore. Deny. Defend. But he would never be able to deny what he had done. There would be much cleanup. He was the worst kind of human.

It was amazing how people started down the path with the best of intentions, and then one wrong step for the right reason sent them another direction. Mitigating risk along the way, with too many doors and options, was a challenge. All it took was one person on the right path to open the wrong door… Then the flood came pouring in.

He was a door away from everything he had worked for his entire life being washed away. His family. His friends. His reputation. His success. His money. He would be stripped of everything. There had to be a way out.

The closet door closed, a little too loudly, and yet he didn't open his eyes. The footsteps moved beside his bed, and he waited for them to leave. But they didn't. He opened his eyes and two hands were now coming toward him.

He grabbed both wrists, and swung outward making his stalker lose balance and fall onto the bed on top of him.

"God dammit! What the hell are you doing?" she yelled, and then her surprise shifted to laughter. "I thought you were sleeping."

"What can I say? Women fake orgasms, men fake sleeping." He gripped her arms firmly, wishing the grip were around her neck, but fearing what he would do if that were the case.

He wished he'd never met this woman. Falling into her bed created far-reaching life changing events, none of them positive.

She ripped the covers from his body. His skin came alive touching the coolness of the room and his body reacted to what would happen next. She pulled free from his grip and grabbed his wrists pinning his raised arms to the pillow. Her body slid between his legs and he parted them. She released his arms and slid her manicured nails down his chest to his best friend. She took him in her hands first, and then into her mouth…

"Ohhh…" he moaned. With eyes closed he pressed his length toward her for the taking.

One of his first bosses had told him to never have an affair with a single woman—*they* had nothing to lose. He never intended to have an affair, so he had let that advice dissipate into the wind. But the morning after their first night, that warning slammed into his brain like a plane hitting the Pentagon. She had all the leverage. He on the other hand, had everything to lose.

*Oh, my God.* If she wasn't such a horrific, manipulative bitch, he could get used to this. He grabbed her head and pulled her close, and moved her in the rhythm he demanded and what he needed. Within minutes he came hard, and dropped his hands to his sides.

She climbed out of the bed and headed to the bathroom. He glanced at his bedside clock—0300. His alarm would be ringing in two hours. He was planning to catch the first flight back to the West Coast.

Diane Nobles returned from the bathroom and turned the master bedroom lights on.

"What the hell are you doing?" he said, covering a face with a hand. "Shut that off."

"I want you to see what you will be missing over the holiday." Diane stood with hands on hips. "I'll be waiting for your return."

He stared, a forced smile plastered to his face. How the hell could he end this? No money, no power, and no job were worth selling your soul. What the hell had he gotten himself into anyway?

# CHAPTER 25

S TRENGTH, COURAGE, AND commitment were all
well and good, but they sure as hell did not prepare a person
for dealing with a full-time job, teenagers, and special projects.
Kathryn knew the rules going in—daily work first, her research
proposal second, and analysis of Flight 42 on the top of the list. She
added cream to her coffee, and returned to her desk.

Other than the basketball game, she had committed the entire
weekend to working the proposal into a format that would be
accepted. Her effort and commitment would be well worth the
sacrifice if they could gather quantitative data to force the airline's
hands in mandating training improvements.

*As if they didn't have enough data so far.*

Her greatest challenge this weekend was the ongoing battle
with the girls to take her car. She would have to give in eventually,
but the weather was turning bad and they had no experience.
Granted, driving would be the only way they would get it, so
she was allowing them to drive to and from school—with her
in the car.

She never wanted to be one of those mothers, but nobody prepared her for being a single parent of teenagers. The worry was overwhelming. Perhaps the incident reports that crossed her desk daily, or the terrorist activity flashing across the television added to her consternation. Nobody was ever truly safe in the world today. She opened her drone security file and got to work.

Time flew by and Kathryn jumped when her alarm rang. She opened flight tracker to see when Don would be landing. His flight was on time and coming into gate C8. She glanced at her watch. If she left now, she could meet him at the gate. On second thought, a table out of view at Anthony's Restaurant might be better.

KATHRYN FLASHED HER ID, and walked through security with the rest of the passengers. Despite her special access, when time permitted she often took the longer route to assess how security was doing. Often this process did nothing more than boil her blood. But today, she was pleasantly surprised at the efficiency and attention to detail.

Within minutes of clearing security, she was standing in front of Anthony's Restaurant.

"Do you have a table by the window?" Kathryn asked the hostess.

"Follow me, and we'll see what we've got."

Kathryn followed the hostess through the restaurant, and when they got to the wall of windows, they turned right. A dozen more tables extended past the windows and buzzed with activity, yet there was one open table at the end of the row.

Once settled into her seat, she texted Don—*I've got a table in the back. Text me when you're here, and I'll come to the entrance. Or, better yet, just head toward the windows, look right and I will see you. I'm wearing a white shirt and black jacket.*

She ordered an iced tea and waited. She checked flight tracker again. They were at the gate. The waitress arrived and refilled her glass, and Kathryn ordered a spinach salad with shrimp. Don's flight had been at the gate thirty minutes now—ample time to get off the plane. He could have run into someone and couldn't get away. She sent another text—*Is everything okay?*

Forty-five minutes later, Kathryn had finished her salad. No word from Don. She pressed favorites, and selected Darby. Within in seconds she answered.

"How'd lunch go?" Darby asked. She had wanted to join them, but Kathryn thought it would be better to not involve her in yet another issue with Global. Darby understood.

"He didn't show up," Kathryn said. "I need you to see if he was on that flight."

"Of course," Darby said.

Kathryn ordered a cup of coffee while she waited for Darby to pull up Global's internal flight information. Something didn't feel right about this. They had spoken the night before and he was more than willing to talk to her. The few details he'd told her over the phone were exactly what Darby had relayed. But she needed more than a he said, she said. She needed recorded documentation from the source.

She still wasn't convinced the captain tried to crash intentionally. Since that event, the captain had been flying a regular schedule. There had to be more to the event, she was sure of it. If she could talk to Don, he could fill in the missing pieces.

"Okay… here we go. What the hell?" Darby said. "He wasn't on the flight. But he didn't call in sick. There's some code…"

"Does it tell you why he didn't take the trip?"

"It will. But I don't know what it means. Just a sec…" Darby said. "Okay. Here we go. Uhh… he no-showed."

Kathryn's blood went cold. "This doesn't feel good."

"No, it doesn't. Hang tight… Okay, I have his home number. Do you want to call, or want me to?"

"I will," Kathryn said. "Can you text me the number?"

"It's done," Darby said. "I don't like this. Pilots just don't no-show. Especially a pilot on probation."

Kathryn paid her bill, walked out of the restaurant, and found a bench. She sat and pressed the number that Darby had sent via text, and within minutes the phone was ringing.

"Hello," a gravelly voice said.

"Is Don Erikson in?"

"This isn't a good time. Can I take a message?"

"My name is Kathryn Jacobs. I'm with the FAA in Seattle. I had a meeting scheduled with him today, and he never showed. I'm just calling to see if everything's okay."

Kathryn listened to muffled talking, without clarity. But one thing she knew—everything was not okay.

Within seconds a woman said, "This is Claire Erikson."

"Claire, this is Kathryn Jacobs. I had a meeting with—"

"I know who you are," she said, and began to cry. Kathryn waited patiently. "He's dead. They said he killed himself."

"What? How?" Her heart climbed to her throat.

"I found him in the garage. Gunshot."

*Oh shit.* "I'm so sorry," she whispered.

"He didn't do this! There's no way he'd ever kill himself."

"Didn't they take his gun after the incident last March?" Kathryn asked.

"No. They never acknowledged he pulled it." She began sobbing, but the words flowed fast. "We're having a baby. He'd have given up that damn job for us. He was willing to risk it all talking to you. Why would he kill himself?"

"He wouldn't."

# CHAPTER 26

A MAN'S LIFE was taken by a gun issued to keep skies safe, not take a life. Then he ended up as a series of numbers identified in a report. Kathryn sat in her office reading the police report. First officer Don Erikson committed suicide with the government issued FFDO weapon: H&K 704037-A5 USP40 Compact LEM 10+1 40S&W 3.58.

She lifted the suicide note—*I can't do this anymore. Claire, I'm sorry. I almost killed everyone on my flight because of my errors. Please forgive me. Don.*

She set the note on her desk, and pushed her chair back. She walked to the window and placed her hands on her hips. *Who the hell killed him, and why?* Nobody who had the resilience and psychology to come forward and report safety ended their life. *What a bullshit note.* She had talked to him. Kathryn knew the truth. His wife knew the truth, as did Darby. Whoever killed him had to know that, too.

They closed Don Erikson's case in less than twenty-four hours. *What the hell is going on?* She watched a Global A330 depart, just as her cell phone rang on her desk. She rushed to answer it.

"Kat, I just had a weird call from Clark. He told me that the company attorneys said because everything in my report was happening in flight operations, they can't do an internal investigation of themselves, so he wants me to talk to an HR safety investigator."

"What'd you say?" Kathryn asked, finding that slightly odd.

"I said yes. I want to answer any questions they may have for clarification. Ray agreed that it would be a good idea to meet with them. It could only help."

"So why are you calling me?"

Darby laughed. "Good point. I'm just thinking if it walks like a duck and quacks, it might be..."

"A duck. Then tell them no."

"I kind of can't. I could. But I mean if they are finally willing to investigate, then I should do my part. Shouldn't I? It's just those little hairs are standing up with this one."

"I'm feeling a few soldier hairs myself." Kathryn wasn't sure about this. Something didn't feel right to her either. She glanced back at the report on her desk. Her head was beginning to throb. Nothing felt right today. One thing she knew, she wasn't one to be giving advice being pulled in so many directions.

After a moment, Kathryn said, "An HR safety investigator?"

"That's probably what's bugging me. Safety is all about human resources. It makes sense. I just didn't know Global was so proactive."

Kathryn sighed. "I'm sure it'll be fine. When do they want to meet?"

"One hour. At the Hilton, down the road from your office."

"You just heard about this, and you're having a meeting in an hour?" Kathryn's brows furrowed, and she squeezed the bridge of her nose. "Presumptuous or efficient?"

"Nothing at Global is efficient," Darby said. "I'm guessing they had this set up for a while and forgot to tell me."

"That makes sense. But are you okay doing this now, with all that's happened?" She placed a hand on the report. Darby was exposing her stoic, light-hearted exterior, but Kathryn knew Don's death hurt her more than she let on.

"I'm not sure I'll ever be ready, but…" Darby blew her nose, and then said, "But I do know this is all part of the crap that's going on at Global. If I don't do everything possible to improve safety, then I'm part of the problem."

"You will never be part of the problem."

They said their goodbyes and Kathryn turned her phone to silence, returning her attention to the report. Seconds later she was interrupted by a knock at the door.

"You have a minute?" Jason asked.

"Sure." Kathryn set the report down and gave him her full attention. "How was your weekend?"

"Long," He said, and pulled out a chair. "Can we talk about what happened to that first officer?"

"I think we should." But her heart felt otherwise. "I can't help but think that I am a contributor to his death."

"How so?"

"If I hadn't gotten involved he might still be alive."

"He killed himself."

"No, he didn't." Kathryn spoke a little firmer than she'd wished. She sighed and added, "He was coming forward. He told me what happened. I know the truth and that should be good enough to open an investigation of our own."

"You don't have proof."

"Since when do FAA inspectors need proof with a verbal discussion. I know what he told me."

"Won't hold water. The guy killed himself. They have a note. They'll call him crazy, and say that it was better in his car than in an airplane. The world will be happy with that, especially after that kid buried his plane into the side of the mountain." Jason stood and headed toward her Keurig. "Do you mind?"

"Of course not. But he wasn't crazy. That captain had problems. Stupidity or intentional, I don't know. But Don pulled his gun to save that flight, and someone wiped the voice recorder clean."

"I have no doubt the company is trying to protect the captain," he said pressing start on the coffee machine. "They're hiding something."

"By killing someone?"

"I'm sure there's more to this. But I'm not sure if we should shift our focus toward solving an assumed murder that occurred in another state when we have so much more on our plates." He lifted his cup, and moved to a seat in front of her desk. "What we're dealing with is far greater than all of this."

Whenever Jason helped himself to a cup of coffee, he always had more on his mind than he let on. But it was times like this that he actually listened to her—when he wasn't rushing.

"Look at the passenger manifest," Kathryn said. "The current secretary of the DOT was onboard, as was the leading contender against Nobles."

Jason sipped his coffee and then said, "You're implying?"

"I'm implying nothing, other than *if* that captain was trying to crash that flight on purpose, it could have been due to the passengers on board."

"Then why not investigate? Why not pull him in for psychiatric evaluation? Why protect him?"

She wondered that same thing. "Why hide the fact that Don pulled his gun on him?"

"Media would have a field day. The FFDO program could lose certification." He stared a moment, and then added, "A risk I'm not willing to take."

*Maybe.* The problem with judgments was they all had them. The decision of what was right and wrong was a gray sliding scale. Don was right to do whatever he could to stop the captain, but did they have the power to hide information for the greater good?

"Are we the judges to make that decision?" Kathryn asked.

"Safety is our responsibility," Jason said. "You and I both know that if a pilot pulls a gun on the other pilot, it could go either direction. Good guy, bad guy. All we can hope for is that they have protections in place to assess the stability of the pilots who receive those guns." He sipped his coffee. "We can't afford to lose that program."

He was right and she found herself nodding as he spoke.

Darby was an FFDO, and she had not only taken the MMPI—Minnesota Multiphasic Personality Inventory—a standardized psychometric test that assessed adult psychopathology and personalities, but she had met with a psychiatrist and attended a weeklong boot camp. Darby hated guns, but she was one hell of a shot. Program management did the best they could to keep solid subjects in the program, but there was always room for error.

"I get why they wanted to keep that quiet." She lifted her pen and tapped it on the desk, wheels spinning. "But would that be enough to kill someone?"

Jason sipped his coffee, watching her over the brim. Seconds ticked passed. "Perhaps. I'm losing faith in mankind. Hell, I question myself every day if I'm doing the right thing. People with the best intentions can be pulled the wrong direction. All we can do is our best."

"I wanted to join the FAA to help create change. To make sure accidents never happened, instead of cleaning up after them. But…" she closed her eyes for a moment to hold her composure. When she opened them, she said, "I feel like a hamster running on a wheel, not getting anywhere."

Jason leaned forward and placed a hand on hers, and squeezed. "Kat, you are making a difference. There's nobody more dedicated than you." For the first time, his touch did not send an unwanted chill through her body.

"Thank you for allowing me access to this report, and the time to review it."

He nodded, and then removed his hand and took another drink of coffee, and set the cup on her desk. Then he sighed. "We can't get funding."

"What?" Kathryn felt like she had been slapped. "Why?"

"Let's just say there are some people who say it's too expensive."

"What price do you put on safety?" This was a hit that she had not expected. "This needs to be done. It's the only way to gather the data to mandate change. Hell, we shouldn't have to do this. We know the problem."

"We don't know anything until we have data."

"Then let's get it."

"I'm sorry, but if there was some way we could do this without government funding, it would be a go. As it is now, it's just not possible."

"I'm sorry," he said again, walking toward the door. He turned and said, "If it weren't for the money, we could have made this happen." He walked out of her office, and she stared at the doorway for a moment.

Kathryn stood and picked up his cup. She walked across the room, dumped the remains into the sink, and held the cup for a moment, wanting to throw it through the window. Instead she set the cup in the sink.

She turned and leaned against the counter, folding her arms. *Who would not want this data?* Her mind shifted to Darby and then to Don. Jason knew that Don had been murdered, but he was letting it go because they have bigger issues? Darby knew the truth about what happened on Don's airplane. Did anyone at the company know that Darby had met with him? They sure as hell didn't want him to meet with her.

Fear trickled into her gut and mixed with anger. She rushed to her desk and dialed Darby, but the phone went directly to voicemail.

"Darby, if you get this in time, cancel your meeting. I don't feel good about this."

She gripped her phone and leaned against her desk. HR was designed with the pretense of employee services. But the truth was, the HR department worked for the company, not for the employee.

Besides, since when couldn't a flight operations department investigate itself for safety issues? She hoped to hell they were not screwing with Darby. She was madder than hell that someone was screwing with her research. Yet a young man was gone, and his death had everything to do with their meeting. Her heart broke for Claire Erikson and her unborn child. Tears broke free and for the first time, Kathryn Jacobs cried at work. She prayed John could find the truth.

# CHAPTER 27

VISIONS OF HIS lifeless body haunted her throughout the night. First, he was on the floor. Next, he was in the car. Then Darby was with Don, holding the gun that shot him. His brains splattered against the glass and across her face, and she awoke with a scream. Ray had held her, and assured her that it wasn't her fault. But she knew better. She shuddered at the memory as she backed down the driveway.

Looking left and right she pulled onto the street, and headed toward the hotel. Nothing felt right about this meeting. But if meeting with Global's safety investigator could help save even one life, she would do it. If Clark were serious about creating change, then she would do whatever she could to help him. Besides, any distraction to stop thinking about Don was welcome.

She pulled onto Highway 99, and merged into traffic. Her car wanted to turn left into airport parking so she could go flying and escape the reality of what happened. If she hadn't called Don, he'd still be alive. Someone knew he was going to talk to Kathryn, and she had put that into motion.

If only she had let it go. But that was the deal with all this—she couldn't. She wished she could be like the fraction of the population that was oblivious, or like the majority who believed nothing would change, so why make the effort.

Blinker on, she turned right into the hotel lot, and drove past many cars until she found a spot. She glanced at her watch—five minutes to show time. She shifted the mirror to assess her face. At least her mascara hadn't run in the last hour. Pushing the mirror back into place she said, "Don, I won't let this die, and I will find out what happened."

She climbed out of the car and threw her purse over her shoulder. One thing she knew, Don was much like herself—he had a fire in his soul to fix whatever had happened, more so than fearing the loss of his job. Not many people understood the difference between the love of flying and job retention. He did. He got it. There were some things you loved so much that you would never allow anyone to destroy, even at risk to yourself. Flying was one of those things.

Darby slammed the door. You never sacrificed love to terrorism. You never ran in fear, and never made decisions based on fear—you made them based on what's right. What happened in that flight deck was nothing short of wrong. The cover-up was worse. Don's death, in light of it all, was horrific.

Raindrops began to fall and Darby ran towards the entrance. Heaven was crying for their loss of a pilot. More than that, she knew the devastation his wife felt—Darby had been there too many times. She walked inside the lobby and sucked a deep breath. *Be strong. Deal with this now. Mourn for Don later. You can do this.*

Smiling at the desk clerk, she walked forward.

"I'm supposed to be meeting Anne Abbott. She apparently has a meeting room?"

The man looked at her with confusion for a moment, and then said, "Oh, the lady from Global?" When Darby nodded, he said, "She's around the corner, in the lobby." He extended a hand.

Darby approached a woman sitting at a table, in the center of the room, with a copy of her safety report in front of her.

The woman looked up and smiled warmly, "Darby?"

Extending her hand Darby said, "Yes. You must be Ms. Abbott."

"Anne, please," she said. "Thank you for meeting me."

"Of course. I'll do anything I can to help," Darby said.

Abbott opened the report and began to flip pages, and Darby's attention shifted to their surroundings.

The room was filling with hotel guests. People sat at tables within three feet of theirs with their coffee, chatting. A couple of businessmen entered and sat to her left. Then a mom, with her two small children rolled into the room, the kids arguing about something, sat on her right. Others were walking past the room headed to the restaurant, all within earshot. This was an odd, and far too open a setting for such a serious and confidential discussion—

"Darby."

"Huh?" Darby's attention snapped back to Abbott.

"Are you okay?"

"Of course." She was just assessing the environment, mitigating risk of their conversation to not hit the wrong set of ears. "I thought we'd have a room. Do you want to go to my house and talk? I'm ten minutes from here."

"No. We should stay. Are you okay with this?"

Darby shrugged. "If you are."

"First, I want to thank you for coming. I know this hasn't been easy," she said with so much compassion and concern. "I've read this report, and what's become clear is what you have gone through. We're going to get to the bottom of all this."

A rush of emotion overwhelmed Darby. The company was finally taking her safety issues seriously. She had spent years trying to create change that resulted in retaliation along the way. From her being called into the chief pilot's office, her simulators set up, to numerous line checks—she had persevered in the interest of safety, despite the warnings.

But Don lost his life. And now there was an angel sitting before her, sent by the company to make everything right. To fix all these issues, and get to the bottom of why the decisions were made as they were, along the way.

Darby's eyes moistened and Abbott pushed a small box of tissues toward her. "Thank you." But she sucked a deep breath gained her composure and didn't touch them. She was afraid if tears fell, she would flood the room for Don.

A woman to Darby's right glanced at the box and then to Darby, and Darby winked and smiled. The woman pulled her attention back to her table.

"So… I've read this report numerous times, and there's a lot in here." Darby nodded, and Abbott continued. "Let's start at the beginning with this checkride you had years ago, where you said the pilot falsified records. Can you explain how that's a safety issue?"

*Seriously?* That statement brought Darby to the table and slammed her into the moment.

"Part of the FAA AQP mandate is that we must show that the system is working. The only way to do that is through pilot assessment. The orals are part of that assessment. They are part of the quality assurance process to not only determine if pilots understand their limitations, but the entire system is designed for continual improvement. This is where the crews' knowledge is assessed."

Abbott stared without changing her expression, and Darby wasn't sure if she understood anything she was saying. "The training assessment process is one of the biggest challenges we have. Many professionals think the way we assess performance is falling short of identifying how well our programs work. Probably because of the thousands of FOQA events and air safety reports that come in annually, indicate otherwise."

When Abbott furrowed her brow at the FOQA acronym, Darby said, "FOQA is Flight Operational Quality Assurance program, where the plane captures performance data." Darby sighed. A safety investigator, at the very minimum, should know that term. "But if we don't even give the required orals, and our instructors skip the pre-brief—and I could give you an entire dissertation on the benefits and necessity of that brief—we don't have a chance to meet our requirements."

"How bad would it be if he only falsified records once, or he only got caught once?"

Darby's eyes widened. *What the hell?* She couldn't believe what she was hearing. "What if you robbed a bank? And you only did it once, or you only got caught once? Would they say, oh, that's fine, you just did it once?"

Abbott clearly did not understand, so Darby told her about a time at Coastal Airlines, when a check airman had pencil-whipped another check airman's checkride. Meaning one check airman was supposed to give a simulator check to the other check airman. He already knew the guy's performance level, so they didn't do the ride, and instead just filled out the paperwork.

An FAA safety audit identified this transgression, and made the company bring back every pilot, for six months, that the check airman who falsified documents had given rides to. He was subsequently removed from training. Accurate record keeping was essential and a serious violation if they didn't do it.

"Okay," Abbott said, and sighed. She then lifted one of her two cell phones, and began to type. "I'm sorry. I've got to take this."

"Kids?" Darby asked. She knew many people held two phones—one for company and other for personal, thus their personal data could never be recorded as company property.

"Children? No. I work," she said. "This is my mom. She had back surgery and I'm concerned she might fall. Sorry about this, it will just be a second."

That was sweet she was caring about her mother, but *seriously...* women did work *and* have families, too. *Culture*, sometimes it took decades to change, and culture was Global's greatest problem. Clearly, the backwards way of thinking was built deep within the company and many employees.

"Okay. Thank you," she said after she rapidly typed a text to her mother. "Can you explain what you meant by AQP?"

Darby focused on keeping her mouth closed, so her chin wouldn't hit the table when her jaw dropped. But she could not keep both eyebrows from rising as her eyes widened in shock. She sighed, and then she explained about AQP, SMS, and safety culture.

Then Darby went through every point in the report and carefully explained the correlation of events to each element of a safety culture, or in Global's case, lack thereof.

"What's going on here is so bad," Darby said, "that everyone in this report was afraid to come forward because of a fear of getting fired."

"Other people have told you they're afraid?"

"Are you kidding? My union rep called and warned me that I had a target on my back. I laughed and told him not to worry that I walked to my gym with a thick book in my coat if anyone took the shot."

"What'd he say to that?"

"He missed the joke about the location of the book and the target. But in a rather loud voice, he told me how he hated Odell, Clark, Wyatt, and the director of training, and how evil Clark was. I don't think he likes them.

"The problem with this company is that we don't have a reporting culture. People are afraid to say anything. That means all safety issues will remain hidden until it's too late."

"Too late?"

"Yeah, when an accident happens. When employees are afraid to come forward, then nothing can change because we fly along with a false sense of security. Unacceptable levels of risk remain in place until the accident happens. Then the industry reacts."

"Are you afraid?"

Abbott had clearly read the report since she had highlighted and written all over it. She must know that the retaliation had continued through the years, and that Darby wasn't afraid to speak out.

"I'm here, aren't I?" Darby said. *Follow your heart for the greater good and it will never fail you,* she reminded herself. "I've had many friends and coworkers warn me. I even got a lunch date out of it. Pretty much the same story, they all told me I was ruining my career. One of my favorite pilots asked what color I wanted my room painted when I lost my job, so I could move in with him and his wife when the company came after me."

"They're threatening you?"

"No." Darby grinned, and a laugh escaped. "These are *friends* warning me to watch out."

"Did you call the police?"

"Why would I call the police?" This was one of the oddest lines of questions that she had ever experienced, or expected. Maybe she thought they would give them donuts for being good citizens.

Abbott looked at her watch, and said, "I've got to get going. My flight is departing in an hour and I've got to get my bags, and checkout out of my room. Sorry to rush. I think I have enough information." She stood and said, "I'll send you a copy of the report when it's complete." She handed Darby a business card.

"You flew in and stayed here last night?" Darby asked.

"Yes. I live in Oklahoma City."

As they walked to the elevator, Darby digested the information they'd just gone over. She wondered who the hell this lady really was, because one thing she knew for sure, was that Anne Abbott had no idea how to spell safety, let alone what it meant at an airline. Her experience with aircraft was no greater than the average passenger that knew a plane had wings, engines, and pilots.

Darby turned toward Abbott, before she stepped onto the elevator and placed her hands on her hips.

"Ms. Abbott, a good friend of mine read this report. She clearly understood the magnitude of it all. She said if anything happened to me, she wouldn't allow my hard work to be in vain and that she would take this to the media."

Darby worked hard to find the words to emphasize the importance and magnitude of all this. "But the truth is, if we have a crash and our airline has done nothing to fix what's going on here, I will take it to the media. We have to do something."

"Okay, then," Abbott said. "Thank you for your time."

Darby watched her enter the elevator and disappear. She looked at the business card. Her eyebrows furrowed. *What the hell?*

# CHAPTER 28

THE CAR HAD a mind of its own and drove directly to Starbucks. After that insane discussion, Darby needed caffeine *and* sugar topped with whipped cream. Besides, there was no way a brain freeze would be as painful as what she had just gone through. *Safety meeting my ass.* She ordered a venti coffee light Frappuccino.

Fifteen minutes later, she was home and settled at her computer in her bedroom. She popped up Global's website and typed in Anne Abbott. Abbott's lack of knowledge on anything safety or aviation was enough by itself, but the business card should have identified her position—H.R. or safety. Instead it said PASS EO.

She pulled her straw and licked the whipped cream and then stuck it back into the hole and sucked. Her fingers typed rapidly. Then she began to laugh. "What the hell?"

"You looking at porn again?" Ray asked, and Darby jumped.

"Oh, my God, you scared me," she said. "Look what I just found."

Ray snuggled up behind her, pressing his body close. "What? A new job?" His hands slid over her breasts.

"Don't you wish?"

"Who's that?" he asked leaning closer. He unbuttoned a button on her shirt and slid his hand inside her bra.

"This is the lady I met with today. The one who Clark said was an H.R. safety investigator..." Darby stood, and he pulled his hand back. She turned toward him, and grabbed onto his belt and pushed him backward toward the bed, as she unbuckled it.

"What does your meeting have to do with pass travel?" Ray asked, unbuttoning her shirt, while she worked on his belt. "You look nice by the way."

"Thank you," she said, with a grin. She didn't often wear business clothes, as she was more of a t-shirt or sweatshirt sort of girl. "You should see me naked."

"Looking forward to it," he said, finishing with her buttons and opening her shirt. He leaned down and kissed her left breast, and held them both.

She backed him into the bed, and when he stopped movement she gave him one last body push, and he fell backward with her on top of him.

He slid his hands behind her back and released her bra, and then whispered, "You have way too many clothes on." He helped her out of her shirt and bra and she tossed them aside. "Don't distract me," she said. "I've got to tell you what happened."

"Can it wait?" he said, sliding his pants down his legs with her on top.

"Nope." She slid a foot between his legs, on top of his pants, and pushed them to the floor, and said. "That lady, Abbott, that I talked to today... doesn't work for H.R. She's not part of safety anything."

"Who was she?"

"She's the manager of the pass travel complaint department. She's also the equal opportunity program manager. Her card says PASS EO."

"Idiot," Ray mumbled.

"Excuse me?" Darby said, arms extended she pushed away from his body and gave him the look. She felt every bit the idiot being had, but for Ray to say it...

"Clark." He laughed. "He's the idiot."

"I'm trying to figure out the point of that meeting." Darby pulled away from him and stood. She unzipped her pants and allowed them to fall to the floor, then kicked them toward her hamper. There wasn't too much that slipped past her, but this one was perplexing. What kind of games were they playing?

Ray lifted his body, leaning on his forearms. "Maybe it's nothing. He was probably just doing this to check off the box, to make you think he's done something."

"Well, I've never worked so hard trying to teach someone about safety culture than I did today. Even Linda understands the ramifications of what's happening, and she isn't a pilot."

"Most people should understand the ramifications of that report. Did you show it to her?"

"Show what to whom?" Darby asked, sitting on the bed beside Ray.

"Show the report to Linda?"

"Of course," Darby said. "She actually wanted to send it to the board of directors."

Once they were disrobed, she nestled into his arms. Then she pulled back and stared at him with a curious look. "Why are you home so early?" It was only three p.m. and he rarely made it home before six, these days.

"I'm going back. I just came home for a quickie."

Darby grinned, and slapped his chest. "You are the most presumptuous man I have ever met."

Ray flipped Darby to her back and placed his lips onto hers, then slid a hand to her breast. The other hand went under her waist and he pulled her close. His lips relocated to her neck and he began nibbling his way south.

She wrapped her legs around him and tilted her head back. "You're on a time clock. How the hell did you get away?" she said, and then moaned.

"Late lunch?" he said as he ran a tongue over her abdomen.

Darby didn't want him to lose his job. He had come dangerously close before. And being demoted had taken a huge chunk out of him. She worried about him, and then she thought of Don. He had been willing to risk his job and do the right thing, but he lost his life for it.

Maybe the meeting today was to see if she would say anything about Don, and they were testing her. Abbott volunteered nothing, and Darby never mentioned him either. Visions of his smile were replaced with his lifeless body. Tears filled her eyes. He didn't deserve the ending he received.

Ray pulled his body on top of hers and they became one. Darby held him and closed her eyes tightly to shut away the visions of Don's death. As hard as she tried to get into the moment and give her all to the man she loved, a tear leaked from an eye and slid down her cheek. She knew Don's murder was her fault.

# CHAPTER 29

TIME WAS THE most precious commodity available to man, and when spent between two worlds it disappeared more quickly than a blink of an eye. Torn between two worlds, John sat in his office trying to focus. But his thoughts drifted to Jackie and their family.

They would have a baby in a little over a month, and he would be a dad. He wasn't sure if he was ready for that. A readymade family was one thing, but the idea of a daughter that he would be responsible for way into his later life, was now sinking in. He could feel her kick—there was life. This was actually happening, and rapidly becoming all too real. Then there was this damn business. He hated lying to Jackie, but now his greatest fear was whether he could keep his family out of harm's way.

His phone buzzed, and he glanced at the number that flashed across the screen. He picked up the phone and strode to his door. He closed and locked it, then answered.

"Where are you?"

"Office," John said. "Seattle." He headed toward his desk.

"Any news?"

"Nothing. First officer is dead. They gave the captain remedial training and he was back flying a week later. Still out there." John settled into his chair. "Union won't let him talk."

"How convenient." A scuffling came across the phone. "Never stopped you before."

"Things are different this time."

"Perhaps. When are you coming back east?"

"I'll be there Monday." John closed his eyes and rubbed them. "I'm taking the weekend off."

It was the day before Thanksgiving and the least he could do, for his family and friends, was to be present for the holiday weekend.

"Don't go soft. I need you focused."

John said good-bye, clicked his phone off, and set it on the desk. He was not proud of what he was doing, but the world was filled with sacrifices. Unfortunately, he was no closer to learning whether or not that Global flight was set up to remove the Secretary of Transportation, or if Global seriously had pilots who were that far behind the plane. A dead pilot wasn't helping.

He sighed, swiveling his chair toward the window and leaned back. Clouds filled the sky, and wind howled beyond the windowpane. If they were after him, that meant one thing—they knew. But nothing had been done since. Perhaps that was nothing more than a warning.

He glanced toward the parking lot. What didn't make sense was why kill the first officer? If the captain were the paid gun, then common sense would be to have gotten rid of him. But he was still out flying. Something didn't fit. Did this have anything to do with anything, or was it an ironic turn of events? No pilots could be that bad. *Could they?* This had to be intentional. *Or was it?*

He thought of Kathryn and all the work she had done on her proposal. It was damn good, too. He hated the fact that they pulled the funding. Timing was everything, and now wasn't the time. But he knew Kathryn and he suspected what she would do next. Then there was Darby's meeting in a hotel lobby to investigate a safety report—*what the hell was Global up to?*

John's phone buzzed again. He swung his chair toward the desk and he smiled at the name flashing across the screen.

# CHAPTER 30

HAPPINESS WAS FOUND by living life with gratitude, and Thanksgiving reminded her of all she had to be grateful for. Laughter and love filled the room, mixing with most incredible smells of a home-cooked meal. Darby stopped mashing the taters and reached for her wineglass. The guys were all in the living room watching the Steelers kick the Colts' butts on the big screen. As much as she would love to be in the living room with them, she needed her friends. Besides, Kat had bought a small kitchen television for times like this.

"Are you done with those?" Kathryn asked, covering the turkey with a second sheet of foil.

"Yes Ma'am. They are lump free!" Darby sipped her wine and then reached for a large serving spoon.

"Let me do that," Linda said, taking the spoon from her.

Darby gave in. She moved to the table, and sat beside Jackie and lifted the bottle of wine. She was filling her glass when Jackie extended a wine glass Darby's direction. Which was followed by Darby's eyebrow rising.

"Don't be judging me," Jackie said, with a laugh. "My doctor said I could have a glass of wine and it would help with contractions."

"You're contracting?" Linda said. "That baby's not due until what... mid-January?"

"Maybe end of December. A month isn't unusual," Jackie responded.

Darby poured a half glass for Jackie. "Well, looks like you're going to pop any day."

"God, I hope so." Jackie placed a hand to her back. "I forgot how uncomfortable this was."

"Wait until you're up all night with a screaming baby," Kathryn said, pulling out a chair and then sitting. "I don't know if it ever ends."

"Are you still fighting with the girls about driving?" Darby asked.

"They're too inexperienced. It's just..."

"Just you can't let 'em go," Jackie said. "Like I should talk. If it were my decision, Chris wouldn't be driving until he's twenty."

"You two," Darby sighed. "Linda, the kids are going to be counting on you to fix their mother's over-controlling behavior."

Linda laughed, and said, "It's one of the hardest things to do. To let go." She finished putting the potatoes into a serving bowl, and covered it with foil and sat at the table.

"To friends," Linda said extending her glass. She glanced toward the door, and back toward the table. "Jackie told me a little about what happened with your safety interview. What was *that* all about?"

"Who the heck knows?" Darby said. "But the manager of the pass travel complaint department investigating safety might not be out of character for Global. They definitely dance to their own drumbeat." She sipped her wine and then said to Linda, "I told her what you said about taking it to the media if something happened to me."

Linda laughed. "Well, I didn't want you to worry that if you drove that beast of yours off the road, no one would follow through." She glanced at Kathryn and winked.

"I didn't tell her that Kat, John, and Jackie read it too." Darby reached for a chip, dunked it into the clam dip, and stuffed it into her mouth. She chewed for a moment and her mind drifted to Don. "After Don was killed, nothing surprises me anymore." Her eyes moistened and Linda placed a hand on her back and rubbed.

"Were you sleeping with him?" Jackie asked. "I mean, back when you knew him."

"I wanted to know the same thing," Kathryn said.

"Inappropriate question, ladies," Linda said. "But thanks for asking." She laughed.

"God, no. He was just a really good guy. Each year he rented an airplane and would spend the weekend giving girls free flights. He and the other guys gave so much time and money. They're incredible." She sipped her wine, and added. "He was amazing. He was just scraping by as a regional pilot, but he loved aviation so much he wanted to share it. He also had integrity, and now he's gone."

"I'm sorry," Linda said, and moved her hand to Darby's and squeezed. "Jackie also told me that you were shut down on your research proposal," she said to Kathryn.

"You need a blog," Darby said to Jackie, with a laugh. "News flash! Updates by Jackie." Yet, Darby was thankful for the shift in direction of the discussion.

Jackie grinned. "What else am I supposed to do, being a beached whale?" She grabbed a carrot stick and dipped it into the ranch dressing. "I've given up on snooping."

Kathryn and Darby exchanged a glance. "You want to tell them?" Kathryn asked.

"No." Darby spread her hands. "You've got the floor."

Kathryn breathed deep and said, "Darby's going to fund my research."

"Are you kidding?" Jackie said. "That's amazing."

"How much will it cost?" Linda asked.

"I haven't figured that out yet," Kathryn said. "But we'll hit six digits without even trying."

"Holy cow!" Jackie said. "Darby… really?"

"Sometimes, you have to put your money where your mouth is." Darby knew that nothing would change unless they gathered the data. Kathryn had a great plan, and for the FAA to pull funding pissed her off as much as that phony safety investigation with Abbott. "What better way to use book money."

Kathryn gave Darby a heartfelt look of gratitude before turning toward Linda and Jackie. "I'm going to write an expanded proposal and layout how we'll conduct the research. Then we'll figure out how much it's going to cost. If it doesn't break the bank," Kathryn glanced at Darby, "I'll take it to my boss and let him know we've got funding."

"You ladies amaze me," Linda said.

DARBY FINISHED HELPING Kathryn clear the dishes and then joined everyone in the living room. Thanksgiving dinner had been perfect, and it was fun having the kids at the table. Now they were in the game room watching a movie, eating pumpkin pie. Darby had her plate in her lap with a piece of pie, piled high with whipped cream.

"Kat, you outdid yourself this year," John said, with an arm wrapped around Jackie.

"She always outdoes herself," Darby said. "That's the reason I've never taken the time to learn how to cook." She lifted her fork with a large bite of pie. "Kind of like… what's the point?" She stuck the pie into her mouth. Pumpkin pie cheesecake—life couldn't get better.

"When do you start flying the new plane?" Niman asked.

"I'm not sure," Darby said. "It's been ten days since my checkride, and I heard they're five to six weeks out."

"That can't be good, can it?" Linda asked.

"Nope. It couldn't be worse," Darby said. "Training is pretty short, and the longer a pilot's away from the plane, the more their confidence sinks and memory fades."

"Like your confidence could ever be reduced," Jackie said.

"We're all in that boat. It's just whether we admit it or fake it," Darby said. "There should be a mathematical formula for time away from training, squared… divided by how many days of training, to the factor of quality that equals the diminished confidence factor."

"My next project," Kathryn said.

Conversation settled around Niman's and Linda's new home, and all the challenges with closing the sale. Darby was glad Linda moved back to Seattle, especially with Jackie getting close to having the baby. If Darby were on a flight, Linda would be extra support if the little one decided to pop out early.

"Have you decided on a name?" Linda asked, changing the subject.

"Darby Junior," Darby said. "It would be so cool. She would be DJ, and male initials for a girl rock."

Jackie laughed, "As much as I like DJ, she's going to get a girl name."

"I'm just saying… when we turn her into a pilot, she'd have a better chance at Global if she had a guy name." Darby winked at Kathryn.

"How about JJ," John said. "She could be John Junior."

"Or RJ," Ray added.

"Whatever her name is," Kathryn said, "she'll be perfect."

"Can I tell him?" Jackie asked Kathryn, snuggling close to John.

"Tell me what?" John asked, glancing between Kathryn and Jackie.

"Of course," Kathryn said.

Kathryn and John had been good friends, long before Jackie had come into the picture. The fact that they worked together, had the same goals, and talked the same language didn't hurt the connection. There wasn't much Kathryn and John didn't discuss, and often before Jackie heard about it. But this wasn't one of those times.

"What's going on?" John asked, his eyes settling on Darby.

"Twins. You guys are having twins." When John turned white, and his chin hit the floor, Darby immediately retracted her statement. "I'm kidding! Just one little lady pilot on the way."

Niman and Ray laughed, and Linda joined them.

"You might need counseling after you're done with this group," Linda said.

"Don't scare an old man like that." John placed a hand to his heart. "I think I could handle any Global flight better than the thought of two babies."

"As much as I would love twins," Jackie said, "it's something that Darby's doing for Kat."

"What hasn't Darby done for Kat?" Ray said sarcastically.

Darby smacked his arm. "Backwards, on that. It's what hasn't *she* done for me."

"Darby's funding Kat's research," Jackie said.

"You're *what*?" John said.

Jackie told John about Darby paying for Kat's research, and Kathryn filled in the details of how they were going to proceed. But as Darby sat back and watched their animated discussion, it was John who surprised her. He appeared less than excited, and was definitely someplace other than the living room.

# CHAPTER 31

THE KNOWN CREWMEMBER line was the best thing they could have done for pilots and flight attendants alike. Flashing her ID, the TSA agent scanned Darby into the system, and within minutes she was through crew security access. She couldn't remember the last time she had gone through airport security as a normal person, unless it was in a nightmare. Tossing her purse over her shoulder, she headed through the terminal toward flight operations.

To say she was going stir crazy sitting around was an understatement. She *needed* to fly to energize her soul, something only pilots could understand. She also wanted to get into that left seat. She had not realized how much she missed it until she sat in the simulator for that first departure. But now she waited.

Most of her time off had been focused on solving Don's murder. She began talking to Claire Erikson daily, trying to figure out if anything else was going on in his life. She pulled Don's previous months' schedules and began calling the captains he'd flown with to see what they thought of him. Then John asked her to back off—he was taking care of this. So, she shifted her attention back to studying her aircraft procedures, and working on her presentation.

What she witnessed within the Global training department was nothing short of pathetic, leaving new pilots short on knowledge and confidence—exactly Kathryn's concern. It had also been over a month since training, and she still hadn't flown the aircraft. Heck, they hadn't even scheduled her O.E. yet.

O.E. was the operational experience that enabled pilots to fly the aircraft for the first time. They had an instructor onboard for guidance, as well as passengers to make the training events profitable. The problem was... five weeks was far too long to go without flying for any pilot, let alone a new captain, and a new pilot needed to reinforce what they learned in the simulator in a timely manner.

Pressing the code into the pad, the red light flashed. She laughed, being locked out of flight operations was a nightmare of another kind. She pressed the numbers again and this time the door unlocked.

Darby found her company mailbox, alias manila folder, and there wasn't much there—a couple of union informational sheets and a training disk. She smiled at the thought of training by disk and wondered which was better—train by disk or train by Google. It was a shame humans were taken out of the training mix.

Making this trek every few days kept her thumbprint on her airport community, and enabled her to say hi to other pilots. She would read the posts on the corkboard, and print bulletins off the computer. Today she had a different mission. She glanced through the office window. R.D. was on the phone. Darby referred to him as R.D. only because he was very proud of his title—Regional Director. She could wait. If she had anything these days, she had time.

At least the time off gave her the opportunity to work on her presentation. That project, however, made her even more frustrated that she wasn't flying, as she *knew* how bad this delay would impact her performance. She stuck her hands into her jacket pockets and smiled when he looked her direction.

When his eyes caught hers, and it registered with him who was waiting, he smiled broadly and then turned his chair, continuing his conversation. R.D. had turned out to be a super nice guy, albeit lacking integrity, was dumber than dirt, and was a pain in her ass. But you couldn't have everything when dealing with management.

Years earlier, he'd disciplined her for bypassing the chain of command. Apparently, when she had gone to Joel, her chief pilot, for something about her book, Joel went over the regional director's head to talk to Odell, the director of flying, who subsequently dumped on R.D. to control her. R.D. had been out of the loop and was pissed at Darby, like it was her fault. That was one of the funniest calls. But it all started with Phil, her union captain rep, talking to Joel the chief pilot when he shouldn't have.

"You bypassed the chain of command!" R.D. had yelled at her over the phone.

"No, I didn't," Darby had said. "I went to my chief pilot."

"I *am* your chief pilot!"

"No, you're not. Joel Iverson is. I don't even know who you are."

"I'm Joel's chief pilot. I'm the regional director!"

"Then if I'd gone to you instead of Joel, technically I would have been violating the chain of command going over his head." He wasn't very happy with that statement. But what could he say? She quickly learned what that was.

"You come to me for everything," he had told her. "You tell me *everything* you are doing even on your days off!"

"Everything?" she'd asked, wondering how far he could take this.

"Anything that has *anything* to do with an airplane, or talking to people, I want to know!"

"So, if I fly a little airplane, or host a flying event, or talk at the Rotary Club?"

"All of it!"

"What if I read *Flight For Control*, again?" she said, with a grin. "It's an aviation thriller."

"If you shit aviation I want to hear about it!" he'd yelled. "I want an email. I want to know everything that you're doing."

"Hmmm. How exactly do I get my aviation poop into an email?" she'd asked. But by the end of the call they had a plan. Darby wondered who else in the company had to write to the regional director and tell him their activities on their days off. She knew the answer to that—no one.

Darby requested that mandate in writing, and he had complied. Thus, for two years, she had been emailing him about her activities. For a joke, she once wrote about her and Ray joining the mile high club, but then thought better of it and pressed delete. The last email she had written was to ask for his assistance in making her meeting happen to report safety.

He declined. Come to think of it, she now wondered if R.D. was the person who had told Phil to talk her out of presenting the report. She had always found it hard to believe that Phil, as a union representative, allowed the company to force her to email her day off activities to the company.

"Knock, Knock," Darby said, tapping on the doorframe after he had finally hung up the phone. "Do you have a minute?"

"Sure," R.D. said, leaning back, with a huge smile. "What can I do for you?"

"My simulator check was five weeks ago, and I've yet to do O.E. Can you get me another simulator session before I fly?"

"We don't do that until six weeks have passed."

"That's in three days."

"You're point is?"

"My point is that December's weather is crap, tiz the season for holiday stress, and I experienced the shittiest training program in my career. I think we could make accommodations."

"You think we should make special accommodations just for you?"

"No," Darby said, placing her hands on her hips. "I think you should make accommodations for everyone."

"Do you know how much that would cost?"

"Do you know how much it would cost if there's an accident?"

He folded his arms, and said, "Do you need anything else?"

She pulled up a chair in front of his desk, and sat. "Yes. Our process of putting pilots on a plane and flying them across the country, without calling it duty to avoid duty time regulations, and marrying them up to an actual trip, violates FARs."

"No, it doesn't. It's legal."

"It's an FAR workaround. Imagine if Regional 39, the flight that crashed in New York years ago... what if the company put that first officer on a flight for non-reported deadhead, but just didn't pay her, because as you say... it's legal. The media would have had a field day." They had learned the first officer had commuted across country to fly that trip the same day, and fatigue was an attributing factor.

"We're doing nothing wrong. We're following the rules."

"No, you're not." Darby stood. "You're working around the rules with a technicality." This was turning out to be a waste of time.

Obviously, he didn't understand, so she tried a different tactic. "It's about company liability. If an accident were to happen and one of these non-duty deadheading pilots was flying, and they'd been on duty for twenty-six hours, that would be something Global would never recover from."

"I disagree," he said. "So how are you doing otherwise? I miss our chit-chats."

*God, he is such a dick.* "I'm going to be giving a talk to divisional leaders per Clark's request. Maybe you should join us."

His stare was unreadable. She wasn't sure if he had that good of a poker face, or perhaps there really was nothing inside his head.

# CHAPTER 32

A HEAVINESS HUNG in the air that grew thicker as the weekend came to a close. Jackie sat on the edge of the bed and watched John pack his suitcase. He was leaving again, and this was getting old. God, she wished they were in the new house, and the baby was safe in her arms. She and Chris could be reading like they used to, and they were waiting for him to come home at the end of the day. As it was, John was leaving, the baby wouldn't be out for three more weeks, and Chris was hiding in his bedroom playing video games.

"I'm sorry, sweetheart." John sat beside her and took her hand. "I knew this was going to be tough, but my presence in DC is… let's just say, not optional."

She squeezed his hand. "I just didn't know how hard it would be with you gone so much."

"Me either." He lifted her hand and kissed it. "Are you going to be okay?" His hand fell to her belly, and he rubbed just as the baby kicked.

"I will be when we figure out a name." She laughed. "Otherwise Darby Junior will stick."

John grinned, and then stood. "I'll be home on Friday and we will have a name by Christmas." He leaned over and kissed the top of her head. "I'm sorry this has been so hard on you."

"As soon as you get your appointment, we'll get settled."

"If," he said. "But yes, soon I won't have to keep leaving."

Jackie stood and closed his suitcase. "Thanks for taking the red-eye. We loved spending the day with you."

"Of course," he said, wrapping her in his arms. "I'm going to miss you."

They stood that way for a moment and Jackie said, "I'm looking forward to Christmas. We really get to keep you through the New Year?"

"Yes. Maybe longer depending when DJ gets here."

Jackie rolled her eyes. "Don't encourage her."

They went downstairs to the living room to wait for John's car to arrive. "I think this is silly for you to take a car. We live so close to the airport. I could drive you."

"I don't want you out on the street at night." He sat on the couch and reached for her. "Are you sure you're okay?" he asked.

She sat beside him. "I actually feel better than I have in a long time. Tomorrow I plan on getting the last of my shopping done, and Chris gets out of school on Wednesday, so we'll find a movie and do something fun. He's been so distant lately."

"Teenage boys. I'm sure I was the same."

"Oh God. Then I really should be worried."

He reached for her hand and pulled it to his lips. He'd been touching her often this weekend. She loved his affection, but it felt as if he were saying goodbye. Just then, lights flashed through the front window.

"Guess it's time," she said.

He stood and adjusted his suit, then headed for the front door, pulling on his long wool overcoat. Jackie followed him and opened the door.

"I'll talk to you sometime tomorrow sweetheart," he said, and gave her one last kiss.

He walked down the path toward the street, and tears sprung to her eyes. She wasn't sure if they came from the hormones, the season, or the fear that she couldn't trust her husband. But something was amiss. Once his car was out of sight, she closed the door and went directly to his office. She pulled the box out of the drawer. When she got the lock fixed, she had them make her a second key.

She was about to open it when Chris said, "Mom, what are you doing?"

"Nothing sweetheart," she said, putting the box back into the drawer. "Just straightening a few things up. Did you finish your homework?"

"Yeah. Like on Saturday." He rolled his eyes and then left the office. Jackie followed, but she hesitated at the door, and then turned out the light. There was always tomorrow.

# CHAPTER 33

LIGHT OF DAY brought renewed hope and a burst of energy. Jackie had just finished cleaning the kitchen and was now working on the refrigerator. On her knees, she wiped the bottom shelf wondering what the heck John had put in that box. It had been sitting on the top of his desk over the weekend, and then it ended up in the drawer again. Whatever he was working on had to be something big. He had not even talked to Kathryn about it.

She stood and returned the eggs to their shelf, as she did the yogurts. She opened the lid on the leftovers from Saturday dinner and sniffed. Then she closed them up, and set them on the shelf. She would have to give up snooping on John. She needed to trust him. Besides, what she didn't know didn't hurt her. *Yeah right.*

Chris was upstairs getting ready for school and Kathryn would be there any moment to give him a ride. The rain was dumping hard, and Jackie was glad to not have to go out this morning. She was also thankful Chris didn't have to walk to the bus. She glanced at the clock, and then yelled, "You almost ready?"

He made some sound acknowledging he'd heard her. Jackie glanced out the window to see if Kathryn was there yet, and she noticed a streak. She grabbed the Windex from under the sink and then sprayed the spot. She grabbed a handful of paper towels and began wiping the window.

Kathryn pulled into the driveway. Jackie waved to her and went to the stairs and yelled, "They're here!"

Jackie tossed the paper towel into the trash. She grabbed her coat and headed for the door to go out and tell Kathryn Chris was on his way. When she opened the door, she jumped with a scream.

Kathryn laughed. "Sorry for scaring you, but I suspected you may try to come to the car," she said stepping into the kitchen. "Sorry for dripping on your floor. How are you feeling?"

"Really good. Thank God, no more morning sickness. It's been a week now." She looked back toward the stairs and yelled, "Chris!"

"Small miracles." Kathryn glanced out at the car.

"Worried they're going to drive off?"

"Wouldn't surprise me," Kathryn said. With her attention back on Jackie she said, "Today's the big day. I'm going to present the final proposal to Jason, and surprise him with Darby's offer."

"You didn't tell him yet?"

"Nope. I wanted the work to be done first. Every detail. I'm also not quite sure how this will work. I think Darby will have to create the project offering funding, and then we apply." She grinned. "We'll figure it out. But the point is we have funding, the final proposal is complete, and we are going to gather our data."

Chris came bounding down the stairs and said, "Bye, Mom," as he headed out the door.

Jackie sighed, and Kathryn gave her a hug and said, "Are you sure you want to do this again?"

"Someone should have asked me that nine months ago." Jackie smiled. But the truth was, the answer would have been yes.

Kathryn ran to her car and Jackie waved, then she closed the door. She walked over to the counter and picked up the bottle of Windex and returned it under the kitchen sink. If John wasn't having an affair, then he was working on something important. Not telling her what he was doing could just mean he was being overly protective of her and the baby. She might be able to bring insight if she knew what that was.

Jackie headed toward John's office. Once there, she sat in his chair and swiveled it toward the drawer. She removed the box and set it on the desk, then pulled the key from her pocket and placed it into the lock and turned.

Her heart sped up and the baby kicked as she opened the box. Placing a hand over the huge mound she said, "It's okay sweetheart."

Jackie could handle *anything*, but not photos of John with another woman. She removed the envelope that was thicker than last time. She pulled out the photos and began looking through them. The top photos were the ones they had already seen. There were also more of Global's CEO—half a dozen. John was following Patrick Lawrence. *Why?*

Then the next photo and the next, were of… blood? She pulled one of those photos close appreciating the beauty of the single splatter. It was kind of weird. Another photo looked like a staging for a movie set. There was a morbid curiosity that brought acid to her throat, but she looked on. Another photo of blood splattered inside a car. Different angles. *Why was John taking pictures of blood?*

The next photo made her gasp. Her eyes widened, and a hand went to her mouth. She fought the bile in her throat.

"Oh, my God!" she screamed, when she realized what she was holding, and threw the photos. She pushed back from the desk and ran to the bathroom with a hand covering her mouth. Dropping to her knees, she vomited into the toilet. She heaved again, and again. Tears were flowing and her stomach contracted, but this time when she heaved nothing came out. The cramping grew stronger.

She sat back on the floor, and that's when she realized it was wet.

# CHAPTER 34

THE JUXTAPOSITION OF noise and silence never ceased to amaze Kathryn after the kids were out of the car. She dropped them off at school and then headed straight to the office. She couldn't remember when she had been more excited about a project than she was now. Part of the excitement was that she could finally use her researcher's background. She grinned. *Who am I kidding?* All she wanted to do was get the data they needed.

No billion-dollar airline CEO, no matter how much power, could fight proof that pilots needed better training. She pulled into her spot and parked her car. Grabbing her briefcase and purse, she ran for cover, holding her briefcase close to her chest. Once inside, she hurried to the elevator, stuck her hand in between the closing doors, and stepped in. She pressed the button to the top floor.

She was one of the few who loved Seattle rainstorms. The sound of raindrops and flow of water filled her with peace. Granted she would rather be inside looking out, but Darby was slowly teaching her how to dance in the rain. Kathryn could not believe Darby's generosity. Far too many people sat around and complained, but never put their neck or pocketbook on the line. Not Darby—she did both.

The elevator stopped on her floor and she headed directly to her office. Once inside she lifted the handset and pressed speed-dial to Jason's private line as she shed her purse and coat.

"Good morning, Kathryn," he said answering the phone. "How was your weekend?"

"Busy," she said. "But I have great news."

"How so?"

"Do you have a few minutes?"

"For you? Of course," he said. "But can you give me an hour first?"

She forced a smile and said, "Of course."

If a person smiled while speaking, the words sounded more optimistic. She leaned back in her chair and sighed. She had waited a long time for this, what was one more hour? Besides, she had a job to do.

She logged into her computer and began searching cyber security. The greatest delay with NextGen was security. The concern that aircraft could be utilized as weapons was huge. While drone management was her job, she was more fascinated by NextGen. It wouldn't be long, however, when drone technology would be the next level of NextGen. The pilots would be nothing but the backup system for that technology in the event of failure or hacking—until they proved it reliable, and then they would remove them.

Kathryn's fingers flew across the keyboard, and she opened her current file and typed *Blockchain—a* data structure that created digital ledgers of transactions and distributed them among a network of computers. Blockchain enabled network users to securely manipulate the ledgers with what they called cryptography, which did not necessitate a master authority.

The Wall Street Journal had an interesting article, and Kathryn proceeded to read—*Once a block of data is recorded on the blockchain ledger, it's extremely difficult to change or remove. When someone wants to add to it, participants in the network—all of which have copies of the existing blockchain—run algorithms to evaluate and verify the proposed transaction. If a majority of nodes agree that the transaction looks valid—that is, identifying information matches the blockchain's history—then the new transaction will be approved and a new block added to the chain.*

"Hmmm." *Interesting.* She wondered as to the power of this type of technology if utilized for NextGen and drone security. The more she read, the more questions she had, but it might just be what they were looking for in security.

While there was no failsafe system, they needed to do something as the industry escalated to the next level of technology. The big players in the blockchain technology were Linux, IBM, and Drake Technologies. She smiled at the sight of Drake's name.

Drake had made it into the Whitehouse, and she hoped to hell his technology business wouldn't fail during his time away. He wasn't wrong about the government being inefficient and in desperate need of change. She also supposed that Niman was correct, and Drake's motivation was self-serving tax-cuts for his business. Yet if this technology were to work, she would have much preferred him to stay where he belonged and help build the future of aviation.

Security was everything and Drake was onto something. However, government legislation could be blocking his progress. With the power he now held, he might just tear down those walls and progress could be well underway to bring NextGen to the market quicker.

Kathryn jumped when her phone alarm rang. She had killed the hour. Slipping her phone into her purse, she headed for Jason's office.

"Hello, Kat. Mr. Bernard is expecting you," his secretary said. "Go right in."

"Thank you, Barbara."

Kathryn entered Jason's office and closed the door. He was sitting behind his desk and smiled broadly at her.

"Before we begin, I want to thank you for the input on the Flight 42 incident." Kathryn nodded, and then he said, "How's the security research going?"

"Good." Then she told him what she'd learned, and her question of whether or not blockchain cyber security systems could find its way into drones, and perhaps airliners. He nodded his head, listening intently. When she was done, she said, "But that's not why I'm here."

He grinned. "I didn't think so."

Kathryn handed him the final copy of the proposal.

"What's this?"

"The final proposal. Logistics. Cost. Etcetera."

He took it and then placed it on his desk. "I told you we didn't have the budget," he said sliding it forward across his desk toward her.

Kathryn smiled. "I have an investor who is willing to fund the project."

He pushed back from his desk, stood, and walked to the window. Then he turned. "We are not doing this. Consider this proposal *dead*."

Kathryn stood, "Jason, you can't kill this. We need this information!" she exclaimed, a little more passionately than she had expected. "You said if—"

"You don't understand," he began, then placed his hands on his hips. "This is not for you to decide."

"Then who? Who the hell's making these decisions?"

"You're crossing a line."

Kathryn was furious. "You told me that funding was the issue. I got you funding." She had never raised her voice in the office before, but dammit, what the hell was going on?

"Kat, I know you worked hard on this. It must be extremely disappointing. But we're not going down this path."

"Disappointing? Seriously?" she grabbed the proposal off his desk. "This is about the safety of our industry and I *am* doing this." Her phone vibrated in her purse, and buzzed.

He folded his arms and stared a moment, and then said. "Not in this office you're not."

"Excuse me?" Had she heard him right? Her phone continued to buzz, but she ignored it.

"If you feel that strongly, then you know where the door is."

"Are you firing me?" Kathryn said, her phone now chiming with a text coming in.

"That's your decision," he said. "And, will you please answer that god damned phone!"

Kathryn pulled the phone out of her purse and read the text. "I've got to go." Holding tight to the proposal, she grabbed her purse and headed for the door. She touched the doorknob and hesitated, looking back she said, "Yes, it is that important."

Kathryn opened the door, exited with as much calm and grace as she could muster, and closed the door quietly behind her. Then she ran like hell.

# CHAPTER 35

HER LIVING ROOM was a Christmas card with music. Silent Night played from the speakers, while flames danced in the fireplace, and lights twinkled on her tree. Darby was snuggled on the couch, wrapped in a comforter. She was reading her training manual, trying to focus without much luck. It had been six weeks and three days since her check, and yet there was still nothing on her schedule for that extra simulator session. Instead of fretting, she was finishing her first cup of coffee and enjoying the comfort of being home for the holiday.

"Darb, want another cup of coffee?" Ray called, from the kitchen.

"Does a rubber duck float?" she called back.

Within minutes he was standing in front of her with a fresh cup, and he traded her for the empty.

"Thank you," she said, and sipped her brew. He had even added hot cream and a touch of sweetness. "You're the best."

"Just keep thinking that," he said, and bent down and kissed the top of her head. "Don't study too hard." Then he added, "I've got to go. Some of us have to *earn* a living."

"Don't tell me about earning a living," she said with a smile. "Wait until I fly the airplane for the first time in a snow storm, with a couple hundred people on board, after not seeing the simulator for a couple months."

"Let me know how that goes," he said with a grin.

Just then Darby's phone rang. "Speak of the devil." R.D.'s number flashed over the screen, and she held up the phone.

"Send me a text when you know your schedule," Ray said.

Darby gave him a thumbs-up as she answered the phone.

The first thing that popped out of R.D.'s mouth was, "You need to come to the office now."

"Why? Did you book a simulator for me?"

"I'm not at liberty to tell you."

"You can't tell me if you booked the simulator," she said, rolling her eyes.

"I can't tell you why you have to come in."

"You have to tell me," Darby said. "You can't just order me around on my day off. How do I know this isn't a crank call?" she grinned, and sipped her coffee.

"God dammit Bradshaw! Get your ass in this office now."

She looked under her comforter and then said, "I'm not sure they'd let me through security right now."

"Why not?"

"I'm kind of naked. But you're certainly getting a little personal."

"You had better be here within an hour."

"I could be there in two. Should I bring my union rep?" Darby asked.

"He's on his way."

R.D. hung up, and Darby called Phil. She learned even less from him.

AN HOUR AND a half later, Darby was on her way to the airport. She did the same ID flash as the week before and, in no time, was punching the code into the flight operations door. R.D., Joel, and Phil were sitting in the glassed-in office. That was the best Global did for transparency. At least it was something. She smiled and then went to her mailbox, but it was empty.

She walked to R.D.'s office and said, "Is this party for me?"

"Sit. Please," R.D. said. He was no longer the angry elf he had been on the telephone, but a kinder gentler version of someone else.

Darby sat with her purse in her lap.

R.D. said, "Is anyone recording this?" When nobody responded, he said, "Joel, are you recording?"

Joel said, "No."

"Phil, are you recording?"

"No."

"Darby, are you recording?"

Darby shook her head no, because she didn't want to be on the recording lying. She pulled her purse a little closer.

"So, what's this about?" Phil asked.

"We have a letter for Darby."

"Do you have another copy I can read?" Phil asked.

R.D. gave him a copy, too.

Darby began to read her letter—*Darby Bradshaw, this is to inform you that under Section 8 of the pilot working agreement, that you have been pulled from flight status because of the company's concern for your ability to hold a first class medical certificate due to mental health concerns. You will be contacted by Dr. Marsh MD, and are required to provide him all your medical records for evaluation.*

"Are you kidding me?" Darby asked. "On what grounds?"

"We don't know," R.D. said in the most sickeningly sarcastic voice she'd ever heard. "It was something you said to Abbott, and that was confidential. But we take safety very serious at Global Air Lines, and in light of what happened with that plane flying into the mountain—"

"I know what I said to Abbott. And this is way out of line," she said holding out the letter. She stared R.D. down, and he looked away.

"How did Abbott know to talk to Dr. Marsh?" Phil asked.

"Who *is* Dr. Marsh?" Darby glanced to Phil, and back to R.D. Then her eyes flashed to Joel, who was sitting quietly trying to disappear from it all.

"Our company doctor," R.D. said, shifting in his seat.

Darby looked at Phil and said, "Let me get this straight. The company is concerned about something I said to the manager of the pass travel complaint department, and they want me to give a *medical* doctor my medical records to assess my *mental* health?"

"That's the process," R.D. said. "Your point?"

"My point is," Darby said, "The only medical records I have are from a colonoscopy last spring, and unless my head is up my *ass*, I'm not sure how an *M.D.* is going to assess my mental health with those records."

Darby's phone began to vibrate and she pulled her purse close.

"This is the process," R.D. said. "You will give him what he wants. We've pulled you from flight status. You no longer have known crewmember status. You can keep your ID, but it really won't do you any good, other than get you into secured areas for employees."

Darby raised an eyebrow at the thought of the company enabling a crazy person to retain their ID and access to secured employee areas. Then she looked at Phil. "Our union allows them to pull this shit without cause?" Her phone continued to vibrate.

"I also want you to know that I knew *nothing* about this when we had our talk the other day," R.D. said.

The reality of what was happening fell on her like a brick wall. She was being pulled from flying for mental health. They were not going to allow her to fly her plane. She had been on a mission for safety, yet they were painting her a villain that would fly a plane into a mountain.

Darby looked at the letter again and realized R.D. had signed it the week prior—two days after their talk. Last spring Phil had warned her that they could use this tactic if she reported.

"I was supposed to give a safety presentation to Clark's divisional leaders." This time, Darby's phone chimed.

"Yes," R.D. said. "Captain Clark asked if you would still be willing to do that."

"I don't advise that," Phil said. "Not now."

They pulled her for a mental health issue, calling her crazy, and yet they wanted her to come to corporate headquarters and give a safety presentation to their divisional leaders? Were they fucking idiots? Her phone dinged again and Darby pulled it out and read her text—*My water broke I'm driving myself to the hospital.*

Darby's eyes popped wide open and she dialed Jackie's number. It went straight to voicemail. She hung up and dialed Kathryn, who answered out of breath.

"Where are you?" Darby asked, standing and throwing her purse over her shoulder.

"Running to the car, heading to Swedish Hospital."

"I'm on my way," Darby said.

Darby ended the call and R.D., Phil, and Joel stared at her as if she were crazy.

"FAA," Darby said, waving her phone. "As much fun as this party's been, I've got a baby to deliver! Talk to you from the mental ward."

# CHAPTER 36

"HOLY SHIT!" JACKIE cried out, and began panting. "Hoo. Hoo. Hee. Hee." She had forgotten how painful this birthing thing was. The baby wasn't due for three more weeks. She needed John! "Hoo. Hoo. Hee. Hee." But the thought of John brought visions of the horrific photos. She forced them from her mind. "Hoo. Hoo. Hee. Hee." She visualized her beautiful daughter. *God, please bring her safely into the world.*

"You're doing great," Linda said, placing a wet rag over her forehead.

"She's too early," Jackie said, and then doubled over and yelled, "Ahhhh." The pain was unbelievable.

"Breathe, sweetie," Linda said. "She's going to be fine."

"Hoo. Hoo. Hee. Hee."

Kathryn came running into the room. "How many minutes apart?" She moved to the side of the bed and touched Jackie's shoulder, and then kissed her cheek.

"They're ten minutes apart. She's dilated to six," Linda said.

Darby came running into the room minutes later and threw her purse on the floor. "What can I do?"

Jackie whaled, "Ohhhh… God! Hoo. Hoo. Hee. Hee." As the pain began to subside, she said, "Where were you both? I called and nobody answered." She was so glad they were all there.

Kathryn sighed. "I was yelling at my boss."

"Why?" Linda asked, adjusting Jackie's pillow.

"He forbids me from doing the research."

"Even if Darby's paying?" Linda asked. "That's crazy."

"Can I get an ice chip?" Jackie asked.

Darby reached for the cup of ice and scooped a couple ice chips into Jackie's mouth. "Did you tell your boss he was a fucking idiot?" Darby asked Kathryn.

Kathryn laughed. "No, I don't think so."

Darby sat on the edge of the bed. "The company pulled me for being crazy. Said I can't hold a first class medical."

"What the hell?" Kathryn said. "What does that mean exactly?"

"It means I can't fly if I'm a mental patient."

"They can't do that." Jackie said. "Those baaaastards! Ahhhh. Hoo. Hoo. Hee. Hee."

Kathryn moved to Jackie's side and rubbed her back. "Breathe, sweetheart. You're doing great."

"Hoo. Hoo. Hee. Hee."

"That's ridiculous," Linda spat. "There's nobody I would rather want piloting my aircraft. What grounds?"

"They wouldn't tell me." Darby held Jackie's hand. "But we'll sort it out."

"Hoo. Hoo. Hee. Hee."

"We'll be on the street together," Kathryn said, rubbing the small of Jackie's back. "You're doing great. Keep breathing."

"You got fired?" Darby asked.

"More or less and... breathe baby..."

"Hoo. Hoo. Hee. Hee." Jackie could hardly talk, but she managed to say, "Was it more or ... less? Hoo. Hoo. Hee. Hee."

"More." Kathryn said. "I walked."

Jackie looked from Kathryn to Darby and yelled, "Ohhhh. Shiiit!" she screamed. "Hoo. Hoo. Hee. Hee."

"I'm thinking the same thing," Darby said. "How are you going to survive without a job?"

"I didn't think that through."

As the wave of pain began to subside Jackie said, "I need one of you to go to the house before Chris gets home."

"I'll get him and take him to my house for the night," Kathryn said.

"Not what... Hoo. Hoo. Hee. Hee." Jackie tried to catch her breath to get the words out, but the pain was on the upward slope. "Oh, my God! I need drugs. I can't do this."

"I'll get them," Darby said, and ran out of the room. She returned with the nurse.

"Let's see how you're doing sweetie," the nurse said. "Oh... my. I think we're having a baby."

*You think?* There was so much more she wanted to say, but instead Jackie blew harder. "Hoo. Hoo. Hee. Hee!" She squeezed Linda's hand and said to the nurse, "I changed my mind. I want an epidural."

"I'm sorry, it's too late. You're dilated to nine and this baby is making her way into the world. Let me get the doctor."

Within minutes, the doctor came rushing into the room and checked her. "Ten! This little lady is in a hurry." The doctor said, "I'm going to let you push in just a minute, so hang tight with me. Okay?"

Jackie nodded. "Hoo. Hoo. Hee. Hee." She reached and grabbed Kathryn's arm and yelled, "Ahhh! "Hoo. Go to the house. Hoo. Hoo."

The doctor said, "Okay, it's time to push. Hang onto your legs and you're going to push with the next big contraction. I want you to give it your all."

Jackie nodded, and Kathryn and Linda were each on a side ready to support her back.

"Okay, here we go," the doctor said. "Let's push this baby out."

Legs bent, she leaned forward, with support of her friends, and screamed, "Ahhhhh," as she bore down hard, holding her legs for support and pulling for leverage. Kathryn and Linda held her upright, supporting her back. "Get the photos!"

"That's good. You're doing great," the doctor said. "I can see her head."

"She has red hair! She's a Darby Junior!" Darby began snapping photos on her cell phone. Jackie was too exhausted to tell Darby that's not what she meant. She laughed, and then she cried. The contractions subsided for what felt like half a second and the wave was coming back.

"Here we go," the doctor said.

"Kat. Photos in John's office... Ahhhhh!" she yelled bearing down again, this time harder than the last. "You can't let... can't let Chris see." Tears spilled from her eyes with the pain.

Once this wave began to subside, she stopped pushing and took a deep breath. Kathryn said, "You found more photos in John's office?"

"I need you to push, sweetie. You're almost there. Give me a good one this time," the doctor said, "and your daughter will be here."

Jackie was nodding in answer and yelled, "Yeeessss!" about the photos. She bore down and screamed... "Ahhhhhh!" Her screams were then replaced with the cry of a baby. Her baby.

Kathryn squeezed Jackie's hand. "Don't worry. I'll take care of it." She would take care of it all. She always did.

"She's beautiful," Darby said. "Look how tiny she is."

Linda touched Jackie's shoulder, "You did good, sweetie."

"Did anyone call John?" Kathryn asked.

"I called him on the way here," Jackie said. "Got his voicemail."

"He called back," Linda said, glancing at her watch. "He's on a flight and should be here within three hours."

The doctor cut the cord and placed Jackie's daughter on her chest. She was so little. She was so beautiful! She was perfect in every way. Jackie couldn't stop staring at her. Tears fueled by emotion began to flow, and Jackie had no idea where they came from—love for this tiny human she had brought into the world, sadness that John wasn't there to experience this with her, or gratitude knowing she would never be alone with friends like these.

Jackie leaned down and placed her lips on her baby's head for her first kiss.

# CHAPTER 37

SURREAL COULD BE the only way she could explain this day. The gravity of all that had transpired would settle in soon enough. Now she had a cleanup mission to accomplish. Kathryn parked in Jackie's driveway and climbed out of the car. She glanced at her watch as she headed toward the front door. The kids would be out of school within the hour, and John would be landing in twenty minutes. He would go directly to the hospital, and she would pick up the kids. There was time. She stuck the key into the lock and turned it.

Linda and Darby were staying with Jackie, while Kathryn picked up Jackie's overnight bag, and took care of the house. She closed the door behind her and headed toward the downstairs bathroom.

The smell hit her first. She looked under the sink and grabbed a spray bottle of Clorox and sprayed the tile, then went to the kitchen and grabbed a roll of paper towels. Returning to the bathroom, she cleaned up the floor, wiped down the toilet, and flushed.

Kathryn stuffed the paper towels into the bathroom garbage can and removed the bag. She washed her hands and carried the bag to the kitchen and set it on the floor. Then she headed upstairs to the bedroom so she wouldn't forget to pick up Jackie's things.

An overwhelming sense of déjà vu encompassed her body. It had been years since she did this exact same process of gathering a bag for Jackie to take to the hospital, but it felt like yesterday. The only difference was, the last time she took a bag for Jackie to the hospital it was to watch her husband die, this time it was to bring a life into the world.

The thought of Greg brought tears to her eyes. Jackie not only lost her husband, Kathryn lost her brother.

Once in the bedroom, she looked around the room. Then she saw it, lying in between the nightstand and the wall. Kathryn picked up the overnight bag, then headed downstairs to the kitchen. She set Jackie's overnight bag on the counter, grabbed the garbage bag and opened the back door. She stuffed the bag into the garbage can, and closed the lid tight.

Back inside the house, she headed straight for John's office. There were photos scattered everywhere. Kathryn began picking them up. There were many more than last time, and many of Patrick Lawrence. *Why is John following Global's CEO?* The million dollar question. More pictures of the same woman as before, with some of her shaking Lawrence Patrick's hand.

Kathryn gasped. Now she understood why Jackie was insistent that Chris should never see these photos. This was Don Erickson. Dead. There was a hole in his face. His blood soaked uniform told all, and the image made her want to vomit.

The first officer from Global flight 42 posed motionless, life stripped from his body. She ran a finger over the photo, as if touching him could bring him back to life. Did he die because he was coming forward with what he knew… or had he learned something new?

"What did you know?" Kathryn whispered to the photo.

She gathered up the other photos, and her brows furrowed when she noticed the first picture of blood. Then another of blood spatter against the window. Shifting her attention from Don's photo to the blood spatter and back again. The blood on the window behind Don was the exit spatter. But why does John have a photo of that?

She sat at his desk and stared at the photo and the pattern his blood had made. This was definitely the impact stain, where the bullet-projected blood splattered against the window. Whenever there was a gunshot wound, there was also an element of back spatter at the bullet's entrance point. She flipped through the photos and found one of back spatter. Then she looked at the photo of the exit point.

Impact spatter varied depending upon the type of gun and where the projectile entered the body, and if the bullet had exited. The entrance wound spatter was a mist, and the larger drops of the exit wound had slammed against the window.

His blood stains against the glass told the story of what happened. She looked at the shape, and visualized the angle of impact, the distance… velocity. What was it? Leaning back, she closed her eyes, took a deep breath to clear her mind.

Something wasn't right. His head lay backwards as if he had been facing forward, but the spatter was more on the side window—it should have been behind him. Had they measured the length of these stains, or location to assess the angle? As the angle increased, the spatter would have elongated. The patterns were wrong.

Hollow point ammunition was used in guns carried on aircraft in order to protect against collateral damage that could be caused by an exit wound. The expanding nature of this bullet caused maximum damage upon entry, but seldom exited the body—especially if it penetrated bone on the way in and would have to penetrate bone again on the way out. The bullet never left his skull, but destroyed his head all the same.

Kathryn opened her eyes and located John's printer, removed a blank sheet of paper and wrote—*Blood. Angle. Head position.* She then looked at the photos again and sighed. Someone turned his head for this photo. Did John do this? Was he there? He had to be. This was definitely a first-response photo. She tapped the pen on his desk, and sighed. She lifted another photo from the desk, a seat from his car with a single drop of blood.

It fascinated her. Why take a photo of a drop of blood? What made this drop unique? She set it on the desk and just stared, trying not to think too hard. The blood had begun to turn reddish-brown, indicating some time had passed. But how much? The shape was more round, as compared to the exit splatters. She squeezed the bridge of her nose, and then looked at it again. The photo held answers. Every photo told a story and this drop was a passive stain that dripped versus spattered.

She stacked the photos and placed them into the envelope and then into the box. Jackie had said the photos that they had first looked at were on the top, and the new ones were behind, but there was no way to know the sequence.

Her phone rang, and she jumped.

"Mom! Where are you?" Jennifer said.

"Oh, my God. I'm sorry sweetie," Kathryn said, looking at her watch. "Is Chris with you?"

"Yep. Flirting with Jessica."

"Stay there. I'm on my way."

Kathryn removed one of the photos from the envelope and put it into her purse. She returned the others to the box, closed the lid and locked it. She opened the side drawer and placed the box inside.

Maybe with the excitement of the baby, and the excessive travel, John wouldn't notice the discrepancy of the photo placements, or that one was missing.

She walked toward the door then turned and assessed his office. What was John up to? Why had he been in the garage, let alone the car, shortly after Erikson had been shot? Had he taken those photos? Or had someone sent them to him? Most importantly, why hadn't John confided in her?

Kathryn's mind whirled with questions. How far would he go to get what he wanted? Had he been pushed too far? Was he willing to give it all up to do what needed to be done, like she was? She wasn't sure, but one thing she had learned in life—nothing was ever as it appeared on the surface. She turned the light off and closed the office door behind her.

# Chapter 38

"HUSH LITTLE BABY don't you cry..." Darby was sitting in a chair beside Jackie's bed rocking the baby and quietly singing. She looked up when Kathryn walked into the room, and could see the toll the day had taken on her. It had taken a toll on all of them. Jackie had spewed a human out of her body, and she actually looked the best. It was approaching ten p.m., and Darby had yet to get a hold of Ray, beyond playing phone tag.

John had made it to the hospital before Kathryn returned. The love in his eyes was a love that many would never experience. When Kathryn arrived with the twins and Chris, they each took a turn holding baby Jo. Her full name was Josephine J. McCallister—the initial J for her middle name was so cool. They named her after Jackie's Grandfather, Grandpa Joe, and the initial, well... that would depend if she was in trouble or not. J for John if she was in the doghouse, and the good girl J would be for Jackie.

Linda had gone home with Niman, and Darby and Kathryn had taken the girls out to dinner. They wanted to give John, Jackie, and Chris time to bond with the baby. Even Chris appeared in awe of the beautiful little bundle. After dinner, Kathryn had taken the girls home, and Darby had come back to stay with Jackie so John could get Chris home, and get some much needed sleep.

"How are you doing?" Kathryn whispered to Darby.

"Good. Mother and daughter have been sleeping for about an hour now." Darby looked at Jo again. "Isn't she beautiful?" She looked up and said, "I like them like this... while they're asleep."

Kathryn smiled. "May I?" She reached for the baby and Darby carefully handed the little package over to her. Once her hands were free, she stood and stretched sideways.

"Hey Kat," Jackie said with a yawn. "When did you get here?"

"Just now. Sorry to wake you."

"You didn't." Jackie yawned again and pushed herself up, in the bed, and adjusted the pillows behind her back. "I don't think sleep will be in my future for a while anyway."

"You had quite the day," Kathryn said, handing the baby to her mom. "We all did."

"You could say that," Jackie said, helping the little one to find a home on her breast. "Thank you for taking care of those photos." Then she added, "What really happened with your job?"

Kathryn walked to the door and closed it, and then told them everything, ending when she said that conducting the research was worth her job. Yet she had called Jason, on the drive to pick up the kids, and apologized for leaving so abruptly. She explained about the baby. Then she told him she wasn't quitting, but she was going to work on the research on her own time. If he didn't like that, he would have to fire her. He said that was exactly what he had to do. The paperwork would be started the following morning.

"Don't you kind of need a job?" Darby asked.

"The truth is... I didn't think he'd fire me."

"But you have kids and a mortgage," Darby said.

She sighed. "I hadn't thought that part through, and the reason why I called him. If I quit, I get nothing. If they fire me, I get an eight-week severance package."

"What about the other forty-four weeks of the year?" Darby asked.

"I'm going to fight it. That'll provide me an extension with pay until the process is complete."

"What grounds is he firing you on?" Jackie asked, switching the baby to the other side.

"That'll be interesting to see," Kathryn said. "He doesn't really have any reason. But the point of standing my ground with him was to do the research. If I don't have access to the system, we can't do a nationwide LOSA. So, what's the point? Hang myself on principle, I suspect."

"LOSA?" Jackie said.

"The line observations."

"Is that the only way to gather data?" Darby asked. "I mean… pilots often behave differently if someone's watching them anyway. It might not even be the best way to get it."

"True," Kathryn nodded. "There are numerous problems with LOSAs but I'm not sure there is any other way."

"Why not just ask them what you want to know," Jackie said.

"That's not a bad idea," Darby returned to the chair. "You could gather survey data."

"But I wanted to observe them to see if they were manually flying, to determine if there was a connection with their level of understanding and confidence to fly."

"Okay. But you don't really know *why* they didn't fly, unless you ask them. Also, what if the weather was down and they had to do an autoland, or had a weak crewmember, or were just tired?

There are a lot of variables, and then you do a twelve hour flight to gather data in the last two minutes and you don't get anything."

Kathryn sighed. "A survey would be better. If they'd tell me the truth on their manual flight habits."

"I could help you now that I'm off work," Darby said.

"How could they pull you for mental health?" Jackie asked. "That's crazy."

"It's kind of scary, too. These guys are powerful... I guess they can do anything." Darby hugged herself, allowing the reality of what had transpired to finally sink in. "I pissed them off by giving them that report. I suspect they're getting even." Darby grabbed her purse and pulled out the letter, and handed it to Kathryn, who read it aloud.

When finished, she said, "The date here is from last week."

"I know. Two days after I talked to R.D. about the illegal duty times."

"So, they thought you were mental last week, but just pulled you today?" Kathryn said.

"Yep." Darby nodded. "Seriously, this is stupid and they're just spanking me. Phil told me last spring he was concerned they'd do this."

"I could never imagine," Jackie said.

"Me either," Darby said. "Besides, when Phil warned me, I actually didn't know what a section eight was."

"Now that you know, would you do it the same way again?" Kathryn asked.

"Hell, yeah."

"Then you did the right thing." Jackie up-righted the baby and rocked her. "But how long will they keep you off?"

Darby shrugged, "I'm guessing a couple weeks. But at least when I go back, they'll have to give me the extra training sessions I wanted, and then some." She moved to the edge of the bed. "Time is a gift. I'll use it wisely."

"This is going to be part of your permanent record," Kathryn said.

That was something that Darby hadn't thought about.

"They'll have to remove it when she's cleared," Jackie said. "Won't they?"

"No, they don't." Darby had learned that the hard way years before. She placed a hand on the baby's back, and thought of Claire, Don's wife. She was due within a month. "What was in the other photos?"

"John had more pictures of the CEO, same woman, and…" She hesitated and then said, "And Don… after he'd been shot."

Darby's eyes widened. "Why would John have those photos?"

"My thoughts exactly," Kathryn said.

"He also had weird blood photos," Jackie said. Tears filled her eyes. "I keep thinking… what if… what if he was involved somehow?"

Kathryn pulled a chair to the side of the bed, and sat. "I thought the same thing while looking at those photos. But the truth is… the love that man had etched in his eyes for you and the baby, and the look he gave Chris when he held her, were not the eyes of someone able to take a life in cold blood."

"How can you be sure?" Jackie asked.

"Faith," Darby said. "I saw the way he looked at you, too. John's a good man and he loves you more than you know."

"But those photos prove that Don had been murdered," Kathryn said.

"How?" Darby asked, standing. "If you have proof, we could find who did it. I could kill the bastard." She placed her hands on her hips and said, "Now that I'm deemed crazy, I could probably get away with murder."

"Don't even joke like that," Jackie said. "You're not crazy."

Darby laughed. But the truth was, there was not much that she could do other than joke. The accusation was on the point of absurdity and she would get to the bottom of it. Until then, she would enjoy her time off.

Kathryn reached into her purse and pulled out a photo. She handed it to Darby. "See this splat, it's a drop."

"You took the photo?" Jackie said. "He'll know."

"I'm going to copy it and get the original into place. He'll be too busy with you and the baby for the next day or two."

Darby looked at the photo. "What does a drop of blood mean?"

"A bullet into Don's head would not have left a drip. That was from something, or someone else."

"Where was this?" Darby asked.

"Passenger seat, close to the door."

"Don's position?"

"Driver's seat. Facing forward, head tilted back."

"Holy shit!" Darby said. "Someone else was in the car with him. And that drop is his friggen blood, isn't it?"

"Yes. I think so," Kathryn said. "And if it were John's blood, I doubt he'd be taking a picture of it."

"Why in the hell didn't they do tests on it?" Darby asked. Kathryn shrugged. "Maybe they did. But I doubt it, or the case wouldn't be closed."

"Let's just tell John what we know, and ask him," Darby said.

"No!" Jackie snapped. The baby startled and began to cry. "Oh, sweetie, mommy is so sorry. Shhhh. Shhh. It's okay." Jackie slowly rocked her back and forth, and within seconds the baby quieted.

"I don't want John to be disappointed in me for getting into his things."

"He already knows you snoop," Darby said.

"This is serious," Jackie said, "and the reason for a locked box."

"I agree with Jackie," Kathryn said. "We'll just keep our eyes and ears open."

Tears filled Jackie's eyes.

Kathryn placed a hand on her shoulder. "Sweetheart, it's going to be fine. Please don't worry."

"I'm not crying because I'm worried," she said, handing the baby to Darby. She pressed the button to upright herself in the bed, as tears streamed down her cheeks. "I'm crying because you two are the bravest women I know." She swiped her hands over her cheeks. "You have both risked so much to do the right thing. Who does that?"

Darby exchanged a glance with Kathryn. She looked at baby Jo She held her breath to hold her emotion in. "We're doing this for you, little one." She kissed the baby's head. "Because we can."

Kathryn held Jackie's hand and squeezed. "If we don't, I'm not sure who will." She sighed, and said, "But I'm madder than hell that this research has been canceled, a murder is being covered up, an airline is risking the safety of its passengers because of shitty training, and now they pulled the final straw by attacking Darby."

"You go Kat," Darby said, grinning. When Kathryn got pissed, she could move mountains.

"My boss didn't cancel this on his own. He was initially excited about it. Someone is pulling his strings and I'm going to get to the bottom of it. I know in my gut that this has something to do with Don's murder and whatever the hell John is working on."

Jackie nodded and then extended her arms for her baby. Darby gave Jo to her mother. Jackie looked up at Kathryn and then at Darby. "I want my daughter to grow up just like you two."

"Not to worry, we'll turn her into a crazy pilot by the time she's three," Darby said, with a grin. "And we'll have her cooking lasagna by the time she's eight."

Jackie laughed. "I'm sure you will."

# CHAPTER 39

HOW THE HELL could everything get so turned upside down? Her life felt like a snow globe, and she hoped that someone would stop shaking it soon. The only good thing was baby Jo being born healthy, a gift she would not overlook. Darby rolled out of bed, pulled her robe on over her red flannel pajamas, and headed downstairs.

Kathryn had bought her one of those funny machines for her birthday many months earlier, and she was finally beginning to love it. She opened the cupboard and decided upon Gingerbread—five days until Christmas, it felt appropriate. She popped the little cup into the slot, stuck a cup into position, and pressed start.

She dumped some cream into another cup, and stuck that in the microwave. Pressing the quick start button, she waited. Within seconds the cream was boiling, and she pressed stop before it boiled over the cup. She poured the hot cream into her coffee. *Now what?*

*Jack Daniels.* She wandered into her living room and found the bottle. After pouring a capful into her coffee, she wandered back into the kitchen. She stirred the concoction, then opened the fridge and pulled out the can of whipped cream, shook it, and pressed her finger on the plastic tip and sprayed. "Happy Holidays." *It might be a little early to start celebrating,* she thought glancing at the clock, but hell—she was crazy. So they said.

Holding her mug with two hands she sipped her holiday cheer and stared out the window, looking at nothing. Heaviness, she'd never felt before, filled her heart. She walked into the living room and pressed the fireplace switch to on. One more sip of coffee, then she set the mug on the table and wandered across the room to turn her stereo on. She stuck a homemade Christmas disk into the slot and pressed play.

Mariah Carey sang *All I Want for Christmas is You.* She turned the tree's Christmas lights on, and began to sway while wishing she were in Ray's arms.

She had returned home just after midnight to an empty house. Ray ended up in Oklahoma City. They were having problems with a 757 down there and they needed his help. He was one hell of a mechanic, but she was pissed at how they used him. She was most upset because they stole him last night when she needed him most. He'd talked to her until the wee hours of the morning, and assured her everything would be okay.

But she wasn't so sure.

The song ended and the next song was *Miss you Most at Christmas Time.* The dancing stopped and she plunked her butt in front of the fire, and reached for her coffee. "I miss you most at Christmas ..." Darby sang, and memories of Keith came flooding back, as tears filled her eyes. It had been four years since he died, but she never forgot. He always trickled back into her mind and heart during Christmas.

You could never replace love, but you could find it again. She sipped her coffee and wondered what the hell she would do while she waited for the Global doctor to call. "This is ridiculous." She had to do something.

"Sitting around and whining in your breakfast alcohol is for losers with a capital L," she said to a nutcracker standing on the mantel. Then she laughed, "Maybe I am nuts." She set her coffee on the table again and ran up the stairs into her bedroom.

She found Anne Abbott's business card on her desk. Darby pulled her cell phone from the charger and headed back downstairs. This time *Santa Baby* was playing on the stereo. She sipped her coffee for a moment, sucked up some courage, and dialed the number. "I may be crazy, but I'm certainly not a chicken."

"Ms. Abbott, this is Darby."

"How are you? I was going to call you today."

"About what?"

"I wanted to tell you that I talked to Dr. Marsh."

"The Chief Pilot told me."

"Oh… well, uh… I wanted to be transparent."

Darby laughed—transparent as combat soldiers wearing fatigues in the jungle. "Why did you tell me you worked for H.R., when you're really the manager of the pass travel complaint department?"

"This is not about me. This is about you."

"Do you know what you did by attacking me for reporting safety issues? You have just reduced the level of safety. Nobody will ever come forward," Darby said a little louder than she intended. Then, with a lowered voice she said, "I feel like I've been raped, and you have put me on the stand defending myself against the rapist."

"Just go with the process. Everything will be fine."

"Fine?" Darby walked across the room. There were so many things she wanted to say to this woman, and yet she wasn't worth the effort.

"I was just concerned that you were okay."

"What does okay mean exactly?" Darby said. "Okay—that nobody is going to give me a line check? Or, okay—that I am not going to fly a plane into the mountains? Or, okay—that I'm not going to hurt myself?"

She stopped pacing and reached for her coffee, and Abbott said, "Yes."

"Yes? Yes to what?"

"Yes to all."

Was she kidding? Then she remembered something that Phil had said. "So, who told you to go to Dr. Marsh anyway?"

"That's not the issue."

"I think it is. You don't have to tell me who… but did someone in flight operations tell you to talk to him?"

"I'm not going to tell you my processes."

"I don't need to know your processes," Darby said, exasperated. "Just if someone in flight operations directed you to talk to Dr. Marsh?"

"I'm not going to say yes, and I'm not going to say no."

That pretty much answered her question.

"Have a great holiday," Darby said, and hung up.

She had never been more disappointed in a human being in all her life. Had they paid her do this, or was she so ignorant to the fact that they were playing her? She tipped back her coffee and finished it. Then she walked to the couch, sat heavily, and stared at the fire. The phone rang and she glanced at the screen. Oak City—corporate headquarters. She rolled her eyes. Could this day get any better?

All she wanted to do was climb the stairs and crawl back into bed until this nightmare ended. She sighed, and on the third ring she answered the phone.

"Darby? This is Rich. Rich Clark. Do you have a minute?"

"Apparently, I have lots of minutes these days." She leaned back on the couch, closed her eyes, and breathed deep, not sure if she should be talking to the enemy.

"That's what I wanted to talk to you about."

"Shoot."

"Joel Iverson said that you still want to give the safety presentation."

She sat upright and an eyebrow rose with a life of its own. "Of course I do."

When R.D. said that Clark still wanted her to give the presentation, she had thought he was blowing smoke up her skirt and had no clue what he was talking about. She'd been wrong.

The real question should be—did they really want a mentally unstable person to be locked in a room with his divisional leaders. Hadn't they heard of going postal? She doubted he'd thought it through. This could only prove one thing—Clark knew she was fine.

"Great. I was hoping you'd say that," he said, in his most charming voice. "I'll have Jane figure out a time that will work for everyone on this end. We'll get it scheduled. Have a Merry Christmas."

Darby went to the kitchen and pulled a chair up to the counter to reach to the top cupboard. Standing on her tiptoes, she searched her mugs until she found the one she was looking for. She pulled it off the shelf.

"Perfect," she said, reading the words. *"You don't have to be crazy to work here, it's part of the benefit package."* She climbed down off the chair, and filled her new mug with straight coffee. She had work to do.

# Chapter 40

THE GIFT OF patience was all she needed this Christmas. That, and a lot of faith that everything happened for a reason and would work out like it should. Leaning back on her bed, Darby opened her training manual to study. At least she could keep her head in the game while the company examined it. But as hard as she tried, she couldn't focus. *This is stupid,* she thought closing the book. She set it to her side on the bed.

Three days before Christmas—she had earned a break.

The discussion with Abbott was as ridiculous as her interview. Lying back on the bed she pulled a pillow over her face. Two weeks of this would drive her crazy. Hopefully they'd get it sorted out after Christmas. She grinned and tossed the pillow. Okay, maybe after New Years—she hadn't celebrated one of those properly since the merger. She should be preparing for the week to come that would include indulgent food, not sitting on her butt whining.

Swinging her feet to the floor she jumped out of bed, and headed towards her dresser to retrieve her exercise clothes. Calories were looming and she might as well eat them guilt free. Besides, a good workout may just be enough to clear her head—or fix it.

She climbed out of her pajamas and into her sweats, then pulled on a sports bra. The doorbell rang as she grabbed her favorite hoody and pulled it over her head. She glanced at the clock. It was a bit early for Kathryn who had kiddos to deal with on Christmas break, and Jackie just got home with a newborn. Pulling one arm into a sleeve, she walked to the window and glanced out. A smile spread across her face.

Darby pulled the other arm through her sleeve while she ran down the stairs, then freed her hair from the shirt, and opened the door.

"You are exactly what I need this morning," Darby said.

"I hope you don't mind me dropping by unannounced like this," Linda said. "I'm on my way to work."

"Are you kidding? Darby hugged her. "In my condition, a free at-home counseling session is exactly what I need."

Linda laughed. "That's not exactly why I'm here."

"What?" Darby gasped. "You're going to charge me?"

"I'm glad they didn't take your sense of humor."

Linda removed her coat and went into the living room while Darby ran to the kitchen to retrieve two cups of tea. After she returned, they settled onto the couch, and Linda stared at her over the cup.

"Is this how you do it?" Darby asked. "Watch us until we boil and crack?"

"I'm going to watch you so you *don't* crack," Linda said.

Darby knew that Linda's psychology degree would come in handy one day, not that it hadn't in the past. Linda had been there through so much with all of them, and she suspected it was Linda that kept Kathryn sane as a single mother of teenage girls. Darby sipped her tea, glad to have Linda sitting with her.

"What's going on here isn't right." Linda began. "I'm concerned on many levels. For multiple reasons." Linda set her cup on the table. "If Global owns the psychiatrist, you can't win."

"Eternal hope of optimism."

"I want you to be optimistic. But…"

The smack of reality hit Darby fast and furious. She had not realized this was a game that she might not win—her career was actually at stake. They were not just playing *with* her, they were taking the core of who she was by challenging her brain, and gambling with what she loved most—flying.

"If… and I'm just saying *if*, whomever they send you to is working for the airline—"

"Like a paid assassin," Darby said, attempting to lighten the situation.

"More or less," Linda said. "The point is, if you talk too much, they will say you are nervous and can't deal with silence. If you don't talk enough, they will say you are withdrawn and isolated."

"What's the perfect amount to talk?" Darby asked.

"That's my point—there isn't a perfect amount. *Whatever* you do or say, they could spin it against you."

Darby furrowed her brows. This was something she had not thought of. She needed time to digest this new nail in her coffin.

"He'll find your soft spot, work on you until he opens an emotion, and then he'll stick a knife in and turn. He'll want you to cry."

"Crying's a bad thing?"

"No, sweetie," Linda said, placing a hand over hers. "Crying is the best thing. But he'll do this to call you emotionally unstable." She reached for her coffee and sipped.

"Well then, I just won't let him get into deep places."

"He'll bring up Keith. If you don't show emotion, you'll be cold, unable to show feeling."

"If I do react to those memories... then I'm emotional." Darby saw this picture clearly. "But how could a trained medical professional do that to someone?"

"Oh, you'd be surprised what people are capable of," Linda said. "I never imagined my husband could be pushed into taking down an aircraft."

Darby stood, walked over to the fire, and wrapped her arms around herself to stave off the chill. Without turning, she said, "I'm kind of screwed, if that's their game."

"It might not be their game," Linda said encouragingly. "But these guys inviting you to give a safety presentation to the divisional leaders know you are anything but crazy. So, we have to ask, why are they running you through this assessment?"

"How the hell could a psychiatrist be involved with their games?"

"A lot of these older guys have been making a killing off the airlines for years. Not to mention, they are still part of the old school. Airlines are not the only group that still partakes in that good ol' boys club."

"Aren't they afraid of getting sued?"

"The risk of litigation for taking down a crazy pilot doesn't compare to the reward. They also have resources, with the airline backing them, to bankrupt the pilot in court. How long could a pilot last after they lost their income?"

"The airlines pay the doctors a shitload of money, and what jury would believe the crazy pilot?"

Linda nodded. "Exactly."

Darby sat heavily on the couch and placed her face in her hands digesting the ramifications of all this. Then she looked up and said. "What can I do?"

"Find an attorney and start procedures now. Being a woman, you have a hell of a lawsuit for sexual discrimination."

"Yeah, but I don't think this is because I'm a woman. I think Clark is doing this because he's an asshole, and he can."

"Have they done this to any male pilots?"

Darby sighed. "I'm not sure."

"Find out. Make this your new research project, as if your life depends upon it." Linda glanced at her watch. "I need to get to the office, but know that I am here for you, for *anything*."

Darby and Linda stood, and Darby hugged her, long and hard. "Thanks. I won't let them get to me."

"I'm counting on that. Also, don't allow this process to make you crazy." Linda picked up the cups. "Isolating someone from their community does horrible things to the mind. It's a form of punishment in the military."

Darby took the cups from her and set them back on the coffee table. "Leave them. I've got time on my hands," she said with a wink.

They walked to the front door and Darby opened it.

Linda hesitated, and then said, "Find that attorney. Arm yourself to do battle. Don't be afraid to use the sex card, because the reality is… I would suspect they do this to women more often than they do to men."

"Why would you think that?" Darby asked, not that she would put anything past them.

"Women are fixers. From what I've witnessed between you and Kat, you both solve problems. That makes you trouble makers in the eyes of a system."

"That's so illogical." Darby folded her arms to stave off the chill.

"It is." Linda stepped onto the porch and said, "But what I witnessed in the medical profession, which I doubt is much different than your industry, is that the men don't like intelligent, high achieving women. It makes them feel... inadequate."

"And that's our fault?" Darby asked. "Did they play with you going through medical school?"

"Oh yeah. They intimidated the hell out of *all* the women. Some of the brightest minds in my class ended up dropping out because of it. These guys killed their self-confidence."

"How did you survive?" Darby asked.

"I've got some years under me," she said. "There's also something about having a husband who murders a planeload of people and leaves you with a teenage daughter that gives you strength. Besides, there's one little secret about confidence."

"And that is?" Darby asked.

"It's only yours to give away. Nobody can take it."

# CHAPTER 41

THEY SAID THEIR goodbyes, and Darby closed the door. She knew exactly what she needed to do, and ran upstairs to get her laptop. Her workout postponed. It was time to find an attorney. First things first, she emailed Neil—a name from her past. They had dated years before under false pretenses. He pretended to be single, and she pretended she'd fallen in love with him. Truth was, she had. However, they had rolled into good friends, allowing that time of their life to dissipate.

He was now divorced and dating a flight attendant, and she hadn't heard from him in months. "My turn to invade your space." She typed a text message to him—

*Neil. The boys are at it again. I gave Clark and Wyatt a safety report… they were apparently not happy. Check my schedule. Look at my status. I need that attorney's name that helped one of our pilots back at Coastal. That guy who walked into the preliminary hearing, and the company backed down the moment they saw him. Happy Holidays! Darby.*

Sitting on the floor, computer on the coffee table, Darby's fingers danced on the keypad as she searched the Internet for an attorney. She wrote down three names and phone numbers. Then she started with the first, but gave up on the third. *This is ridiculous.*

Each paralegal said more or less the same thing—because the airline had a binding contract with the union, that contract preempted state and federal court. What that meant was, if their contract allowed the company to pull this crap, they could, despite federal and state laws that said otherwise. The Railway Labor Act took away pilots' rights and gave complete control to the airline. Somehow that didn't make sense.

Darby stood and stretched. Mental health was a hot topic since the pilot for German Wings flew into the Alps, but not something to use as retaliation. The public would assume pulling her was a good thing if the company convinced the world she was a threat. Only those who knew Darby would know the truth and support her.

Yet fear of what had happened would fuel the general public's opinion. Then again, she did have her book on the national best sellers list for many months. Those people would know her and how she thought. They would know what she was doing was for the right reason. She would have public support, at least from those who had read her book.

Yet how the hell could Global possibly use a disability as a form of retaliation?

The ding of her text startled her and she grabbed her phone. Neil—*I can believe it. Attorney's name—Jackson White. Hang in there. I'm proud of you. Happy Holidays.*

Darby swiped the tear away, not knowing where it came from. She Googled White and found his number. Within minutes the phone was ringing.

"Is Jackson White in?"

"May I ask who's calling?"

"Darby Bradshaw. I'm a pilot for Global."

"Is he expecting your call?"

"No. But my airline pulled me on a trumped-up mental health issue after reporting safety, and I—"

"Wait. Are you the pilot who wrote that book?"

"*Inside the Iron Bubble*... yes."

"Oh, my God! That was so good," the woman said. "I'm working as a receptionist while attending graduate school. My dad's a pilot and he had me read it."

"Thank you," Darby said, with a smile. "That book may be part of why they're doing this."

"Assholes." When Darby laughed, she said, "Sorry. I hear stories like this all the time and it pisses me off. Let me see if Mr. White will take your call."

Darby already liked this office. They definitely got ample points for their receptionist. Maybe there was a light at the end of the tunnel and it wasn't a train. She sat on the floor in front of her computer and placed her phone on speaker so she could type while he talked.

"White. How can I help you?" he asked when he came on the line.

"My name is Darby Bradshaw and I gave my company a safety report. They subsequently pulled me for mental health accusations."

"Have you been fired?"

"No. But I was pulled from the flight line pending a mental assessment."

"Here's how this thing's going to go down. They will pay some quack to fail you on the mental assessment. Say you're mentally unfit. If for some reason you pass, then they'll keep you out long enough to mess with your performance. They'll screw with you in the simulator," his voice boomed. "I've seen this all too many times. I've got two of these cases going right now."

"Are they men or women?"

"I'm not at liberty to say."

"But there has to be something I can do now."

"I'm sorry," he said. "But when they fire you. Call me back, then I can help."

Darby leaned back on the couch, stunned by what she'd just heard. This was criminal on so many levels. She stood and headed straight for the kitchen. She pulled her sports bottle from the dishwasher, filled it with water, and added a packet of acai berry energy drink. They were going to fire her. *How the hell could this be legal?*

Waiting to do something until after they fired her felt like going into battle unarmed. Who would knowingly get shot so they could fight for their life while they were bleeding to death? None of this made sense.

Somehow shaking her sports bottle made her feel better. Perhaps it was the image of ringing Clark's neck. Her phone rang in the other room and she ran to get it.

"Hey, sweetie," Ray said. "I have some bad news."

"It's one of those days." Darby rolled her eyes. "Shoot."

"I've got to stay down here for another day. I'll wrap up Friday and be home on Christmas Eve."

"I'm sorry," Darby said, not having the heart to tell him what she'd learned—there was nothing she could do, and the doctor could be a hired gun. He was going through enough with Global, and working him out of town until the holiday was more than enough on his plate. "I hope it's not all bad." She picked up her tennis shoes and moved to the couch.

"Actually, it's not. But we can talk about that later. How are you doing?"

"Excellent. Going to the gym to pump up so I can be ready to kick a little ass."

Ray chuckled. "That's my girl. As long as it's not *my* ass."

"Only if you deserve it," she said, pulling on a shoe. "What time are you going to be home?"

"Not until 4:30. Can I meet you at Kat's?"

"Sure." Kathryn was hosting Christmas Eve dinner, but they weren't eating until 5:30. She pulled on her other shoe. "Do me a favor. If you see Clark, tell him he's not going to get away with this."

"The next time I see Clark, he's going to need someone to surgically remove my boot from his ass."

# CHAPTER 42

DECEMBER 24, 2016

INDULGENCE WAS THE new word of the day. Darby leaned back on the couch with Ray, feeling like a fat cat. Kathryn's prime rib had been outstanding and the mashed potatoes and gravy were like none other. Jessica, Jennifer, Chris, and Linda's daughter, Francine, were nestled on the game room couch watching Chevy Chase's Christmas Vacation and eating roulage—a Kathryn specialty.

Dinner conversation was light and nothing of Darby's ailment came up. They had not told the kids yet. Kathryn hadn't even told them about losing her job. Those details would be saved until after the first of the year. Then her attention shifted to John. *What in the hell was he up to with those photos?*

Half of her wanted to ask, but the other half didn't have enough wine with dinner to be classified as a good enough excuse. That discussion could be saved for a later date. Besides, he looked so cute holding the baby.

"How's fatherhood treating you?" Darby asked.

"Easy for me. Jackie does all the work."

"Don't let him fool you," Jackie said. "He's up every night changing her diapers and bringing her to bed so I can nurse."

"Is she sleeping in your room?" Kathryn asked.

Jackie nodded. "At least until she's six months old. They say a year, but... I think she'll do just fine in her nursery."

"Maybe three months," John said, and Jackie grinned, giving him a sideways glance.

"Did you find an attorney?" Niman asked Darby, and Linda nudged him.

"It's okay," Darby said. There was nothing she would keep from any of them. She filled everyone in on what she had learned. Kathryn already knew, but Ray was the most surprised at the helplessness of it all.

"Why didn't you tell me?" He asked sitting up and turning towards her. "This is crazy."

"I didn't want to add to your angst at work. It sounded like you had your hands full down there."

"Do you work in other bases often?" Linda asked, and Darby mouthed *thank you*.

"Sometimes." Ray stood and walked to the bar. He poured himself another rum and Coke. "Can I get anyone anything?"

Kathryn exchanged a look with Darby, and Darby shrugged. She had no idea what was up, but Ray had been unusually quiet during dinner.

Ray walked over and stood by the fire. "It wasn't all work. I actually had an interview."

"For a promotion?" Jackie asked.

"Why didn't *you* say anything?" Darby asked. That was not at all like him. "Back into management?"

He shook his head and took a long sip of his drink. "I had a pilot interview."

"How the hell did *you* get a pilot interview?"

"Darby!" Kathryn snapped.

"No. She's right. I'm not military. I only have general aviation hours… and I have over 8500 flight hours."

"That's a lot of time," Niman said. "I didn't realize you flew that much."

"Every weekend for the previous twenty-some years, and then some."

"He doesn't fit their profile," Darby said. "They hire pilots with low-time, preferably military, or kids with flight hours from college." She didn't mention the fact that he had a record with Global for looking the other way when a couple employees stole millions from the airline.

"You're the one who told me I should become a pilot," Ray said to Darby.

"Yeah, but I was thinking with Alaska or United or something. I never imagined Global would ever consider you. Especially knowing me."

"They did more than that. They offered me a job."

"Oh, my God!" Kathryn said jumping to her feet, and she gave him a hug. "This is huge."

Jackie stood and hugged him, too, and everyone said congratulations. But Darby just stared with her mouth hanging open. "Congratulations!" she said at last, with the largest smile she could muster. She lifted her glass to him and then took a very long drink.

This was huge. But Darby couldn't help feeling out of sorts. She wasn't sure if it was because he'd kept this from her, or because she was flat out jealous. More than that, *why the hell did they hire him?* Clark and the boys all knew they were an item. If anything, that would have screwed him, *not* gotten him a job. Something was up, and she doubted it was Santa in the chimney.

DARBY AND RAY had taken an Uber home, and the ride had been quiet. Darby bobbed with the ocean, remembering that even the biggest waves never tipped her boat. But this was something that she had never expected—her without a flying job and Ray having one. Her boat had been dumped upside down on the beach.

Once inside, he went to the bathroom and Darby changed her clothes. After she was in her holiday pajamas, she headed downstairs and turned on the fire and the Christmas tree lights. She pulled a blanket around her shoulders, and sat in an otherwise dark room in the silence of the flickering lights, trying not to overthink this.

Ray walked down the stairs and hesitated. She didn't turn to look at him. She smiled when she heard the pop of a cork. When he entered the living room he was carrying a bottle of champagne and two glasses.

"I'm sorry I didn't tell you," he said pouring the first glass. "I just knew that with all that's going on it would make you feel bad. Hell, I felt bad." He filled the second glass. "But I couldn't give up this opportunity."

"I get that," she said. "But... I still don't understand. You and I both know how these guys roll. Knowing me should have kept you *from* getting that job."

"They gave it to me, with the unspoken words that I'm on their team."

"You sold me out for a flying job?" She jumped to her feet.

Ray laughed. "No. I just kind of rented you out."

"What the hell?" Her hands were on her hips, and she counted to ten. "How cute am I now?"

He grinned. "Gorgeous. Which makes me really afraid."

"Fuck you. This isn't funny."

"I know it's not," he said, patting the couch beside him. "Let me explain."

Darby stood with arms folded. "I'm listening."

"I applied over six months ago, after you put the bug in my ear. I love flying. Why not get paid to do it?" He sighed. "I'd heard nothing. Then while I was down there getting briefed on the status of the project this week, Clark dropped into the hangar. He excused everyone and said he wanted to talk to me. Said that he'd seen I applied."

Darby sat beside him. "Don't you see what he's doing?"

"I do. But how the hell could I turn this down?"

"I guess you couldn't. But what do you have to give him in return? Naked photos of me?"

"Nope. Keeping those for myself," he said, placing a hand on her leg. "Clark said that he took care of me for a reason, because I showed my alliance. He wants to continue that relationship."

"What the hell does *that* mean?"

"They didn't fire me before because they thought I was keeping quiet. I always suspected Clark was part of that deal with the parts, but I could never prove it. Yet I *think* he thought I knew, and I was protecting him."

"He's such an arrogant asshole."

"To say the least."

"So, what are you going to do?" Darby said.

"I'm going to continue my relationship and show my alliance." He handed Darby a glass and he lifted his. "To the woman I love."

Tears filled Darby's eyes as they toasted their glasses and sipped their champagne.

"But what happens when he wants something?"

"I'll be noncommittal until I get off probation."

"That's going to be a year *after* you start training." She looked into her glass and then up to Ray. "Nobody can keep it up that long. Not even you." She smiled. "But it might be fun trying."

He grinned. "Well, if he forces the issue. I'll play the recording for him."

"You taped him?"

"Damn right." He nodded. "I'll continue to do so each time the asshole opens his mouth." He sipped his champagne, and sighed. "He'll probably fire me for violating company policy, but I'll cross that bridge when I come to it."

"As if they don't violate enough policies." Then she said, "It might be fun to play with him."

"Sweetie, as fun as that would be, whatever game they're playing, I would avoid it."

"Yeah, but you just stepped in the middle of their chess board."

# CHAPTER 43

THIS SCREAMING COULD drive anyone crazy. Darby paced the tile floor, humming to Josephine. She kept a bounce in her step, but maintaining sanity was getting harder with each moment. How the hell did she get here? Truth be told, she had no idea what she was really getting into. Visions of a mental ward slipped through her mind. Just when she thought she was about to go over the edge, a door opened in the distance.

"Thank you so much!" Jackie said, rushing into the room. "I couldn't imagine going to the doctor smelling like that. Or leaving her alone to cry."

"Is this normal?" Darby asked, handing Jackie the baby. "She's pissed about something."

"I thought it was it colic," Jackie said, bouncing her. "Shhh, shh, shh. But now I'm not so sure." She took the baby to the living room and sat on the couch. "Hopefully the doctor will know."

The baby had been sleeping peacefully when Jackie made breakfast for John and Chris. Then John took Chris to school. Instead of taking care of herself, while the baby slept, Jackie took care of her family. Once they were out the door, Josephine decided she was going to make her presence known.

"Want me to go with you?" Darby asked.

"No. We'll be good. But thank you," Jackie said, changing the baby's diaper.

"Fourteen days old. It's hard to believe." Darby sat next to Jackie. "Too bad John couldn't go with you."

"I can't get too dependent upon him," she said, sticking the tapes on the diaper. Then she wrapped Jo like a pea in a pod, and stuck her to a boob. That quieted her.

"How much time off does he have?" Darby asked.

"I think three weeks."

"He has three weeks off, but he's at work?"

"My thoughts exactly." Jackie's eyes shifted to the baby. "But something came up and he had to go to the office."

"Did he say anything about the photos?"

"Nope. Nothing." Jackie gently rubbed the baby's back. "Thank God for that. But something feels off between him and Kat. It's kind of uncomfortable."

"Did you ask her about it?"

"She says it's nothing, other than she's worried about the photos." Jackie placed the baby upright and patted her back. "But it's John who's weird. Every time I bring her up, he changes the subject."

"I'm sure he has a lot on his mind." Darby glanced at her watch.

"You need to go?"

"Not really." *Not these days.* "I've been waiting for a call from Phil, my union rep. He's been on a trip. Should've landed an hour or so ago."

"What's the next step with all this?"

"I'm not really sure," Darby said. "I have a chain of emails from an ALPO attorney. I ask a question. She responds to that question only. That opens another question. She responds. And then—"

"I get the picture," Jackie said. "Why don't they just send you a step by step process in one document?"

"Because that would make sense." Darby sighed. "I think I have to wait for Global's doctor to meet with me. Then he'll decide what to do." She stuffed her hands into her hoody pockets. "I just thought I would have something scheduled by now."

"I hope you sue them," Jackie said. "Do you mind holding her while I get my jacket and purse?"

"Of course not." Darby stood. She took the baby who was peaceful now. Exactly how she liked them. The moment Jackie left the room Darby's phone rang. She stuffed her headset into her ear, and answered.

"Sorry it took me so long to get back to you," Phil said.

Darby rolled her eyes. He could have emailed her. The only reason he didn't was he didn't want a paper trail. "How long's this process going to take? I feel like I'm pulling teeth with the union attorneys." She spoke quietly.

"I'm not sure," he said. "But you brought this on yourself."

"Excuse me?"

"I told you they would do this."

"So that makes it right?" Darby snapped. "Because you told me?"

"You could have let the union take your ideas and slowly feed them to Clark and Minor, enabling them to make them their own."

The baby stirred and she didn't want her to wake up. Darby held her close and swayed right and left, and right and left. If she started screaming again, Darby wasn't so sure if she wouldn't join her. "This has been going on for years. We don't have time. We're going to have a crash," she spoke in a sing-song voice, to not scare the baby.

"You don't know that. Besides, I told you not to have that meeting."

"That's what you're concerned about?" Darby said, just as Jackie came into the room. Darby rolled her eyes and handed her the baby.

"Take your time. Help yourself to anything," Jackie said, buckling the baby into her seat, while Phil raged in her ear about how Darby never took his advice. Darby nodded to Jackie and handed the diaper bag to her. She opened the door and closed it behind her.

Once she was gone, Darby opened the fridge to see if there were any adult beverages. "Bingo," she said when she found a Diet Pepsi, interrupting Phil's tirade.

"Excuse me?" Phil said.

"I have one question. Why did you say you *knew* they were going to do this? Who told you that was the plan?"

"Huh… Oh… well, it wasn't that I knew, per se. I just heard some things. It's just a logical next step, or I could say it was more of an available tactic. You've been an irritant to them. Let's just say this was an option open to them that they theoretically could do. But… uh, I didn't really know for sure."

"An option? Are you effing kidding me?"

"Dammit, Darby. You can't expect to tell these guys they are idiots and think they'll allow that to slide."

"I didn't call anyone an idiot!" Darby spat. *At least not to their faces.* But she was getting really close to changing that with this phone call.

"You showed them how screwed up they were."

"We have airline directors who have to be coddled or their feelings get hurt?" Was he frigging crazy? What was this, the second grade?

"You need to learn how business works."

"I have *so much* to learn," Darby said sarcastically, pulling the tab on her soda can. She took a drink to calm her emotions and prevent her lips from moving.

"Change takes time."

"We don't have time," Darby said, setting the can on the counter. "Oh, let's just kill a few people in the process. Speaking of which, what are you doing about Don's murder?"

"That was a suicide."

"Bullshit. Who told you that?" She said. "Someone who knows how business works and wants to coddle your feelings?"

Phil hung up on her. Darby's mouth opened wide. Now that was a first. Okay, perhaps she should not have been a smart ass to him, but the truth was, he wasn't there to help her or anyone else. He wasn't on the side of the pilot, or of safety for the passengers. He was just part of the political world doing what he did for money and power for himself.

He was there to silence her.

She lifted her Pepsi and leaned against the counter and drank. Then her phone rang—Phil.

"Hello?" Darby said.

"I'm sorry about that. I'm just frustrated. I'm doing my best to help you. But you just don't listen to anything I have to say."

Darby sipped her drink, wondering what to say next.

"Darby?" he said. "Are you there?"

"Yep."

"I wasn't sure if you hung up."

"Nope. I don't do that." She paused to drive her point home. "But I do listen. I just don't take your advice when I disagree."

"I was right about them giving you a section eight."

"You were. But what *you* don't understand," Darby said, "is that even if I *knew* without a shadow of a doubt they would do this, I would not have done anything differently."

The moment of silence gave her reason to believe that he hadn't understood that point before.

"You shouldn't have talked to Clark on the phone. You should not give that presentation."

"They already pulled me. What harm could possibly come from me giving a presentation now?"

"You don't know what these guys are capable of."

"Apparently you do," Darby said. "So enlighten me."

"There are things, that, uh… I can't say."

"Of course you can't. But you have no problem talking to Joel about *anything*."

"What does that mean? Joel's a good guy."

"A good guy and a chief pilot who talks to his buddies in management." She sighed. This conversation was getting nowhere. "So how long is this process going to take?"

"Not sure."

"So, I just wait for Dr. Marsh to call me?"

"That's all you can do."

"Would you answer a question?" Darby asked.

"Depends what it is," Phil said, with a laugh.

"If you told your wife not to walk after dark and she did, but then she got raped, what would her reaction be when you told her that it was *her* fault because she didn't listen to you?"

"That's entirely different."

"How so?" Darby raised an eyebrow.

"Because, this wasn't a rape."

"Bullshit! They screwed me without my permission," Darby

snapped. "They violated my rights and took part of my soul. What do you call it—business?"

"Just hang in there," Phil said. "On a lighter note, do you know what abused women have in common?"

"What?" Darby said, flatly. She'd heard this joke before, but there was no way in hell he would actually speak the words. Not with this going on.

"They just don't listen."

*He really did not just say that.* Darby rolled her eyes and said goodbye, ending the call.

That was the reality of what was happening here. The world had become politically correct, and everyone smiled and said the right thing. Yet the disrespect for women ran deep. If a man didn't listen, he was being proactive and assertive, but a woman deserved to be put in her place and thrown away. She must be crazy to not listen.

Darby pulled her coat on and grabbed her purse. Violence against women ran deep, and the reason she was part of Zonta International. Her mother had been abused, which was the reason she had kicked her father out, and thus Darby joined the group to help prevent that violence worldwide. She headed outside. The wind was gusting something crazy.

Zonta was a leading global organization of professionals that empowered women worldwide through service and advocacy. Recognizing women's rights, they strive to help them to achieve their full potential in a world where no woman would live in fear of violence. Most people envisioned violence as physical. But psychological violence was equally as bad and often led to suicide.

Nearly half of all women in the United States would experience psychological aggression by someone in a close relationship. Add the workplace to that equation and those statistics were more than frightening. Seated in her car she gripped the steering wheel with both hands, and placed her forehead against the coolness of the leather.

Darby never imagined in her wildest dreams that her company would do this to her, when all she did was submit a safety report on their operating practices identifying failures in safety culture. They were in the process of psychologically tearing her down. Perhaps it was damn time to show them exactly what she was made of.

# CHAPTER **44**

JOHN COULD HAVE denied the request to come into the office this morning, but he needed a little peace and quiet. His daughter had some lungs on her, and a hell of a lot to say. He still felt guilty forcing Jackie to handle it all. However, if he didn't take care of business life as they knew it would change. The controller suggested it would be a good idea to show up, and John had learned, years ago, to listen to his advice.

Climbing out of the car, he glanced around the dark parking garage. The lack of light was one of the reasons he appreciated this location. The only movement was a red Subaru heading down the ramp as it left the garage. He grabbed his briefcase, closed the car door and headed for the stairs. Once at the bottom of the stairwell, he stepped onto the sidewalk and waited for the light to change. Walking across James Street, he glanced back assessing the garage where he had just parked, and then walked inside the building. He blended in with the Monday morning crowd.

Today they were meeting in the Seattle office, hidden within the walls of the King County assessment building. He pressed the button for the eighth floor. The NTSB building was minutes from his home, near Angle Lake and across the street from the Hampton Inn. But when discussions necessitated confidentiality, they moved to the city. It was far easier to slip in and out of Seattle without being seen. There were also no signs indicating this office existed.

John opened the door and expected to see the Seattle controller only. Instead the controller had a visitor. He knew instantly who it was by the scent of her perfume. But how the hell she had arrived in Seattle without his knowledge was completely unacceptable. That would be dealt with later.

"John, glad you could make it." The controller smiled. "You know Diane."

Diane Nobles stood facing him, with a smile plastered across her face. "Good to see you, again, John." She extended a hand, and John took it.

She held his hand with too much familiarity, a bit too long. John pulled back abruptly, and didn't miss the controller's glance between the two of them. "Good to see you, too."

"Diane has great news," the controller said, returning to his seat. "She has decided to make her home in Seattle for a while."

"We need to focus on the Seattle area," she said. "It appears Global is having a few problems." She extended a hand to an empty chair. "Please join us."

"Why not Oklahoma City where they're headquartered?"

She smiled, but her eyes narrowed before she spoke. "We'll call it multi-tasking with the Seattle FAA office."

"How long are you staying?" John asked, pulling the chair a couple feet away from Nobles, and positioning it at an angle facing them both.

"That depends," she said. "President Drake should be announcing the selection in a month or two."

What game was she playing? John did his best to show no reaction. However, one thing he knew, if that woman was in Seattle with his family there, he would not be leaving town any time soon.

"Perhaps you could find a fixer upper in White Center," John said.

"Sounds lovely. Thanks for the advice. I'll look into that."

"It would fit you perfectly." John folded his arms.

The controller glared a warning to John. White Center was once considered Rat City, and the controller knew exactly how John felt about Nobles. He just didn't know why.

"Well, then," Nobles said, adjusting her jacket. "I'd like access to all your files on Global."

"What files?" John said.

"You haven't been investigating them?" she asked demurely. "Looking into the report on Flight 42, perhaps?"

"No."

"It was my understanding one of the FAA's top players, Mrs. Kathryn Jacobs, emailed you those files."

John glanced to the controller and then returned his attention to Nobles. "Mrs. Jacobs emailed me the *same* accident investigation that my office generated, because I was getting on a plane. Nothing secret."

"Confidentiality is important," she said. "Was that all she sent?"

"That report can be accessed as it's public record." He would not dignify her question with an answer. *What the hell is she doing?*

"Not until it's closed."

"Did I miss something here?" John asked, raising his voice. "Aren't investigations *our* responsibility, then we give *you* our recommendations?"

"John," the controller said firmly.

"It's fine, Brad," Diane said. "Let him speak."

This time, John gave the controller a look. Nobody was on a first name basis with the controller. He returned his attention to Nobles.

"If you have a problem with any office, clean your own house," John said. "You have no jurisdiction here. As a matter of fact, your presence could be interfering with our processes."

"I thought we made it perfectly clear that you were to stay away from Flight 42, due to your personal involvement." She stood and shifted her attention toward the controller, "Brad, as always it was a pleasure seeing you again."

John remained seated as she left the room, more as a slap in the face to her arrogance. They were all expected to rise for the mighty queen. Once she was gone, he stood and closed the door.

"DC is done. No more trips back East."

The controller nodded. "Consider it done."

# Chapter 45

A FINE LINE separated the difference between killing time and relaxing. Darby knew which side of that line she sat on. The morning found her sitting at the kitchen table with one foot on the chair, painting her toenails passion pink. The bottle of black had yet to be opened, but she would put that to good use also.

"Do you really have to do that here?" Ray said. "That shit stinks."

"Yep," she said, carefully touching the pinky toe. "This is where my toothpicks are."

He closed his manual and sighed. "I'll bite. Why the hell do you need toothpicks?"

"I'm going to paint tiny airplanes on my toes. I need the fine tip." She placed the brush into the jar and closed the lid tight. Then she lifted her other foot onto the chair. Legs extended, she examined her work.

Ray stood with his coffee mug and headed for the machine. "Want one?"

"Yes, please."

"Can't we get a real coffee pot?" he said grumbling. "It would be nice to be able to poor two cups instead of waiting."

Darby stared at him. How the hell he could be in a bad mood? He was studying for a dream job and she wasn't flying. Hell, she hadn't even gone to see Dr. Marsh yet, and it had been thirty-five days since they pulled her. Actually thirty-nine, if you counted the date R.D. signed the letter. Or if you went back to the date of Abbott's first concern for her mental health, they left her hanging for sixty-two days. Dates, numbers, and timing had become the focus of her life and were driving her crazy.

Ray set her coffee on the table in front of her. "Thanks," she said pulling her feet to the chair she was sitting on, legs bent, careful not to bump her toes into anything. She wrapped her arms around her legs, lifted her cup, and sipped.

"Yoga while drinking?" he said, pressing the button for his cup. "That's a new one."

"It works," she replied. "So, how's training going?"

"Frustrating."

"I can tell."

"Sorry."

Darby shrugged. "It's okay. But what's the problem?"

Ray had whizzed through systems training with his mechanical background. Darby helped by putting everything into operational perspective. The flight instruments were a piece of cake, as he had more advanced technology in some of the general aviation aircraft he flew. She couldn't imagine him having a bad time learning anything.

"This damn upset recovery training," he said opening the manual.

"I didn't have that." She dropped her feet to the floor and looked closer. "They've got it in the syllabus already?"

"They're being proactive, because that's how they roll with safety," Ray said mockingly. "What bugs me is the stall training wants us to push and then roll wings."

"And you want to roll your wings level and fly out of the stall, don't you?"

"Shit yes. If someone's in a tight descent, close to the ground and turns to capture the localizer and overbanks, they are already disoriented and behind the power curve. If you have them push, while still overbanking, they could wrap that turn tighter and induce an accelerated stall. Close to the ground it's a death sentence."

"Preaching to the choir," Darby said. "But the advisory circular states to reduce the angle of attack and then roll. You'll be fine, if you just do what comes naturally." She took another sip of coffee, eyeing him over the brim. "So, what's *really* bothering you?"

He pushed away from the table and stood. "I don't want you to give that presentation."

This had been their ongoing argument since they'd scheduled it, yet he hadn't said a word about it for three days. She'd been counting to see how long he could go before bringing it up again. He'd said he hadn't talked to Clark since he began training. She wasn't so sure.

"I've got to," she said, folding her arms. "Or all this will be worth nothing."

"What good is it worth anyway? You toss and turn all night, and the nightmares… I'm afraid this is going to drive you crazy."

"Going to?" Darby said sarcastically. "Too late for that."

"Be serious for once in your life!" he snapped. "You haven't flown for how many months now? This isn't going anywhere." He placed both hands on the table. "Besides, I don't know if I want to fucking fly for this company, knowing you are home going through this shit."

"Don't let me take your joy." Darby's eyes filled with tears. "This is happening to me. Not to you. Don't make me responsible for your career. This job, and airline, is a good thing for you, and you know it."

Her phone rang, but she didn't recognize the number. "I'll take this in the living room."

She sucked a deep breath to gain her composure, and walked to the living room, duck-footed, leaving Ray in the kitchen. She answered.

"Darby? This is Tom."

"Tom?" her mind whirled. "Kat's Tom?"

He laughed. "I like the way you think."

Tom was a pilot Kathryn had dated for a few months the year prior. But when Kathryn learned he'd gone to prison and asked Bill for permission, she shut that one down. What was Bill... her father and Kat fifteen? She had not dated since, and the last time Darby saw Tom was Christmas dinner at Kat's, a year ago.

"To what do I owe the pleasure?" Darby asked sitting on the couch.

"I noticed you're off the schedule with some company administrative code. What's up?"

Darby told him what had happened with the report, the meeting with Abbott, and her being pulled for mental health. She told him about the pending presentation in less than one week, alias potential doomsday.

"So, what are you doing now?" he asked. "I mean while you wait?"

"Watching the paint dry," she said, leaning down and touching her toenails. "Mostly working on the presentation."

"These guys don't play on the same ball field. Be careful."

"So I've heard. The worst part is that I miss flying. I'm not sure how much more of this I can take."

"I get it," he said. "When my wife kicked me out and I moved into a dump, I did more than watch paint dry. I drank a lot when I wasn't flying. I began gambling. Made lots of bad investments. It was pretty ugly."

Darby knew the outcome of what he had become, and always thought he'd just scammed people and lost everyone's money. She had even warned Kathryn about him. The truth made her feel ashamed. "I'm sorry," she said. As much for his loss, as for the opinion she had formed without understanding why.

"You're doing the right thing reporting safety," he said. "Nobody else will."

His statement caught Darby off guard. She appreciated his words, more than she could express. Fresh tears sprouted to her eyes. Everyone was telling her not to go forward because she would dig a deeper hole. She dreamt of that grave nightly.

"I hope so," she said, wiping a tear. "It's been taking a toll. I know intuitively that I'm going to be okay, but at night... well, let's just say I'm haunted."

"Been there for different reasons, but I get it."

"How are you doing now?" Darby asked.

"Climbing out of the hole I dug. But," he said, lowering his voice. "If they had pulled me from flying at the time, I probably would have taken a gun to my head, or jumped off a cliff."

Darby understood completely. That cliff was getting closer each day.

"Flying kept me sane. If I had to sit in that apartment, alone without my family, without the ability to do what I loved, and... for how many days has it been?"

"I was in training before, so working on three months now."

"Shit. I don't know how you're doing it."

"One day at a time. Plus, I've got Ray and my friends to keep me sane."

"How's Kat?"

"Good. But she quit her job because…" The words came out before she realized what she said, and stopped short.

"Why in the hell would she quit her job?"

"Let's just say differing opinions. But I'm sure it's temporary."

"Anything I can do?"

"Forget that I told you," Darby said, leaning back on the couch. She stared at the ceiling.

He laughed, and said, "Consider it done."

TOM HUNG UP the phone. He truly felt sorry for Darby. More than that, he hated himself. He stood up from the bench and pulled his jacket tight. The weather was already turning bitterly cold in Walla Walla. He walked down the sidewalk with hands in his pockets. He hesitated a moment and then reached for the door. He entered the prison. Bill Jacobs was expecting his visit.

# CHAPTER 46

THIS SHOULD BE a moment of excitement, having completed such a daunting task, but at best, all she could do was breathe deep. Kathryn had just finished the first draft of her survey questions. She would test them on Darby and Ray to assess validity, and then modify them as necessary. The next challenge would be getting the survey to the pilots. She'd lost her security clearance into the airport, and that could be problematic. Darby, however, could get through on her employee ID.

Closing her eyes, she shook her head. Why in the world they would allow a person suspected of mental health issues to use employee access to the airport was a mystery to her.

Kathryn pushed away from her desk and headed to the kitchen for a glass of water. There was only one reason they were keeping Darby out of the simulator. They wanted to destroy her proficiency and kill her edge as a pilot. Kathryn filled a glass from the faucet and drank.

As much as Darby loved to fly, she feared this was destroying more than proficiency. They were stealing a piece of her soul. Kathryn prayed that the destruction wouldn't be permanent. Time would tell, depending on how far Global Air Lines would go.

She glanced at her watch, wondering if she should review her questions one more time, or... A knock brought her out of her reverie. She set her glass on the counter and headed to the entryway. When she opened her front door, Kathryn was startled to see Jason standing before her. *What the hell?*

"Subway delivery," he said holding up a bag. "May I come in?"

"Oh… uh… yes," she said, stepping aside to allow him to enter. She closed the door behind him. "What are you doing here?" Working unsuccessfully to hide the anger in her voice.

"Bringing you lunch, and to apologize."

Kathryn glanced at the bag, and then at Jason. "Let's go to the kitchen," she said walking that way. Once there, she grabbed a couple plates out of the cupboard and set them on the table. Then asked, "What can I get you to drink?"

"Water's fine."

She pulled another glass out of the cupboard, while he sat at the table and unwrapped the sandwich. She filled his glass, and then joined him.

"I hope turkey's okay," he said, setting half on her plate.

"My favorite."

"I know."

They exchanged a look, and Kathryn picked up her sandwich. But she didn't take a bite. "Why are you really here?"

"I heard what they're going to do with you."

Her eyes widened. "Already?" She had not expected the results of challenging the termination to move through the channels so quickly. The expectation was that she would have at least another five or six months.

"They can't fire you."

Kathryn smiled, a huge weight fell from her shoulders. "Then I get to return."

"They're going to eliminate your position."

"Then I'll get another job."

"No, you won't." He stared at her for a moment, and took a bite of his sandwich.

The reality of what he said hit her in the gut. She wouldn't get another job because she would be blackballed.

"How the hell can they do this?" Kathryn said, pushing her sandwich away. "This is bullshit."

"I'm sorry," he said. "If you come back before the ruling is official—"

"What's the point if they're cancelling my job?"

"If you were on property and I moved you to another job before the ruling became public, and your position was shutdown, then you'd be safe."

"Then what? They shut that position down too?"

"Perhaps. But it would buy time. At the very least, cancelling the job would buy you two months of severance."

"Why do you care?"

"Because I care about you," he said. "I think this sucks and I hate that I have anything to do with it."

"Who is doing this?" she asked. "Why?"

He glanced down to his sandwich for a moment, and then looked up and said, "I'm not exactly sure who's pulling the strings. I'll find out, but I need time."

She took a bite of her sandwich. The effort it took to eat was well worth the time she needed to think. She could survive with the mortgage and feeding the kids until John was in position, but if he didn't get it… She wasn't sure how long she could make ends meet. This was happening far too quickly.

Darby would help financially, but Global was headed down the path to fire her, too. She would need her money to fight her own legal battle. They could run her through the court system for a very long time wiping out everything she had. Then she thought of the twins, Chris, and the baby. She knew what she had to do.

"If I come back, I want to continue the research," she said. "I've finished the survey and all we have to do now is get it to the pilots. No expense on this one."

"Not if you're part of the FAA you can't."

"Then I can't come back."

"Kat…"

"Please. Don't try to convince me otherwise. There's more to this."

"Explain it to me, then!" he spat, startling Kathryn. He relaxed and said, "I don't understand. What about your kids? Plain ass survival?"

"This is *all* about the kids," she said. "I've told them what happened, and why I don't have a job. If I go back now, then I'm selling right for wrong, for a paycheck."

"Your kids need to realize a mortgage has to be paid, and food put on the table."

"Don't tell me what my kids need," she snapped.

With all the injustice in life, everything was imploding. The chaos of the world, the insanity of what they were doing to Darby, and the apparent fight to keep pilots as minimally qualified as possible, made no sense. A young man was murdered and his child would never know him.

"What's really going on here?" Jason asked.

"I feel that if I don't do the right thing, for the right reason, my kids won't have the…" She hesitated to find the words to explain how she felt.

Finally, she breathed deep and calmed her emotions. "The kids need to understand that life is more than money and power. It's about integrity, caring for others, ethics, morality, and compassion. I need to *show* them that if we don't stand for something, we will fall for anything."

# CHAPTER 47

WHY NOBLES WANTED to see Kathryn the day after Jason showed up at her door, was beyond her. There was nothing she wanted more than having the structure of a real job, with a paycheck—except for a safer industry, that is. But something felt wrong about this meeting. Nobles had to know that Kathryn and John were friends, and they had worked together over the years. Then there was Darby. Yet, curiosity got the best of her.

Lifting the blinker lever, she turned right and pulled into the parking lot, scanning for a spot. Stopping short, she waited as a car backed out, and then parked. She climbed out of her car, and headed toward the building. She walked around the corner and down the path to the front entrance.

Kathryn placed a hand on the door, hesitated a moment, and then breathed deeply, pulling open the heavy door. Once inside, she scanned the seating area, where only men sat waiting for their tables. She glanced at her watch—she was ten minutes early.

"Are you Kathryn Jacobs?" the hostess asked, and she startled.

"I am."

"Ms. Nobles has already been seated. Please follow me."

Kathryn followed the hostess. Many people got what they wanted in life with persistence and due diligence, but at 13 Coins restaurant, *nobody* was ever seated without the entire party in attendance.

Extending a hand toward the table, the waitress said, "Enjoy your meal."

Kathryn froze. A million thoughts ran through her mind, and she worked hard to shake them off. This was the woman in John's photos, shaking Lawrence Patrick's hand. *What the hell?* John was following the woman he was in competition with?

"Kathryn," Nobles said, sliding out of the seat and extending a hand. "It's wonderful to finally meet you."

"It's nice to meet you, too," Kathryn said, shaking hands and then sliding into her seat. "Thank you for inviting me, especially under the circumstances."

"Of course," Nobles said, with a wave of her hand. "This meeting is long overdue."

Nobles did not appear to be the villain that John had implied. She seemed perfectly charming, professional, and… very well put together. There was still no word on who would become the Secretary of Transportation, but Kathryn could see that John had strong competition.

The waitress arrived, and Kathryn ordered a bowl of soup and an iced tea, and Nobles ordered a salad. Kathryn lifted her water glass and sipped. She would wait and allow Nobles to speak first. This was her meeting.

"This is a bit awkward," Nobles finally said, "but I want to apologize on behalf of the agency for what has transpired."

Apologize? That wasn't what Kathryn had expected to hear. Kathryn's eyebrow rose as she scrutinized the woman before her. The waitress set their iced teas on the table and stepped away.

Nobles continued. "Mr. Bernard explained your research, and I want to say that it's a fabulous idea. Might be exactly what we need." She sipped her water and then said, "I would love to see your work come to fruition."

Kathryn's foot began tapping and she worked to settle it. "I can't tell you how good that is to hear." She placed a napkin on her lap. "I've shifted to a survey instrument and I'm close to completion. Administering it will be the next step. But..." She hesitated.

"Now is not the right time," Nobles said flatly.

"Why not? Far too many issues over the years have occurred that have not been addressed. Pilots are short on knowledge and skill, and it's been an ongoing..." Kathryn stopped short. Nobles knew all this, and she had for twenty or more years.

The waitress arrived and set the salad and soup on the table. She offered them fresh ground pepper. When she was gone, Kathryn said, "I'm sorry. I didn't mean..."

"That's quite all right." Nobles stuffed a bite of salad into her mouth and chewed. Then she sipped her tea, silence ticking between them. "I was young. Idealistic." She hesitated a moment and said, "Can I share something in confidence?"

"Of course." Kathryn touched the napkin to the edges of her mouth.

"I tried to do something back when I received that report so many years ago. Hell, I didn't have a background in human factors, but anyone could see that automation was going to be a problem for humans." She closed her eyes for a moment, and when she opened them, they were filled with remorse.

"I was told to back off. Let the chips, or planes, fall where they might. The airlines didn't have the financial resources to increase training. They were barely surviving, and I was ordered to enable them to manage their own operations, as they saw fit."

"But there were known issues." Kathryn let her diplomacy fall to the floor. "Doing something could have stopped numerous crashes." Thousands of people would be alive today if Nobles had taken action.

"God, I know that. There's not a day that goes by that I don't think about those lives lost and know that I have blood on my hands. But the truth is, there was nothing I could have done, not at the level I was at anyway. Not to mention being a woman. I knew the system and the bullshit. The good ol' boys club."

Nobles sipped her tea, watching Kathryn over the brim, and added, "I would have been fired, just like you. The only way to create change was to be flexible, and wait for the appropriate time. I accepted my orders with the knowledge that at the end of the day, I could be influential where it would count."

"John feels the same way," Kathryn said, before realizing the words escaped.

"He's a good man." Nobles nodded. "Half the time I'm not so sure that he wouldn't be best in the position." She stared at her plate and pushed the lettuce around a bit and then looked up. "I know that in the right place and time I could make a difference, and make up for those souls that haunt me daily because I followed orders."

"Orders," Kathryn said, with a sigh. "How do you do it? Especially when you know it's wrong?"

"You believe in the system. You play ball. You realize that if you're benched, you can't do anything."

Kathryn nodded. She knew exactly what Nobles meant. Despite her ability to work on the research on her own, she wasn't sure that if she gathered the data they would even use it. John would, and from the sounds of it, so would Nobles... but at what expense? Would being out of the game be her kiss of death and some government bullshit prevent the data from being used anyway? There was a high probability.

"Jason asked me to come back yesterday."

"I know. I sent him."

"I supposed he shared our discussion?"

"That's why I'm here." She stared into Kathryn's eyes with concern. "We need you back. We won't dissolve your position. But you must stop this research."

"You said that it was a great idea."

"The concept is exactly what we need." She sighed and set her fork on the plate. "The problem is, there are some powerful people who don't want this to happen, not now. You're being faced with the same dilemma I was, so many years ago."

"Why would anyone not want to improve training?" Kathryn didn't know how far to push Nobles. "Is it money? Solving the training issue doesn't have to break the bank. It's as if someone wants planes to crash."

Nobles laughed. "God forbid the day that happens again." Her eyes bore into Kathryn's and then she said, "It's my turn to apologize."

"No apologies necessary," Kathryn said. Her husband had been at the heart of destruction—driving planes into the ground to prove a point. "As long as I'm alive, that will never happen again." She sat a little straighter. "Bill Jacobs is the reason I must finish what I started... my redemption for the lives he took."

"I get that. But at whose expense?" Nobles asked. "I have the power to bring you back, if you shelve the idea."

Kathryn's mind whirled. Was she willing to die on her sword for no reason? Then again, she could tell them she was not working on it, get her job back, finish the instrument at home, and have Darby help gather the data. They wouldn't be the wiser. Or would they?

"It hasn't been announced, but there is a good chance I will have the secretary position. There would definitely be a place on my staff for someone like you."

Kathryn's blood went cold. She had just been offered a bribe with terms. "Contingent upon following orders, giving up the research, and first returning to the department?" she asked.

Nobles nodded. "Yes." She lifted her napkin and wiped her mouth, and glanced at her watch. "I'm sorry I've got another meeting. Please finish your lunch. The bill has been taken care of. Order some dessert." She reached out and covered Kathryn's hand with hers. "You've got a long career ahead of you. This moment shall pass. Look at the big picture. You can let me know first of next week."

# CHAPTER **48**

IT WAS EINSTEIN who said that the world was a dangerous place to live. Not because of evil people, but because there was nobody willing to do anything about them. The truth was, there *were* people willing to do something. Kathryn poured Darby a glass of wine and then another glass for herself. She set them both on the table. She wasn't quite sure what to make of her meeting with Nobles. She pulled a plate out of the cupboard and filled it with carrots, celery, broccoli, and fresh sliced red peppers. She added a dish of ranch dip in the middle and placed that on the table.

Darby held her glass and stared into her wine.

"You okay?" Kathryn asked, slipping into her chair beside her.

Darby startled and shrugged. "I just keep thinking what if..." Tears filled her eyes. "My union rep called today. He yelled at me, again. God he's pissed that I'm going to give that presentation next week. But I think he's more pissed because I'm not listening to him, and his feelings are hurt."

Kathryn reached over and placed a hand on Darby's. "Sweetie, you look tired." She stared into Darby's eyes. More than that, it was as if the lights had gone out of her spirit.

"I am tired. I started waking up with nightmares when Don died. But when they pulled me, they got worse." She sipped her wine, thinking about the nights she'd been facing. "I know that everything will work out, but nobody gave that memo to my subconscious." To change the subject, she said, "Tell me what happened with Nobles. What's she like?"

"She's the woman in John's photos."

"Holy shit!" Darby said. "Why's John following her?"

"Hell if I know."

Kathryn regrouped her thoughts, and told Darby about Jason's visit first, and his asking her to return. Then Nobles basically said the same thing. Both requests with one contingency—stop the research. Then she told Darby about the offer of a position under the DOT.

"An effing bribe." Darby said, "Do you really think Nobles sent Jason? He doesn't work for her, does he?"

"That's what's bugging me. I don't think so. I tried to check the organizational chart on the website, but I don't have full access anymore so I can't see the real chain." She twisted the stem of her wine glass. "It sounded like she was calling the shots, yet she implied that someone above her was. Jason said he didn't know who it was, but would find out."

"I can't believe they'd think you'd cave." Darby reached for a carrot and grinned. "Did you ask her if she wanted an autographed copy of my book?"

"I actually thought about it," Kathryn said with a smile.

"What? Caving or giving an autographed book."

Kathryn sighed. "I thought about going back."

"How could you think about giving in?" Darby said. "If you do that, then Don's death would be for nothing. My reporting would be for nothing—"

"Hear me out," Kathryn said. "I'm *not* going back. I thought that I could play their game and continue to work on the side, but there's one reason I won't."

A pounding on the front door interrupted her line of thought, and Kathryn said, "I'll be right back. Eat something."

Kathryn walked to the living room and opened the front door. "John?"

"May I come in?"

"Of course. Darby's in the kitchen," she said, stepping aside. "Want a glass of wine? We've got food too."

John didn't show any intention of moving from the entryway. "No thanks."

"Are Jackie and the baby okay?"

"They're fine," he said, stuffing his hands into his pockets. He looked like he wanted to kill her. Maybe that's why his was securing his hands so he wouldn't.

"What's going on?"

"What the hell were you doing having lunch with Nobles?"

"Excuse me?"

"Stay away from her."

"She was trying to talk me into coming back."

John lowered his voice. "You don't know what you are playing with here. Don't see her again."

"God dammit John. If you want me to understand, then explain it to me!" Kathryn snapped. John had been keeping far too many secrets, and now he's telling her how to manage her life? Who she could see? "They're offering me my job back!"

"They?" John said, furrowing his brow.

"Yeah. Jason came by yesterday with the same request." Kathryn folded her arms. "They're going to fire me, and I don't have the six months I thought I did. They have approval to tank me right now with nothing."

"You didn't tell me that," Darby said.

Kathryn turned. Darby was standing in the doorway. "Apparently, someone high up wants me out. Both Jason and Nobles were trying to help. All I have to do is quit what I'm doing and—"

"Scrap your research," John said, placing both hands on his hips. "Not forever, but for the time being."

"That's what they said, too." Kathryn eyed him warily. "Why is it that the FAA, and now the NTSB, doesn't want the data that could drive industry change?"

"What the hell's going on?" Darby said. "You have—"

Kathryn gave Darby a look of—*Don't you dare defy Jackie's secret.* Darby got the message, and silenced.

John clearly noted the exchange. "I have *what?*" John asked.

"You have to know how important this is." Darby stepped closer. "Kat's research is needed. And she can't back down. My effing airline has pulled me for mental health and I have yet to hear anything from them. They just pulled me out, and put me in an isolation hole. All because I reported safety. But Kat... she can make a difference."

"Have you spoken to Global's doctor yet?" John asked.

Darby shook her head. "Nope. It's been thirty-six days. They must be real concerned huh? Maybe we could shift our focus and go nail the bastards who are doing this to me."

John assessed her for a moment, and then he shifted his attention back to Kathryn. "I'm sorry this has happened to you."

"Sorry doesn't pay the bills."

"Are you going back?" John asked.

"Should I?"

"Yes. Get your job back. Tell them you've dropped this, and just get life back to normal."

"How can you say that?" Darby said. "You'd never sell *your* ethics. You can't ask Kat to!"

"Dammit Darby! Don't be so naïve. Everyone has to sell something at a point in their life to survive, or to just get out of their own hell hole."

Kathryn folded her arms and assessed John. Something was up, and it was far beyond selling her ethics. "Tell me what is going on. Seriously, what's the big deal about doing research? Hell, they could bury it anyway. There's something else afoot here."

Darby looked between John and Kathryn and then glanced at her watch. "I've got to go. Thanks for the wine and nutrition."

"Please get some sleep."

"I will." She leaned in and hugged Kathryn. "Take no prisoners," she whispered.

Once Kathryn closed the door behind Darby, she turned to John. "I want to know everything."

John placed a hand on his hip. "How long was Jason here?"

"An hour or so."

"Did you leave him alone at any time?"

"I don't think so, why?"

"I'll send a team to sweep your house tomorrow."

"Do they do windows?"

John's glare told her he didn't think she was funny. She folded her arms and stared at the man she thought she knew. Why the hell would John think Jason bugged her house? She had never seen John like this before—argumentative, angry, and unwilling to talk to her. Perhaps the new baby and sleep deprivation were getting to him. Or maybe he knew he wasn't going to get the position.

# CHAPTER 49

ONE MOMENT DARBY was in a plane and the next she was free falling. "Nooo!" she yelled, startling awake. She bolted upright in the darkness, and reached over for Ray. But he was gone—her greatest fear with all that was happening.

Dropping her feet to the floor, she rubbed sleep from her eyes and glanced at the clock. It was 0500. She thought about going back to bed, but even sleep didn't bring her comfort these days.

To have her mental health challenged was an atrocity that she never believed they would use, or fathomed they could pull off. But with each day this fiasco continued, and without any word as to what was happening, she wondered. The process was driving her crazy. Perhaps that was their intention.

Standing, she lifted her robe off the chair, pulled it on, and headed downstairs. Anxiety for her meeting grew. Her union rep's warning about the Section 8 came true. Did he also know what they had planned for her in Oklahoma City? She had no doubt. Did Ray? She wasn't so sure.

None of this fit her mental model of how life worked, especially in today's world. She felt as if she were in a cage, waiting for her death sentence. If only she knew something—anything. But what she knew was, they were going to screw her over. She knew that with all her heart. The question was whether she would allow them to or not.

The kitchen light was on and Ray was sitting at the table reading a flight manual.

"Good morning," he said when she entered. "Coffee?" he asked.

She nodded and sat in a chair, staring at his manual as tears filled her eyes. He stood and made her a cup of coffee. She got teary-eyed far too often these days. But she wasn't giving up. If they wanted her to pull on the gloves and fight, she was game. She wiped her eyes with the palms of her hands.

"You okay?" Ray asked, setting her coffee in front of her. He opened the fridge, removed the cream, and added some into her cup.

"Yep," she said, sipping her brew. "Why are you up so early?"

"Kind of hard to sleep with what's going on in your head at night," he said, reaching out and touching her hair. He tucked a strand behind her ear. "I really think you should cancel your flight today. Give up on that presentation."

"We've been over this a zillion times. If I back down, all of this will be for nothing."

"There's only one reason they're bringing you down and that's to screw with you," he said, pulling the plastic container from her coffee machine. He stuck it under the faucet and filled it with water.

"Or covering their ass, because Wyatt and Clark can't deny what's in that report. They're acting like they're taking this seriously, to remove suspicion that they put this mental scam into motion."

"This presentation won't get you off the mental list," he said, replacing the container and then putting his cup into position.

"I know that!" Darby snapped. "But there might be one person in that room who has half a brain and might just hear what I have to say. If this can create change, then my efforts won't be for nothing." She was so frustrated with all this. "Have you talked to Clark?"

"Nope," he said, shaking his head, as his cup filled.

Darby stuck her pinky into her mouth and nibbled a fragmented nail. He knew something. He had to. Why was he so adamant that something would happen if he didn't know?

"I'm worried about you," he said, sitting beside her. "This is eating you up, and—"

"And you know they're up to something?"

"No. I'm afraid that you will do or say something that will get you into more trouble."

"Like this is my fault?"

"Sweetie, I didn't say that."

"Phil said it was my fault because I didn't listen to him."

"Phil's a leech on a baboon's ass. He's a political suck up who doesn't give a shit about anyone but himself."

"He's pretty effective sucking baboon ass." Darby smiled at the visual of Clark and Wyatt as baboons, as she sipped her coffee. "I just want to be prepared, but…" she sighed. "I can't believe that Dr. Swamp hasn't contacted me yet. It's been almost six weeks, and nothing."

"Swamp?" Ray raised an eyebrow.

"Dr. Marsh. Global's doctor."

Ray laughed. "At least you haven't lost your sense of humor."

"It's laugh or cry." She sipped her coffee. "I've been crying way too much."

"I know, sweetie," he said reaching over and covering her hand with his. "Since you're hell bent on going, what's your game plan?"

"I'm going with President Drake's motto—if someone screws you, you screw them back. And when they hurt you, just go after them as viciously and as violently as you can."

Ray's eyes widened. "You're kidding... Right?"

Darby sipped her coffee and eyed him over the brim. She was kind of kidding, but the thought sounded appealing once the words escaped her mouth. "Why not? They're trying to take me down, why can't I get even? Hell, I'm getting screwed without even getting kissed."

"The government pulled your gun. Right?" He said with a smirk.

Darby laughed. "Nope. Actually, they haven't. They're just a little behind the pace. But I'm not sure how to get it through security without known crewmember access."

"I wouldn't do that if I were you."

She shrugged. Darby had many friends that would carry a bag through for her and they didn't need to know what was in it, Ray included.

"These guys are idiots," Darby said. "Think about it. They pulled me for mental health because they're afraid of what I might do? Then they allow me to keep my company ID, and access the crewmember line. Then invite me to corporate headquarters along with a half dozen divisional leaders locked in a room with me."

"Now I know you shouldn't go," Ray said, with a chuckle.

Darby set her cup on the table and climbed onto his lap. "I'm so glad we had this conversation," she said wrapping her arms around his neck. "I'm feeling better already."

Ray theatrically groaned. "I've created a monster."

Darby laughed. "No monster. Not yet anyway." She laid her head on his chest. "But it's amazing how having a plan, despite how nefarious it might be, gives hope."

# CHAPTER 50

SOMETIMES JUST TAKING a deep breath helped. This wasn't one of those times. Kathryn busied herself in the kitchen, trying not to worry about Darby. She glanced at the time again. Darby's meeting was in an hour and a half, and she should be up by now, working out or playing on her computer. Silence was not like her, especially today. She had sent her three text messages that had not been answered.

"Hey Mom," Jessica said, wandering into the room. "What's wrong?"

Kathryn laughed. "Am I that transparent?"

"More than you know," she said opening the fridge. She grabbed the milk carton.

"I can't get ahold of Darby, but I'm sure it's nothing."

"What's nothing?" Jennifer asked entering the kitchen.

"Darby's missing," Jessica said, pouring a glass of milk. "Want one?"

Jennifer nodded. Kathryn said, "She's not missing. She's in Oklahoma, not answering her phone."

"I'm proud of her," Jennifer said, taking the milk from her sister and pouring another glass. "You don't think they'll permanently screw her over, do you?"

"Jen!" Kathryn said.

"Sorry." Jennifer glanced at her sister who rolled her eyes.

"We need to talk to you about something important," Jessica said, shifting attention from her sister's language.

Kathryn leaned against the counter and folded her arms, knowing exactly what that something important was… the broken record they'd been playing for months.

"It's been over three months since we earned our licenses," Jennifer began.

"The weather's great," Jessica added.

"And it's our big game on Saturday and we want to drive to it. We feel like idiots. Nobody understands why we have our licenses and can't drive." Jennifer sipped her milk.

"Besides, it's getting hard to protect your reputation," Jessica said.

"Jess!" Jennifer gave her a look.

"Well, it's true. I'm going to have to come clean and tell the world my mother is over-controlling and doesn't trust her kids."

"Why don't you just tell them your mother loves you and she doesn't trust those other drivers?" Kathryn forced the smile down. The girls were getting creative. "Besides, I thought you were going out to lunch with John and Chris, and then to the game?"

"They'll get over it." Jennifer pulled a couple bowls out of the cupboard and set them on the counter. "A bunch of girls are meeting beforehand, and it would be great to go."

Jennifer grabbed the Cheerios box and filled the bowls. "This is a big game. Think how great we would do if we had confidence that our own mother trusted our abilities!"

"Oh God," Kathryn said, with a laugh. "I was going to surprise you. Darby, Jackie, Linda and I are going out to lunch before the game. Darby's driving and I was going to let you take our car."

Both girls squealed at once. "You're the best," Jennifer said, hugging her.

"Yeah, thanks Mom," Jessica said. "Think we could…"

Kathryn's look silenced Jessica, who then stuck a bite of Cheerios into her mouth and grinned while she chewed.

Speaking of Darby, Kathryn really needed to find her. She left the girls in the kitchen and wandered to the living room, and dialed Darby's cell phone again. It went directly to voicemail. She then dialed the hotel and asked them to ring her room.

Waiting through the endless ringing was futile. She wasn't answering. Then she dialed Ray. When he answered, she asked, "Have you talked to Darby this morning?"

"Nope. She's not answering."

"Think that's weird?"

"Shit. All this is weird. But…" Ray hesitated for a moment and then said, "She was in a better mood when I put her on the plane yesterday, better than she's been since this all started."

"I don't feel good about this silence."

"I'm sure she's fine."

Kathryn said goodbye and dialed John. Darby was not doing okay, and each day she grew worse. Granted, she put on a brave facade. But the reality was that clipping her wings was killing her from the inside out. It was like watching the sun slowly burn out a little more each day.

When John answered, Kathryn said, "Do you have any recon on Darby in Oklahoma?"

"Excuse me?"

"Darby was supposed to be giving a report," she said, glancing at her watch, "in an hour and a half, and she's not answering her phone." She placed a hand on her hip, sorry to have made the recon comment. But dammit, if he knew something, he needed to tell her. "This is not like her. She's not been herself since they pulled her, and…"

"And what?"

"Darby knew the truth about Don. I'm worried." She sat heavily on the couch. "It may be nothing, but something's going on with her."

"Have you called the hotel?" John asked.

"Yes, but she doesn't answer that phone either."

"Call them again and tell them to send security into the room. Have them break down the door if they have to. Tell them if they don't, you'll get the fire department there and empty the hotel."

Kathryn hung up from John, dialed the hotel, and asked for the manager.

# CHAPTER 51

HE NEVER WANTED to lose touch with humanity, but somewhere along the journey he became lost in an ocean of greed. Lawrence Patrick, the CEO of Global Air Lines stood in his office looking at the third world outside his window. They had built the training complex and corporate headquarters in the worst part of town because property values were the most economical. Everything was always about money. But each day he looked out his window, a streak of guilt wormed through his soul. How much farther would they go with this? How much was enough? How many lives would be lost? He'd chosen this office location for a reason—a reminder of humanity.

His buzzer rang, and the secretary's voice broadcasted over the intercom. "Sir, your wife is here."

"Please send her in, Rose. Thank you."

The door opened and Lawrence walked toward the door. "Sweetheart, what do I owe this nice surprise to?" His wife rarely came to the office, in order to keep the airline out of their family life. "Is everything okay?"

"I wanted to talk here, because I don't want this to enter our home."

His eyebrow rose and his interest piqued. "What is it?" he asked, as he guided her to the couch. They had been married for thirty-five years, but she never failed to surprise him.

She sighed, opened her bag and pulled out a book—*Inside the Iron Bubble*, and laid it on the coffee table. "This was a fascinating read. Darby Bradshaw is one of your pilots. Is this crap going on at Global?"

He stared at the book a bit too long, and then glanced back to his wife.

"So this *is* Global." She sighed, and then stared at him long and hard. "Dammit, Lawrence. Do you realize that with SMS in place, you'll be personally accountable for all this?"

He knew quite well that with Safety Management Systems, the accountability and liability would shift to the CEO, no matter the size of the operation, and despite corporate insurance. It would only be a matter of time, 2018 to be exact, when the first crash occurred where families could sue the CEO as well as the corporation.

"We could lose everything," she said. She stood and placed her hands on her hips, and looked down at him. "Are they doing anything to her?"

"What do you mean?"

"Don't play dumb with me. I know exactly what has occurred at this airline prior to the merger." Spreading her arms wide, she said, "When this was set in motion, I did a little research of my own. And this book indicates that much of this B.S. is still occurring."

He sighed. "It is bullshit, and I'm tired of it." He would not tell his wife how deeply his roots grew, but he wondered if she already knew. He looked into her eyes and said, "I just don't know how to get out."

"Retire. It's as simple as that." She returned to the couch and held his hand. "Nobody, and I mean nobody, can stop you from retiring. You can walk away. From everything."

He assessed her and her eyes never left his. She knew more than she had let on. She was an amazing woman. No matter what, she had stuck with him.

"How many millions do we need?" she continued. "Besides, if you don't retire, you're going to have to restructure this airline to protect yourself."

He laughed. "Perhaps we should put you in charge."

"Well, if there is one iota of truth in this book, then I'd fire the entire flight operations management team, as well as the director of training, and then find an outside union to keep the airline honest."

He sighed and took the book from her. "That's what this place needs." No truer words had ever been spoken about Global Air Lines.

"Is it worth it Larry? I mean is this all really worth it?"

"No. It's not." He stood and walked to the window and looked down at the reminder, below. Within moments she was standing beside him.

"Oh, my God," she said, and a hand covered her mouth. "It looks like a slum out there. I had no idea."

"The property value was right. If you don't look, you don't see it." He reached over and took her hand. "It's getting more difficult every day to wear a suit that's worth more than the homes out my window."

She turned to him and took his other hand. "We can lock up the house and go to Tahiti for a month. Sit on the beach in the sun, and figure out what's important in life."

He pulled her into his arms and held her tight. "I already know what's important, my love." He knew exactly what needed to be done, and he would do it. He only hoped it wasn't too late.

# CHAPTER 52

"OH MY GOD, I hope she's okay," the front desk clerk said rushing to room 311. The hotel manager and security guard followed. Once they arrived, the manager pushed her aside and knocked on the door firmly and yelled, "Ms. Bradshaw?" He slid the key into the slot and opened the door, but only inches. The inside latch was in place. "Break it in."

The security guard slammed his weight into the door. Nothing. He body slammed a second time, and the wood crackled. The third slam broke the latch free and the door swung open, slamming against the wall. Within seconds, lights were on, and the clerk was running into the room.

"There she is!" the clerk yelled. "Darby, are you okay?" the clerk said shaking her arm.

Darby opened her eyes and shrieked, bolting upright. "What the hell!"

"Oh, my God! We thought you were dead," the clerk said.

Darby's eyes darted from the clerk, to the strange men standing in her room. "I was sleeping." She glanced at the clock. "Oh shit! I'm late!"

Darby jumped out of bed thankful she was wearing her pajamas. "I've got to get to the training center. Can you hold the 9:30 van?"

The manager and guard exchanged a look, but they all stood there staring at her. The message light was flashing on the hotel phone, the receiver hanging from the cord lying on the floor. Her phone was on the nightstand, dead. She plugged it in and said, "Please. I've got to hurry. I've got twenty-five minutes to get ready."

She ushered them out of the room, shutting the door behind them. The security latch was pulled out of the wall and hung on the door, leaving a hole in the wall. *That's going to be fun to fix.*

Shifting gears, she jumped into the shower and out as quickly as possible. She pulled a brush through her hair, then grabbed the hair dryer with one hand and began blowing. The other hand administered makeup. Within ten minutes her face and hair were as good as they would get, and she hung her head upside down for the final blow.

Ten minutes to go. Darby could dress in five. She opened the closet, grabbed her pants and pulled them on. Dress shirt and blazer were next, then socks and shoes.

She closed her computer, grabbed her power cords, and stuffed everything inside her computer bag. The presentation copies were stacked on the desk. She slipped them into the bag.

One more, quick look in the bathroom mirror. She grabbed her cell phone, stuffed it into her purse, picked up her bag, and headed downstairs. Lipstick could wait.

She smiled brightly at her saviors standing at the front desk. "Thank you! Could you let maintenance know the latch needs fixing?"

The van was waiting when she flew outside. She climbed in and moved to the back row for an element of privacy. She ignored the voicemail messages, and called Kathryn.

"Darby! Are you okay?" Kathryn asked. "What happened?"

"I was sleeping," Darby said. "But thank you for putting the troops into motion or I would have slept through my presentation."

"What the hell happened?"

"I was reviewing my presentation last night. I wanted to get a good night's sleep. But I was still on Seattle time, so I took a couple of Tylenol PM's. That didn't work, so I took a third and topped it off with a melatonin chaser." Darby chuckled. "That worked."

A moment of silence was Kathryn's way of saying that Darby knew better. Instead she said, "I was worried about you."

"When I tell you about my nightmare, I'll take your worry to a new level."

"More of the same?"

Darby sighed. "Let's just say that last night the dreams shifted. Instead of me dying, Clark and his boys did."

Kathryn laughed. "That doesn't sound like a nightmare to me."

"When you know who killed them, it would."

"You need to talk to Linda."

"I plan on it," she said, as the van pulled into the training center. Darby flashed her ID, and then said, "Oh, and yesterday Dr. Cesspool called and wanted to see me."

Kathryn laughed. "How'd he know you were in town?"

"My thoughts exactly," Darby said. "I told his secretary that I was preparing for the presentation and needed to focus. I was unavailable."

"Good for you," Kathryn said. "When are you going to see him?"

"After the meeting today."

"You'll be fine. Just hang in there, and know that I love you. I'll call Ray and tell him you're good," Kathryn said. "You focus, and knock 'em dead."

"That might have been the last thing Ray said to me last night," Darby said with a grin.

# CHAPTER 53

THANK GOD THE presentation was over. Everyone had left the room, and Darby was packing up her computer in silence. Her nightmare was not too far from reality. It just ended better for the divisional team—they lived. Clark introduced her exactly as if she were speaking at a grade school, asking the kids to pay attention and be respectful. Which meant one thing—if respect and listening wasn't a given for adult leaders, they lacked a learning culture.

The meeting had lasted three hours. What a brain drain, and a huge waste of time. They had no interest in changing. Without a doubt, Clark put this in motion at the direction of legal. But she did her best and that was all she could do, even though the divisional leaders behaved like hostile hostages.

The Cheshire cat in her dream was there too. But instead of grinning at her, he turned his back to the screen, and stared her way, glaring. At one point, she asked him to look at the screen. He said, "You said everything was in this packet." She replied, "Yes. But paying attention to the screen is preferable to you glaring at me." He turned his attention to the screen.

The director of training tested her at the beginning by challenging everything she said. Darby finally told him, "I know this is difficult for you. If you feel uncomfortable, then you can leave and read the report on your own. If you continue to interrupt, we'll never get through this." Clark perhaps understood his team better than she did—grade school behavior.

She glanced at her watch. The doctor had told her to come over whenever she could make it. Six weeks of nothing, and then out of the blue he had an extremely flexible schedule. Today. Tomorrow. Whenever. It just happened to coincide with her presentation. She rolled her eyes and walked out of the boardroom directly to Clark's office and knocked on his door.

"How'd it go?" he asked smiling broadly. Warm. Kind. Interested—and completely full of shit.

"As well as could be expected," Darby handed him a copy of the presentation, with an envelope inside.

"What's this?"

"Your bill."

"What do you mean, my bill? What's Airline Safety International?"

"A company I'll form one day. Now it's just a holding place for safety information."

"But I didn't hire you," he said, shifting his weight. "You can't give me a bill."

"Captain Clark, I'm fighting for my sanity. Anyone who put this much work into a presentation and worked for free would be considered crazy."

"But we're paying you to be off." His face reddened.

"You didn't pay me to do this. You pulled me from work." Darby said, grinning. "Just open the envelope."

"No," he said, handing her the envelope. "Then I'd have knowledge."

Darby attempted to hold her expression neutral. In some circles, knowledge was actually construed as a good thing.

"I began this work a month before you pulled me. I'm quite certain any pilot you pull for special projects is paid."

She couldn't care less about the money, but this exchange was quite funny. If anyone observed them from a distance it would appear as they were having a jovial conversation. His smile was as broad as was hers. But if those observers could see the thought bubbles, his would say—*You bitch*. Hers would say—*You are such a moron*.

The fact that he wouldn't open the envelope was funny. She shrugged and realized this conversation was futile. His bill was a thank you note for allowing her to present and hopefully they could create positive change. Darby decided since she'd thoroughly pissed him off, perhaps it was time to leave. She had a doctor's appointment.

She found her way to the elevator and waited for a moment before the door opened. A woman stood inside.

"Good afternoon," Darby said as she entered.

The woman smiled sweetly. Recognition dawned. "Are you Darby Bradshaw?"

"I am," Darby said, with a sigh. "But lately, those are tough shoes to wear." She assessed the woman for a moment. She was too well dressed for the training center. "Speaking of which, yours are gorgeous." Then Darby added, "I'm sorry, do I know you?"

"No," she said, reaching into her bag. "I read your book and loved it." She pulled a copy of *Inside The Iron Bubble* out her bag. "Would you mind autographing it for me?"

"I'd love to," Darby said. They stepped off the elevator and Darby pulled a pen out of her purse. "Who should I autograph it to?"

"Doris Patrick."

Darby began writing and then she said, "Are you?"

"Guilty as charged," the woman said. She glanced down the hall and back to Darby. "I was here to discuss your book with Lawrence, today."

*"Seriously?"* Darby said. "Does he have the power to get my medical reinstated?"

"Your what?"

Darby proceeded to tell her the Reader's Digest version of what happened, as they walked toward the lobby. "So, now I'm off to see the company doctor."

"I'm sorry," Doris said, touching Darby's arm. She looked as if she were going to say more, but thought better of it. Then she said, "Thank you for the autograph."

"You're welcome."

Doris walked out the front door, where a car waited for her. The driver opened the door and within moments she was gone.

"Ready to go?" the voice said, and Darby startled.

The union training representative had offered to drive her to the union offices, where coincidentally the company doctor's office existed. They were all one big happy family living under one roof. She was not sure what to expect with the doctor. But the fact that the CEO's wife had read her book, loved it, and was meeting with him about it, gave her renewed hope. Hope she hadn't felt in a very long time.

# Chapter 54

A CALM MIND brought inner strength, and Darby needed all the strength she could find. Unfortunately, adrenaline was still running wild in her veins from the presentation. The thought of doing yoga appealed on so many levels. She glanced at her watch. Waiting for Dr. Marsh was not helping her calming process.

Linda had said her nerves about meeting him were valid because he worked for Global, and he most definitely was not on her side. But the truth was, she kicked ass at the meeting, didn't lose her temper, and did not kill anyone. She also learned more about Clark, and his process of keeping reality out of his vision.

Besides, she was looking cute too—businesslike and all. She turned the page of the magazine just to be doing something.

Sinclair slipped into her mind. *What the heck happened to him?* If she could find him, maybe he was pissed enough about getting kicked out of his office to rat out the King Rat. If only life were that easy. She suspected he was amply rewarded and would be back flying the line. Something she should be doing. Then again, maybe the jilted girlfriend or a pissed off wife could help her cause. If he wanted to fight dirty, she would too.

"Darby, the doctor will see you now," the receptionist said.

She set the magazine on the table and then headed into his office.

Dr. Marsh appeared pleasant enough and had a kindness about him that would be hard to articulate. She wanted to ask him why something so important, such as her mental health, could be postponed for six weeks, but she also didn't want to come off as combative. Her fuse was burning.

"Thank you for coming, Darby."

"Of course," she said. *As if I had a choice.*

"So, tell me what's going on."

"I wrote a safety report that someone didn't want to read, and they put it in motion for me to see you."

"What's your concern with the company?"

"Where do I begin?" *The beginning.* Darby told him of her interest in safety, the essence of her book, and what she'd learned doing her research. She explained SMS and safety culture, as well as Global's shortcomings. "My greatest concern," she said, "is that we're going to have an accident."

"You fear this? Any reason for that concern?"

"We've come close, so many times. And last spring we almost buried a 737 at the end of SeaTac airport."

He raised an eyebrow.

"You didn't hear about that?"

He shook his head no.

"It came within seconds of impacting the ground. The first officer ended up dead a couple months ago. Gunshot. It was in the news." She fought to maintain her composure thinking of Don. Every time she asked John about the murder, he always assured her that, despite the case being closed, the NTSB was still working on it.

"I heard about that," he said, nodding. "I didn't know the history, however."

She gazed into his eyes looking for any tells.

"We also had a flight where the pilots went around three times because they didn't understand the A330 operation. Then another fight where the captain wiped out the moving map, during short final in instrument conditions." She sighed.

"What do you think the problem is?"

"An old school mentality, with an attitude of *this is the way we've always done it*, and a huge dash of ego that prevents any suggestions that weren't invented by them from being considered." Darby sighed. "Experts estimate that we're going to have an unprecedented number of accidents between 2020 and 2025 due to system complexity. But our training program is the real problem."

He rubbed his face, and then drummed his fingers on the table without saying anything, so Darby continued.

"The reason the FAA is mandating SMS is to improve safety. But there has to be a solid safety culture, which Global is lacking. So, I wrote a report to let them know where we could improve. Then numerous people warned me not to give it to them."

"People warned you?" he asked, leaning back and crossing one leg over the other.

"Yeah. Pilots told me to watch out and said that I had a target on my back. A few of my girlfriends warned me that I would ruin my career." She folded her arms.

"What'd you think they would do to you if you reported?"

"Well, my captain rep warned me that they would do this section eight thing to me. But that's still hard to imagine." Darby paused, shaking her head. "You can't fire people for reporting safety, so I figured they'd give me line checks, or set up my simulator. They've done that before."

"Were you afraid?"

"Obviously not. I reported."

"Point taken."

"My motto… show up prepared and there's not too much they can do. Besides, pilots should always show up prepared, regardless if we're going to get a line check or not."

"How do you feel about all this?"

"Cognitively, I know I'm fine, and this will all work out. But I've been waking up with nightmares, so it's worked its way into my subconscious."

"Any specific dreams you want to talk about?"

"Nope." She shrugged. "I usually can't remember them."

He nodded. "I'm sure you don't do drugs. What about drinking?"

"Socially."

"Coffee?"

"Of course," she said. "I live in Seattle. Starbucks country."

"Any health problems?"

"None. And I allow my AME to run any test he wants. I don't actually have another doctor."

"Who's your AME?"

"Dr. Johnson, from Seattle."

"I know him. Good man." He folded his hands in his lap. "I was supposed to have you sign a release so I could gather all your medical records. But I'm not going to do that."

Darby nodded. This day was turning out much better than it started.

He covered his mouth for a moment. Then he leaned forward with elbows on his desk. "I think this is all a huge misunderstanding," he said. "But the problem is I can't release you because I'm not qualified. I'm an MD, not a psychiatrist. That letter will be in your file for the rest of your career, and if something happened to your plane, say in four or five years from now, through no fault of your own, they would come after me for signing you off."

He wasn't going to release her because of *his* liability? But wasn't *he* the one that started this process? Perhaps this discussion should have occurred before they put a letter in her file.

"I've got a friend in Chicago. Let me talk to him. I'll tell him what's going on, and he can conduct the evaluation. We'll get this resolved quickly for you."

"Thank you," she said. "Will I have to do cognitive testing?"

"You know about that?"

"I do." She had six weeks to learn a great deal about a lot of things.

"Dr. Wood will decide on that." He wrote down another name and number for her. "Contact my good friend at ALPO Aeromedical. Let him know what's happening. If Dr. Woods wants you to do cognitive testing, we'll find someplace close to Seattle for your convenience."

He handed Darby the slip of paper. She read the name and then stuck it into her bag. *Why did Global's doctor have a good friend at ALPO Aeromedical?*

"Don't worry about anything. My good friend at Aeromedical and my good friend in Chicago will take care of you. Now, let's get you out of here and onto your flight."

Darby glanced at her watch. She had forty-five minutes until departure and without known crewmember access, she had zero to no chance of making her flight. But she could try.

# CHAPTER 55

"DRUMROLL PLEASE," DARBY said, standing at Kathryn's doorway watching a historic moment. Kathryn was giving the car keys to the girls to drive alone for the first time. They were awesome drivers, but she was an even better mom. It would never be easy.

"Drive directly to Annie's house. Nobody else in the car. Then directly to the game and home."

"But if we win, everyone is going to Red Robin," Jessica said.

"*When* you win, then we'll add that to the schedule," Kathryn said, handing the keys to Jennifer.

Darby took pictures of the key passing moment and said, "Hashtag Freedom."

Kathryn gave Darby *the look,* and asked Jessica, "Did you call Chris?"

"I did," Jessica said. "He said that John was upset. Not sure why, cuz Chris wanted to go with a friend anyway."

"I'm sure it was something else," Darby said. "He's got a lot on his plate."

"I love you both," Kathryn said, hugging Jessica and then Jennifer.

"Jeez mom, we're just going to a basketball game," Jessica said, rolling her eyes.

"Well, you look pretty hot in those shorts," Darby said, slapping her on the butt. "Who's Annie?"

Jessica laughed and wiggled her butt, and Jennifer said, "She's our team captain. We're all meeting at her house first for our game meeting."

"Please drive safely," Kathryn said.

FORTY-FIVE MINUTES LATER, Kathryn, Darby, Linda, Jackie and Jackie's sidekick, baby Jo were sitting in a booth at 13 Coins with a feast laid out before them. The baby was sleeping and Darby could not believe how big she had gotten.

"That doctor you met sounds really nice," Jackie said. "This should be over soon."

"God, I hope so," Darby said. "But they scheduled me for cognitive testing on Monday.

"Here in Seattle?" Linda asked.

Darby nodded, stuffing a bite of salad into her mouth. "Do you still have time to talk after I'm done?"

"How about dinner?" Linda said, lifting her coffee cup. "I think we should stay away from the building."

Darby couldn't agree more. Linda had an office in the rehab center, but talking there felt too formal, and she doubted they'd be allowed a glass of wine.

"I don't feel comfortable with them pushing you through this so fast," Kathryn said. "After a six-week delay, now it's a rush."

"Can you study for it?" Jackie asked.

"Dr. Marsh doesn't think so," Darby said, sipping her iced tea.

"But I did a little recon on the Internet and depending upon what they do to me, yes, a person could prepare for this test, if they had time."

"That's probably why the rush," Kathryn said. "Not that I'm paranoid."

"Get a good night sleep," Linda said. "With no sleeping aids."

Darby laughed. "I do them so rarely; they hit me hard." She stabbed a piece of crab, and shifted the conversation. "Jackie, was John upset when the girls told him they weren't going with him?"

"Yeah. More irritated. He'd been in his office arguing with someone on the phone, and I think that's what he was mad about."

"Any more photos?" Kathryn asked.

Jackie touched the baby with one hand, and then stabbed a piece of fruit with her fork. She didn't look up, and acted like she didn't hear the question. Buying time or ignoring, were equally as incriminating.

"There are more!" Darby said. "Spill. What are they?" She was thankful there were no photos of the visions from her nightmare.

All eyes drilled into Jackie. She was toast.

"Can you tell us?" Linda asked.

"Some were of Kat. At her house with her boss."

"What?" Kathryn said choking on her orange juice.

"You were eating… Subway," Jackie said.

"John was taking pictures through my window? How the hell didn't I see him?"

Jackie pushed a piece of melon across her plate. "I don't think they were through the window." She stabbed the cantaloupe. "The window was in the picture. They came from inside."

Kathryn and Linda's expressions were as surprised as Darby's. John was watching Kathryn from inside her house. That could only mean he had a video camera going. *But why put the still frame photo in the box?* None of this made sense.

"I need to see those photos," Kathryn said. "Is John going to the girl's game?"

"He wouldn't miss it."

"Then let's swing by your house on the way," Kathryn said. "It will take ten minutes tops."

"What if he catches us?" Jackie said.

"We'll just say you needed something for the baby," Darby said.

"Yeah, but two cars and all of us?" Linda added. "How about Kat go with Jackie, and you and I go in my car to the game."

"Now you're learning how to plot with the best of them," Darby said. "We'll do John recon."

"Something doesn't make sense," Kathryn said.

"Nothing makes sense to me," Jackie said.

"I've been wracking my brain to figure out what the big deal is with my research. It's as if they sent out the National Guard to prevent us from knowing that it rains in Seattle. We already know what we'll find with performance."

"Maybe they're afraid if you're *not* working for the FAA, then you could tell the world," Darby said.

"Perhaps. But if I'm working, and conduct the research, why not just bury it like Nobles did years ago with that report?"

"That's probably why they want you back," Darby said. "To control your work and shut you down."

"I think Ms. Diane Nobles met with you to determine if you could be managed, or if you are a wildcard," Linda said. "Did you give her any reason to believe either way?"

Darby could see Kathryn's gears kick in. Fear flashed through Kathryn's eyes.

"If this gets out, then everyone in the world will know they're playing Russian roulette while climbing on a plane," Darby said. "And the FAA has done nothing to fix it."

"If they find Darby crazy, they could order her publisher to pull her book," Kathryn said. "Who would keep a best-selling book on the shelf that was written by a mentally unstable person?"

"I couldn't even self-publish because I don't own the rights," Darby said.

"But if the public knew Kat was fired because of her research, that could create a media sensation," Jackie said. "It might help."

"But the government could spin it against her," Darby added.

"This is making me ill," Linda said, placing her napkin on her plate. "Global's attempting to discredit Darby and the FAA's trying to silence Kathryn, leaving the traveling public in the dark."

"They're not going to silence me," Kathryn said and looked at her phone. "It's 11:40. We have time to swing by your house, Jackie, to look at the photos. If I can determine where John put the camera, I can find it. Then we'll go to the game."

"Kat…" Jackie said. "There was another photo you might not like." All eyes turned her way. "It was that pilot you dated last year. Tom I think his name was."

"What the hell?" Kathryn snapped.

Guilt overwhelmed Darby, remembering her phone call with him. She'd planned on telling Kathryn, and then forgot. "He called me two weeks ago to see why I was off, and asked about you."

Kathryn's eyes flashed between Jackie and Darby.

Jackie glanced at her plate and then up to Kathryn. Her face an ashen color, she said, "He was standing outside Bill's prison, reaching for the door. He was going in."

Darby's stomach rolled and she thought she was going to throw up.

Kathryn raised a hand to get the waitress's attention, and at the same time her cell phone buzzed with a text message. She glanced down and then cried, "Oh, my God!"

# CHAPTER 56

HE LEANED AGAINST the pillow reading the newspaper, half-listening to the news on the television, and glanced at the clock. He was waiting for a sign to proceed, so he could get the hell out of there. He had places he had to be, and people were counting on him.

Once the shower started, he glanced toward the bathroom door and jumped out of bed. He opened his briefcase, lifted the papers and pulled up a flap exposing a compartment. He removed the electronic device, and a knife. Then he grabbed her purse.

Reaching to the bottom of her bag he poked the knife through a corner. He separated the microphone into two pieces, and stuck one through the hole from the inside and then connected the other piece on the outside. The spot mirrored one of the many studs that covered her purse. She would never notice. He moved all contents back into place and returned the purse to the dresser.

The shower shut off and he quickly climbed back into bed. Then he saw the knife and scrambled to get it, just as the door opened.

"What are you doing?" Diane asked, emerging from bathroom.

"Nothing much," he said, turning toward her. "Just going over some work." He closed his briefcase and then turned his attention toward the television.

With a towel on her head, she glanced at the briefcase then she shifted her attention to the television, too.

KOMO 4 News flashed—breaking news. "Live from Des Moines, Washington," the reporter said. "This is quite a scene. We have two young ladies trapped in a car. Officials are attempting to cut the power lines. The entire City of Des Moines is without power."

He grabbed the remote and increased the volume, as the reporter pushed hair out of her face. She glanced at the crash and then toward the camera. "Witnesses said that the car came flying through this intersection, running a red light," she said extending her hand. "The fact they missed passing cars was nothing short of a miracle. Now we can only hope these girls are alive."

"Kathryn's car," he said. "The kids!"

"She's never allowed them to drive it before."

"You've been watching her?" he said. "If you had something to do with this…"

She rolled her eyes and continued to dry her hair with the towel.

"What the fuck have you done?" If those kids were harmed and he had anything to do with it, he would never forgive himself. "They're just kids!"

She chuckled. "Maybe that'll be enough to get her in line," she said tossing her towel to the bed, and moving behind him. She snuggled up close, and wrapped her arms around his waist.

"I've got to go," he said, pushing her aside.

"Do what you must." She returned to the bathroom and closed the door.

He pulled his pants on, and then his shirt. His eyes were glued to the television, watching the emergency team cut the wires. He pulled on his socks and slipped on his shoes. He wanted to rush out the door, but he couldn't remove his eyes from the television. Those kids—what would happen to Kat if she lost them?

All he wanted to do was get the hell out of this room. He grabbed his coat, his briefcase, and the keys from the dresser.

She emerged from the bathroom, wearing a robe. "When will you be back?"

"It's over."

"When I say it is."

"You disgust me," he said. "If you had anything to do with this—"

She folded her arms and said, "Don't threaten me."

"This is the end. I'm done." He opened the door, exited, and slammed it behind him. Once outside he ran to his car.

# CHAPTER 57

IT HAD BEEN four hours since the crash. Darby leaned against the wall, watching Kathryn pace the waiting room floor. John sat on the couch with Chris, and Jackie bounced the baby. Linda stood with her back to the room, staring out the window. Niman was transferring between operating rooms from Jessica to Jennifer.

Images of this hospital scene roared through Darby's brain, and visions of Greg's charred body filled her mind. Tears leaked from her eyes and she felt as if she wanted to vomit. These girls had so much life to live, and were so beautiful and smart. How could this have happened? *Please God, save them.*

John's phone buzzed and he looked at the screen. He stood and walked to the opposite corner of the room before he answered. With his back to them, he spoke low so nobody could hear what was he was saying. The call ended quickly and he turned.

His attention turned directly toward Kathryn, pain filled in his eyes.

"What?" Kathryn said, which came out as gasp of desperation.

He walked over to the table and pulled out a chair for her, and then sat in the one beside it. Kathryn glanced at the chair for a moment, and then walked over and sat beside him.

Darby followed and pulled out another chair, as did Linda. Jackie stepped closer, still bouncing the baby.

Chris looked up from the couch "Did you hear something about the girls?" he asked.

"No. Just work stuff," John said. Then Chris returned to a world of his own.

John spoke in a low voice. "The brake line was cut. Appears it started in your driveway. Not a big cut, but effective enough. It was cut to leak slowly."

"I drove it on Friday."

"We'll see if there are two drip points in the driveway. That'll give us a better time stamp as to when it occurred."

"Who'd want to hurt the girls?" Kathryn asked, more to the Universe than to John.

"Nobody," Darby said. "John was supposed to take them in his car. Jackie was picking up Linda. You were driving me." She pushed back from the table, and stood. "Someone wanted to hurt you, or me. Or both of us."

"Who knew you'd be driving with her?" Linda asked.

"Besides you?" Darby began. "Jackie, the kids, Ray, and… John." She glanced John's way.

Kathryn turned toward him. "Who else has been watching me? I want answers now, dammit. Did you find a bug in my house after Jason was there? Or did you remove your camera instead?"

John stared her way, eyes not blinking.

"Do you have surveillance cameras in my driveway, too?" Kathryn snapped. Her anger was focused on John, and it was probably 100% deserved.

"What does that mean?" Chris asked, now standing at the table. "What's going on?"

John's eyes flashed to Chris then back to Kathryn. "We've got an ongoing investigation, and I'm sure this has nothing to do with it. But if it does, we'll find out."

"I should have never let them take the car." Kathryn covered her face with her hands. "I'll never forgive myself."

Linda reached over and touched Kathryn's arm.

The door swung open and Niman entered the room. He glanced toward Linda first, and then to Kathryn. John stood quickly, and extended a hand to his chair for Niman.

Niman sat beside Kathryn and placed a hand over hers and squeezed. "The girls are going to be fine."

Kathryn's shell finally broke and tears flowed. When she could speak, she said, "What's the extent of…"

"Minimal considering. Jennifer has a broken leg. She was driving and must have had that brake pedal all way to the floor when they slammed into the pole. Jessica's left arm is broken. Looks like she may have flung it left to block her sister from flying forward. The airbag did its job. The roof impacted the blow of the pole, so the weight didn't slam on them. There was head trauma, but nothing too extensive, or to worry about. They're both in surgery for their limbs, but with time, they'll be as good as new."

"They're going to be fine," Jackie said, tears falling. "They're going to be fine." She held the baby close, who decided to wake up and join the sobbing session.

Even Chris's eyes moistened. "Can I see them?" he asked.

"How about tomorrow," Niman said. "They'll be in surgery for a while longer. The doctors will set their limbs, and we should keep them quiet tonight."

"Will you tell them I was here?" Chris asked.

"Of course I will," Niman said. "But for now, I think the fewer people the better. I've coordinated a room for them to be together, and we'll watch them through the night."

Darby knew all too well what that meant. They were not out of the woods. There was no way she would leave this hospital until the girls were awake and talking.

"I'm going to get the baby home," Jackie said, setting her in the car seat. "Chris, why don't you come with me? We can come back tomorrow."

Chris glanced at Niman, and then John. He turned to his mother and said, "Okay. Let me carry her for you," as he reached for the baby.

"I'm going to head home, too," Linda said. "Call for anything."

"I'll walk you out." Niman turned to Kathryn, and squeezed her shoulder. "I'll stay until the girls are moved into their room."

Kathryn touched his hand on her shoulder. "Thank you."

Linda bent down, and gave Kathryn a hug and kissed her head. Then she and Niman left the room.

John sat beside Kathryn. "We need to talk." Then he looked at Darby.

"What?" Darby said, sitting in a chair beside Kathryn, wrapping an arm through hers. "The hell if I'm leaving and not hearing this first hand."

# CHAPTER 58

A FAMILY WALKED into the waiting room, and silenced John before he began. Kathryn didn't want to leave the floor until the girls' surgeries were complete and she knew they were safely tucked in for the night. Darby doubted she'd move from their sides until they were safely home. But she had an idea.

She found Niman, and he worked his magic to enable them to wait in the girls' room. He sent a pot of tea and coffee their way. For some reason, Darby was feeling guilty drinking coffee, after Dr. Marsh asked her if she drank it. As if coffee had anything to do with mental health.

A foldout bed was in the corner, and three chairs were placed at the end of the beds. Darby walked to the window and stood by Kathryn, who stared out at the scene beyond.

"The girls will love this room," Darby said. "The view's great." She glanced back at the male nurse passing the door, attempting to cheer Kathryn up.

Without looking her way, Kathryn said, "Are you talking about the mountains, or the nurse's station?"

"They're kind of cute," Darby grinned. Then she said, "Kat, they're going to be fine."

"I know they are," Kathryn said, glancing at John and then back to Darby. John stood outside the room and was talking to someone on the phone. "I'm not sure I want to know what he's going to tell me. I don't know if I could forgive him if he put the girls in harm's way."

"There's only one way to find out," Darby said. "Let's drink the tea before it gets cold, and find out what the hell he's been up to."

Kathryn and Darby relocated from the window to the chairs, and Darby poured them each a cup of tea. A few minutes later John saw them sitting and ended his call.

"Sorry about that," he said, as he returned to the room, closing the door behind him. He sighed heavily and pulled up a chair.

"Tea or coffee?" Darby asked. He gave her the 'are you effing kidding me' look, and she poured him a cup of coffee. "I'm just saying that there are some medical circles that think this stuff could indicate mental health problems."

He took the cup and drank. Darby knew a delay tactic when she saw one.

"John, what's going on here?" Kathryn finally asked.

"Where do I begin?" he said, pulling a hand through his hair.

"The beginning," Kathryn said.

"I was never up for the Department of Transportation secretary position. I was announced under false pretenses to see if we could pull out Diane Nobles."

"What the hell!" Darby said. "For what?"

"We've been watching her for a long time. Someone inside the FAA is allowing the airlines to self-regulate to an abysmal level of performance. That started back with AQP, when airlines were allowed to design their own programs and track their own performance." He paused for a moment. "Then the Oklahoma City

FAA office, overseeing Global, began filling with retired Global captains, and things got worse. Diane's name is all over this."

"What does this have to do with the photos you've been taking?" Kathryn asked.

"I know Jackie, uh… explores. I knew she would show you, and I wanted you to follow the trail."

"You intentionally wanted Jackie to see a gunshot victim?" Kathryn said.

"No. I wanted *you* to see it, to know it wasn't suicide."

"That's just wrong on so many levels," Darby said. "But kind of brilliant."

"Why didn't you just tell me?" Kathryn said, exasperated. "You could have shown them to me and told me what the hell was going on."

"I couldn't. Someone's monitoring me. I'm not sure if they're in my office or yours, or how they're doing it. But Nobles *always* has too much information. That was the only way I could think of to get that info to you." He sighed. "I had you send me the Flight 42 report to see if they tracked it."

"Did they?"

He nodded.

"But why put a camera in Kat's house?" Darby asked.

"We suspect Jason Bernard may be involved, too. We've watched him enter Nobles hotel room on numerous occasions. But then, again, so has Lawrence Patrick. I suspected that Jason might try to meet with Kat after she quit."

"Does this have something to do with my research?"

"Probably everything. Nobles told us to back off the investigation of Flight 42. She adamantly wants you to stop what you're doing. She carries more weight around the system than anyone. You'd think she already was the secretary of the DOT."

"That's why you were so upset when I met her for lunch."

"I think she hired the hit on Don, but I can't be sure."

"The head of human factors of the FAA killed Don?" Darby snapped. "Why?"

John shrugged. "We don't have proof, but for all intents and purposes signs are pointing that way because of what he was going to bring forward."

"How the hell did you get photos of Don before the police got there?" Kathryn asked.

"You were meeting with Don, and I wasn't sure as to the extent of Bernard's involvement and what you'd carry back to your office," John said. "Erikson had the answers. I needed to know if that event was intentional. I decided I'd do an interview of my own, at his house, before you met with him. His wife led me to the garage, and that's when we saw him. I ordered her to call the police. While she was out, I snapped photos. I knew instantly he hadn't killed himself."

"Why weren't you in the report?" Kathryn asked.

"I walked out before the police got there."

"Jesus, John! You could have ended up in jail for that." Kathryn placed a hand over her mouth.

"Does any of this have anything to do with my mental health?"

John looked Darby's way. "I'm not sure. You might be crazy all on your own."

"Not funny," Darby said, as she lifted her teacup. Neither were the thoughts of someone taking her gun to her head, and faking her suicide, too. They would say she was so distraught and crazy that she killed herself…

"I'm sorry," John said. "I think they're trying to discredit you. Coincidence is overrated."

"Could Nobles be getting even with me?" Darby asked. "I mean... if she and Patrick are pillow talking, she's pissed that I wrote about her, he could be pissed too, and she told him to do this."

"Patrick's not someone to be told what to do," John said. "But for the life of me, I can't figure what that hell Diane's motive is for holding down pilot performance. Clearly training is flailing, and the FAA is watching it happen."

"Money. They're lining the CEO's pockets by cutting training," Darby said. The thought of Tom's photo in front of Bill's prison slammed forward.

"How does that benefit Nobles?" John asked.

Darby shrugged. "But what about the photo at the prison?"

"We're not sure," John said. "Maybe Bill and Tom are friends, nothing more."

"Huh," Darby said. "When Bill's concerned nothing is that simple."

Kathryn glanced between Darby and John. Then she said, "The FAA's charter was for airline survivability. But now airlines are more than surviving, they're thriving. Everything is outsourced, pilots are training themselves at home, and simulator sessions are minimal. Planes are more efficient than ever, and stock prices are soaring. How much money is enough?"

"Technology has also reduced the cost of training," Darby said.

"True, and technology is Nobles background," John said. "Thus, we know what's happening, but we don't know why. That's why I was tasked with figuring it out. Players are Nobles, Patrick, Bernard, Clark, and... Bill."

"I ruined your plan by walking out, because I became a wildcard."

"Let's just say your departure put a snag into the mix." John leaned forward on his knees. "But then again, it might have pushed the rats out of the hole. When they sequentially contacted you, begging for you to return, I realized they were nervous. But this," he said glancing at the empty beds, "now I know what they are capable of."

"We should've known with Don's death," Darby said.

"We have no evidence," Kathryn said quietly.

Just then they wheeled Jennifer into the room. "Mom," she said, and started crying. "I'm so sorry."

"It's okay sweetheart. This wasn't your fault." Kathryn brushed her daughter's hair back and kissed her forehead. "I'm so thankful you're okay."

The nurses moved her to the bed, and removed the gurney from the room. Jennifer said, "I tried to stop, but the brakes didn't work."

"We know, honey. It's okay. I love you."

"Where's Jess? Is she okay?" Jennifer asked with a look of fear that Darby had never seen before.

"She'll be here soon," Kathryn said. "She's fine."

"Speak of the devil," Darby said, stepping aside as they wheeled in Jessica.

"Did I miss the party?" she said, words ever so slurred. The nurses lifted her to the other bed. Then they became busy adjusting IV's and connecting monitors for the night.

Kathryn rushed to her side and kissed her other daughter. "I love you," she whispered.

When the nurses left, Jessica said, "So, I guess you're not going to let us drive again."

"Probably not until your limbs are healed. Then we'll get you back out there."

Darby stepped between their beds, kissed Jessica on the forehead, and then moved to Jennifer's bed and kissed her. "I love you guys, and you scared the hell out of me. Don't do that." She wiped a tear and said, "I didn't want to leave your mom alone. But now you two can keep her company. I'll see you tomorrow."

Their eyes were both already closing. She turned to Kathryn and opened her arms, and gave her a long hug.

"Thank you," Kathryn whispered.

"I'll see you tomorrow," Darby said. "I'll be here in the morning, so you can sneak out for a break." She knew Kathryn wouldn't be moving from the room anytime soon, for any length of time.

John stepped toward Kathryn, and said, "I'm sorry."

"This wasn't your fault," Kathryn said, giving him a hug. "But we're going to figure this out and nail whoever did it." She glanced at the girls and back to John. "Can we get—"

"It's already done," John said. "I'll stay until security gets here."

# CHAPTER 59

LIFE WAS A crazy ride and there were no guarantees. Darby was just thankful her prayers were answered and the girls were okay. She sat in the waiting room doing what she was getting really good at—waiting. The Rehabilitation Institute was across from the Seattle Center. The Museum of Pop Culture, MoPop, Key Arena, and the Space Needle were all within four city blocks. She wondered if there was some connection between this location and head injury patients. The best part of this location was—Linda was someplace in the building.

She dressed in business attire to make a good presentation, yet she felt as if the other inmates were thinking she was a doctor. For the onlooker, she could be waiting for a job interview—professional exterior attempting to exude confidence—but a basket of nerves feeling her entire career was dependent upon this interview.

The truth was, if this were an interview and she failed, her life wouldn't be over. With what she was doing here, it would be.

"Ms. Bradshaw, the doctor will see you now."

Darby followed the receptionist to a back room and took a seat. The doctor was sitting behind a desk. She was cute and couldn't be more than twenty-five, maybe thirty years old. Darby settled into a chair and the woman turned her chair toward her.

"Hi, I'm Dr. Reece."

"Darby. Nice to meet you."

"How was your weekend?" she asked.

"An adventure, to say the least." When Dr. Reece's look encouraged her to continue, she did. "My best friend's teenage daughters were in a car accident. It was pretty bad. They're over in Swedish now. I spent most of my weekend there."

"Are they okay?"

"They will be. Their spirits are pretty low. Sixteen-year-old basketball players. One with a broken leg and the other with a broken arm. The next game they miss, they'll feel like their lives are over."

"What do you think?"

"I think they're lucky to be alive," Darby said. "This is nothing but a thunderstorm temporarily grounding them. Sometimes we have to wait out the storms in life, too."

"Do you know why you're here?"

Darby nodded. "I created a safety report and gave it to someone in management who wasn't too happy to receive it."

"What makes you think that's why they pulled you?"

"Well, to begin with my union rep warned me of this exact tactic five or six months before they did it."

"Why did you do it then?"

"The most often asked question," Darby said with a smile. "I couldn't live with myself if I knew what was happening and didn't at least tell them what I knew."

Darby gave her the condensed version of safety culture. Shared with her the old-school culture of the airline, more the good ol' boys club. She told her about what was happening with Kathryn and the FAA. She almost told her that the brake line was cut, but she remembered her promise to John.

Dr. Reece had a few of her own boy club stories to share, too.

A young girl walked into the room and Dr. Reece said, "This is Brenda. She'll take you through the testing. Then I'll gather the results and write up my report."

Darby followed Brenda down a long hallway. They passed many closed doors and walked into a room at the end of the hall. Brenda closed the door. The first test was to look at a picture and then draw it—lines, diagonals, circles, flags and more. It was a complex doodle art piece, and kind of fun. She did pretty well, too. Then the testing began.

By the time Darby emerged from the fourth room, it was lunchtime. She was physically and mentally exhausted. She walked into the break room and saw a fridge and microwave. She could have brought so many more options for lunch, had she known. As it was, she brought a couple pieces of fruit.

Two other inmates were sitting in the room. Then the door swung open, and in came a man carrying a stack of pizza boxes. Soon the room filled with people. She had been wrong; she dressed better than many of the doctors.

This was Joe's last day party. He no longer had to come to rehabilitation. Joe offered her some pizza and she accepted.

"May I ask what happened to you?" Darby asked Joe.

"Car accident," he said. "Couldn't ... uh... talk when I got here. Look... at me now." He spread his hands. One hand didn't move too high off the table, but it moved. "I'm... slow." He grinned. "But heard good things... uh... take time." He laughed. His speech was slow and deliberate, but his smile spread through his eyes. "Glad to... uh... be alive."

"We're proud of you Joe," said another guy, in worn-out jeans, who placed a hand on his back. Darby wasn't sure if he was a doctor or patient. The room was full of hope and inspiration from people who'd fallen victim to life, but were not giving up.

Then Joe asked her why she was there, and Darby told them the story. Talking with them, she realized how lucky she was. She had her health, mental and otherwise.

Thirty minutes flew by and she inhaled two slices of pizza. Wishing everyone good luck, and they her, she hugged Joe, and then exited.

The second half of the day was clicking a tapper with her left finger as fast as she could, and then the right, then the left. They were timing and comparing scores. Vocabulary was interesting, and she got all the words except for one. The worst part was, she knew the word… it just sat in the back of her brain and she couldn't pull it forward, more due to exhaustion.

"Close your eyes," Brenda said. "When I say go, I want you to mentally count to sixty and tell me when to stop." Darby breathed deep and Brenda said, "Go."

Eyes closed, Darby silently counted—one and two and three and… then thirty-two, thirty-three, and when she got to sixty, Darby said, "Stop."

"Oh, my God!" Brenda said. "Nobody has ever gotten that perfect before."

Darby smiled at her accomplishment, and opted not to remind her they were in a brain injury facility. There could be a good reason she was the only one who handled that task to perfection.

She sat at a machine where numbers flashed one at a time on a screen and then she had to recite them backwards… sometimes three numbers, sometimes five. The hard part was a reflex game to keep the ball in the center of the screen, as it moved left and right. It kept moving right and she'd tap left to get it to come to center, and then it would jump full left. The same thing would happen bringing it right—frustrating as hell. Then she gave Darby a blank piece of paper and asked her to draw the picture from earlier in the morning.

"Can I see it?" she asked. Brenda shook her head no. All she could do was the best she could, which was certainly substandard. If they had told her to remember it, she would have done much better.

Finally, the easiest test was the last. Brenda showed her drawings of simple items and asked her what they were. When she showed her the fourth picture, Darby's mind drew a blank.

"I know what that is," she said. "But I can't find the word. I am mentally done." She wanted to cry.

Brenda closed the cards, and the word came. "Tongs," Darby said. Then she sighed, "My brain's fried. Is this normal to do this much testing in one day?"

"Oh no. The human brain can't process this much information in a short amount of time."

"Then why the heck am I doing this?"

Brenda shrugged. "We have one more test. The MMPI."

The MMPI was the Minnesota Multiphasic Personality Inventory, a standardized test to assess personalities, screen job applicants, and apparently utilized for mental health assessment. This was the test she was looking forward to. Darby had been invited to a private Facebook of female airline pilots, a forum where women celebrated their accomplishments and vented their concerns.

She had learned that Global had a pattern of downing female pilots on this test. She'd taken this test when she was employed with Coastal, and again when she passed her FFDO psychiatric evaluation.

Darby smiled as she began reading, knowing she, too, would have failed the profile of military pilot by acknowledging she liked to read romance novels, liked to paint, enjoyed gardening, loved to paint flowers, and take bubble baths. She also didn't really like reading auto mechanics, but loved driving cars. Then she came to an important question.

Brenda was sitting in the room grading her tests, and Darby said, "I found my first paranoia question—do you think someone is out to get you? I'm not sure what to say."

"Just answer it honestly."

Darby smiled. "I wouldn't be here if at least one person wasn't." Darby checked yes. But she was also not stupid, and didn't answer yes to any of the other questions that pointed toward paranoia. Which proved one thing—an intelligent brain could game the MMPI if the individual knew what they were looking for. She answered it honestly, and knew that truth would be her best defense to all of this.

Once complete, Darby had been in the rehab center for seven and a half hours—one hour talking to the doctor, and thirty minutes for lunch. The remainder of the time, it felt like a six-hour, non-stop checkride with emergencies she had never seen. She finally understood how the pilots in that Air France crash felt—sensory overload combined with fatigue. She prayed she had not pulled the stick in the wrong direction.

"Can you tell me my scores?"

"I'm sorry," Brenda said. "I don't have enough letters after my name."

Darby just stared her way. Defeated. Exhausted. Not sure what to say to that. So, she said nothing. But Brenda must have felt her pain.

"Let's just say you were the first person taking this test who didn't swear at me, or at a machine." Brenda gave her a small smile. "Your scores are fine."

# CHAPTER 60

DARBY ARRIVED AT the Edgewater's Six Seven restaurant first, and ordered a glass of red wine. She sat on the balcony and looked out over the Seattle piers at Puget Sound. The sun was setting beyond the Olympics, and she breathed deep attempting to release the day's tension. She sipped her wine, noticing a distant ferry silently working its way her direction.

"Sorry I'm late," Linda said, touching her shoulder. Darby jerked, ever so slightly, her nerves a little on edge. Linda pulled out a chair, and ordered a martini.

"Did you see the kids today?" Darby asked, pulling her coat tight.

"They're doing great. The basketball team was there, and they're the stars of the moment." She paused a moment. "We'll be there to catch them when this bubble bursts."

Darby nodded, hoping Linda would be there catch her, when her bubble burst.

The waitress arrived with Linda's drink. "I'll have a window table for you in about twenty minutes."

"Thank you," Darby said, and reached for her glass.

"How'd you do today?"

"I have a good sense of time."

"You'll have to explain that one," Linda said, with a smile. She sipped her drink. "So, what time do you go in tomorrow?"

"I don't. I finished today. Tomorrow I fly to Chicago to see the psychiatrist."

"Neuropsychological testing in one day?" Linda said, a shocked expression on her face. "That's a ten-hour test and designed to be conducted in two, five-hour days."

"Apparently, Dr. Marsh wants to help me get back on the flight line quickly."

"He took over six weeks to see you. Then he forced a two-day test into one day, without time for you to prep, and he's flying you to Chicago the next day?" Linda leaned forward. "I don't trust him."

"So answering that someone was out to get me on the MMPI, might not be too far off base." Darby said. "We could put the list on the wall and throw darts as to who it might be."

"This is more than your career," Linda said. "Someone tried to kill you and Kathryn. You should be doing something to protect yourself."

"Uber." Darby sipped her drink, and said, "But you'd better be careful or they may come after you next, for being paranoid."

Linda laughed. "Are you paranoid if they're really out to get you?"

"Touché." Darby raised her glass toward Linda's and they clanked them together.

"I understand you've been haunted by nightmares. With a doozy last week."

"You could say that," Darby said. "I carried my gun to the presentation in my purse. Then I cut the bottom off of my plastic Pepsi bottle, stuffed my pantyhose inside, taped it, and then put the gun into the bottleneck end. I asked everyone if they would come forward and tell the truth. They wouldn't, so I killed them all."

Oh, my God," Linda said, "That's fascinating. How did you learn how to make a silencer?"

Darby laughed and almost choked on her wine. "Out of that entire story that's what was fascinating?"

Linda nodded, and Darby said, "Long story as to how the subject came up. But I learned how to do it at a Ninety-Nines conference, from a delightful couple who liked guns."

"Do you like guns?"

"No. I hate them," Darby said. "They scare the hell out of me."

"Then why are you an FFDO?"

"I don't like anything controlling me, so to give an emotion that kind of power seems fundamentally wrong." She thought for a moment, and then added, "But the training was incredible. I think every pilot should go through it, gun or not."

"Those dreams you're having are normal," Linda said. Then she lifted her glass and looked out to the bay as the ferry, Darby had been watching, approached, sounding its horn. Moments later she turned her attention toward Darby again. "No matter how strong you are… the fear of losing something important in your life is inside of you. The time it comes to the surface is when you are most vulnerable, while sleeping and you can't shove it down."

"The fear of losing it all is slipping into my daytime, too." She sighed. "I'm not sure if Dr. Marsh was really on my side, either. His putting me in isolation for a month and a half, and then slamming me through this rush to be tested, felt wrong to me. But I'm trying to stay positive."

Linda's hand covered Darby's and it stayed in position. "What else is bothering you?"

Darby swiped a tear. "I feel like an idiot. But Ray's in training now, and I want to be happy for him. But…"

"You're jealous."

"Yes! He has my life. I want my life back."

"You have a life, sweetheart," Linda said. "It's just taking a different path right now. No fault of your own, and somewhat like the girls' event. We don't always have control, which I guess is more difficult for a pilot to accept."

Darby chuckled and dabbed a napkin under her eyes. "No kidding."

"The point is, you do have control over some things right now. If you can channel your energy into doing something positive while this is going on, then your focus will shift to strength, versus nightmares of being the victim. Which I think your subconscious is now feeling desperate enough to fight back because it thinks it lost everything. But *you* haven't."

"I could start another book, and begin writing about this."

Linda nodded. "That would be great idea. And it would help you to work through your feelings with all this, too."

"But what if they really fire me, and I go from living my dream to grounded without passing *Go* for my two hundred bucks?"

"Have you ever been broke before?"

"Oh, hell yes. Do you know how much flying lessons cost?"

"You survived. And you, my dear, are not about the money. If you were, you would never have put your job on the line by going forward despite all those warnings. You did this because it was the right thing to do."

"It's never been about the money. It's who I am. Flying is… It's in my soul and part of me. My identity. Without that, I have no idea who I would be."

"You would be Darby, and you would spread your wings in another direction."

Darby wanted to believe her, but it was hard to imagine another life. The waitress arrived and moved them into the dining room. Darby hadn't realized how cold it was outside, until the warmth of the restaurant embraced her. Once their meals were ordered, Linda shifted the conversation.

"Did you find an attorney?"

"I tried, but there's a little problem with our system. It's called the Railway Labor Act."

Darby explained to Linda that the Railway Labor Act that passed in 1926 with a second and last amendment in a 1936, prevented attorneys from taking an airline case because they would too often get kicked out of court.

Under the act, the airlines, with a pilot contract, use the collective bargaining agreement with arbitration and mediation for strikes as well as labor disputes. Basically, everything was to be settled internally. The problem was, the airline owned the process. The jury and judges were pilots paid by the airline, and open to the same retaliation if they didn't play the game.

"Match that all up with Global's working agreement, where this section eight was instilled sixty years ago, and it's hopeless."

"Are you telling me that airlines are protected by a ninety-one-year-old act that was last amended eighty-three years ago, with a sixty-year-old clause in your contract?"

"That's exactly what I'm telling you."

"But what about all the human rights laws, and discrimination, and the fact you can't fire people for an unjust cause, etcetera?"

"They don't exist for the airlines." Darby lifted a roll out of the basket and said, "Global actually has a clause in our contract that says a pregnant pilot has to go on disability."

"You're telling me these young women are utilizing their disability insurance for a natural human life function? And they won't have any remaining if they get sick later?"

"Not only that, but they are not allowed to use their pass travel privileges while pregnant, because they're considered sick. The policy is you can't travel when you're sick."

"This makes *me* sick! Are you fucking working in the dark ages?"

Darby laughed long and hard. She had never heard bad language spew from Linda's lips. Which proved one thing—there was a first time for everything.

When she could speak again, Darby said, "That's about the size of it. Clark got one of our pilots pregnant. She was a new hire, working in his office as his assistant. Word flew on the flight line that he would be gone. Everyone was excited, kind of like—ding-dong the witch is dead. But at the end of the day, he stayed and she went."

"This is wrong on so many levels."

"You know what else is wrong? This is not the first time Global used this tactic. And they're not the only airline doing it."

"You need to go to the media with this."

"Oh, I will," she said. "All in due time. So far, many of the pilots I found who went through this ended up retiring. However, I did find three other women, all at different airlines. Two just got their jobs back after years of hell, and another is still fighting for hers. Then I connected with a group of guys from one of the largest airlines in the world, and they are going through the same thing."

"This is amazing," Linda said. "Can't the FAA help?"

"You answer that question. I found a case, many years earlier, where the pilot was actually fired from Global. After many years of pain, exhaustion, and financial drain through the court system, she won her lawsuit. Global's doctor was subsequently fired for his part in the transgression." Darby sighed. "Global had stopped firing people, but I suspect they are now paying the medical system to do their dirty work."

"Shift the liability," Linda said. "Where'd Global's doctor go?"

"I'm not going to pass judgment until I know all the facts, but let's just say he's still lurking the medical halls, very high up. The reality of my story is that I'm a thorn in their side and one they're trying to permanently remove."

"Why hasn't your union helped?"

"Just as Global owns the FAA, they control the union. My union rep never stood up for me, along the way, to stop this train. Now it's too late. They all know how bad training is... yet they never do anything. They all run in fear. Phil warned me about the section eight, so I'll give him credit for that. But he never told me why he thought they would do this, and now he blames me. He's holding something back."

"Sweetie, I'm sorry."

"Don't give up hope," Darby said, spreading butter on her roll. "You've inspired me to write another book, and I might even get into law school to fix this system."

# CHAPTER **61**

TIME WITH LINDA always put life into perspective. Then a quick visit with the twins made Darby realize that her issue was not arms and legs. She would find a way to get back to flying, and make sure this never happened to anyone, ever again.

Once home, Darby went directly to her computer. She opened her email account and Justine, one of the captains pulled for mental health, had written—*Darby, I am sorry this is happening to you. I have just a minute, and will respond more later… But for now, I wanted to give you my attorney's contact information. He can help. You're not alone.*

She copied the law firm's name, and pasted it into her browser. When the page opened, she scanned the attorney's credentials— impressive. She filled out a form with her name, phone number, email address, and then explained her issue. The last thing she typed was—*I thought there was a whistle blower law to protect employees from this type of thing. Why do we have to be fired first?*

The phone rang. Darby stuck her headset into her ear, and the phone into her sports bra, so she could pack while they talked.

"How'd training go today?" Darby asked Ray, while opening her suitcase.

"Pretty good. I now have renewed respect for what you've been doing."

"Well, you're having fun aren't you?" she asked, standing in front of her closet figuring out what to wear for the psychiatrist.

"The best time of my life."

"I know." Darby said, maintaining a smile so he could hear her inner joy.

"I'm sorry, sweetheart. How was testing? Are you crazy yet?"

"They're working on it." Darby sat on the bed and closed her eyes. "Imagine if your two-hour simulator session, was a six-hour session of electrical fires, hydraulic failures, and engine failures with stalls and TCAS, combined, with warnings firing every thirty seconds, and you had no checklists and weren't trained first."

"Was it really that bad?"

"Worse. What if they showed you a picture at the beginning of your training, and had you draw it? Just some abstract lines, waves, a flag, circles... nothing that made any sense, but complicated all the same. Then you did all that training, six hours worth, and during the debrief they made you draw that picture from memory."

"Holy shit. This is just nuts." He sighed. "How're the kids doing?"

*Safe subject*, she thought. "Good as can be expected." Darby returned to her computer. "Did you talk to Clark or Wyatt since you've been there?"

"Yep. Clark, that asshole, has everyone fooled."

"Not the pilots," Darby said.

"True. But they still kiss his ass."

"Holy shit!" Darby said.

"Holy shit, they kiss his ass?"

"I just got an email from an attorney. Ever hear of an Air21?" Darby said, as her fingers frantically typed, with her new word search. There it was. "It's the whistle blower law."

"I thought you had to wait until Global fired you to get an attorney."

"I'll be damned," Darby said. "Air21 is the Wendell H. Ford Aviation Investment and Reform Act for the 21st Century under 49 U.S.C. §42121."

"Huh?"

"Oh, the FAR code squiggly line thing. But it's a joint FAA/OSHA program that says it extends beyond discharge and compensation loss, to changing the terms of my job. I don't have to be fired. Retaliation includes, if the terms, conditions, or privileges of employment have changed because I reported internally. Holy cow, I think grounding me and pulling my known crewmember access changed the terms of my employment. I'm protected under this law."

"Do you really want to spend money for an attorney on this?" Ray said.

"Hell, yes! I'll be damned if I will allow them to get away with this."

"I'd bet anything, that law was designed for the airline to win."

"Stop being so negative," Darby said, returning to the attorney's email. "But, I've only got ninety-days since this thing started."

"My point exactly. How long has it been?"

"Forty-nine days, six hours and thirteen seconds. Going on a lifetime."

# Chapter 62

IMAGES OF *The Shining* flashed through her mind as she stepped off the elevator and looked down the long hallway. She walked the length, and looked left and right. More hallways protruded out both directions. She located the numbers to the offices, and turned right. She found herself in front of Dr. Wood's door, and knocked. No answer. The door was locked. The building was silent, no activity from any of the dozens of doors she had passed. Her nerves were firing on every cylinder.

Darby had arrived at Chicago's O'Hare Airport the night before, and then she cabbed it for forty-five minutes to some hotel in an outskirt county, which turned out to be another thirty-minute drive to the doctor's office the following morning. Her night was short and restless, and when her alarm went off at 0600, it was 4:00 a.m. by her body clock.

Linda's words of warning echoed in the back of her brain as to how he could twist anything the direction he wanted to prove his case. If he was paid to find her crazy, she couldn't win. She could only be optimistic and pray he had integrity.

The girls were being moved home today, and Darby should be there with them instead of here. This entire process was infuriating.

John set security up at Kathryn's house. His team found a bug—someone had been monitoring Kathryn's communications. Yet it had not been her boss, as the video had captured his every movement during his visit—unless he'd set it earlier. Then she thought of Don—he had been murdered and yet they closed the case. That could only mean that someone in the police force in Oklahoma City was involved. John said he was still working on it, but she was beginning to doubt they would ever get the bastards who killed him.

She shifted her weight from one foot to the other and then leaned against the wall. *What the hell is going on?*

On more than one occasion, the union had mentioned someone claimed she was paranoid, and that was the core of this issue. But for the life of her, she couldn't figure out why. She reported the issues. It was others who'd warned her.

Yet she still looked up the definition of paranoia online—*a mental condition characterized by delusions of persecution. It may be an aspect of chronic personality disorder, of drug abuse, or of a serious condition such as schizophrenia in which the person loses touch with reality.* The final statement made her smile—*suspicion and mistrust of people or their actions without evidence or justification.*

There was plenty of justification for concern with all the warnings she'd received, and plenty of evidence to the accuracy of her report. She glanced down the hall. A little man strode her direction and stopped in front of her, he stuck a key into the lock before he looked her way. When he spoke, he came across soft and gentle, but very slow.

They made their introductions, and Dr. Kenneth Wood opened the door to his office. Papers and books were stacked on the single desk that was pushed against one wall in a front office filled with crap. No receptionist. She followed him to the back office with more of the same. But this room hosted two chairs, a desk, bookshelves, a single window, and another disorganized mess.

Darby began to sweat. Not from nerves, but the temperature. It was hotter than hell.

Chicago hosted temperatures dropping to 19 degrees Fahrenheit outside, yet it felt as if she were in Death Valley—one of the hottest places on earth. She removed her overcoat, and wished she'd warn anything other than a sweater. While he shuffled papers, she removed her sports jacket. Sweat trickled down the inside fuzz of her sweater, making her skin crawl.

Perhaps it was this entire process that was getting under her skin.

"I'm going to record this session," he said. "Do you have any questions?"

"Why we are here, would be a good place to start."

"Ohhhh," he said, slowly. "Why do *you* think we are here?"

"I was warned six months ago they could do this if I presented a safety report," Darby began. "But Dr. Marsh said this was a misunderstanding. He also said that he had a friend in Chicago that he'd talk to and explain what was going on, and would send me to him because he as an MD, wasn't qualified to release me." Dr. Wood nodded in agreement. "So here we are."

"Well, let's get started. Do you have any siblings?"

"Four stepbrothers and sisters."

"Where do you fall in age?" he asked writing numbers one through four on the page

"In the middle."

"The middle?" He looked at her quizzically. "What number is that?"

"Three," Darby said fighting a smile. This was a far easier test than the cognitive testing.

He circled number three on the page and then wrote Darby's name under the number. When she realized what he was thinking she said, "Wait. You asked how many siblings I had. I said four," Darby clarified. "That means there are *five* children in the family and I would be number three. The middle."

He melodramatically erased her name with an audible huff, and added the fifth number on the page. "That's why I have to do this in pencil." Then asked her their ages, as well as the ages of her parents, aunts, uncles, cousins, and entire family tree.

Darby's family was her aviation community and Ray, Kathryn, Jackie, Linda and their families. But she did the best she could, having not been in touch with many of them for years. Her siblings were two of her Dad's wives' kids—none of his biologically.

After they spent forty minutes establishing this family tree and ages, he asked, "Any drug abuse within the family?"

"Nope."

"Alcohol abuse?"

"Nope."

"Mental disorders?"

"None."

"Bi-polar disorders?"

"Is that different from a mental disorder?" Darby asked crossing her legs. He stared, and she added, "Nope."

"Okay then…" He scribbled notes on a paper.

"Why did you want to know the ages of my family members?"

"Well…" He spoke slowly, as if she were two-years-old and helping her to track his thinking. "As you know… I asked about their mental health and drug and alcohol issues, which is often hereditary."

"So, if you would've asked if my family had any issues first, then we wouldn't have had to play the 'what's their birthdate game' for the better part of an hour?"

He stared without response. Glared might be more appropriate. She opted to not question him as to the validity of stepbrothers and sisters, and why he'd never ascertained if they were blood relatives or not.

Dr. Wood turned toward a foot-tall stack of papers piled on his desk and pulled a sheet off the top and said, "Read this."

Darby took the paper and read the post concerning mental health from her blog. She'd posted that in response to the pilot who had flown into the mountains.

"Why did you write this?"

"I didn't write it."

"Yes, you did. It came from your blog."

Darby took the paper and pointed to the header as she said, "See this name? See where it says, 'Please welcome my guest speaker today as she shares her concerns for mental health?'"

"Oh... well, uh... do you agree with it?"

"Yes, as a matter of fact I do." Darby wiped sweat from her forehead, and onto her pants.

"Could we turn down the heat? Please," she asked.

"No, I'm sorry. It's on or off."

Then he drilled her with random questions that had nothing to do with mental health. She answered his interrogation questions the best she could. He was very concerned that she had come from a broken home and wondered how her mother managed without her father there.

"So your mother left you alone and went to work at night?"

"I'm assuming I had a babysitter and wasn't alone."

"How could she do that?" he asked, sounding incredulous that her mom could do such a thing as being a working mother.

"Well, it's like this. She called a teenager to come to the house and…" she said, answering a stupid question with an equally stupid response. In light of the glare he threw her way, she changed directions and said, "She needed to pay bills and to feed me."

"Did she express her milk for the babysitter to feed you, while she was gone?"

"I was a baby, so I couldn't actually attest to that information. However, I'm fairly certain that I was in fact fed or I might not be sitting here today."

This line of questioning went on for hours. She fought hard to maintain composure when she got to Brian's and then Keith's deaths. Linda was correct. Someone was feeding him information and Dr. Wood worked hard to push her over the edge. He pushed, and pushed, and pushed some more.

She held it together. Sweat dripping beneath her clothes. Her pants and shirt were soaked.

When the day was almost done, she realized he had been nodding, raising eyebrows, and shaking his head in response to her questions, so as to not verbalize his answers on the recording.

"Oh… here's a good question for you *West Coast people*," he said. "What are your religious or political beliefs on suicide?"

*What the hell? We West Coast people?* Since when does a person's political or religious beliefs dictate mental health? Unless they were cult driven. "I don't have political or religious beliefs. I have personal beliefs." Darby folded her arms and stared.

He challenged her on the safety report where she stated that the loss of an autopilot and autothrust did not dictate an emergency aircraft because manual flight should be a core skill. He'd told her she was wrong about the pilots not having an autopilot, and that nowhere in the transcript, the company had sent him, was that information present.

"They couldn't get the autopilot engaged," Darby said, frustrated. "They flew to destination and then declared an emergency." She wiped sweat on her pants. "All I'm saying is, if that were an actual emergency they should have returned to the departure airport. But pilots should know how to fly. That is not an emergency in visual conditions."

"Read this transcript. Tell me where it says there's no autopilot."

"The first paragraph. See where is says we lost the autoflight system?" Darby couldn't believe she was arguing with this imbecile.

"What's an autoflight system?"

"An autopilot and autothrust." Was he serious?

"You're wrong! They had the autothrust."

"No, they didn't," Darby said, folding her arms. She was so hot, she felt faint.

"See here, where it says the autothrust was unreliable?" he said, emphatically. "That means they had it, it was just not reliable."

"No sir, they did not. We don't use unreliable autothrust; we disengage it."

Global had data to show that the pilots did not have the ability to hand fly or manage a fully automated aircraft—so said the thousands of safety reports that came in annually. The training department included that module to encourage the pilots to declare an emergency if they lost their automation. Apparently declaring an emergency was a lot cheaper than providing adequate training.

What did any of this have to do with mental health? His questions concerning elements in the report, clearly identified a lack of knowledge, as limited as the lady from the pass travel complaint department.

Darby did her best to educate and inform, answering all his questions. He shifted to challenging her flying career. Grilling her on her first job, and then he moved to the second.

"Okay, so your second job was less challenging than your first."

"Please don't put words in my mouth. Who said my first job was challenging? I was flying airplanes and it was awesome!"

"Hmm. Are you religious or spiritual?" he asked. "Have you ever had an experience?"

Oh, she was having an experience with this asshole, all right. Ken Wood was a friggen idiot and did not deserve the title of doctor before his name.

Instead of saying yes, she decided to share with him a time she sat on the beach on the Oregon Coast. Her experience was enjoying the magnitude of the ocean crashing upon the beach, with fog wrapping around the lighthouse and mist lightly falling.

"Dr. Wood, have you ever been to the Pacific Ocean?"

"Uh... well. I... uh..."

"That's not a difficult question. Either yes, or no." She glanced at her watch. She had been in this interrogation approaching six hours now. No food. No bathroom breaks. Nothing but attack, after attack, after attack, while he cooked her to death. She was done.

"I, well... uh... I have seen the Atlantic Ocean."

"You've never gone to a medical conference in Hawaii? Never wanted to see the Pacific Northwest? That's God's country," she said, shocked. "Perhaps it's *those* West Coast people that scare you away?"

He stared for a moment and then said, "What do you think of all this?"

"What do you mean?"

"With all that's happening, how do you feel? How does it make you feel?" He moved in closer, pulling his chair into her space. "I want you to express your feelings."

"I feel like I've been violated."

"What do you mean?" he asked staring her down. She was the stare-down master, but he was creepy. Hell, even his office was creepy.

"How does it really make you feel?" He leaned closer.

"It makes me feel like I've been raped. Like I'm on the stand and being prosecuted for reporting!"

"Ohhhh, does it now?" he said, leaning forward, putting his face within twelve inches of hers, and glued his eyes to hers without blinking.

Not blinking, and maintaining his gaze, her silent mantra kept her strong. *Don't cry! Don't look away! Be strong!* His effort to push her over the edge had failed, for all he knew.

When they were done, Darby walked out of the office. She headed down the elevator and stepped outside. The freezing cold slapped her in the face and she began to shiver something violently. The moisture on her body became supercooled.

After she called for a cab, she dialed Kathryn.

"How'd it go?" Kat asked.

"These fucking people are seriously trying to have me put in a straitjacket," Darby said. And for the first time since this started, she cried, really cried. Her emotions and tears, springing on her daily, never dropped more than one or two tears down her check. But now she couldn't stop crying.

She wasn't sure if her tears were fatigue induced due to the marathon interrogation, or the inappropriateness of his questions. The pain of someone killing Don, the reality of what could have happened to the kids, and her fear for Kathryn… felt heavy on her chest. She'd gone from a weekend from hell to marathon cognitive testing, and then this bullshit interview.

They had broken her.

The realty that a medical professional could be paid off to do what he had just done was nothing short of criminal. None of which assessed her mental health, but had everything to do with pushing her to the edge of a cliff so she would jump.

# CHAPTER 63

THEY SAY CHANGE is inevitable and nothing lasts forever, but to walk away from the empire he had built felt strange. Lawrence Patrick had just left the Oklahoma City Airport and was entering the on ramp to I-44. This had been one of the most difficult decisions of his life. He knew the only way to save his name was to get out. How many more millions did he need anyway? Doris was correct. Enough was enough. The entire fucking empire could implode at any time. He had sold hundreds of thousands of shares of his stock, and he was set for life.

His cell phone rang, and he pressed answer on the car speaker. "Yes?"

"Just heard the news"

Lawrence smiled. "Word travels fast in this industry."

"I'd heard rumors a few days ago. Tried to call."

"I was busy. Had some loose ends to clear up." He merged onto I-44 north bound. A black SUV sped past, cut in front of him and then slowed to a normal pace. *Damn drivers,* he thought. "There's a reason I normally hire a car."

"What next?" Clark asked.

"Take some time off. Maybe take Doris to the Caribbean for a much deserved and extended vacation." A call from Nobles flashed on the screen. "I've got to take this."

Lawrence switched calls. "What is it Diane?"

"It's official? I never believed you would actually do it."

"I told you I was getting out of the airline business."

"People say things all the time, but they rarely follow through."

"Not me. If anyone should know that, you should."

"That I do." Diane sighed. "You're making a mistake."

He laughed. "I'm not falling off the face of the earth. I'm still going to be the Chairman of the Board."

"Perhaps."

"What the hell's that supposed to mean?" he said, trying to switch lanes in attempt to get around the SUV.

"We had an agreement. Early retirement was not in the fine print."

"Things happen."

"I'm not one to forgive or forget," Nobles said.

"Croft will do a hell of a job. He won't change anything."

"He knows?"

"No."

"Then your guarantees are as worthless as your word."

The SUV slammed on its brakes. Patrick reacted by slamming his foot to the floor. His Escalade turned sideways and tires squealed. Skidding, he looked out the passenger window. The semi from behind hit the tail of Lawrence's car with such force, his car veered toward the railing.

He smashed into the railing, and the airbag slammed into his body, knocking the wind out of him. Everything moved in slow motion.

The semi-trailer broke free. The truck jackknifed, hitting his car with so much force his head jerked sideways, slamming it against the side window. His car crashed through the guardrail, nose first toward the Oklahoma River. He pulled his seat belt tight, and hit the electric switch to open his window as blood dripped into his left eye.

# CHAPTER 64

THE COMFORTS OF home were many, and should never be overrated. Darby was content to be sitting on her couch with a cup of hot chocolate, in contrast to her visit to the nuthouse. Ray would be joining her in less than a week, but it wouldn't be long until he would be out flying her airplane, without her. She thought about getting a pass and traveling with him on his first trip. But then again, he might need to keep his head in the game.

She lifted the can of whipped cream and sprayed a fresh mound on top of her cocoa. Pointing the remote at the television, she began scanning the channels, stopping on the local news channel— KOMO 4. Her phone rang and she muted the television.

"You alive?" Kathryn asked.

"Whipped cream is involved, so I'm thinking yes." Darby slurped some cream off the top of her mug. How are the girls?"

"Great since you did their nails."

"Passion pink works for any ailment."

Kathryn had convinced her to spend the night in Chicago to get a good night's sleep after she'd missed her flight home. The next morning, Darby bought a first class ticket on Alaska Airlines. Linda had said she needed that cry and a good night sleep, she had been right. After returning to Seattle, Darby drove directly to Kathryn's for a bit of normal. She painted the girls toenails, ate pancakes, and then returned home for a much needed nap.

"Do you want to join us for dinner tonight?"

"Thanks, but I think a soak in the hot tub and a good night's sleep might be just what I need, and… holy shit!" Darby sat upright and unmuted the television. "Channel four! Lawrence Patrick is dead!"

"What the hell?" Within seconds Kathryn said, "Oh, my God."

The reporter said, "We're here in Oklahoma City where the CEO of Global Air Lines has just been pulled from the Oklahoma River. The only witness, the driver of a semi truck, told us that Lawrence Patrick drove directly toward the rail, then slammed on his brakes and spun into the truck driver's lane. The driver of this huge rig did all he could to stop."

With a hand to her ear, the reporter listened to her headset. "We're getting some news here. The word is that he may have been sick. Could the CEO have done this on purpose? Did he end his life because he was ill? Or was this just an unfortunate accident?"

The reporter looked toward the river. The camera followed, zooming in on his car, and then focusing back to her. "Lawrence Patrick was just nominated the CEO of the year. He merged two of the world leading airlines into one, and built Global into a premium product. He will be sadly missed by those of us in Oklahoma, and around the world."

"Kat, do you think…" Darby said, but couldn't finish the words.

"I'm not sure what I think, but I need to call John."

Darby dialed Ray, and he answered on the first ring. "Did you hear?" she asked.

"I fucking can't believe it," Ray said. "Clark was telling people he had cancer and didn't want to live with it."

"The hell with that," Darby said switching to CNN. "If you get sick and have the money he did… you don't give up."

"I guess not," Ray said.

"There's actually *nothing* that could have caused him to kill himself," Darby said.

"How do you know?"

"Because people like Lawrence Patrick never give up. You don't become CEO by rolling over or driving off a bridge. It's all about a person's character."

# CHAPTER 65

WHEN ONE PHONE rang with Kathryn's name on the screen, and seconds later his other phone rang with the controller—he knew there was a problem. He answered the controller's call, and fifteen minutes later he was slipping into the Angle Lake office. The controller was sitting in the room without lights. The sun had just set and shadows cast eerily across the wall.

"What the hell's going on?" John said, not bothering to turn on the lights.

"If I knew what it was, it would have ended yesterday," the controller said leaning back in his chair, arms folded.

"There's no way in hell Patrick committed suicide." John placed his hands on his hips. "We'd better damn well figure this out, before we add any more bodies to the list."

"Eventually everyone on our list will be dead. We can select him by a process of elimination."

"This is not the game of clue," John said. If only it were that easy. "We damn near lost Kat's kids. We could've lost her. We have nothing definitive on Erikson's death, and a key figure on our list is dead."

"Maybe he killed himself. Feeling guilt for what he was doing."

"What the hell *was* he doing?" John asked.

"Enabling the airline to train their pilots to half-ass standards." He pushed back from his chair and reached for a bottle of scotch. "Want one?"

John nodded. "Global Flight 42…" He sighed. "I'm telling you that we are knocking on the door of a major catastrophe. I don't know if that was incompetence, or…"

His boss poured a couple fingers into a glass and handed it to him. "My vote is Bernard."

"I'm not so sure," John said. "But, if so, he's in it with Nobles."

"You sure there isn't a little professional jealousy there?"

"Fuck you," John said, and sipped. She'd be the last person to be jealous of, position or not.

"She's a bitch, but a well-connected one at that," the controller said.

No truer words were ever spoken.

"Would it be out of line to pray she's not involved and she's the next to go off a bridge?" John asked with a grin.

"You two sound like an old married couple."

John tossed back his drink and said, "Well, then it's time to divorce the bitch."

# CHAPTER 66

WITH MONEY AND power involved, anything was possible. Jason suspected his days were numbered, and he needed protection. More than that, he needed to help Kathryn. He never imagined they would have proceeded with that threat. Lifting the remote, he clicked off the living room television and headed toward his office.

He stopped by his wife's room on the way. "How's she doing?" he asked the nurse.

"We had a good day, today."

He nodded. "I'm not sure what I'd do without you."

"Make sure you're home by 3 p.m. on Monday and you won't have to worry about that."

He laughed. "I wouldn't miss it. I'm going to do a little work. Then I have to step out for no more than an hour or two. Are you okay until eight tonight?"

"Of course. Take your time."

Once inside his office, Jason closed and locked the door. He opened the closet, pulled out the recording equipment and ejected the flash drive. He held it in his hand and wrapped his fingers around it, deciding how to deal with it.

The technology existed with options to record and save an electronic copy to the cloud, but he wasn't sure on the security of that system. This was something he'd never intended on getting out. He wanted it for his knowledge only. He placed the flash drive into his top desk drawer and locked it, then stuffed the key deep into his pocket.

In his wildest dreams, he had never imagined what Diane was capable of, or how high her power went. Everything fell into place and he understood more than he wanted to know. Now he needed to decide what to do with the information. He turned his office lights off, and headed toward the front door. He pulled on his overcoat and stepped out of the house.

He backed his car four feet down his driveway and then put it into park. Leaning over the seat, he opened the glove compartment and grabbed a flashlight. He climbed out of his car and shined the light where his car had been parked. The driveway was clear.

At what point would he be construed as paranoid and thrown into the nuthouse? He climbed back into his car and backed down the driveway, knowing exactly where he needed to go, and what he needed to do.

# CHAPTER 67

BLOOD BOILING, JASON didn't care who saw him as he pulled into valet parking. He gave the young man a twenty-dollar bill and said, "I won't be longer than ten minutes."

He took the elevator to the 15th floor and walked down the hall and knocked on the door.

"Now this is a nice surprise," Diane said, opening the door. "I suspected you'd be back."

He pushed into the room and then closed the door. "What the hell are you doing? Those were children you damn near killed. And Lawrence Patrick, too?"

"Excuse me?" she said folding her arms, eyes narrowing.

"This will end now. If you touch those kids, or if Kathryn Jacobs ends up with so much as a scratch on her head, that will be your end."

"Threats are unbecoming. You have no idea what you're dealing with."

"I know more than you think."

Her eyes pierced his soul. What scared the hell out of him was that she had followed through with the order to get rid of Patrick, and Kathryn was the next on the list. He would do anything he needed to protect Kathryn. He had thought firing her would keep her out of harm's way. He had been wrong.

"How much more blood do you want on your hands?"

"A few more drops couldn't hurt," she said. "What's with you and Jacobs anyway? She's been nothing but a pain in the ass."

"She's a good woman trying to do the right thing." He already knew how far Nobles would go. Now he needed to figure out how to stop her. "Don't do it," he said. His words sounded more as a plea than the demand he'd intended.

An eyebrow rose. "Where'd you get your information?"

"It's called protection," Jason said, folding his arms. "It stays buried as long as you lay off Kathryn Jacobs, her family, and Darby Bradshaw."

# CHAPTER 68

PAJAMA PARTY WAS the best way to describe the scene. They had moved the girls into the game room, until Jennifer's leg healed enough to navigate the stairs, thus it was one big campout. Darby was helping them get dressed, and settling them in to do their homework. They were still sore, but the attention from their friends made that bearable. She would have to talk to John about getting an older and not so good-looking guard outside the house to get Jessica away from the window, or she'd fail her studies.

"You two set?" Darby asked.

"Yep," Jennifer answered. "But I can hardly wait until we get back to school."

"I never thought I'd hear you say that," Darby said with a laugh. "But you're going to have to get up and get dressed before noon."

Jessica groaned theatrically. "Thanks, Aunt Darby."

Darby headed to the kitchen where Kathryn was sitting at the table reading her survey questions.

"Almost done?" Darby asked.

"Close. Thanks for reviewing these from a pilot's eye. I appreciate your feedback."

"I might invalidate your data, being mental and all," Darby said opening the fridge. "Seriously, the problem with this is the pilots might not tell you the truth about their performance."

Kathryn laughed. "Well, that doesn't say much for your species."

Darby removed a bowl of leftover macaroni and cheese, happy Kat still considered her in the special group of being a pilot.

"Well, the pilot species is often fatigued which sucks for the memory," Darby said, putting the bowl into the microwave. "Not to mention, the lack of an incident can be remembered as good performance."

This was not unlike an industry that based safety on the lack of an accident. Darby explained that pilots also judged their performance on making it to their destination without incident. Despite the errors made with a close call, landing long, or just getting lucky, the truth was that highly automated aircraft masked marginal performance. People also remember their positive performance more so than the negative.

"Nothing's ever easy," Kathryn said. "Did you get the Air21 filed?"

"Yep, and if Global decides to fight this and take it all the way to court, it might dent my bank account," she said, pulling up a chair beside Kathryn. "But as long as I live, I will never allow them to do this ever again."

"It's scary they could do it in the first place."

"It feels like Nazi Germany and they're ushering me into the gas chamber."

"They know we're friends since the last fiasco with the director of training," Kathryn said, tapping her pen on the table. "Do you think they could be doing this to pull our attention from something else?"

"Like hiding Don's murderer, stopping your research, or derailing the safety report? Of course." Darby stuck a bite of macaroni into her mouth. She wouldn't put it past them. "I know John doesn't like Nobles, but I think Clark has his thumbprint all over this one, at least for my issue."

"Could Clark have killed Lawrence Patrick?" Kathryn asked.

"I wouldn't put it past him," Darby said. "My first meeting with Clark and Wyatt, they told me that they worked closely with Nobles. The more I think about that statement, it almost felt like a warning."

"Warning or not, I don't trust any of them," Kathryn said.

"What are you going to do about Nobles?

"I left her a message that I'm giving up on this project, asked to get my job back, and that I would love to be part of her team."

"Holy shit. Does John know your plot?"

"It was his idea."

Darby's eyes widened as she scraped the last of her pasta out of the bowl. She wasn't so sure that lying would be the best thing with this group. She hoped to hell John and Kathryn knew what they were doing. Darby stuck the fork into her mouth, and licked it clean.

"I also want to go to the memorial with you," Kathryn said. "We could pull a rat out of the pile down there."

"What about the girls?" Darby said, excited to have company.

"I'm taking them to Jackie's," Kathryn said. "I'll feel better having John there, and security will go with them."

The doorbell rang, and Darby and Kathryn jumped. Darby laughed at their reaction and said, "Post traumatic stress disorder."

Kathryn left the room and a few minutes later she returned with a box. No return address, but Jason's name was on the packing slip.

"Careful. Could be a bomb," Darby said.

Kathryn hesitated a moment, and then opened the box. She removed a package wrapped in bubble wrap, and then opened it. A gorgeous wooden plaque, with a gold engraved center emerged from the plastic.

Darby took the plaque and read.

"In honor of Kathryn Jacobs. On behalf of the Federal Government, your integrity and diligence for aviation safety will always be admired and respected. Your efforts to make Aviation Great Again will always be remembered. Federal Aviation Administration 2017."

"This is really nice," Darby said.

"Yes, it is," Kathryn said, her eyes narrowing. "But I guess this means it's permanent—I'm done, Nobles must have changed her mind."

"Kat, just go talk to him."

"What am I going to say?" Kathryn sighed. "I already left a message for Nobles." She tapped her spoon on the table and then said, "Do you think my conversation with John was overheard?"

"Maybe." Darby walked to the sink and rinsed her bowl. "Talk to Jason. He seriously likes you. He may not have known that Nobles made you that offer, and this was premature. You could go now. I'll stay with the kids."

Kathryn returned to her seat and glanced at her watch. "No. I have too much to do before we go tomorrow." She lifted the plaque and read Jason's words again, running a hand over them. "But I will go Monday after I drop the girls off at school."

# CHAPTER 69

THE CHURCH WAS filled with hundreds of people. Clark, Wyatt, Odell, and numerous other management pilots sat in the front row in full uniform, hats included, their wives beside them. This was quite the show. Doris sat to the right, surrounded by her family. God, Darby felt bad for her. She knew what it felt like to have someone ripped from your life unjustly. It couldn't help but change you.

Darby and Kathryn settled into their seats.

Clark spoke about Lawrence's accolades as a CEO, and all that he had contributed to the airline. His children took turns speaking about their dad. It was odd seeing his business suit removed, revealing a normal person with a family. But everyone had a life outside of work, and now Darby witnessed the other side of the man. She wished she'd known him.

"Is Nobles here?" Darby asked Kathryn.

"I haven't spotted her yet."

Nobles worked closely with the airline, as Clark and Wyatt had made clear during her initial meeting. John had many photos of them together, too. One would think she'd make an appearance, if for nothing but respect.

The slide show filled multiple screens around the room. One of Lawrence's best friends spoke of their days as little boys, and their shenanigans. Photos of him as a baby, some of him in high school, water skiing, college, snow skiing, marriage, the births of his children, and then him with his grandchildren sequentially filled the screen. With each photo, Lawrence Patrick became more of a human beyond the airline executive.

When the service was over, Kathryn and Darby worked their way forward so Darby could talk to Doris. Clark looked her way and she smiled sweetly, giving him her best fuck you look.

Clark nodded and then it registered that it was Darby. She wanted to laugh at the shift in his expression. Yet the guy had balls as he stepped forward instead of running away.

"I'm surprised to see you here," he said.

"They haven't put me in a straitjacket yet," Darby said. Kathryn fought a grin, but her eyes never wavered from the man.

"I'm, uh… just surprised you'd come all the way down, under the circumstances."

"You know what you're doing is illegal," Darby said, folding her arms, her eyes never leaving his.

"We've done nothing wrong," Clark said. "We're paying you."

"Paying me?" Darby grinned. "You apparently haven't heard of Air21."

That's when she saw it—a shift in his expression. He hadn't heard of Air21. He didn't know that a change, in terms and conditions of her job, was also considered retaliation. Just because an employee was paid, did not make it right to retaliate.

A woman's voice spoke, "Darby?"

Turning her back on Clark, Darby took one step sideways, and positioned her body between Clark and Doris and said, "I am so sorry." Then she introduced Doris to Kathryn and they shook hands.

"I'm sorry for your loss," Kathryn said.

"Thank you." Fresh tears sprung to her eyes. "We were planning life after retirement, not this."

Darby spread her arms and hugged Doris, and said, "He didn't kill himself."

Doris whispered, "I know." She pulled back and reached for Darby's hand and placed a paper in it. "Can we talk after everything settles down?"

"Yes, of course," Darby said, as someone stepped in and grabbed Doris's attention. Darby glanced down at the paper—a phone number. When she looked up, Clark was standing against a wall in the distance staring her way.

# CHAPTER 70

*WHO THE HELL does she think she is?* Clark climbed into his car and slapped the steering wheel. "That fucking bitch." He breathed deep, gathering his composure. How the hell did Darby and Doris know each other? He had no idea. What the hell was an Air21 anyway? Bradshaw was full of bullshit, and this was more than likely one of those times. He unlocked his cellphone, located the number and pressed call.

"What can I do for you?" Dr. Wood asked.

"Did you get her tests?"

"I did," he said. "They were surprisingly good. Forcing her into a one day event didn't work like we'd thought."

"Do you have to use them?"

"No."

"Have you had a chance to look through the information I sent?"

"Yes. It was helpful."

"What about the interview?"

"She was argumentative, but not considered a mental issue... no more than the standard personality disorder of most women."

Clark laughed. "How long can you run this out?"

"As long as you need."

If Global had to take her back, Clark could keep her out of the flight deck long enough to destroy her performance. Hell, he never wanted to see her on company property again.

"Can we remove her permanently?" Clark asked.

Dr. Woods was silent for a moment, before he responded. "Yes. I could build that case. But I'll need time."

"Take all the time you need." Clark's wife walked out of the building, and Clark said, "I have to go."

After the service, Clark's wife had stepped into the restroom, and he'd said he'd meet her at the car. Now she was coming his way and she didn't appear happy. It was always something with her.

He had seen his old assistant sitting in the middle of the group of pilots, yet he looked past her. His wife was a perceptive lady. His assistant's smile fell flat when he showed no recognition of her, but she knew the deal. They all knew their time at Global would be limited if they ever said anything. The company proved that many times over. Hell, they just fired two women for reporting their boss for touching himself at work. All they had to do was keep their mouths shut. What could be more simple than that?

His phone rang. "Yes?" he snapped without looking at the caller.

"We need to talk."

# Chapter 71

SUCCESS BEGAN WITH doing what was necessary. Walter Croft knew that all too well. He sat at Lawrence Patrick's desk, assessing where to begin the cleanout process. Personal effects would go to Doris and the rest... he would have to assess the importance. As the chief financial officer, he knew most of what was going on from a financial aspect. Anything else, his boys were down the hall for assistance—Wyatt, Clark, and Odell.

He'd wanted and expected to get the CEO position years earlier, prior to Lawrence's arrival. They had promised him one day. That day had arrived. Now he had everything he wanted, but the magnitude of it all hit hard. Perhaps once he was fully moved into the office, it would feel more real.

He set desk photos into a box for Doris. Then found an envelope with personal cards. As much as he hated to, he opened the envelope and began reading. Nothing that Doris shouldn't read would find its way into her home. She was going through enough pain. He knew Lawrence better than his brother, and was sure he'd find nothing incriminating. But sometimes people were full of surprises.

Once he'd sorted through the personal effects, he set them aside and rang Rose.

"How can I help you Mr. Croft?"

"Walter, please," he said. "I've got a box of personal effects for Doris. Could you set up a car to take them to her?"

"Of course. When would you like to—"

"Actually," he said. "I think I'd like to take them myself. Please contact Doris and ask her a good time to drop by."

Lawrence's desk was surprisingly neat, but there were drawers filled with documents of some sort or another. Legal had advised Walter to bring anything questionable to their attention. Half of him wanted to tell legal that perhaps they should clean out the desk. But truth be told, this was an excellent way to get his fingerprint on what was happening within the airline at the CEO level.

Rose knocked on the door and opened it. "I thought you could use a cup of coffee," she said, setting a tray on the corner of the desk. "Doris is expecting you at three-thirty."

"Thank you." She was about to turn, but hesitated. Walter asked, "Are you okay?"

"It's just hard to imagine I won't ever see him again."

"I feel the same. We all do."

"I can't imagine what Doris is going through."

"She'll get through this. She's strong," he said. "Thank you for the coffee."

Rose walked out of the office. He stood, and stretched. With a cup of coffee, he walked to the window—*heaven in the center of hell.* This location had been his idea. The price had been right, and now he wondered if it had been a good idea. He'd also wondered why Lawrence had chosen this location for his office.

Walter returned to his seat and glanced at the incoming mailbox, sitting on the corner of the desk. He would start with the current mail, and then would dig into the drawers. He opened a manila envelope and pulled out a report—SMS and Safety Culture, an Ethnographic Study on Global Air Lines. There was a personal note inside—*I've done the best I can. The rest is in your hands. Now I must focus on saving my reputation and my career. Darby.*

With his coffee in one hand and his document in the other, he leaned back and began to read.

By the time he reached the end of the document his coffee was cold and his blood pressure was high. He pushed back from his desk and stormed out of his office. He headed down the hall and walked into Clark's section.

"Is Clark in?" Walter asked Jane. When she glanced to his door and nodded, he stormed into Clark's office unannounced.

"Walter, what can I help you with?" Clark said, jumping to his feet.

He closed the door firmly, and then slammed the report onto his desk. "What the hell is this?"

"I, uh... I'm not sure," Clark said lifting the report. His face reddened slightly. "Oh, this is the presentation one of our pilots gave to our divisional leaders."

"What does she mean she has to save her reputation?"

"We've had concerns about her. Pulled her for administration action concerning her mental health."

"This work doesn't appear to be that of a person with mental issues." He folded his arms. "What did she do at the presentation, go nuts?"

"Uh... well, we pulled her first, and then legal advised us we should go forward with the presentation."

"You pulled her *before* she gave the presentation, and you still brought her in?"

"We had to. Legal suggested we give her an opportunity to present this information to avoid litigation."

"She reported safety issues, and *then* you pulled her from flight status, and then you brought her down to give a formal presentation?" He had to be hearing this incorrectly.

Clark nodded. "Yes, sir. We had reason to—"

"You brought someone you accused of having mental health issues, into headquarters, to give a presentation to our divisional leaders?"

"Yes, sir."

"Are you fucking crazy?"

Clark's composure shifted ever so slightly, and he said, "Legal suggested…"

Walter reached for the report and pulled it from Clark's hands. God dammit. Was he working with imbeciles? What the hell were they thinking? This is not how he needed to start his career as a CEO.

Walter sucked a deep breath and then said, "Nothing in this presentation had better be true, and if it is… you had damn well better fix it yesterday!"

"Yes sir. I'm looking into this. We take safety very seriously, and—"

"Don't give me that safety crap. I've been with you guys for a very long time," he said. "You've helped to keep the numbers right… but this? If any of this is true, then you've gone too far."

This report was a liability that he had not expected. When safety management systems were in place, he would be personally liable for all this. No wonder Lawrence Patrick decided to retire.

He was fucking mitigating his liability.

"We've done our best and I've got a good team," Clark said, regaining his composure.

"If we're this close to burying an airplane because of shitty training practices, or because instructors are falsifying records, or we're moving pilots around the world connecting them to flights, keeping them on duty for god knows how many hours and not calling it duty, this will bite us in the ass." He was furious.

"You wanted numbers," Clark said, folding his arms. "They come with a price."

# CHAPTER 72

SECURITY WAS PARKED across the street in a silent vigil. Yet Kathryn remained in place watching the girls walk up to the building, friends bombarding them from every direction. She understood John's confusion as to why the FAA was allowing the airlines to run amok. Intuitively, nothing made sense. But the more she thought about it, the clearer the answers became.

Airline CEOs had to be paying Diane Nobles to create legislation and look the other way, enabling them to cut training. Poor performance was a byproduct, and if Kathryn proved the training was the issue that would be the end of the game for them all. Granted, performance issues were well noted and documented, but the industry blamed pilots and not their training.

The next step would be to check Nobles' bank account. But if she were pushing money overseas, they would never see it. Don was going to open the door by going to the media, and he was killed for it. Patrick got nervous enough to retire, and Diane couldn't have any liability out there, so she got rid of him.

Kathryn had never received a message from Diane about coming back to work or being part of her team. Jason's gift of 'goodbye we loved you' spoke volumes—she was done. Kathryn suspected that Jason learned what was going on, and she would get it out of him. Maybe they could have lunch. She smiled.

On the surface, it appeared that Jason Bernard was playing on the wrong team, but she wasn't so sure. He was sincere when he came to her house. What also bothered her was that Jason was at first supportive of her idea. He loved it.

Diane Nobles was convincing about her being young and vulnerable when she buried that report, many years earlier. She also appeared extremely remorseful. There was only one way to find out. She would put her trust in Jason Bernard and see where the cards fell. She would not give up on him.

The girls finally stepped inside the building. Kathryn glanced at the security guard, who nodded, and she put the car into gear and pulled onto the street. Her next question was about Darby being pulled for mental health. If Darby was right about Nobles and Patrick's connection, pulling her could have been Global's way to discredit her report. Then again, Darby probably just bruised Rich Clark's ego and pissed him off. Stranger things have happened for revenge.

Kathryn knew one thing—she would talk to Jason, attempt to get back inside and begin a little investigation of her own. Her research was all but forgotten at this point. There was something far bigger that needed to be addressed. She parked her car in her old spot and headed into the building straight for Jason's office.

When she arrived, Jason's secretary was nowhere to be seen, so she knocked on the door and opened it. A body was slumped over in the chair with blood everywhere. She rushed to his side to check vitals and the head fell backwards.

"Oh, my God!" Kathryn gasped. It was Diane Nobles. Her throat was slit.

Kathryn's heart beat rapidly and her legs began to shake. She didn't know if she should scream or cry for help, but instead she froze; shocked by the sight of it all. She sucked a deep breath and gathered her wits.

Once upon a time, she had been an NTSB first response team member. Working airline accidents, she thought she'd seen everything. She'd been wrong. But her instincts took hold and she began scanning the area.

Glancing to the floor, she saw the weapon. "What the hell?" Kathryn said, and rushed to the door and closed it, leaving bloody footprints across the floor.

She opened her phone and called John. He answered on the first ring.

"I'm in Jason's office. Diane Nobles is dead. The knife on the floor is mine."

"Did anyone see you go in?"

"No."

"Take the knife and get out of there."

"But... John..."

"No buts. Put that knife into your purse, and get the hell out of there. I'll meet you at your house."

Kathryn's mind spun wildly and she attempted to slow her breath. She lifted a piece of paper and picked up the knife with it, and wrapped it the best she could. Then she put it into her purse.

Her shoes had walked through the blood. She stepped on her tiptoes, and twisted and turned over the footprints to obliterate them. Then she stood on one foot and removed a shoe, and stepped to a clean spot on the floor. She removed the other shoe. With both shoes in her hands she hurried to the sink and pulled a paper towel down, placed it over the faucet and turned the water on, then rinsed the blood from her shoes.

She then pulled a handful of paper towels down to dry them. Her heart raced wildly and she worked quickly. Once her shoes were clean, she put them on. She placed the paper in the sink with water still running, to ensure the towels would become soaked to remove her fingerprints.

Kathryn threw her purse over her shoulder and moved to the door, careful to avoid the blood, and opened it. Nobody was in the lobby. Where in the hell was everyone? She locked the door, wiped the lock and door handle with her shirt, and closed it. Then she wiped her prints off the outside handle and headed for the stairwell—her best chance of not being seen.

# CHAPTER **73**

LEAVING A MURDER scene was a crime, but Kathryn would be no good to anyone in jail. She pulled out of the parking lot. How the hell John had convince her to take the murder weapon, she had no idea. She needed to talk to Jason. He had the answers. Had he done this? No way in hell, not in his own office. She sucked a deep breath and turned right, and headed toward his house. He lived twenty-five minutes away, but if she hurried, she could be there in twenty. He'd have the answers.

Why the hell was Diane in his office? Who had access to her knives? Just then her phone rang.

"Did anyone see you?" John asked.

"I don't think so," Kathryn said. "I'm going to Jason's to ask—"

"Dammit Kathryn, get home!"

"But…"

"There's no but. His house is burning. You don't want to be anywhere near there."

She pulled off to the side of the freeway to think, and red lights immediately flashed from behind. "Shit. The police are pulling me over."

"Keep it cool. Call me back."

Kathryn rolled down her window. "Yes, sir?"

"Is there a problem Ma'am?"

"No, sir. I had a phone call I needed to make. My daughters had been in an accident and this is their first day back to school."

"May I see your ID?" he asked.

Kathryn glanced at her purse not sure how deep her wallet was buried, or how much blood would be on it. She reached inside, and got lucky. She opened her wallet without removing it from her purse and removed her license. His radio blared. He glanced away just long enough for her to wipe the blood off the back of her hand onto her pants.

He returned his attention toward her, and she handed him her license. He looked at it for a moment and then said, "Thank you for being conscientious." He returned the license, and rushed back to his car, turned on his siren, and sped off. She began to shake. What the hell had she stepped into?

She called John. "I'm clear. Heading home, and scared as hell."

"I'll meet you there."

# CHAPTER **74**

DARBY PACED IN the driveway waiting for Kathryn to arrive. She had a key, but no way in hell would go inside alone with all that was happening. A minute later, John pulled up and parked behind her car.

"Kathryn called you," he said, climbing out of his car. His words were more of an obvious statement than a question.

"What the hell's going on?"

"Someone's set her up for killing Nobles, perhaps Bernard too."

"Why?"

"They're getting scared and cleaning house, I'd suspect."

"No. I mean, why would Kat kill them?"

"They fired her. She was getting even," he assessed Darby. "But you had access to her house, and killing people for your friend wouldn't be out of line for a person with mental health issues."

Darby's eyes widened. "They couldn't possibly say that. Could they?"

"If Kathryn had called the police, they'd learned it was her knife. You had access. Yes, I think that could have been a reality."

Just then Kathryn pulled into the driveway, opened her garage door, and pulled into the garage. John and Darby followed, and she closed the door behind them.

Once inside, Darby said, "Get out of those clothes and throw them into the washer. Give me your purse."

She grabbed Kat's purse and carried into the kitchen and dumped the contents into the sink. The knife clanked on the aluminum. There was blood on her wallet and brush. "Shit," she said under her breath. Darby pulled on rubber gloves, grabbed the bottle of bleach under the sink, and a white rag from the drawer. She soaked the towel and wiped down her wallet. Then soaked her gloves in Clorox and dried them. She opened the wallet and removed all Kathryn's cards and money.

Once the purse was empty, she turned it inside out and wiped it down with Clorox. Darby took the wallet and purse to the laundry room and dropped them into the washer. Death to leather, but there would be no evidence. She could throw them away after they were clean. She ran back to the sink and grabbed the brush. She dropped that into the washer, too.

"Where's Kat?" she asked John.

"Upstairs showering."

"All her clothes in here?"

John nodded and Darby noticed her shoes. Shaking her head, she dropped them into the mix, and then dumped detergent in and started the washer. She returned to the kitchen and washed the knife with Clorox, handle included. If they were setting her up, there would be no fingerprints to nail her now.

She put the knife into the dishwasher, which was half full, and started the load.

Kathryn came walking into the kitchen. "Thank you."

"No worries. Apparently, I might be covering my butt too." Darby lifted the bloody paper. "Not sure what to do with this."

"We'll burn it," John said.

John took the paper to the living room with Kathryn, while Darby finished cleaning the kitchen sink. When done, she hurried to the garage, opened the car door, and wiped down the floor mat in Kat's car. When complete, she returned to the laundry room. She paused the washer, added the towel and her rubber gloves to the mix, and closed the lid to resume the cycle.

By the time she got to the living room, a fire was glowing and the paper was gone. There was something to be said for a real fireplace.

They all sat by the fire, listening to it crackle. Then John said, "Turn the news on."

Kathryn turned the television on and they watched Jason Bernard's house burn. The media broadcast that three bodies had been found. All dead. Arson. But the actual cause of death yet to be determined.

"Let's hope their throats weren't slit first, and one of your knives isn't in there, too," John said. "This puts a new twist on what's happening."

John thought the degradation of performance was setting up for NextGen, which would eventually remove the pilots from the flight deck and shift to drone technology.

"I thought Nobles was being paid off by the CEO's," Kathryn said. "Looking the other way for a buck."

"That theory can't be overlooked," John said. "Don going public, with his captain's performance problems, would have opened a huge chain of events and led to an investigation, further identifying poor training practices pointing to her."

"But Don said it was intentional," Darby said, and Kathryn nodded.

"That's why Tom visiting Bill in prison had us all wondering,"

John said. "We're watching him, too."

"Ever see Tom with Clark?" John shook his head no, and Darby asked, "Do you still think Nobles killed Don?"

"I'm not sure," John said. "We knew she didn't have the background in human factors, but assumed she was making honest mistakes. But murder? Now... I just don't know."

"Ahh, the advent of a just culture," Darby said. "If you make an honest mistake, no harm, no foul. You get away with it."

"Exactly," John said. "But the question is, who put her there and why? This could go back thirty-plus years. Why her? What's the motivation? Again, were they honest mistakes, or did she know exactly what she was doing?"

"Technology," Kathryn said. "That's her background. Drones are going to be the future. There's no better way to build a case for drone technology, than to show how bad pilots are."

"Does that mean all airlines could be involved?" Darby asked changing channels on the television, looking for the murder she might be convicted of.

"Maybe not intentionally," Kathryn said. "Perhaps they're just doing what the FAA allows them to do, and what's expected of the CEOs—do it as cheaply as possible. Then they blame the pilots."

"What we don't know is who's running it all," John said. "My boss is not off the list yet. Nor is the current DOT secretary, or Bill." He sighed. "But whoever it is, they are cleaning house."

"I think it's Clark," Darby said. "Rumor has it, he's evil." She pressed the button turning the television channel to CNN, and froze. "Oh, my God."

# CHAPTER 75

THAT WAS IT! How could she be so blind? Darby threw the remote onto the couch. She ran outside and opened her car door, thankful her purse was still sitting on the seat, with keys inside. She grabbed it, and ran back inside. In the living room, she pulled out her wallet and began removing the contents. "It's Drake."

"What are you talking about?" John said. "What's Drake?"

"He's the puppet master," Darby said, now digging through her purse.

"I could say he's guilty of a lot of things, but how the hell does he have anything to do with any of this?" Kathryn asked.

"Stand by," Darby said, finding and opening the paper. She dialed the number and the phone rang three times before Doris answered.

"Doris, this is Darby Bradshaw. I need your help."

"What is it darling?"

"Do you have the slides from the memorial?"

"I have a copy of the entire presentation on my computer."

"Could you email it to me?"

"When do you need it?"

"As soon as possible," Darby said, and then gave Doris her email address.

After Darby ended the call, John asked, "Who was that?"

"Patrick's wife." She turned to Kathryn, "I need to use your computer."

They moved into Kathryn's office and opened her laptop. Kathryn powered it up and then moved aside for Darby to take her chair. She logged into her Gmail account and said, "Drake, Nobles, and Patrick went to school together."

"Drake Technologies," John said.

"He's got the most to gain by moving to pilotless aircraft," Kathryn said. "He's been working on this technology for years. I never—"

"As president, he'd control the DOT secretary position. He could ensure his technology would be at the forefront," John pulled up a chair and sat heavily. "Not only that, he could establish legislation for full drone operated airliners."

"But why kill Nobles?" Darby asked, typing the password into her account. "I get that if Lawrence bails early they would off him. But if Nobles was in on this, then why kill her?"

"She could have become a problem, and he'd found someone else to put in her place," Kathryn said, leaning with one hand on the desk looking over Darby's shoulder.

"I've got it," Darby said, downloading the photos. Once they were in the computer, she began tapping through the presentation at rapid speed until she came to the one she was looking at. "See!" she said, enlarging it. "There they are. Much younger, but this is definitely the three of them. They all went to George Washington University together."

"So, we place them in college together, what does that prove?" John asked. "It's nothing but speculation."

"It's a crumb on the path," Kathryn said. "We might not prove anything, but we know."

"What do we do now?" Darby asked, sitting back and folding her arms. If the President of the United States was involved with this, the pilot group could kiss their careers goodbye to drone technology.

"We press on as normal," John said. "Go about the rest of your day as if nothing happened. If there's anything in Bernard's house, it won't be found for days."

John stood and walked to the window and looked out. "If no one saw Kat leaving the office, she should be okay." He turned toward them. "All we can do is wait."

"Can you shift your investigation toward Drake?" Kathryn asked.

John stared into Kathryn's eyes far too long before he spoke. "We don't have power to deal with the president."

"He's going to get away with this?" Kathryn asked.

"Probably," John said. "We'll be on whomever he puts in the DOT position. We'll find something. Eventually."

Eventually was not good enough for Darby, but what could she do? She had a battle of her own. She glanced at her watch. "I have to go. Ray's landing soon and I want to meet him at the gate."

"What about security access?" John asked. "I thought they took yours."

"They took my known crewmember status," Darby said. "I can go through the employee line with my ID."

"Don't look at me," Kathryn said, when John scowled. "I'm on the same page."

Darby had no time for a discussion as to the security of mental health patients slipping inside the bowels of the airport with a company ID. They were correct. But in her case, she wasn't overly worried.

"If you end up in jail tonight, call," Darby said, giving her a hug before she ran out the door.

# CHAPTER 76

HIS WORLD WAS imploding, and it appeared there was nothing he could do about it. John was watching the news in his bedroom waiting for Jackie, hoping to learn something new. Chris was in his room listening to music, and Jackie was putting the baby down for the night. The truth was… he could be on the top of the suspect list. His boss was probably thinking that exact thing.

How the hell had they never suspected Drake? It was so obvious. If Nobles or Patrick had known of John's involvement, Drake did as well. His days were numbered within the NTSB. Hell, they may just be numbered altogether. He suspected that Kathryn wasn't out of harm's way either. Her knife being used to kill Nobles was a warning of another kind.

Jackie walked into the room and joined him on the bed. John muted the television and then told her everything—from the details of the investigation, to the truth about the photos. He had been followed and tracked closely, and he had needed Kathryn to know what was happening so she would understand the magnitude and keep her eyes open within the FAA office.

He couldn't tell Kathryn… he couldn't tell anyone, not even Jackie. Now it didn't matter because they were all but done, if, in fact, Drake was the heart of the problem.

"So, we're not moving to Washington DC?" Jackie asked, touching his leg. "There's a bright side to everything."

John chuckled. "Yes, there is."

"I know you wanted it, despite it being a farce," she said. "You would have been good."

John lifted her hand and kissed it. "Perhaps."

"I'm sorry that I snooped." Jackie sighed.

"You did nothing out of character." He wrapped an arm around her.

"Thank you. I think," she said, elbowing him.

His getting wrapped around the idea that he could have become the secretary altered his focus and blinded him to the truth. He was a fool. Fools fall hard.

"So now what?" Jackie asked.

"I keep doing what I'm doing, until Drake decides to have me removed."

"Could he do that?"

"Absolutely. He has proven he can damn near do anything he wants."

"What are we going to do?" she asked, laying a head on his shoulder.

"I'll figure something out."

"You and Kat could start your own safety consulting business," she said. "You could hire Darby to help, if they don't let her return to work."

"That's an option."

Jackie was always a bright light, and he wasn't sure how he got so lucky to have her in his life. He only hoped that he could protect her. There was no doubt Drake knew he was on his trail. The high-tech bug in Kathryn's house should have been his first clue.

"Our next lead will be whomever Drake selects as the DOT," John said. "Maybe he will leave a trail."

"Speak of the devil," Jackie said. "He's on television."

John grabbed the remote and unmuted the television.

"I'm disappointed and surprised at the loss of a valuable servant to the government and industry," Drake said. "Miss Nobles has been a value to the FAA for many years. She'll be missed."

"Word is," the reporter said, "that you were to announce Diane Nobles as the new Department of Transportation secretary."

"Nobles was on my list, but not at the top," Drake said. "However, she would have done an excellent job if selected."

"Who is on the top of that list?"

"John McAllister, from the NTSB." Drake looked directly into the camera. "We'll see what he's capable of."

"What the hell?" John said, jumping to his feet.

Was that a threat? He froze the television and played back the section when he said—we'll see what he's capable of. That bastard was looking directly at him. A blatant challenge.

John's phone rang... his boss. He pressed deny, and turned toward Jackie.

She was staring at the television with her mouth open, tears flowing down her cheek.

"Sweetheart, why are you crying?" He touched her hand and she jerked, ever so slightly.

# CHAPTER 77

THERE WAS NOTHING like a hot shower to bring clarity. Darby stood under the water with a million thoughts rolling through her mind. She was more than frustrated with everything. Bodies were dropping, she and Kat were being set up, and the guy at the end of the spear was the President of the United States. This took Clark's crap to a new level—unless, of course, Clark was part of it. But they had no proof of anything.

If this was all a plan to disparage pilots in order to promote automation to the public, the world was in trouble. Removing pilots from the flight deck and replacing them with ground-based, remote-control gamers was a mistake that could move terrorism to the next level.

The visions of possibilities filled her mind and she shuddered at her thoughts. She would do her best to ensure that pilots would remain at the control of airplanes. But there was not a hell of a lot she could do if she were tried and hung as a mental patient.

How the hell Drake could put money above and beyond the world's safety was beyond her—unless he planned on controlling the world. She turned the shower off, and a chill crept through her body.

Darby dried herself off, and pulled on her robe. She released her hair from the pile on top of her head, and pulled a brush through it. Ray was in bed watching the news.

She stepped into the room and watched him for a moment. It felt good to have him home. Instead of jumping his bones, they had spent the afternoon talking and enjoyed a leisurely dinner. Their behavior was far too civilized for the chaos surrounding them.

Darby climbed on the bed and snuggled up to him. He slid a hand inside her robe. His touch sent a chill of another kind through her body. His mouth found her neck, and he nibbled. He untied her belt and opened her robe, and rolled her on her back. He grabbed each wrist and held her firmly, and kissed her gently. She tilted her head back, and Drake's face filled the television and his voice echoed the room. She closed her eyes.

"I'm disappointed and surprised at the loss of a valuable servant to the government and industry," Drake said. "Miss Nobles has been a value to the FAA for many years. She'll be missed."

"Word is," the reporter said… as the news echoed in the background.

"John! Oh, my God. Did you hear that?" Darby said, shocked.

"My name's Ray," he said with a laugh, nibbling her ear.

She pushed away. "Drake just announced John as the DOT." Sitting upright she continued to focus on the television, and Ray pulled her back to continue his mission, to have his way with her.

"This position is essential," Drake continued. "It's my goal to make aviation great again."

"Fuck!" Darby yelled.

"That's what I'm trying to do," Ray said. "Give a guy a chance."

"I can't believe I missed this!" she yelled, pushing away and scrambling off the bed. Darby ran to her closet and pulled on a pair of sweats. She pulled a sweatshirt over her head and sat on the bed pulling her socks on.

Ray sat upright, pissed.

"Get dressed!" she said, you're coming.

"Where?"

"Kathryn's."

Ray stared at her for a moment, then climbed out of bed and lifted his pants off the back of the chair. Rushing out of the house was clearly not his goal for the evening he'd planned. But damn it, she needed him with her.

Darby pulled her shoes on, and ran downstairs. She slipped into her down jacket and threw her purse over her shoulder. Waiting for Ray, she called Kathryn.

"Did you see the news?" Darby asked.

"I did. John's the new DOT... how the hell—"

"Not sure, but I know how to pin this on Drake," Darby said. "Ray and I are on the way to your house now. Don't let anyone come in but us."

Ray walked to the top of the stairs, still in stocking feet and no shirt. Darby gave him her best look of exasperation at his delay.

"I'm going to wait here."

"What? Why?"

"Because I'm tired. I only have two days home, and I really need some sleep." He placed his hands on his hips. "Wake me up when you get back."

Darby raced to her car.

# CHAPTER 78

DARBY WAS PISSED that Ray wouldn't go with her and wondered where that had come from. But there was no way in hell she would spend one minute trying to convince him. More importantly, she hoped she was right.

Her mind whirled a thousand directions. John had been made DOT secretary, and that could have been motive enough to off Nobles. John also had access to Kathryn's knives.

"Oh shit." Darby dialed Kathryn's phone, and said, "Did you call John?"

"He's on his way."

*Shit.* The light turned green and Darby looked both ways and then flew out of the intersection. "Is there any way possible he could have had anything to do with this?"

"I thought that for a moment." Kathryn sighed. "But at the end of the day, if someone like John could fall that hard, then I'd lose my entire faith in humanity. I just can't go there."

"I hope to hell you're right."

"What do you know?"

"I'll show you when I get there."

In no time, she was turning onto Kathryn's street, and minutes from her house. Up ahead, John was pulling into her driveway. *Let's hope humanity wins,* she thought.

Darby pulled into Kathryn's driveway beside John's car. He was doing something inside his car, and she didn't stop to find out what it was. Instead she ran up to the porch. Kathryn stood in the open doorway and Darby flew past her and into the kitchen.

Dropping to her knees, she opened the tool drawer and pulled out a flathead screwdriver and a hammer. When she jumped to her feet, Kathryn and John were watching her.

"Where'd you put the plaque?"

"Huh?"

"That thing you got from Jason," Darby said.

"My office, on the wall behind my desk."

Darby ran to her office and pulled it off the wall. She looked at the back, then the front. Then shook it. Nothing. She dropped to the floor and set the plaque on the ground before her. Propping it between a knee and the desk, she put the corner of the screwdriver to the edge of the gold plate and swung the hammer at it. One tap. Then two. She found another angle and tapped again.

"What the hell are you doing?" John said.

"Make aviation great again," Darby said. "That's Drake's slogan. Why would Jason use it on Kat's plaque?" She whacked the gold plate one more time and it popped off.

"Oh, my God," Kathryn said, her hands covering her mouth.

Behind the plaque rested a flash drive. Darby removed it from the security of its case. She held it up and said, "I suspect everything we need to know, we'll find in here."

# CHAPTER 79

HER HEART NEVER pounded so hard. She suspected what they would hear, but feared more of the unexpected. Darby placed the flash drive into Kathryn's computer, under John's initial protest to take it into official evidence. She and Kathryn had told him that they could make a backup copy on the computer for added protection, just in case it disappeared once he turned it in. The convincing moment was their suggestion that John's boss could be involved.

"*Welcome,*" the voice said.

"Drake?" Kathryn asked, and John nodded. "*It's good to finally meet you. Miss Nobles says wonderful things about you.*" Darby envisioned him stepping forward to shake someone's hand. Moments later he said, "*That will be all. Thank you.*" Footsteps and then a door closed.

"*Lawrence, join us. Please,*" Drake said. She could hear rustling and then Drake said, "*To success of long-term plans, may they only be the beginning to great fortune.*"

Darby pressed pause. "This doesn't make sense. He knew Lawrence, why act like he was just meeting him?"

"Security was with them," John said. "It was a show. Let's hear this out."

Darby pressed play and the audio continued.

*"Lawrence. Are you okay?"* a woman said.

"Nobles?" Darby asked, and Kathryn and John nodded.

*"I'm done."* Darby recognized Lawrence Patrick's accent anywhere.

*"What do you mean you're done?"* Drake said. *"We haven't come this far for you to back out."*

*"This entire situation is out of hand. You were here for one reason only. To ensure Diane got the DOT position. This was not your license to kill."*

More rustling and Lawrence said. *"You murdered one of my pilots. What the hell are you doing to Kathryn Jacobs and Darby Bradshaw?"*

Kathryn and Darby exchanged a glance.

*"Look in your own house for Bradshaw,"* Diane said, *"But I will handle Jacobs."*

*"By hurting her kids?"* Lawrence snapped. *"I'm retiring. I'm done with all of this!"*

A chill wormed under Darby's skin, and she reached over and touched Kathryn's hand—ice cold. She squeezed it, and Kathryn glanced her way with moist eyes.

*"You can't retire,"* Drake spat. *"Your ass is as deep as the rest of us."*

*"What the hell are we doing, other than improving Drake Technologies bottom line?"* Lawrence asked. *"This is more than creating pilot error, this is about killing people."*

*"For God's sake,"* Diane snapped. *"You knew what you were getting into."* A long pause, and then Nobles continued. *"You have control of your airline. You don't need the FAA to regulate you into providing adequate pilot training. You have that power all on your own. If you lose an airplane, look in a mirror."*

*"Let's stop pointing fingers,"* Drake said, more calmly now. *"You*

*loved the power that position brought. You loved the money. But we're not done. Two years, that's all we need."*

*"Maybe five,"* Diane said, and then, *"I'm just saying… security has been a challenge. When we get that conquered, the shift will begin full force, and quick."*

*"Hang with us until NextGen is in full swing,"* Drake said. *"We need you for a few more years."*

*"I'm sorry. I can't do that."* A few moments later Lawrence added, *"I've created a press release, and will announce that the CFO will take my place."*

*"When?"* Diane snapped.

*"Not soon enough."*

Footsteps, rustling, and moving around but no words were spoken. They waited and a door closed.

Darby asked, "Can we prove anything with this?"

"He accused one of them of killing Don. We don't know which one. We know they were up to something, and someone at Global is playing with Darby, and either Drake or Nobles tried to kill Kathryn," John said. More rustling and then conversation began again.

*"I'm done with him,"* Drake said.

*"He'll come around… You know how he's always been."* There was a bit of clanking, and it sounded as if she were pouring something.

*"Not this time."* Drake's voice was farther away, and then footsteps brought him closer. *"We can't afford any holes. I've got four years, and if we don't move quickly, we're screwed."* Drake's voice was up close now.

*"So he retires. How bad could that be?"*

*"Depends."* Silence for a moment and then he asked, *"Do you know anything about the CFO?"*

"*The epitome of a bean counter type,*" Diane said. "*He'll more than likely, not change anything.*"

"*More than likely?*" Drake said. "*I have not given my life for a more than likely!*"

"*This was not part of the initial plan, either,*" Diane said. "*But it works. It suits you. Time creates changes and we'll handle them. Besides, I told you when we started this he'd be the one that would bail. Why do you care now?*"

"*We thought it'd be you.*"

"*Fuck you. This was my idea. Why the hell would I back out?*"

"*Patrick's an idiot to give up everything that we've worked so hard for.*"

"*Maybe so. But we don't need him. I've got a good working relationship with Clark and Wyatt. Besides, Global's director of training is incompetent.*" Diane laughed.

"I'll vouch for that," Darby said.

"*The truth is, Lawrence is better off retired than growing a conscience.*"

"*Will we be ready?*"

"*All reports indicate that pilots have lost their flight skills. They're minimally proficient. We'll have the public primed when the time comes.*"

"*What happened with the Jacob's woman?*"

"*Wrong place at the right time. I think she'll back down now.*"

"*Think? We can't risk thinking.*" Moments ticked by and then, "*When I make you secretary, will Bradshaw's book be an issue?*"

"*It's already old news.*" A great deal of rustling and static occurred, and she said, "*Besides, the boys are taking care of her in a rather unique manner.*"

"Good."

Then, after what felt like forever, Drake said, *"When this comes to fruition, his conscience could come out of retirement. I want him gone."*

*"What?"*

*"You heard me."*

*"But Lawrence is—"*

*"God dammit, Diane!"* Drake yelled. *"I want all loose ends tied up now."* There was background noise. Then Drake spoke again. *"The stage has been set. If training doesn't improve in another two years... rapid growth, new equipment with new pilots, and massive retirements... incidents will continue until it's time."*

Diane chuckled and then glasses clinked. *"To making aviation great again."*

There were audible footsteps, and then silence.

John pressed pause. "We've got them. Conspiracy to commit murder."

"Why just conspiracy?" Darby said. "What about murder?"

"Depends what else is on this tape," John said.

"Nobles said she was working closely with Wyatt and Clark, and that they were dealing with me in a unique manner. Isn't that enough to nail their asses?" Darby asked.

"They're supposed to work closely with her," Kathryn said. "I doubt it."

"We might have enough to create speculation," John said. "We'll get them."

"I'll make some coffee," Kathryn said. "We could be in for a long night."

# CHAPTER **80**

NOBODY CAN DRIVE you crazy unless you give them the keys—the saying on her favorite mug. Despite holding tight to hers, it had been nine months since they had first pulled her for mental health, and still no word.

Mental health was nothing to play with, and if they really thought she had a problem they owed it to her to expedite this process. The truth was that most people could be called crazy for stepping outside the norm, but it was insanity the world should worry about.

President Drake negotiated a resignation in lieu of an impeachment by filling in the holes. He ended up in a medium security penitentiary in Lompoc, California. The murky waters of his ordering Diane Nobles to employ a hit on the CEO clouded the issue. He would be out in a matter of years.

Nobles, on the other hand… there was plenty evidence that she had orchestrated Patrick Lawrence's death. They'd found a hole where the bug had been placed inside her purse, but the equipment was gone, burned in Jason Bernard's house.

Don's death remained a suicide, despite evidence from the tape, which identified that someone from the Federal Flight Deck Officer program had killed him.

Nobles knew Don was coming forward because Jason Bernard had told her, and she needed him dead for self-serving reasons. She convinced an unidentified source that if Don came forward telling the world he pulled his gun on the captain, that would be the end of the FFDO program. Sustainability of the FFDO program killed Don Erikson. Instead of announcing to the world that a government had a murderer walking free, suicide was easier.

Darby sat at her table and sipped her coffee in silence, watching her birds dance at the feeder. John had explained that Drake had the power to utilize government resources to make people disappear, in the interest of government security. That government security line was a piece of gray yarn—soft and fuzzy and easily moved.

John took the Department of Transportation secretary position, yet they allowed him to set up a Seattle office. He split his workweek between Seattle and DC, which enabled him to be home Thursday through Sunday. It worked for now and enabled Jackie to stay put and Chris to complete another year in his school.

Darby's phone rang, and she glanced at the screen and smiled.

"What sane person could live in this world and not be crazy?" Darby asked.

"Excellent question," Kathryn said, with a laugh. "I'm sorry I've been so busy. If feels like forever since we spoke."

"That's okay," Darby said. She understood. Kathryn had been promoted into Jason's position and was busier than ever learning the ropes. So much so that the girls drove themselves everywhere, and were ecstatic.

"Any word on your status?"

"None. But Global is changing many of their processes," Darby said. "They're fixing most everything from my report."

"Then what you did wasn't for nothing," Kathryn said.

"True."

Darby sipped her coffee, wondering when she would ever get to fly again. She filed the Air21, but the government was so backed up, she was still waiting for the progress. Winning that, however, wouldn't get her back to work. Hell, it would do nothing other than say Global was wrong and couldn't do this to her. She was beginning to wonder if it was, in fact, a law for the airlines. Her returning to work was in the hands of that quack in Chicago.

"So, how's data collection going?" Darby asked.

"Don't get me started," Kathryn said. "John's bound by red tape, but we're working to make this an FAA mandate for all U.S. airlines to administer to their pilots."

"It's going to happen, isn't it?"

"Eventually," Kathryn said. "Then we'll enforce improved training."

The current FAA mandates were a start, but never addressed pilots' understanding their equipment. Holding airlines accountable for training was the answer. Pilots would no longer be automatically blamed for poor performance if they were not provided the tools to do the job.

"Any word when Ray will be based in Seattle?" Kathryn asked.

"Nope. But he's having fun getting sand between his toes."

Darby and Ray were working on the long-distance relationship scenario. He opted for an East Coast bid, and spent most of his days and nights in Florida on reserve. She understood—beach time was important to him. But what would happen to them? Time would tell.

"I think it's time you start pushing for your results," Kathryn said. "The longer they keep you off, the more challenging it will be for you to pass your check."

"Yep. I know," she said. "I countered that hand and bid the Boeing 777 in Portland. When I go back, they'll have to give me a full meal deal on training."

"Why didn't you tell me?

"You've been busy. I didn't want to bother you."

"You never bother me," she said. "When's your mediation hearing?"

The mediation hearing was the company process to determine if they had the right to do this—a bought and paid for process where the airline held the outcome. The definition of a kangaroo court.

"Who knows, they keep changing the dates. They said Abbott's been sick for months."

"Karma's a bitch," Kathryn said, with a chuckle.

Darby laughed. "Yes, it is. But the entire process is more of a lesson in futility."

"How so?"

"Clark is still running around Global, and he owns the pilots on the mediation board."

"We have to find a way to get rid of him," Kathryn said.

"Time's on my side," Darby said with a laugh. "Besides, pay backs are hell."

# EPILOGUE

FEDERAL CORRECTIONAL INSTITUTION
LOMPOC, CALIFORNIA
SEPTEMBER 6, 2017

LIFE WAS A game, where a true master controlled all the moves. There was nobody more in control than Thomas Drake. He sat in the courtyard, his face raised to the afternoon sun. His personal bodyguards were standing by, providing him comfort to close his eyes and enjoy the moment.

Thirty years earlier he, Diane Nobles, and Lawrence Patrick met in graduate school. Her passion was technology, Drake's business, and Patrick's legal. One drunken night they'd made a plan to run the airline industry. But nothing occurred exactly as planned—it had worked better.

Lawrence Patrick had shifted from law into the airline business, where he became the CEO of an international airline. The original plan was for Drake to take that path. Instead, Drake found running an electronic company his forte and turned it into a billion-dollar business, creating parts they would need for the future of aviation. When Lawrence merged the two airlines, he doubled their efforts overnight, controlling the world's largest airline.

This had been Diane's idea, with a vision that computers would one day replace pilots. He'd contemplated bringing her into his organization, but knew she would be more valuable in the FAA. She had moved into human factors, a subject she had no knowledge of—technology was her expertise. However, there was no better way to ensure safety reports were buried, and move the system to self-monitoring, where airlines were assured to take advantage of every shortcut they could to bolster the bottom line.

Together Diane and Lawrence paved the way for a speedy decline in performance to meet NextGen technology. She assisted with the pilot shortage by putting into motion an increase in the required hours to 1500. Airlines were forced to hire pilots who had the flight time and not necessarily the skill. At the same time, experienced pilots were retiring.

They kept wages low at the regional airlines, and the essence of the Railway Labor Act prevented those pilots from striking, or preventing the airline from taking care of someone who steps out of line, like that damned Bradshaw. Salaries had plateaued, and anyone with a brain would choose another career for the money. The shortage was blooming. Those flying kept silent to maintain their status.

Setting pilots up for failure by providing them minimal knowledge and training was the plan. But automation was becoming too good and even a below-average pilot could manage with nothing more than an incident. The night he'd learned about Captain Bill Jacobs' involvement crashing those planes, inspiration struck.

When the time came, they could help the world lose faith in their pilots so they would fully accept drone technology to carry them to their destination. His company had the technology to manage aircraft from the ground, and despite what Diane said about being five years behind with security, he could push that to market, too. It was all about smoke and mirrors.

Hell, his twenty-year sentence would be dropped when he was ready. Until then, he could conduct business as usual from his cell. There was nothing he didn't have access to within these walls. Everything he wanted was delivered, including people.

A shadow crossed his face.

"Heard you wanted to see me," the man said.

"You're blocking my sun," Drake said, not opening his eyes.

The man moved to the side and warmth covered Drake again.

"What can I do for you?" the man said.

"Depends who the hell you are."

"Captain Bill Jacobs."

Drake opened his eyes and a smiled spread across his face.

# ACKNOWLEDGMENTS

BRINGING A BOOK to life takes a team. People often wonder how I do it all—I don't. I have people who help. My team is phenomenal in every way, and I am ever so grateful for them and their assistance. They are the reason this book made publication in 2017. Thank you all!

**Carol Singleton** has been working in the aviation industry for many years, and is now a flight attendant at a major airline. More than that, her son is a pilot. Carol's passion is aviation and support for safety. Carol performed the first read and edit of *Flight For Sanity* while this novel was in the roughest form, and she provided insightful comments that impacted the novel. I cannot thank her enough, as she did this while flying over the holidays.

**Captain Kathy McCullough** is actively supporting female pilots and is involved in many social groups with her efforts. She recently published her first book, *Ups and Downs*, a story of her life and many challenges women faced in aviation in the early days. She is an advocate of making aviation a female friendly place, and is the ISA+21 communications chair. In her busy schedule she took the time to do a detailed line edit, and had the courage of a good friend to make comments on passages such as, "info dump," or "delete this paragraph." She's also an excellent editor. I cannot thank her enough!

**Nathan Everett** is my go to guy for his final editing talent, with an eye for perfection. This time he recommended dumping an entire chapter—I did! When I contact Nathan, I never know where in the world I will find him. Literally. But, this time I got pictures. Oh my… he was having fun. But he still worked me into his schedule. His talent and assistance in bringing this work to life, was perfectly timed. He is a master of publication, and is always willing to work my projects into his schedule. He can be found at elderroadbooks@ outlook.com.

**Kayla Wospschall** is my middle daughter and my cover designer. Her talent never ceases to amaze me. She illustrated our first children's book: *I Am Awesome, the ABCs of Being Me.* This book is amazing. All proceeds go to her non-profit startup: The Children's Museum of Central Oregon. Where hands-on learning using STEM education is the focus. If you want more information email her at kwopschall@ gmail.com.

**Dick Petitt**, my husband of 35 years, felt like he lived this story. He read, edited, and gave me great feedback throughout the entire process. There is no greater support system than my husband. He always places everyone else's priorities above his own, and never complains if I'm up late with a deadline, or doing homework. He also plays scrabble with me every night.

**Captain John Nance**, **Dr. Chris Broyhill**, and **Captain Eric Auxier**—I am honored to have these captains, and best selling aviation authors, give me their valuable time to read and endorse *Flight For Sanity*. Especially when they are all in the middle of projects of their own, and extremely busy.

# BOOKS BY KARLENE PETITT:

THE *FLIGHT FOR...* Series
>
> Aviation Thrillers that read like a mystery
>
> *Flight For Control*
>
> *Flight For Safety*
>
> *Flight For Survival*
>
> *Flight For Sanity*

COMING IN 2018: *Flight for Justice*

MOTIVATION:

> *Flight To Success, Be the Captain of Your Life:*
>
>> *"When you fly toward a dream*
>> *embraced by passion in your soul,*
>> *the clouds part, the sun shines and*
>> *the rainbow guides you to*
>> *your deepest desires."*

CHILDREN'S:

> *I Am Awesome, The ABCs of Being Me:*
>
>> *I can be an* Astronaut
>> because I am Awesome.
>>
>> Stars shining bright,
>> up in the sky.
>> I want to fly to the moon,
>> And ask them why.

KARLENE PETITT is an international airline pilot who is type-rated, has flown, and/or has instructed on the B747-400, B747-200, B767, B757, B737, B727, and A330 aircraft. Petitt is a 38-year veteran of flying, and has worked for Coastal Airways, Evergreen, Braniff, America West, Guyana, Tower Air, and Northwest Airlines. She is currently based in Los Angeles on the B777, awaiting training. Petitt lives in Seattle, is the mother of three, grandmother of eight, holds MBA and MHS degrees, and is an ERAU PhD candidate in aviation with a safety focus.

KARLENE IS AVAILABLE to host aviation discussion groups, join book clubs, or speak at your meetings. Please email her at

KARLENE.PETITT@GMAIL.COM

to schedule your next event. And check out her blog for more writings at KarlenePetitt.com.

Lightning Source UK Ltd.
Milton Keynes UK
UKOW01f0657170217
294649UK00001B/55/P